MILLIE ADAMS

REGENCY
Scandalous
Society Brides

MILLS & BOON

MIX
Paper | Supporting
responsible forestry
FSC® C001695

Published by
Mills & Boon
An imprint of Harlequin Enterprises (Australia) Pty Limited (ABN 47 001 180 918), a subsidiary of HarperCollins Publishers Australia Pty Limited (ABN 36 009 913 517)
Level 19, 201 Elizabeth Street
SYDNEY NSW 2000
AUSTRALIA

Printed and bound in Australia by McPherson's Printing Group

CONTENTS

Books by Millie Adams

Harlequin Historical

Claimed for the Highlander's Revenge
Marriage Deal with the Devilish Duke

Millie Adams also writes for Harlequin Modern.

Visit the Author Profile page
at millsandboon.com.au.

Claimed For The Highlander's Revenge

Millie Adams has always loved books. She considers herself a mix of Anne Shirley (loquacious but charming and willing to break a slate over a boy's head if need be) and Charlotte Doyle (a lady at heart, but with the spirit to become a mutineer should the occasion arise). Millie lives in a small house on the edge of the woods, which she finds allows her to escape in the way she loves best—in the pages of a book. She loves intense alpha heroes and the women who dare to go toe-to-toe with them (or break a slate over their heads).

Author Note

What if a lady were promised to a duke and found herself married off to a Scottish Highlander instead? That thought was the inspiration behind this story. Beauty and the beast stories are a firm favorite of mine. And I loved the idea of taking Lady Penelope's dreams and expectations and turning them upside down.

I've always been fascinated by this period of history, and it was fun to delve into some aspects I was less familiar with. Revamped Scottish castles and Scottish military uniforms, for example. But what captivated me most were the characters.

Lachlan is a big brute of a man, scarred by years spent in war, the devastating loss of his mother and the sins of his father, which contributed to the ruin of his clan. He's a far cry from the sophisticated duke Penny expected to spend her life with, but of course, he's exactly what she needs.

What I loved most about their journey was that Beauty doesn't simply tame the beast—the beast makes Beauty a bit more fearsome along the way. And it's that discovery of strength in the heroine that makes writing stories like this such a joy.

I hope you enjoy my fierce Scottish warrior and his resilient lady as much as I did.

To Harlequin, for being my dream
come true in so many ways.

Chapter One

England—1818

Lady Penelope Hastings was sitting in the drawing room, eating buttered toast, when she discovered she had been sold to a barbarian.

'I'm afraid there's nothing to be done.'

That was all the explanation offered by her father, Lord Avondale.

If there was one thing Penny knew from experience, it was that the situation was never ideal when her father began by stating how limited the options were. When her mother had died there had been *nothing to be done*. When he had dismissed her favourite governess—the only person in the household with whom she shared a connection—there had been *nothing to be done*.

When she had been young and full of dreams, and she had brought him a small, wounded bird in the hope that she might save it, he had barely given her a glance.

There is nothing to be done.

She felt a bit like that wounded bird now.

'I'm not quite certain I understand the full implications of the situation.' She looked at her toast and found it was no longer appealing. She set it back down on her plate.

'You are no longer to be married to the Duke of Kendal. There is... It is only that I thought the man dead and I did not imagine I would have to honour any prior agreements.'

'This is the first I've heard of any agreements.' She folded her hands in her lap and affected a bland expression. There was no point or purpose to arguing with her father. At best, protestations fell on deaf ears. At worst, she often caught the edge of his temper.

Penny had no wish to engage with her father in either state. And so, it was best to remain bland. Her emotions upset him. So much so at her mother's funeral that he had locked her away for days after.

And so she had learned to lock her feelings away. She felt them still, echoing inside her chest like a cry in an empty room. But no one could see them. No one could use them against her.

Later, she had learned this particular method of dealing with him. Rational responses. Forcing him to repeat his statements multiple times. She'd read once about negotiating tactics in war and had internalised the lesson.

Her father's one virtue was that he was in possession of a rather good library. More for vanity than his actual use, but she'd made use of it and often.

Books had been her companions growing up in this house where her father was rarely in residence and staff came and went like spirits in the night.

She'd long suspected the disappearance of staff was due to lack of payment, for she knew they had joined the ranks of the peerage who had title, reputation and a position in society, but no money to support any of it. Their home was a metaphor for the position. Stately, large and crumbling inside.

The ornate, tarnished gold that adorned the ceilings and

door frames seemed a mockery of what they were now. All gilded with no substance.

The paper hangings in the drawing room had been a rich blue once, faded now to a mottled navy. What had formerly looked like expensive, damask silk now looked like worn paint. It didn't much matter, as her father hadn't entertained here since her mother's death when Penny was five.

Her father didn't have to announce their dire straits for it to be obvious to Penny.

Penny wasn't a fool. She spent her hours reading and watching. When there was someone around she talked to them. Servant, chaperon, even the falconer who lived on the estate. She would talk to anyone. She hated silence. Silence created fertile ground for terrible memories and awful feelings to rise up to the surface, and that didn't accomplish anything. However, asking endless questions was the simplest way to find common ground with a person and she'd discovered that not everyone was like her father. Not everyone told her to be quiet the moment she made a noise. And so, she asked. And asked and asked.

How the household worked. What London society was like. How long it took for an egg to become a chicken.

She remembered everything.

It might not soothe her loneliness, but it helped her put together a clear picture of the world. Of the reality of the situation she and her father were in.

'I did not require your opinion to be given, Penelope, you did not need to be consulted. But you will marry the Scot.'

She was in disbelief. Her face was hot, as if she'd stuck it in the fire where her toast had just been made. Her hands were cold as ice, as though she had some grave illness.

It felt a blessing because it was better than the absolute despair that was just beneath it. But there was no point giving in to that, nor the rage she could feel beginning to churn inside her.

She didn't know what horrified her more. The fact her hopes were being burned to the ground before her eyes, or the fact that she was having difficulty controlling her response.

If she spoke out of turn, her father would fly off into a temper and then not only would she be less an engagement to a duke, she would know nothing of her current situation.

Her father, when challenged, was all bluster and rage and no useful information at all.

'Have you spoken to the Duke of Kendal, Father?' she asked, choosing her words and tone carefully.

She wanted to yell. To scream and cry and fling herself on the ground like a child denied a sweet. But being a child, free to release emotion whenever it welled up in her chest, had ended when her mother had died.

Mourning was supposed to be worn on your body. Signified by the colour. It wasn't supposed to overtake who you were. To run rampant through your chest leaving jagged, painful wounds that felt as though they would never heal.

She had learned to keep her feelings hidden away. She had a jewellery box that had been her mother's and, while she'd inherited no jewellery—all sold to pay the estate's debts— she'd treasured the heavy wooden box with its gold lock since she was small. She kept stones and feathers inside, little trinkets she'd collected on the grounds. Treasures her father couldn't sell, but that marked the years of her life, years spent wandering the grounds alone. Things that mattered only to her.

When her mother had died, she hadn't understood. One of the boys who worked in the stables had told her it meant her mother was being put in a wooden box under the ground. She'd started to wail. A deep, painful sound that had come from the depths of who she was. And her father…he'd been so angry. He'd screamed at her to stop. Uncaring of all the servants who witnessed it. He'd carried her into the house and set her in the centre of the great hall and yelled at her, but she hadn't been able to make her tears stop.

He'd banished her to her room, and roared at the staff she wasn't to come out until she'd stopped crying.

And there she'd stayed. For nearly three days. She'd felt as though she was in that wooden box the boy had said her mother was in. She'd felt buried in misery. And then she'd taken her mother's jewellery box down from her vanity and had brought it into bed with her. Held it close against her chest. And when she'd had a feeling that was too big, too bright and sharp to be contained in her chest, she'd imagined locking it away in that box.

She hadn't cried since then. Not for years. She simply put her feelings in the jewellery box. With all the stones and feathers and other precious things she could not afford to let her father touch.

It was what she did now. She imagined locking all of her fear, her anger, her sadness, away. Those feelings wouldn't help her now.

'No,' he said. 'Not yet, but there is nothing—'

'Only,' she said, cutting him off, trying to disguise the desperation in her voice, 'I am certain the Duke will know what to do and will have some means of assisting us as our engagement is common knowledge. And I have purchased my trousseau.'

Paid for by the Duke, of course, as her father could never have provided her with the trappings required by a duchess.

And the Duke's family...his sister and his ward, his mother. She was supposed to live with them. She was supposed to have real friends.

The bit of toast in her stomach was now sitting heavily.

Penny's engagement to His Grace, the Duke of Kendal, had been her father's greatest triumph. It had been evidence to him that perhaps having a daughter had some value.

For him to dissolve such an arrangement and offer her

hand to a soldier, a Scottish soldier at that, spoke of a situation so desperate she could scarcely fathom it.

She loved the Duke and everything he represented. Everything about him. From his lovely manners to his exquisitely formed face and his perfectly manicured manor. The one good thing her father had ever done was put her in the position to secure the match.

It had come as a shock to her. She'd never been given a proper debut. It was a match borne from geographical luck and she was not foolish enough to think otherwise.

The Duke's grand country estate was only an hour's ride away. One day when she'd been out walking she had discovered the Duke's sister, lost and covered in mud. She'd brought her back to the house and given her tea and toast.

It had been a great shock when the Duke himself had appeared to ferry his sister home.

His mother had sent her thanks and an invitation to tea.

It had been the beginning of something Penny had never even dreamed of. A fantasy too fine for her to have ever spun for herself. Perhaps, she might have dreamed it, but only if she imagined first that she were someone else and not simply Penelope Hastings.

She would never know the full circumstances of why exactly the Duke had chosen to marry her rather than a girl who had graced London's ballrooms for the Season. Though as she had got to know him she had made some guesses as to why.

Penny knew she was beautiful. Along with that empty jewellery box, beauty was the only thing her mother had left her. She knew, though, that it was not her beauty that appealed to the Duke of Kendal. Rather she imagined he took great pleasure in circumnavigating the rabid mothers of the marriage mart and finding himself a wife who was respectable, free of scandal and entirely his choice.

Her father's pleasure in the match was self-serving on his part and she knew it. She also didn't care. Without a good marriage she would be left with nothing. It was a matter of survival. She had expected to be forced into marriage to a toothless old man whose lack of hair on his head was to be compensated for by the gold in his purse.

She had expected something like *this*.

And to be given the Duke, only to have him *replaced*, was a blow to her heart, her hope, her pride, that she had not expected.

Her father had found a way to be worse than her every expectation.

Because he had given her something sweet, a dream spun from sugar and gold, then burned it to dust before her.

She'd been sure her father had lost the ability to hurt her. Disappoint her.

She'd been wrong.

'He has informed me that he will be procuring a special licence. And after that, you will return with him to Scotland.'

Without thought, Penny pushed herself back from the table and sat for a moment. Then she stood slowly, the room tilting as she did, though her feet remained firmly planted on the ground.

She was not only losing her future husband, but also the plans for her future. The beautiful jewel box of a withdrawing room at Bybee House was not faded. Rather the paper hangings were a cheerful pink, with gold detail and ornate marble like twisted vines over the walls and ceilings. She'd already imagined sitting there for hours and sewing, reading, petting a cat.

She had planned on getting a cat. One she would keep in the house and not out in the barn simply to trap mice.

To say nothing of the Duchess of Kendal, the Duke's mother, who had become so dear to her. His younger sister and his ward, who had become such good friends to her. Who had made her feel as though she might not have to be lonely any more and she could have friends that existed out-side the pages of a book.

She hadn't felt like that in a long time. Not since…well, not since Lachlan. A servant who had worked on the estate. He'd been nearly ten years her senior, she was sure of it. But he'd been kind to her. Her first experience of a friend.

He'd once helped her save a bird. He'd let her trail after him and ask endless questions that would have caused most men to be sharp or short with her. He'd been there. A place for her words to go so she didn't have to sit in silence.

Then one day he'd gone. No explanation. No goodbye. It might as well have been death.

She'd mourned him.

Only this time she'd done it inside. For she knew better than to ever show her pain.

She did the same now, her hands folded in her lap, her face betraying nothing as the vision of the life she'd hoped for burned before her. And she had no idea how she might make it right.

Lachlan Bain was a patient man. The years had hardened him, changed him. Battle had scarred him. Destroyed what had once been good inside him.

But it had also sanded away the edges of youth. Impa-tience, hot-headedness. Like a broadsword made in fire all that remained was sharp, cold steel.

For years he had carried his rage inside him, a reckless heat that had driven him in battle. Had driven him beyond. The years had dimmed the motivation for that rage. Some-where on the muddy battlefields he had forgotten where his anger had come from. It had spilled over into all the things around him, the atrocities of war.

The innocent lives he'd failed to save.

But he'd learned to harness it. Honed it into a sharpened blade he'd used to cut down the enemy.

He'd let the memory of the enemy who had ignited the rage in the first place fade.

But when news of his father's death reached him, he was reminded. It had taken him six months to ready his business to function without him. Six months to begin putting his plans for revenge in order.

And his blood burned with all the red-hot rage that had existed inside him these long years. It had not truly gone away. The fire had only been banked. And now it glowed red.

Before he returned to Scotland, before he returned to the Highlands to restore his clan to their former glory, he would collect the debt owed him.

He had heard whispers among London's high society, happy enough to share the tables in the gaming hell with him though he knew he would never be invited to any ball-rooms, that the Earl of Avondale had made himself a prestigious match for his daughter.

A match that was far above what an impoverished man with his reputation should have been able to manage.

A duke.

The man was puffed up in his pride over his triumph.

Lachlan knew the Earl had nothing else of value. Nothing but his daughter.

He remembered the girl. She had been pretty in that way a doll might be, but had looked terribly fragile with her blonde hair, so light it was nearly white, and her wide, blue eyes the colour of a robin's egg. He had felt pity for her. As much of a hardship as it had been to work for the Earl as a lad, he imagined being a child in that mausoleum that passed for a manor house was worse.

Lachlan knew all about useless fathers. And he had deemed the Earl worse than useless.

He had felt pity for the girl then and he might have felt guilt for using her now if he were a different man.

But he was not.

He was a man of battle. A man who had the courage to be all his father could not. A man who refused to sit back and fill his pockets while his people went without.

He had gone into battle to fight. He had gone into battle to die.

But over the near decade he'd spent fighting, he'd gone from being a boy who'd been beneath the contempt of the Englishmen around him to a brother in arms.

The necessities of war, and his own skill, had found him advancing through the ranks until he was a captain. He'd been in command of a group of men, most Scottish like himself, and they had fought hard, in kilts, for their oppressors. And through those acts had earned respect none of them had even wanted.

But in war, they'd all become the same. He could not stomach the death of a young man any easier if he was English. Covered in mud and blood, they were the same.

And when he'd saved a young peer who'd been injured in a battle, had stayed with him in a ditch all night while gunfire exploded around them...

He had found himself a decorated war hero and a very rich man. Which made his options when it came to revenge that much richer. It also presented the possibility of being able to restore that which his father had nearly destroyed.

He had a plan. He could not afford guilt.

Guilt was a luxury afforded to men who were both rich and titled. Of course, men less likely to feel guilt did not exist, as far as Lachlan could see.

The girl's father was only lucky he'd decided on this action, rather than separating the man's head from his shoulders.

When he had ensured that his horses were secured in the stable—a stable that was all too familiar to him from his time spent on the Avondale estate—he made his way to the house.

It stood as grim and imposing as it ever had. An English manor house was a far cry from the impassable stone keeps in the Highlands, where he had been the son of a chieftain. Disgraced though he was in Lachlan's eyes, his father had been a man who retained an air of power. And in his homeland, no door was ever closed to Lachlan.

In England, it was another matter.

Though the years had shifted English sentiments on the Scots, after seeing how bloody well they fought, it was still clear he wasn't a member of the upper echelons of society here. War hero or not.

For three years he'd been building his shipping empire and he could buy access into any London club he chose, but like many merchants...he would never be considered on equal ground with smart society. He'd no mind to try. He enjoyed frequenting the gaming hells and putting more coin on the table than the peerage could.

Enjoyed forcing them to interact with—and lose to—a man so beneath them.

A rebellion against his father and his fascination with the English.

But the time for games was over.

It was time for him to leave. Time for him to go back home.

Though, perhaps the memory he had of his homeland was one that wouldn't stand all these years on. If he were greeted by swords and pitchforks, he wouldn't be terribly shocked.

If the clan imagined he were anything like his dead father, he wouldn't blame them at all.

His father had squandered his money, the money of the clan, the money of his people, trying to live life like the English peerage, drinking it away in pubs in Edinburgh while those they were sworn to protect starved, their ancestral homes falling down around them in disrepair.

It might be too late and there might be too little left for him to bring salvation now.

But defeat was not in his blood.

For good or ill.

Neither was mercy.

As the Earl of Avondale was discovering.

It was time for Lachlan to go home, but he would bring with him a souvenir. The greatest prize of the man who had nearly destroyed him.

He could think of nothing sweeter.

Lachlan's mother had sent him to England, using a connection forged by his father, to gain him a position with the Earl. She'd sent him without his father's knowledge or permission. A great dishonour, his father would think. To send his son to make money to replace the money he was squandering.

But the Earl had cheated Lachlan. Left his labour unpaid. And he could not return home a failure. So he had stayed. Waiting for the man to make good and in that time his mother...

She had given in to despair.

She had taken her own life.

His father bore the brunt of that guilt. But the Earl of Avondale had played a part in it and he would pay for that part.

Lachlan went to the door and knocked. He could have barged in. He had no patience for waiting around. But he would be let in here. Admitted by servants. A station he no longer held.

He could buy this manor, he could buy the Earl of Avondale, twice over. He bowed to no man.

Their fortunes had reversed and he intended to make the other man feel the weight of it.

The butler who answered the door was the same man who had been here when Lachlan was a boy of fifteen. He remembered him as being rather imposing. A hawkish face and broad shoulders, which Lachlan recognised now were padded.

The man's black eyes no longer looked intimidating, rather Lachlan could see a depth of exhaustion there he would not have appreciated as a boy.

He felt no pity. It was the price to pay for working for the devil.

He didn't judge the man, either, as Lachlan had once found himself in the Earl's employ.

'Mr Bain,' he said. 'The Earl is expecting you.'

'Captain,' he said. 'Captain Bain.'

His ranking in the British Army, which he used only because it gave him some satisfaction to exceed the position this Englishman insisted on placing him in.

The man's lip curled ever so slightly. If the man recognised him as the boy he had been, Lachlan couldn't be sure. But he recognised a Scotsman and it was clear he found him beneath contempt. Yet the man had no choice but to admit him entry and so he did. Lachlan looked around the entry that he knew at one time had been grand. Now the wallpaper was stained and peeling, the flowers warped and swollen from moisture that seeped into the walls here. Apparently even aristocrats could not find insulation from the damp.

Before he could take another step, a door flung open and a woman all but tumbled into the space in which he was standing. She straightened, pressing her hands down over her skirts. Hands that were clearly shaking.

'Steady, lass,' he said.

His voice clearly provided her with no comfort. Wide, blue eyes met his and he could see fear there. He was used to men looking up at him with fear. He was quite accustomed to being the last thing a man saw. He had a reputation for being brutal in battle and it was well earned.

But he derived no joy from frightening small women.

It took him a moment to realise that this woman was his newly betrothed. He had not seen her since she was a girl. But he could see traces of the child she had been then. She still had a small frame, delicate. Her cheeks were no longer round, but her eyes were the same blue and the stubborn set of her chin remained.

Her dress was a simple, pale shift, the same milk white as her skin, the neck low and wide in that way that was so fashionable. He had wondered more than once if men were responsible for the current sensibility since it offered a tantalising view of female flesh.

He had not expected her to be *beautiful*. Beautiful seemed too insipid a word.

She was like a faery. It seemed that gold glowed beneath the surface of her skin.

She was infinitely lovelier than he had imagined she might be. He had not thought the collection of limbs she'd once been could be reassembled into something quite so pleasing.

She was still slim, her pale blonde hair like gold, her eyes the sort of blue found in the deep part of the sea. Mysterious like the ocean, too. He could see her fear, but there was more. A strength and stubbornness and something he could not define.

A depth he had not expected.

That, he supposed, had always been there. The magic behind her stubborn bearing. Most vulnerable beings would find themselves crushed living with a man such as the Earl. Yet she had seemed to retain her stubbornness and he found it admirable.

But while he could see her defiance, he could also see her fear. A pulse racing at the base of that delicate throat. It angered him for a moment, that her body betrayed her in such a way. The source of her life there to be seen. So easily crushed if a man was of a mind.

Had he been a different man he might have felt pity for her. But he was not a different man and pity had no place in his life.

'*You,*' she said, her expression changing from one of fear to shock.

That one word contained many.

'Aye,' he said. 'You've spoken to your father, then.'

'That's not what I mean,' she said. 'It's you. You're the boy.'

She did remember him. He had wondered if she might when he had wondered about her at all and it had been only for the briefest of moments. He had thought of her only in terms of a tool he might use to exact revenge.

A might bit more difficult now that she stood before him, clearly a woman and not a chess piece.

Most women, he found, displayed what they wanted from him, or didn't, with immediate clarity. Fear, lust or greed an immediate flash in their eyes and smile, with nothing else beyond.

But not this woman.

He knew what manner of man her father was. Living beneath this roof would have been enough to break even the strongest of men, yet here she stood, her back straight, her shoulders square.

She was unexpected in every way, though she should not have been.

A neglected child with a broken wing of her own, she had occupied herself saving animals on the estate. Curious, he'd thought at the time. For she so clearly needed rescuing, yet she concerned herself with the plight of other small, vulnerable creatures, not seeming to recognise she was kin to them.

Recognising that did not change his intention.

Though the flare of lust he felt when he looked upon his future bride was a welcome and unexpected addition to his revenge.

'The boy who used to talk to me. The boy who helped me save the bird,' she added.

'Yes. I suppose I should be flattered that you remembered. But you will find that I'm not a servant any more. Neither am I a boy. I'm Captain Lachlan Bain, Chief of Clan MacKenzie. And you are to be my bride.'

Chapter Two

Penelope had run straight from fireplace and...well, right into the enemy.

Except, the enemy was a man she had once considered... nearly a friend. Her only friend in the whole world, once upon a time. Oh, if her father had known it would have meant disaster for them both. But he hadn't. She had been careful, sneaking out of the manor during the day when her father was otherwise occupied. When he had left her to her own devices, left her without a governess, she had nothing else to do.

So, she had made the hours pass picking across the fields that surrounded the property. And she had often rescued wounded animals she'd found there.

Lachlan had helped her.

She'd thought him an angel. She'd loved his funny accent and the way the sunlight caught the curls in his hair. She'd loved the way he'd smiled at her.

She'd been quietly destroyed when he'd gone. Another brush with grief.

It was tempting for a moment to think he'd come back for

her. He *had*. But she knew it wasn't like that. She could look at him and know.

There was almost nothing of the boy she'd once known left in him.

She didn't remember him being quite so tall. But then, she'd been a child when he was here and to her, everyone seemed tall. That he still towered over her now seemed notable.

She knew for a fact he had not been quite so broad.

His hands were battered and scarred, a great, raised slash extending from his neck down beneath the collar of his white shirt. A shirt which was open at the neck and revealed quite a bit more of his chest than was at all decent.

He wore a kilt with a green tartan, a sword at his hip, and a sporran clasped with a badger's head.

She knew that the kilt was common dress for Scottish soldiers, but it was very rare to see a man wearing one for a social call.

She looked to his face, hoping to see someone she recognised. Hoping to see Lachlan as she'd known him somewhere in those eyes.

But they were hard as flint, his mouth set into a grim line. As mysterious and frightening to her as the Highlands themselves.

If she had hoped to find an ally in him, she suspected she would be disappointed. Because this man was not soft. She couldn't imagine him bending down to help a small, distraught child save a doomed bird. No. Instead, she could imagine that large hand wrapping itself around the vulnerable creature and crushing it.

She thought to use the same tactic with him that she used with her father. Rational, reasonable negotiation.

'I am engaged already,' she said, trying her very best to look beset by regret. 'A sad truth. But that will make a betrothal between you and me quite difficult.'

'Nothing difficult about it, lass,' he said, his voice rich and low. She remembered the accent, but the voice had definitely changed. She could feel it echoing inside her chest and she did not like it.

He had come into her home and filled the space here. Now he was invading her as well.

'Your father owes me a debt. And money will not suffice.'

'I don't understand.'

'It's not for you to understand. It's for you to do as you're told.'

Well, rational did *not* seem to be working. He certainly wasn't giving her any answers that she could hold on to. Nothing about this made sense to her. He had been a boy, a servant when he had left, and now he had returned, saying that he had some sort of hold on her father.

'I'm not certain I understand,' she said, keeping her tone exceedingly patient. 'You see, when you were here last you were a servant. You can see how I might be having some difficulty connecting how you went from there...' She circled her hand and then pointed at the floor. 'Here.'

'I saved the neck of the right rich man while fighting in the war. His parents were exceedingly grateful. They gave to me what your father promised and did not deliver.'

'What?'

'I worked for your father for years. Sweat and blood, lass. There were no wages paid. I was nothing but a penniless boy in a foreign land unfriendly to me based on my origins. I had few options when I arrived, less after I'd spent a year here, with all the money sent by my mother long since gone. And when I approached your father about the lack of payment, he promised me a merchant ship, if only I were to work three more years.'

'That's... I can't imagine that my father would pay a boy something with that sort of value.'

'He didn't,' Lachlan said. He smiled, but there was nothing at all nice in that smile. 'He lied. And he sent me off with nothing. After years of promises. Years of working for nothing. I had no means of getting home and, by the time I was through here, by the time I realised that nothing would come of this, that I had wasted those years, my mother was dead.' His lip curled, the expression savage. Thunderous. 'And there was nothing I could do to save her.'

'I'm sorry about your mother,' she said. 'Really. I know what that's like. My mother's dead, too.'

'Are you trying to appeal to my softer side? Because you're wasting your time, lass. I haven't got one.'

'That's not true. You did.' He had and it had meant everything to her at the time. Everything to a girl trapped inside herself.

'That boy you knew is dead.' Those words were haunting, but had they been spoken in anger, had there been some discernible emotion on that face of his, they might have been less terrifying. But it was the emptiness there, the way his face seemed carved directly from rock, as immovable and unreadable as a sheer cliff, that made her soul turn to ice. 'He died somewhere on a battlefield in Belgium. The man who stands before you wants nothing but revenge before he returns home for absolution. I got my ship, but I paid for it with blood. And I've made my fortune. Which means I have the power now. And your father has none. He has nothing. And I've purchased his debts. Sadly for him I've made you the price.'

'But why?' she asked. 'If you have the money, then what difference does it make?'

'My mother is dead. And I would have your life for hers.'

Fear rioted through her. 'You don't mean to... You don't mean...'

'You're no good to me dead.'

'Honestly,' she said, losing track of strategy altogether, 'I probably wouldn't be any use to you alive. My father often tells me that I'm useless. Save my beauty, of course, which I find to be quite a hollow comfort.'

He stared at her, his eyes cold, and she realised it was perhaps not good of her to speak of her own beauty. But truly, now, it meant nothing to her at all.

She cleared her throat and continued. 'It must be said, I accomplished some sort of usefulness when I secured an engagement to the Duke of Kendal.'

'If Kendal found you useful, I imagine I can find something to do with you.' The words were rough and hinted at a mystery she didn't fully understand.

One that made her stomach shiver and the hair on her arms go up on end.

She pushed the unwanted sensations down deep. 'I'm not entirely sure he found me useful. But his sister likes me quite a lot and so does his mother, and...'

'I'm not interested in the particulars of an engagement that no longer exists.'

'Then perhaps you would like to tell me about the particulars of this one.'

He took a step towards her. 'You are right. Your father was very proud of your engagement to the Duke. His highest achievement. And a pathway out of debt. It brings me great joy to deprive him of both of those things.'

'So I'm...simply revenge to you? A pawn? No regard whatsoever for the fact that I had plans. For the fact that I'm supposed to be getting married to somebody that I'm actually quite fond of. It doesn't make any sense. You...' She sputtered, trying to think of some way she might appeal to a humanity she wasn't certain he possessed. 'You *saved a bird*.'

'That is the second time you've mentioned the bird. I confess I don't remember much about you as a child, but I do remember your chatter and I had hoped you'd grown out of that.'

'It's not chatter!' she protested. 'The bird matters.'

She was no longer able to keep her feelings, her frustrations, wholly locked away. The bird, the truth about Lachlan as she'd known him, had been her only hope.

She was so very tired of glimmers of hope, faintly shining in the distance, only to be snuffed out.

'You *helped* me save the bird,' she said again. 'I came and I found you and you were working in the stables. I had found a small bird that had fallen out of its nest and you helped me save it.'

'You are applying far too much meaning to it. I was simply a servant doing his best to keep the mistress of the house from reporting to her father that I'd disappointed her. I still thought I was saving my family then, my clan. I still had a heart in my chest. I think what you'll find is that what war can do to harden a man, to change him, is beyond understanding. There is battle, yes. But what happens in that battle turns men into beasts and what those men will do to the innocent is beyond comprehension.'

There was something utterly cold and desolate in that tone, something that chilled her from the inside. But she refused to back down. She met his gaze, hard as it was, and would not look away. 'I don't understand how the same boy who could help me save that bird would do something so utterly barbaric as to force me into a marriage that I don't even want.'

'You haven't even seen the beginning of how barbaric I can be. And if you think I care about your feelings any more than I care about the plight of a bird, you are gravely mistaken.' His tone was laced with iron and there was a promise in those words that she could not quite untangle. It made strange waves of tension begin to radiate low in her stomach, spreading out through her limbs. 'I care about two things, lass, and your feelings are not among them.'

His eyes were green. Deep and dark and unfeeling. When she had seen him standing there she had been struck by a sense of the familiar. But the longer she looked, the more that feeling drained away.

Until all she could see was a stranger.

He was right, he wasn't the boy who had helped her. The boy she'd thought she'd befriended all those years ago. The boy whose absence she'd once mourned. She had thought it impossible to find herself in a colder situation than the one she had grown up in. But it seemed that she had.

Perhaps that wasn't fair to her father.

He had kept her fed and clothed. He had not sent her away. He had not struck her. She was lonely. But loneliness was not fatal.

'Are you spiriting me off to Scotland to be married right away?' She lifted her chin, trying not to appear frightened.

But she was frightened.

Still, she knew a bit about dealing with feral dogs and showing fear was a certain way to get bitten.

She had no desire to be bitten.

Not only that, she didn't want him to have the satisfaction of her fear. He hated her father. How much more joy would he get from his revenge if she cowered? If she wept?

The only control she had was in what she chose to keep hidden and what she chose to show.

Still, fear wound itself around her in cold coils like a viper.

Marriage, and all that it entailed, was a mystery to her in many ways. She could vaguely remember her mother and father speaking to each other. Her mother had always seemed pale and drawn. The sort of lonely Penny often felt. She could not remember her parents together. Many girls could take cues from the way their parents acted together—good or bad—and try to ascertain some of the mysteries therein. But she had not even had *that*.

She had felt confident that the Duke would make it right. That he would treat her with patience and that he would help her understand not only her duties as a duchess, but as a wife.

She had no such confidence in a man like Lachlan Bain.
What would he want from her? And how quickly?
Her entire body trembled at the thought.

She had such vague ideas of what passed between a man
and a woman. She was a voracious reader and it was a topic
she found quite curious. Her father's study was mostly absent
of books that contained such topics, but she had a skill for
finding mentions of copulation. Between horses. Chickens.
Every so often hints at it between men and women.

She knew just enough to be mortified by the thought and
little enough to feel as if she might as well know nothing at
all.

'No, that is not what I have in mind. I have no patience for
the reading of the banns, but I will purchase for us a special
licence. We can get married immediately.'

'What is the purpose of that?'

'A wedding in a church. Legal in England. Gossiped about
in England.'

'I think you're underestimating the power of an elopement.'
She didn't know why she'd said that. She didn't *want* to elope.

'Not at all. But I take great joy in forcing your father to
witness the event. At the same church where you might have
married His Grace.' Somehow the Duke's honorific sounded
like an insult on his tongue, the slight twist his accent making the word sound a vile curse.

She frowned deeply. 'You're playing a game.'

'Perhaps. One of logic. Chess, I think.'

'I don't fancy being a chess piece.'

'I don't think a chess piece gets to choose which game it's
a part of. And that is all you are. A pawn.'

She had thought it impossible to be dismissed any more
thoroughly than she often was by her father on a given day.
Lachlan Bain proved it was in fact possible to make her feel
yet more insignificant. Not a skill she would have listed as a
high priority in a husband.

'Will I be given a chance to speak to him?'

'Your father?'

'The Duke.'

'I don't own your time yet, lass. If you've a desire to go and speak to him, that's your decision.'

'How very generous of you.'

Her toast was now rebelling in her stomach.

Did they eat toast in Scotland? She didn't know. In all her reading she hadn't studied the food of Scotland. She hadn't thought it would be relevant to her. It turned out it was desperately relevant.

'Do you eat toast?' The question came out quite a bit more plaintively than she had intended. Of course, of all the things she could have asked about, the presence of toast should perhaps have fallen to a lower priority.

It seemed imperative at the moment, however.

That granite face contorted into an expression of shock, if only for a fleeting moment. And were she not half so distressed she might take it as a victory.

'Toast?'

'I don't know very much about Scotland. My father's library is thin on the subject.'

'Oh, no,' he said. 'No toast. Nothing but haggis and porridge.'

She felt ill.

She suddenly wished she had been able to enjoy that toast more, if toast was about to become a rare commodity in her life.

'Well, I'm certain there will be many things to adjust to.'

'I see you've met.'

Penny turned and saw her father standing in the doorway. He looked a stranger to her. They had never been close and his gaze had never held any great affection for her, but even that sense of familiarity that she'd had from living within the same walls for so many years was absent now.

This man was selling her to pay his debts.

This man had put her in an impossible situation, where her life would only be given value if it saved his.

It hadn't been any different, of course. Her marrying the Duke of Kendal. In her father's eyes, it had been his accomplishment. The value in her existence.

But at least she had wanted that.

She did not want this. Not at all.

But the big Scottish brute was correct. If she refused, she wouldn't be marrying the Duke of Kendal anyway. The Duke was utterly and completely above reproach. His reputation was spotless, not just because he was insulated as a man of high position, but because he was a man of the greatest of integrity.

There had never been rumours of improper behaviour, secret children, gambling or any of the other vices that often gripped the peerage.

If she were to be disgraced, her family name and reputation damaged, the Duke would want nothing to do with her.

No matter what, there would be no saving that relationship.

So she had to swallow hard, had to lower her eyes to avoid allowing her father or Lachlan to see the distress in them. And she had to give the consent that Lachlan had been so confident she would give.

It burned at the last remaining vestiges of her pride to do so.

She was her father's property. Pretending otherwise was a luxury of the past. Remembering Lachlan's words about chess pieces, she had to reluctantly acknowledge to herself that she had been a far happier chess piece when she had been in a different game.

But when you were a chess piece, you did not get to choose. And any illusion of freedom had been just that. An illusion.

All that was left was her pride. The walls of that shiny jewellery box she'd built to hold all her pain.

She would not allow it to break now.

There was no point weeping. When she had been a be-reaved five-year-old there had been no point to it. She'd wept and wailed and gained only her father's ire. She doubted she'd get anything more at twenty-two.

Penny had had, for a few sweet months, hope in a softer future at Bybee House. A life that had seemed too beautiful to be hers. And lo, it had turned out that it was.

But that hope had only existed inside her for such a short time, by comparison to what she knew best. Grim acceptance.

She knew how to protect herself. She knew how to find worlds of information in books, a salve for her soul in one-sided conversations. A sense of accomplishment in saving animals about the estate.

She knew how to move in limited quarters with grace and skill.

In short, she knew how to survive.

She would survive Lachlan Bain as she had survived ev-erything else.

'Everything is settled then,' she said softly. 'I accept your very generous offer of marriage.'

Chapter Three

Her father had told her expressly that he would speak to the Duke, but she felt that she had to speak to him. She felt that she owed him some sort of explanation. It occurred to her as she approached the house that the Duke might not care at all for her explanation. But something had driven her here, far too late in the day and without a chaperon, which she knew would have been a death knell to her reputation were it not already to be killed at the hands of a Highlander.

She ached.

She felt as if she were dying. She had planned a life here. Over the past space of time the Duke had been courting her she had easily slipped into imagining what it would be like to call this place home.

It was the grandest residence she'd ever beheld. Nestled into rolling green hills, surrounded by lakes which provided fresh fish and backed by a forest filled with stags and boars, ensconced by great gardens that provided fresh herbs and vegetables, as well as cheerful English blooms, and orchards filled with apples, the estate was well able to sustain not only itself, but nearly all of the homes in the vicinity.

The limestone façade was stately without being imposing, the great white pillars that flanked the doors giving it the gravity of a Grecian temple. And indeed, the man the residence contained had the quality of a god.

It was warm inside, always. So much more comfortable than the manor house in Avondale could ever be. Adjacent to the great hall was a great, sweeping staircase with frescos of heavenly bodies painted along the walls and looming overhead. She'd always found it to be slightly intimidating. As if the man were really a god and was thus surrounded by angels.

There were many parties given at Bybee House, though she'd always had the sense the Duke was not the driving force behind them. Or rather, his desire for parties was not. They were something he did, rather, to please his family and to continue maintaining appearances fitting for a man of his status.

The Duke's father was long dead. Hugh Ashforth had assumed the title at twenty and had set about restoring the dignity to his family name that his father had destroyed with a life of debauchery, or so Penny had heard the servants whisper. The Duke's mother remained in residence, along with his much younger sister and his ward.

Penny had grown close to them all. She had never been surrounded by women in such a way. And it was that which had given her such a strong sense of home. Of family.

For the first time in her life she had felt as though she would be part of one in a true sense. But not now.

She shrugged off the brief fear that she might cause a scandal by turning up alone after dark. What did it matter? She was hurtling headlong into a scandal and there was no stopping it.

Lachlan was right.

That she would abandon the engagement of marrying the Duke to marry a soldier—a Scottish soldier—was going to create waves that would roll throughout all of London, if not all of England.

None of it would have mattered had it only been her. But she was betrothed to the Duke of Kendal. That would ensure that the scandal was far-reaching. She was sorry that it would touch him. It would. There was no avoiding it.

And she could not offer a full explanation, not without dragging unsavoury aspects of her father's character into the foreground, and a good portion of the reason she was marrying Lachlan in the first place was to avoid such a thing.

But she wanted to say goodbye. To this man who had never as much as touched her ungloved hand. This man who had made her feel as though she might, on some small level, matter even a little bit.

A man who had given her hope for a future that was softer, more civilised, and warmer than any reality she had yet inhabited.

She blinked back tears. Her throat had felt raw the entire day, as though she was coming down with an illness, though she suspected it was simply despair.

After she knocked on the door, she was ushered inside immediately, her arrival announced promptly.

The Duke was in residence, which was a blessing, she supposed. He could have easily been in London, seeing to business.

She had to wonder if part of her hoped that he might've been, if what she truly wanted was a chance to say goodbye to her friends, his sister and his ward.

Her heart thudded a dull rhythm, echoing in her ears, as she stood in the entry of the home that would have been hers. She gazed at her surroundings with longing.

The lovely marble floors, the walls the colour of a robin's egg. It was beautiful. Though she ignored those frescoes, because she felt now as if the angels judged her.

But it didn't matter now. It wouldn't be hers. And neither would he.

It wasn't long before the Duke appeared in the entry. He was a tall man, his fine clothing perfectly tailored to suit his athletic figure. A navy coat over a white shirt, buckskin breeches and the finest boots she had ever seen. He was impeccable, even at home.

Though, she supposed she should expect nothing less of him. He was ever mindful of his image. A man in his position never did know when company might arrive.

There was a hardness to his handsome face though, a severity and sternness in his eyes she had never had directed at her before.

She understood at once.

Her father had been here already.

'I needed to speak to you…'

'Without a chaperon?' The note of judgment in his voice was unmistakable.

With the angels looming overhead, he made a thunderous picture. He was the sort of man she'd found it difficult to look at when she'd been on good terms with him. Now, having earned his displeasure, it was nearly impossible.

She took a breath and pushed her fear down deep. Locked it away. 'I didn't want to rouse Mrs. McCready from her bed, so, no. I felt this was important and it could not wait.'

'And I find propriety to be important. As ever. Regardless of the situation we find ourselves in.' He turned his head slightly. 'Beatrice, perhaps you would like to formally bear witness to this interaction, as a female relative who is lurking in the shadows to eavesdrop on the conversation anyway.'

She heard timid footsteps, and then Lady Beatrice Ashforth appeared from an alcove, her hands clasped in front of her, her expression sheepish. Knowing Beatrice as she did, Penny didn't believe her friend was sheepish at all.

She had first met Beatrice covered in mud and distraught

in a field, out exploring without her brother's permission. The Duke of Kendal disliked it when anything moved without his say so.

A sickly child, Beatrice had spent her life being cosseted and overly protected. Prodded by doctors and barred from playing outdoors, exerting herself or upsetting herself. Beatrice did not like to do as she was told.

Beatrice was also loyal to her brother with all that she was.

'I have spoken with the Earl.' His tone was dark and forbidding and she would have never ascribed those words to him before. He had always been polite. Solicitous.

A man who had never taken a liberty beyond taking her gloved hand in his to help her down from a carriage.

Now, she did not know where that man had gone.

'I assume he explained—'

'About your affair with a Scottish soldier?' The words were clipped, short and shocking. 'Yes.'

'My...*what*?'

He had done it. Her father had taken a burning arrow and fired it directly into the fortress of her reputation, not caring at all that it would reduce her to ash. Destroying his reputation would have taken hers along with it, but it was only her... Yes, he was keeping his own hands clean by making it her sin.

She had never thought him cruel, but this was cruel. Or the act of a truly desperate man. But she had never thought he would sacrifice her like this.

She had always felt as though he'd protected her at least.

But it was only ever physically.

He had locked her in that room with her grief when her mother had died, willing to let her sob until she was ill, alone.

This was much the same.

'Do not worry,' he said. 'I have no desire to see your reputation in tatters. Your upcoming marriage will do that for me.'

And he would not have to sully himself with base gossip.

He didn't say it, but it hung there in the air. All of the men involved would manage to stay above it.

The closest he'd come to debasing himself was saying the word *affair* at all. A word that touched on dark, illicit acts that Penny couldn't even form imagery for in her mind.

And he believed she had done it.

That's what happens when you're a chess piece...

'I bid you goodnight,' he said, turning and leaving her.

She could only stare after him, the sound of his footfalls on the marble floor, along with the air of disdain lingering behind long after he was gone.

A piece of her heart withered as he left.

Hope. Extinguished.

The life she'd dreamed of vanishing around her.

If the very walls of the manor dissolved she would not have been surprised in the least.

But they remained. And worse still, so did her friend.

Her friend, who she knew would be...perhaps not her friend now.

Penny turned to Beatrice, who was still standing there, looking pale, large eyed and filled with confusion, hurt. Anger. Beatrice had been her friend these past months, but any kinship they might have shared was gone now. Stolen by Penny's father's lies. And she would have to be content to let the Duke believe them, as contradicting them might cost her father his very life.

Surely Beatrice should know the truth. Beatrice, who had scarcely ever had a Season due to the overprotective nature of her mother and older brother. A childhood spent in ill health had caused all of them to treat her as a rare and fragile flower. Penny knew that Beatrice resented it and yearned for a more normal existence, hence her wanderings in the forest. Penny understood that. The wildness that was deep inside her.

She had thought they recognised it in each other, though they had not brought themselves to speak of it. Penny had been afraid to. If she gave away too much of what she was before her marriage to the Duke…well, she'd been sure he'd find her lacking.

It didn't matter now.

And what she needed in the moment was not the Duke of Kendal. She needed Beatrice's friendship. For she found as she stood there, the thing she grieved the most was the loss of her friend. Beatrice was the first woman she'd ever befriended. She'd been so lonely and having someone else her age to speak to had only ever been a dream until they'd met.

'I had to speak to him,' Penny said softly.

'You don't deserve to speak with him,' Beatrice said, her voice like ice. 'Not ever again. I will never forgive the blow you have dealt my brother's pride.'

'It's not as it seems,' Penny said. 'My father has put me in an impossible position.'

'And I'm certain that your affair with a Scotsman has nothing to do with the impossible position you're in.' She had never known her friend to speak with such acidity.

'Affair?' The truth didn't offer up less humiliation, for her father had left her exposed. Even if she absolved herself of immorality, her friend would know how callous her father had been in this. But she could not let her believe she would have betrayed the Duke. 'Never. I was sold. To pay my father's debt. But my father clearly wishes to put my own reputation on the altar and not his own.'

There was a pause. Beatrice looked at her sceptically. 'Is that the truth, Penelope?'

'I have no reason to lie. The end result is the same either way. And I could not tell your brother. Lachlan Bain…the secrets he knows about my father, the debts my father carries, they could cost him his life. At the very least his home, every last vestige of respectability. And my reputation would go down with it as well.' She felt as if she were on the edge of a void. 'There you have it. I doubt your brother could have truly married me after all. Pieces of the truth would have come forward no matter what. If not from Lachlan, than from somewhere else. Your brother would never marry a woman connected to scandal. There was never any protecting me, I suppose.'

'Isn't it a father's job to protect his children?' Beatrice whispered.

'I don't know.'

'Neither would I. But Hugh has certainly always protected us.'

She nodded, her throat tightening. She wondered when the Duke would have given her permission to call him by his Christian name.

She wouldn't know now. She would never say it.

Hugh.

His name burned bright inside her and it hurt.

'No one has ever protected me,' Penny said.

Not even the Duke, because he had to protect his family, his reputation. But she had loved him and he had not defended her. He had believed the lie because it was easy.

She'd been so certain this was love. But how could it be when it had been bound up in the way she'd felt safe and protected by him? By the way he'd brought her into his family? Now he had removed his protection. All of it.

Every man around her cared for his own ends and never hers.

'Will he hurt you?' Beatrice asked. 'Because if so then your father's reputation can go to the devil. He won't allow it.' She meant her brother and Penny thought it lovely Beatrice believed that. But after seeing the coldness in his eyes... Penny did not. 'He will not allow you to be carried off by a barbarian.'

'I... He's not a stranger to me. As a boy he worked on my father's estate. He's as a stranger now, but I don't believe he would harm me.'

She didn't know. Not for certain.

She thought of the way he had filled the entry hall, all broadness and power, with a sword strapped to his hip and his tartan proclaiming that he was a foreigner in this land. Foreign to her in every way.

She could not say for certain if *that* man might harm her.

But the boy who had helped her with the bird... He would not have harmed her. And perhaps, even if it were buried deep inside him, that boy still existed. She could only pray it was so.

'Please tell Eleanor goodbye. And...explain to her? I couldn't bear the thought of either of you hating me. And that's why I needed you to know. I have never had friends. The two of you have been the dearest to me. And of all the things that I mourn because of the dissolution of this engagement, that friendship was of the highest value.'

She found herself being pulled into Beatrice's embrace. 'I wish there was something I could do. I could always appeal to Briggs.'

The Duke of Brigham, Hugh's friend, who Penny understood was like a brother to him. He was a notorious rake and every time Penny had been in his company he'd made her smile. But these men...they were second only to the Prince Regent.

They could not understand what it meant to be in her position. Even her father's. They would be shielded by rank. As evidenced by the Duke of Brigham's reputation. That it was spoken of with laughter, not with cruel disdain.

'There's nothing left for me,' she said, feeling pressure gathering behind her eyes. 'My reputation is destroyed. Where would I go?'

Emotion was a knot in her chest and she would not let it unravel. She would not let herself sink into melancholy.

'We could find something...'

She let out a hard breath, though it did nothing to loosen

that pressure in her chest. 'At the cost of your reputation, per-haps Eleanor's. I won't allow you to take such a risk.'

She wished she could ask it. But she could not. Not in any good conscience. Finding that centre, that bit of purpose.

'It is enough,' Penny said, 'to know that you would. To know that I had such a friend.'

'Write to me,' Beatrice said. 'Promise.'

'Assuming that a letter can be sent from where I'm going.'

Her friend squeezed her hand and Penny tried not to think about the fact that she knew nothing of where she was headed. If she would just descend back into loneliness the way she had before. She'd had so much hope bound up in her mar-riage to the Duke. In joining his household and being part of something.

Now her entire future rested in the hands of a man who might as well be a stranger.

A man who was either intent on harming her or bedding her.

And, truth be told, she could not decide which prospect frightened her most.

Obtaining a special licence had been easy enough. Money, that was all it took.

As a boy he'd had wealth. He hadn't realised it was being stolen from the clan. But it hadn't taken the same shape in the Highlands as it did here in England. Or perhaps that was simply a boy's perspective. He'd wanted for nothing. If his stomach growled, food appeared. If he needed clothes, he had them. Warmth, shelter, all of it was there.

It was only as he got older and his father was in the castle less and less, spending money away from their homeland and on drinks and whores in Edinburgh, that he began to realise.

But that didn't matter now. Now, he had the money he needed and in this instance it made the process much shorter and simpler. The reading of the banns could be avoided completely. Which suited Lachlan's purposes. He wanted to publicly humiliate the Earl of Avondale, but he also felt the urge to get back home.

Home.

He had sailed the world over these past years. Had fought on foreign battlefields. His fortune had been earned both in valour there, and in trade on the seas, but he had not gone back to the Highlands.

After the death of his mother there had seemed little point.

He knew that his father would continue on his path. Destroying the once-proud name of their clan, a name that had belonged to Lachlan's mother and was badly used by his father, who had come by his position as chief through marriage. He had squandered any of the wealth the clan had ever possessed, that which was not taken from them already in the uprising.

The rent he had charged the farmers, who were responsible for feeding their people, had been nothing short of criminal. And all so that he could rub elbows with English aristocracy. Lachlan was well aware there were those within his clan who would consider him no less of a traitor, not simply for bearing his father's blood, but because he had fought with England against Napoleon. Because he had worn the uniform of a British soldier.

The uprising had been before Lachlan's time, but there were those who remembered and remembered it well. Lachlan's father was clearly not one of them, as he had taken to the excess of the English peerage with much enthusiasm.

Lachlan's aim was to restore that which had been damaged. He did not know if it were possible.

But when he returned, it would be with money and it would be with a bride.

Not for the first time he wondered if an English bride would cause difficulty, but he had to lay some hope in the idea his clan might see merit in him bringing a Sassenach back to a Scottish castle to live *their* way. For wasn't an English wife evidence that he might just as easily have stayed in England? Particularly one of aristocratic blood.

But she was his trophy. He saw it clearly. He would make his people see it, too.

And he had no intention of carrying on a bloodline. Not with her. Not with *anyone*.

There would be no bairns.

He would fix that which had been damaged. And he would return leadership of the clan to his mother's family when he went to the dirt. His cousin, Callum, had kept the clan going in his absence, even before his father's death. Callum, his children and their descendants, they could rule.

The problem now was resources, so depleted had they become.

He had learned all that he needed about managing industry as he had built his merchant fleet and he had capital enough to invest in his homeland. And his people.

But after that…

It was best if the name Bain died with him.

He was the only surviving child of his parents' union.

That in and of itself seemed a sign.

All of his brothers, dead at infancy, both before and after him. But he had survived.

He had survived childhood and he had survived war, he assumed for this purpose.

So, he would see it done.

It gave him deep satisfaction to go into this English church wearing his tartan. It was true that sentiments had changed regarding Scottish dress and custom, but he still bore the scars of a time when it had not been so readily accepted. His land bore the scars of war he had not seen with his eyes, but had lived through the consequences of all his life.

His loyalty could never entirely be to England. His blood flowed from the Highlands.

He ascended the stairs of the church and pushed the doors to the sanctuary open.

The priest was already in residence.

'And where is the bride?' Lachlan asked.

'She has yet to arrive,' the priest said. 'And when she does, I will want to be sure she is entering into the marriage of her own accord.'

'What a complicated concept,' Lachlan said. 'Do we do anything of our own accord, Father, or is it all some higher power?'

Lachlan himself knew what the highest power was. Money. Greed. In his case perhaps his motivations were honourable, but he did not think it was because he was a superior manner of man to his father.

Rather, just an angry one.

Angry that his mother had been so disgraced she had taken her own life. Angry that the Earl of Avondale had failed to give to him the compensation that was promised and therefore had prevented Lachlan from returning home in time to keep that tragedy from happening.

It was anger that drove him. And a strong sense of how powerful, wealthy men destroyed the lives of those around them on a whim.

No, Lachlan was not a better man. He was just angry at men like his father. And that did colour his actions.

It was then the doors to the church did open again and his bride appeared. She wore a gown in blue silk, the colour like china making his little bride seem yet more fragile than she had when last he'd seen her. Her hair was tied back simply, something about the style drawing his eye to the elegant line of her neck. To the curves lower still.

It took him a moment to remember the Earl was even there. He was next to her, the distance between the two of them palpable.

'So, you've come,' he said.

'Yes,' she said. 'You made it quite clear that there was no other choice.'

The priest began to speak, as if to object. 'You consent to the marriage now, don't you, lass?'

'I *am* here. I didn't come to attend a service.' He did not know why he was pleased that her sharpness remained.

'There you have it,' Lachlan said to the priest. 'From her own mouth.'

Her father said nothing. Lachlan had thought he couldn't despise the man more, but in that he was proven wrong. The only opposition the Earl had voiced to Lachlan marrying his daughter related to the loss of the connection with the Duke of Kendal. It had nothing to do with Penelope. Her happiness. Her safety.

His own father had not cared a wit for his own either, but Lachlan was a son. He had been born to be hard, born to be a warrior.

A man should offer more protection for his daughter.

He deserved to wonder about her well-being. If he ever would.

He deserved to fear for her.

There were no words of reservation from the Earl. And the priest seemed placated as well, beginning the wedding invocation at once.

Lachlan had attended weddings in the Highlands, as a boy, but he'd never been to one in England. As with all things, he'd made a study of it. Often he found the expectation was that he would be an uneducated brute. He took great pride in proving to Englishmen that he was, in fact, an *educated* brute.

Lady Penelope spoke her vows with a clear voice that verged on defiant. As if she refused to show any sort of weakness. He had to respect her for that.

He had purchased a simple ring. When the time came, he slid it on to her finger. He was surprised by how very soft her hands were. By how fragile she felt.

Such a strong little thing, she was. And yet...

So easily breakable.

'With this ring I thee wed, with my body I thee worship and with all my worldly goods I thee endow.'

There was something in her eyes when he said that. A fleeting shock followed by something akin to fear. Perhaps it was the moment settling over her. The realisation that it was done. For all her bravery could not withstand this moment.

He should not be looking at her face. He should be looking at the Earl. For it was not his bride's fear and loathing that he craved. No. It was her father's. But he found he could not look away from her, from the very real consequence of his revenge.

But he would treat her well and he knew that. He'd given her no indication that he might, but he would.

He was not an abuser of women. No matter how deep his anger, that was something that would not change. And perhaps life in a castle in the Highlands was not the same as life for a duchess in London might be, but she would want for nothing.

Except bairns.

But her hand was still resting in his and her skin was soft, and he had not anticipated being affected by such.

He was a man. He had physical needs and he dealt with those the way he dealt with all things. As a transaction. Money changed hands and pleasure was shared by both. But he was not looking for softness when he bedded a prostitute. He was looking for the basest, lowest form of release and he found it.

It had nothing to do with soft, delicate hands.

And certainly nothing to do with large eyes that seemed to offer a window to his past life.

The marriage bed was about duty and he would see the marriage consummated as it must be. But a young virgin would have no knowledge of how to please a man. However pretty she might be, she'd hold no candle to the trained whores he was accustomed to.

He had no doubt he would have to seek his pleasure outside of the union. But it was nothing to him. Vows easily spoken that didn't reach his heart.

As he thought of the hollowness of those vows, the marriage was done. Legal before God and, more importantly, recognised by the church.

Which meant it would have to be recognised by all of England.

Avondale's daughter officially belonged to him.

He looked at the man, his face drawn with sorrow and defeat, and a surge of triumph rocked through his chest. She was his.

No longer a pawn to be used by the Earl, Lady Penelope Hastings belonged to Clan MacKenzie now. Whatever the people thought of his Sassenach bride was no concern of his. He would command their acceptance. For she was his, owed to him by a man and a country that had tried to strip him of his pride. Of all that he was.

She was his token.

His token of fifteen years spent in exile while he earned his way back to his home.

She was his payment.

He could think of nothing more upsetting for the Earl, a man who prized his lineage, a man who had secured such a boon of a marriage, a near miracle really considering his financial status.

And Lachlan had stolen it from him.

And now, he would steal the man's daughter physically as well.

'It is a long journey to the Highlands,' he said.

'What about my…my things, my…?'

'I've had new things purchased for you. Anything you will need is already in the carriage.' Because he would damn well see her taken off from the church in a near-parade that would rival anything the Duke could have provided for her.

He was not a boy any more. Avondale didn't own him. England didn't own him.

His bride didn't move. It was as if she were rooted to the spot. She didn't cling to her father. Her father would have offered her no comfort and he knew she wasn't fool enough to think he might.

'Your carriage waits, Wife,' he said.

Still she did not move.

'Your carriage might wait, but I will not.' He picked her up then, her weight insubstantial. And still he could not quite get over the softness.

She made a noise halfway between a squeak and growl, clinging for a moment to his shirt before releasing her hold on him and going limp, her hands dangling at her sides, her expression one of fury. 'I can walk,' she said, as he began to stride towards the church doors.

'But you weren't.'

'I would have!'

'I was tired of waiting,' he growled, pushing the doors open, early morning sunlight washing over them both.

The carriage was just outside, two shiny black horses, a driver and footman. When he saw Lachlan approaching, the footman scrambled down the side of the carriage and held the door for them. Lachlan deposited Penelope inside and she moved to the far corner, putting as much space between the two of them as possible. 'You were waiting for all of ten seconds,' she said.

'No,' he said, his voice like a stranger's. 'I've been waiting for fifteen years. I will wait no longer.'

Chapter Four

Penny curled deep into the corner of the closed carriage. And she looked across the space—not quite enough space for her peace of mind—at the man who was now her husband.

This man who was a stranger.

She was alone with him. She had never been alone with a man who was not a relative in her entire life. And yet, she was ensconced in this carriage, with this man. Panic clawed at the walls of her chest and she did her best to suppress it.

Fought to envision that little jewellery box. To find a way to lock her panic in there.

It was the vastness of the unknown.

Of what lay ahead with the wedding night itself and…how that was changed by him being the groom.

He was untamed. So very male. Foreign and large and utterly savage.

Everything that lay ahead of her now was unknown.

And that was when it occurred to her. 'Did you bring anything from my father's house?'

He looked at her, his green eyes cool and filled with disdain. 'It is unnecessary,' he said. 'Anything you need will be provided for you.'

'But my... My mother's jewellery box. I want to bring it with me.'

'It is not my concern, lass. I'm hardly going to make a journey back to your father's house for a trinket.'

'That trinket is the only thing I have of hers,' she said, squeezing her eyes shut for a moment. She wasn't afraid she would cry. There was no purpose in crying. It would accomplish nothing. She had trained herself to keep tears back long ago.

But her eyes burned and she felt awash in helplessness.

There was nothing she could do. Nothing to be done, as her father was so fond of saying.

She was being carried away from everything she had ever known and there was absolutely nothing she could do to fight against it. She couldn't fight him. And even if she did, there would be nothing left for her to return to. The Duke of Kendal would offer her no shelter. Her father... Her father had been willing to let her reputation burn. She couldn't go back to him. Her pride prevented it.

Her fate was tied to Lachlan Bain. He was her only protection now. He was all she had.

She did not even have her mother's jewellery box, after all.

'Where are we going?'

'To the Highlands,' he said, as if the question was the most foolish thing he'd ever heard.

'I didn't mean in the long term. I meant tonight.'

Tonight.

The word echoed inside her and she pushed her feelings of disquiet away.

How long would he torture her? How long would he draw all this out?

'We'll head to a coaching inn. I hope you find the carriage to your liking. Because it's a rather long trip to Scotland.'

'I know,' she said. 'What I mean to say is, I am aware that it is quite the trip. I've never been.'

'I thought your father's library was sparse on the subject of Scotland.'

'It is. But there is quite a lot of information on carriage routes.'

'How very interesting.'

'It's not really. But I had exhausted everything else.'

At least now she had some idea of the road they would travel, the dangers it held and the distance they would traverse. Cold comfort, perhaps, but given all the rest of the unknown that was laid out before her, knowledge of the road felt like no small thing.

She could feel a gap between them and she had to decide what frightened her more. Being near him, or the sheer scope of all that wasn't known.

It was the unknown, she decided. And there was only one way to solve that.

Questions.

'Do you really not have toast? Because it's a very simple thing to make. Only you put the bread on a fork and—'

'I'm not confused as to how to warm bread on a fire,' he said.

'Well. You said you didn't have it.'

'Yes, and somehow I've spent a fair amount of time discussing it.'

'I don't feel this is an unreasonable amount of time given to the subject.'

'I do.'

And with that, the subject ended. She was beginning to think he was lying to her about the food.

'There's no need to be mean,' she said.

'There's no need to be nice either.'

Her lips twitched. Making conversation with him was like trying to talk to a stone. Fortunately, she had quite a bit of practice conversing with stones. Small animals, household staff. A great many things that were not inclined to answer her back.

'I don't know about that,' she said. 'It might make the journey more pleasant.'

He didn't respond to that at all. And she found herself gazing out the window, allowing herself to sink into the rhythm of the carriage. It was quite soothing, as long as she didn't think about where it was carrying her to, and it didn't take long for her to begin to drift off.

When she awoke, the dark was drawing low outside and the carriage had stopped.

There was a large, white-stone building bearing a sign that said Old Crown Coaching Inn, but it might as well have simply read: doom. And perhaps that might be seen as a bit dramatic, but Penny's heart was in her throat and she didn't feel one could be overly dramatic in such a situation.

The door to the carriage opened and the footman reached out as if to help her, but Lachlan moved quickly, exiting the carriage. As Lachlan moved, the footman froze, as if he could tell by his master's bearing that his movements were disapproved of.

The man moved aside and it was Lachlan who reached his hand out to her.

She found it nearly impossible to reach her own hand out to meet his. And that was when she found herself gripped around the waist and lowered slowly down to the ground. His strength was overwhelming. She felt engulfed by it, even after such a brief touch. He was so large and broad, and lifting her seemed no more difficult than lifting that injured sparrow from all those years ago.

She felt a glimmer of hope yet again. And she was as terrified of it as she was in need of it.

Because perhaps, just perhaps, that boy wasn't gone after all.

Because in his strength there was gentleness. Because he had not crushed her in those large hands of his.

She looked up at him and he looked away.

She swallowed hard.

'Come, lass,' he said, making his way towards the door of the inn.

She followed.

He issued orders to the innkeeper as if he were still in the army and the man, small and stooped, obeyed as if it were his commission.

The inn itself was clean, with heavy dark wood tables, filled with people. The beams that ran overhead were the same colour, the darkness lowering the ceiling and giving the place a cosy feel.

'I've never stayed in a place like this before.'

'Never?'

'No. I travelled so infrequently. To London occasionally, yes, but it's only three hours in a carriage, so we never stayed overnight on the road. And when Father wishes to spend time in London we rent a town house.'

Likely the reason they had not been in a couple of years. Her father wouldn't have the funds to rent them a place any more.

The innkeeper led them up a narrow staircase, down the hall, and it was then that the walls began to close in around her. She was headed to a room, a small room, with this very large man and everything was beginning to seem as though it was tilting over on to its side.

The door to the room opened and against the back wall was a bed that seemed far too small, made of the same heavy wood as everything else in the place. There was also a chair and a small table.

'I will see to my men and the horses,' Lachlan said. 'And that you're brought some dinner.'

With that, he left the room and she could breathe again.

Maybe she would get a reprieve tonight.

Even as the thought entered her mind, she was certain it wasn't true. Lachlan had no reason to offer reprieve.

She understood it was the way of things. She'd had a brief, short conversation on the subject with the Duchess, but it hadn't satisfied her curiosities. Penny had asked her one afternoon. She'd been a bit nervous, but nerves always made words come easier for her.

The older woman had seemed taken aback for a moment, but then had sat her down and looked at her with kind, grey eyes.

'You were such a small thing when your mother died, weren't you?' she'd asked.

Penny had confirmed it with a mute nod of her head and a pit of disquiet in her stomach.

'She didn't have the chance to speak to you. To tell you what would be required of a wife.'

'I tried to find out, but the servants wouldn't answer my questions. There is precious little in books and I'm very curious about—'

'You'll be fine, my dear,' she'd said, squeezing Penny's hand tightly. 'It is the natural way of the world and while knowledge might do something to ease your nerves, it is not required.'

'Is it not?' she'd asked, feeling unsettled that the one person she might have been able to question didn't seem to think Penny needed much in the way of answers. 'Only I feel that there is so much to learn and I want to know so I can be better prepared.'

Penny liked to hoard knowledge. It was her one source of power. She felt quite cross at her father for not keeping books on the subject.

The Duchess had patted Penny's hand, her expression cool, but the colour in her cheeks had mounted, betraying a small bit of discomfort. 'Men, well, you know, my dear, men are physical creatures and of course they come to the marriage bed with the benefit of experience.'

Penny had found that to be a source of deep irritation. But she'd said nothing.

'He will know what to do,' Her Grace whispered. 'If you find yourself in distress, simply think of something pleasant to pass the time. You are doing your duty as a wife and that's a thing to be pleased over. You might think of ways you can rearrange the household, as it will be yours.'

Penny had not found that at all reassuring.

She found it even less reassuring now because she could not think of anything pleasant in the presence of Lachlan Bain. There was no household to ponder rearranging. Even if there were, it wouldn't be enough to blot out his strength and outrageous maleness.

She hated not having a plan.

She nearly laughed. What plan could she possibly have? She'd been married off to a man she'd known only as a child. A stranger. She was going to Scotland when she'd been meant to go to the estate down the lane from the one she'd spent her life in.

She was supposed to be a duchess.

And now she'd been married off to a…to a barbarian.

He would claim his husbandly rights and she didn't know what it would entail. She didn't know how to manoeuvre herself into an active position in this situation.

He had all the power. And while enduring was a particular talent of Penny's…

She was still utterly terrified.

She felt vulnerable in a way she hadn't since childhood. Of all the things she resented, she perhaps resented that most of all.

She wrung her hands, pacing the room. But then a maid from the kitchen appeared, spiced wine and stew on a tray, which she set down on the table and left with a curtsy.

Penny found that though she was distressed, she was ravenous, and the stew, which was accompanied by a thick slice of bread, was very welcome indeed.

But when she was finished eating, it settled in her stomach like lead. She paced around for a moment, not sure what to do, then it occurred to her that she should probably get ready for bed while he was not in the room.

Of course, she didn't have anything to sleep in.

She didn't have a nightdress and was meant to be sharing a room with a man, and she felt as if she might actually expire from concern.

She stood there, rooted to the spot. The idea of taking off her dress, of stripping herself down to her chemise and letting her hair loose, knowing he would see her...

He would see more than that.

The heavy door to the room opened, this time with no knock, and Lachlan stood there, his massive frame dominating the doorway. On his shoulder, he carried a trunk.

'Tired?' he asked.

'Just a bit,' she said, her voice more of a croak.

She felt as though her feet had been cursed. Transformed into iron weights that kept her fixed to that exact space in the centre of the room.

When Lachlan entered, she wanted to move away from him, but found she could not.

'I told you, I had some things sent ahead.' He set the trunk down near her. 'Clothes for the journey. A nightdress. I assume you'll be wanting one.'

'I'm quite comfortable at the moment,' she said, curling her fingers into fists.

Her dress suddenly felt heavy and ill-fitting, her skin itchy. She was not comfortable in the least. But there was no nightdress, no matter how soft, that would fix her current situation.

He nodded once. 'As you wish.'

With heavy steps he crossed the room and went to stand

by the bed, his back to her. Then he began to remove his clothes. The flame from the oil lamp nearest to him flickered, the light touching his muscles as he stripped the white shirt from his body.

She couldn't look away.

She knew that she should. Except...should she? They were married. And this was marriage. That he would remove her dress and he would... He would cover her, the way that she had seen animals do. She shivered, fighting against fear.

No matter that she had told herself it might not occur, she had known that it would. This bed was a marriage bed by virtue of the fact that they had said vows today. There was no getting around that. She was not a child and she knew the way of things. The way of this.

She knew the mechanics and purpose, as it applied to animals, and she knew it was much the same way for humans. Though her mind couldn't make sense of how those things shifted between man and woman, rather than stallion and mare.

She knew it was a woman's duty to produce children in a marriage. To be available to her husband in the ways he demanded. She might not know the specifics of those demands, but she knew that much.

The truth was, a woman in her position was required to be innocent in order to be desirable. In order to be the sort of woman who would be deemed worthy of marrying a man and bearing his children. A woman in her position's entire life centred on this act. If anyone thought she might have done it without the proper vows being spoken, then her entire life would be ruined. If she failed to secure a husband, then her body would be the currency by which she secured her protector.

And it was considered inappropriate for her to know the details of the act itself.

It suddenly seemed desperately and wholly unfair. Had

her mother been alive, she would have asked her why it was the way of the world.

But her mother was dead. And as her father was so fond of saying: there was nothing to be done.

This man was her protector. And this was the cost of that protection.

But she found she couldn't simply think her way through this. She couldn't push her feelings away or lock them up tight.

Worse than the fear, she found she was transfixed by him. By all the unknown that he represented. By this wild and unyielding bend in her life's road that she had never seen coming.

She would have been a wife in only a month's time, but to another man. These were mysteries that would have been answered for her soon, but she had a feeling it would have been different than what was about to transpire with Lachlan.

But she didn't know enough about it, enough about men to know how.

Except she had felt the safety with the Duke that she did not feel here.

Because Lachlan had a wildness that radiated from the very centre of all that he was.

A wildness that stood in stark contrast to that cloistered upbringing of hers.

He was everything that she had learned to turn away from. Everything that she had spent her life repressing. For she had learned to spend her life walking an invisible, narrow cobbled street and if she took a turn off it, it was only when she was away from the sight of her father.

Whenever she felt an emotion that was too large, she shut it away. Whenever she had a burst of energy that would be too loud, she pushed it down.

She had the feeling that Lachlan Bain never pushed down a thing.

He turned then, not moving his hands to the kilt that he wore over the lower half of his body. She could see his whole chest, those broad shoulders, muscles that spoke of hard labour. A strange thing, how fascinating such a thing could be. A simple physical feature like muscles.

He was a man and therefore physically stronger than she. He did labour, therefore, he had developed that strength.

These were easy lines to draw, yet there was a response that it created inside her body that had absolutely nothing to do with these facts. It was all simple appreciation for his form that made her stomach feel warm and her limbs feel languid.

How could she feel that and fear at the same time?

And she was still unable to move.

'Do you need help preparing for bed?' His voice was much softer than she had heard it before.

'I…'

'You've a lady's maid at home, have you not?'

'Yes,' she said.

'And usually she helps you get ready for bed?'

'Of course.' Her gown had tiny buttons down the back. Getting out of it on her own would be a graceless pursuit.

'I'll be assisting you, lass.'

He crossed the small space, coming perilously close to her as he bent and opened the trunk. From it he produced a simple, white night shift and a beautiful ivory hairbrush, far finer than anything she'd ever owned before.

'Sit,' he said, gesturing to the vanity that was shoved against the back wall.

And for some reason, now, her feet were capable of movement. And slowly carried her to that vanity, where she sat as he'd commanded.

She could see him behind her, large and impossibly broad. And she could see the reflection of her own fear looking back at her. Her eyes wide, dark half-moons beneath them as though someone had bruised them.

When he touched her, she jumped. Her lips parted and she despised the woman in the mirror. The woman who looked so fragile, so upset by the moment.

But his touch was gentle and it was clear he did not want her fear.

Something about that realisation made her shoulders relax. He said nothing as he began to remove the pins from her hair, curling locks falling down over her shoulders in golden waves.

'Aye,' he said, the word full of rough approval. 'I thought your hair would be a glory.'

He said the words as if to himself and not to her. They did not seem to require a response, so she did not give one. He lifted his hand, the ivory brush clutched tightly, looking far too delicate in a fist that she knew could easily wield a broadsword. Brute strength, leashed, as he began to comb her golden curls.

Her heart fluttered uncontrollably and she felt pain. Real, undeniable pain radiated through her.

For when had someone last been tender with her? She'd had a lovely governess for a while. And she'd had a calm, soothing voice. She didn't like to think of her, because losing her had hurt.

She'd gone away because the money had gone away.

All the care she'd experienced since the death of her mother had been bought and paid for.

And now her father had…he'd paid a debt with her and it was as though the floor had become the ceiling, to experience this, from him.

She had expected him to be rough. Callous. Uncaring.

He was such a large man. He could easily kill her with a firm press of his thumb to her throat. He had made it no secret he was angry. That he hated her father.

This was not what she had expected. And more than that,

she had not expected her own response to it. A deep ache that made her chest feel as if it was being torn in two.

He was compromising every wall she'd built up inside herself. She was stronger than this. She'd had to be. She'd cried all the tears out of her body when her mother had died.

And then there was him.

She hadn't cried when Lachlan had gone. She'd already let go of tears then. But he had given her a sense of friendship she hadn't experienced before she'd met him, and at nine his departure had left her devastated.

That he'd come back into her life only to destroy it, only to break barriers she'd built in part because of him, made her want to lash out.

She didn't want his care.

His care had mattered when she'd been a girl. And he'd left.

It didn't matter why. He didn't care for her, why should she care at all for him?

'I loved him,' she said, the words tumbling out of her mouth. 'Just so you know.'

Thinking of the Duke made her feel calm for a moment. Safe.

Until she forgot he was no longer her ally.

His home was no longer her haven.

His family would no longer be hers.

'No concern of mine,' he said. 'It's not your love that I'll be wanting tonight.'

'And you don't mind if my affections are with another man?'

'I have a hard time believing it's him you'll be thinking of. And it's not love that will make you cry out with pleasure.'

His words sent an arrow of sensation down low in her stomach. She didn't understand what her pleasure had to do with anything. She only knew enough about male jealousy and possession to know that it might bother him if she loved the Duke. 'My heart is with Hugh,' she said, his name feeling a strange impertinence on her lips.

'Aye,' he said. 'But your body's with me.'

The words felt a betrayal of the tender act of him combing her hair. Yet he kept on, his movements not coming any more hurried, not shifting into anything rougher.

She hated it. She wanted him to be angry.

It was easier to stand strong against anger.

'Beautiful,' he murmured as he parted her hair and shifted it over her shoulders so that it hung long and curling below her breasts. Then he began working on the small buttons on the back of her gown, letting the fabric go slack, then fall to her waist. It revealed her stays. Left one less barrier between them.

Her heart pounded a thick and heavy rhythm in her throat.

She fought to hang on to her anger, but fear...and something that felt closer to curiosity, rolled through her, beginning to eclipse it.

'Do you know of what happens between a man and a woman?' he asked, his voice rough.

'I know everything,' she said, keeping her chin tilted upward, her eyes steady with the mirror. She would not look at him.

And she would not give in to weakness.

'Everything?' His words held a hint of mockery. 'That is quite a lot.'

'I told you,' she said, the words wooden. 'I love another man.'

Perhaps if he believed she was ruined he would send her away. Ruined was the worst thing a woman could be, after all. Ruined was one thing you must never be, as then a man would not want you.

Lachlan did not react.

'I see,' he said. 'Then I shall expect you to teach me a few tricks. I have been to some of the finer whores that England has to offer, but I dare say not even they know everything.'

She shivered, disquiet moving down her spine like a wave.

His hands moved to the front of her body, where he unlaced her stays with steady hands and threw the small garment aside, leaving her in nothing but her chemise.

Rough hands went to her shoulders and the garment went down, only her hair covering her breasts. Her entire back was bare and she could feel the heat of him against her skin like a roaring fire.

'I will make a bargain with you,' he said. 'I'll not punish you for your lies. And I'll not treat you as you're asking to be treated. Because it's clear to me that you are nothing more than a frightened virgin and you don't know what it is you're tempting.'

'And what is my portion of the bargain?' she asked, the words barely a whisper.

'Your body.'

It felt an impossible ask.

'We're strangers,' she said.

But that was as close as she could bring herself to ask that he postpone the act. She knew the duties of a wife. She knew what was expected of her. He might not be the husband that she had anticipated, but he was the husband she had.

She knew there were no negotiations to be had. Not here.

Rough hands went to her bare waist and she waged a battle within herself against the desire to run. Against the desire to lean into his touch. She fought to remain still.

'We are not,' he said. 'I helped you save a bird.'

She had nothing to say to that.

No man had ever touched her like this. No man had laid his hands upon her bare skin.

And now these rough warrior's hands were resting against such an intimate part of her. She felt dizzy with it.

With those strong hands, he guided her upwards so that

she was standing. Then he pushed her gown down her body, letting all of it fall to the floor.

He did something very unexpected after that.

He growled.

The sound rumbling in his chest, vibrating through her.

Her entire body went cold, then hot. Shame rioting through her.

She felt exposed and terribly afraid.

She was afraid to look at her reflection in the mirror because the woman there would be naked. While her hair might be concealing her breasts, the rest of her was terribly exposed. She didn't want to look at his reflection either. Didn't want to see him impossibly tall and ferocious behind her.

He moved closer to her and she could feel the heat and strength of his body. One hand was still on her waist and it moved, making its way around to her stomach, where he spread his fingers wide and pulled her back against him.

He was solid and hot like a furnace. He bent his head down and pressed a kiss to the back of her neck.

A shocked sound escaped her lips and heat radiated from where his mouth had touched, like the spark from a fire had landed on her skin.

She felt strange. Lightheaded. And then those rough hands moved over her skin, his calluses brushing over her stomach as he shifted and pressed another kiss against her, this time below the first.

Pinpricks of sensation broke out over her body.

His words echoed inside her. Pleasure.

She had never heard pleasure connected with this act. Not for women. She knew that men were not supposed to be held responsible for their desires. But even then, it wasn't presented as pleasure as much as a natural instinct that could not be denied.

But he spoke of pleasure as if that was something she could expect. As if it were something that mattered.

And it didn't feel bad, the press of his hands on her. His mouth to her skin.

It didn't feel bad at all.

She could feel her nipples grow tight and a restless ache began to build between her legs. She looked up at the mirror and her eyes caught his. There was a black flame in those green depths and it startled her. She looked away, but it was no better, because she caught her own reflection in the mirror then. Golden hair cascading over her breasts, her slim exposed midsection with his large, dark hand resting there possessively. The pale thatch of curls just below.

Her heart was thundering wildly, threatening to gallop right out of her chest.

'Perhaps you don't know everything?' he asked.

She said nothing to that. She found strong arms wrapping themselves around her body, her bare skin against his naked chest. Then he lifted her off the ground as if she weighed nothing. 'You are my wife,' he said, the word filled with an intent sort of possessiveness.

She found herself being carried over to the bed, deposited in the centre of it. This was it. It would be it. That part that came with roughness and heaving, which she had of course witnessed between horses.

But he did not cover her. Instead, he stood back and looked down on her.

She fought the urge to cover herself, because again, she despised that fear. She didn't want to show him that she felt vulnerable. She wanted to find a way to go inside herself. To think of something pleasant. To remain passive and to keep herself from reacting. It seemed a better thing than weeping, which was what she truly wanted to do.

With methodical hands he divested himself of the kilt. There was nothing beneath it.

His male member stood out from his body, large and thick, and she knew that was meant to go inside her body and she had no idea how she was supposed to accommodate such a thing.

It didn't seem possible. Couldn't be possible.

But hadn't Her Grace said all a woman had to do was lie back?

That *he* would know what to do?

She had never heard of a woman being torn asunder on her wedding night, so she supposed she was in no more danger of it than anyone else. Though, he was Scottish. And it was entirely possible he was simply larger than most men. Entirely possible that an Englishwoman was not made to accommodate such...vast maleness.

But when he came down on to the bed, he was beside her and reached out, taking a strand of her hair between his thumb and forefinger. It was not what she had expected. He looked at her, those eyes intense, and she felt she would have rather he'd simply done what he needed to and got it over with.

It seemed preferable to this. This long stretch of time, this suspended moment of agony where her innocence remained and her questions were only half-answered, taking her closer to truths that were hidden from her, without revealing them entirely.

'Put your hands on me,' he said.

'I...'

He wrapped one large hand around her wrist and brought it to his chest. His skin was hot, his heart raging beneath. He had hair on his body. She could feel her own heart thundering the same rhythm in response. But he wasn't nervous, surely. So why was his heart working in time with hers?

He made that same growling sound he'd done before, then he lowered his head.

His lips had never touched hers. Her lips had never touched anyone's.

His mouth was firm and masterful, slow, coaxing movements instructing her where words would have failed. He angled his head and then he did the strangest thing of all. He slipped his tongue between her lips.

She gasped and drew back. 'I don't think that's a done thing.'

He chuckled, the sound strained. 'It is. Believe me, it is.'

'But *why*?'

'You have to let me show you.' He brought his mouth back to hers again and this time, when his tongue parted her lips, she did not pull away. This time, she allowed him to lead with a slick, startling rhythm. Like a waltz. And she was lost.

Her skin felt hot, her body flushed as if she was sick.

But she didn't have time to think about it too long, because then he brought his hand to her breast, his calloused thumb moving over the tightened bud there.

It created a restless ache in her that no one had told her about. Was this what he meant? Was this the pleasure?

'I was told...' She tried to catch her breath. 'I was told that I was supposed to think of household chores during this act.'

'I thought you were going to think of your man?'

Her man? It took her a broad space of time to remember who he was speaking of, because the only man in her mind was the one in this room. The one whose hands were creating dark magic inside her.

'His mother said I should think of duty.'

'I'll have you think of me,' he said.

His mouth went down over hers again, this time rougher. Harder. Deeper.

Everything he was doing, everything he made her feel, didn't seem as though it should be possible. Ladies did their duty and that was all.

It was men who had appetites.

Yet he made her feel hungry.

That's what it was like. Hunger pangs. But in low, intimate spaces.

Then he moved his hand, settled it between her thighs and she arched her hips up off the bed, trying to escape him. But he was too strong. He moved his fingers between her feminine crease, with startling ease. She was slick there. Wet.

It made her feel a blooming sense of heat and shame and she didn't even know why.

He felt no shame. His hands were sure and he began to move his thumb in slow, decisive circles. And she was lost. Lost in the pagan rhythm that he created there. She could no longer resist, could no longer find shame in the fact that he was a stranger and the fact that her body was responding in ways she hadn't known were possible. Somewhere, in the gauzy, confused mists of her mind, she realised that everything she'd ever been told about being a woman was a lie.

This was why women fell.

This was why there was such concern about ruination. It wasn't about a simple, accidental step into a darkened alcove. No. It was about the temptation that might wait there. She hadn't realised that. Because the way it had all sounded, it seemed a woman could not be tempted.

But his hands were temptation. His wicked mouth was temptation.

His muscles were a temptation. They were not simply a physicality. They were magic.

A sort of magic of masculinity that called to the feminine in her.

It went so much deeper than societal roles. So much deeper than body parts.

She felt something building inside her, foreign and delicious, and she found herself moving her hips in time with his fingers, chasing that nameless sensation inside her.

It was like a bowstring, pulled taut. And it stretched and stretched until she was certain it could go on no longer.

And that was when the release came. And she soared.

There was a great, gasping sound in the room and it took

ages for her to figure out that it was coming from her own mouth. That *she* was the desperate, whimpering creature she could hear as if from a distance. That she was clinging to him as though he might anchor her to earth. She was shattered. And she didn't know if she would ever be able to be put back together.

He said nothing. He only regarded her with those eyes. Then he shifted his touch between her legs and breached her, one finger sliding deep inside. The invasion was strange, but not painful. Until he added a second finger to the first and she found herself gasping for breath.

'Best to make sure you're as ready as you can be,' he said, his voice rough.

She felt a flutter of terror in her breast, but then he had moved and was over her, the blunt head of that most masculine part of him where his fingers had been only a moment before. She nearly cried out in protest, but then his hips surged forward and she cried out in pain as he entered her.

This was what she had expected. And everything that had come before had been a cruel trick. This was why a woman needed to lie back and think of housekeeping. Because nothing could have prepared her for the pain she felt at his invasion.

Her eyes stung with tears.

Tears.

She fought to hold them back because she would not give this man her tears. But he had invaded her.

Why did any woman *ever* fall?

Was it because of the promises made with masculine hands that were not kept with masculine members? She wiggled against him, fighting it. Fighting against him. Because it was better than crying. She would not cry.

He made a low sound, comforting, as if he were trying to steady the horse. And she bucked against him in anger because she was not a horse and refused to be soothed.

'It will get better,' he said.

It wouldn't. He was lying. But he didn't move, his body resting heavily atop her, his hands pinning her wrists down to the mattress. She began to settle, the tears that had been threatening to spill from her eyes receding. And along with it, the pain.

She slowly began to grow accustomed to the size of him inside her.

And then, inexplicably, as she grew accustomed to him, she felt something more.

Not pleasure, not like before, but a strange sensation of being bonded.

She could not remember the last time she'd been held by another person. Not until he had lifted her in those strong arms and brought her to the bed. And now he was surrounding her. Now he was in her.

She had been lonely. So lonely for so long. And the only end to that loneliness that she had seen was through her marriage to the Duke. She had ached so much to belong to that household filled with wonderful women she could talk to. Whom she could confide in. Women who might understand her, who would not make her keep all that she was locked away in a box inside her heart.

But how could she be lonely like this?

There was no way to be closer to another human. Nothing separated them. Nothing. Even their breath mingled together as he stared down at her.

And he would give her children.

The thought made her heart lift.

The thought of having the Duke's children had made her happy. Of having a family. But he'd come with family and so part of that need had been fulfilled with them. Lachlan...

She'd been certain she'd been facing a future of unimaginable loneliness, but she had not thought of children.

She could still have that. That connection. She could be a mother.

The idea made her ache.

She'd lost her mother when she'd been a girl and she could never have a mother's arms hold her again.

But she could hold a child.

Could offer comfort. Care. Love.

Could give all those soft, painful emotions that had spent years building inside her, locked away.

For the first time she thought perhaps this was not the prison sentence she had first imagined it to be.

Then he cupped her face and kissed her.

It was sweet. It was sweet and deep and tender, and she relaxed into it. Into him. It was wonderful. Those kisses.

Only moments before she hadn't understood. But she did now. This restless, deep need to be as close as possible.

And when he began to move inside her, she found it didn't hurt.

Rather it built a slow, aching rhythm somewhere deeper than the one that had come before.

He gripped her face, kissing her deeply, before pressing his forehead hard against hers, his movements becoming unrestrained. Gone was the tenderness of only a moment before. And somehow… Somehow it seemed right.

Because this wasn't sweet or tender. It was primal and it was quite the most intimate thing two people could share. She found herself arching to meet his every thrust, found herself moving against him, shamelessly.

Shameless.

Had she ever been shameless in all her life?

No.

She had always fought against her nature. Against all that she was.

She had spent so much of her youth wanting to disappear. And everything in her was wrong for the life she'd been forced to lead. The daughter of a man who wished her invisible...who wished her gone instead of his wife, that much was certain.

Everything she was. Everything within her was shame.

But not now. Not with *him*.

And when the cry of pleasure rose up in her chest, she did not push it down. She did nothing to silence it. She let herself shudder gloriously and held nothing back.

He pulled away from her and she clung to his shoulders. He shuddered against her, his breath hot against her neck, as he seemed to find a release similar to her own, culminating in a feeling of warmth on her skin. And then he pulled her against his body for a brief moment, dropping a kiss to her forehead, the moment unexpectedly tender, but all too brief. Before she could revel in the simple touch, he released her.

'Sleep,' he said, getting out of bed.

His departure felt abrupt and a personal insult, somehow.

'What?' She felt shattered and dishevelled and had no earthly idea what had just happened.

'I need to be sure everything is prepared for tomorrow. We leave early. Sleep.'

'You won't stay?'

'You don't need me.'

He began to collect his clothes and she could only lie there on the bed, watching as he did.

Now the shame was back. She felt small and wrong somehow, because certainly had she done right he would want to stay with her.

Then she felt angry that she would care at all. Why did she want him to stay? She didn't know him or care about him in any way. And what had happened between them wasn't...

It wasn't knowing someone.

And it was certainly nothing large enough to take away a lifetime of shame and loneliness. She had been foolish to think otherwise. Even for a moment.

He left her there and she curled in on herself, doing her very best to try to press her shattered pieces back together.

She hadn't known.

She hadn't known that the physical act between a husband and wife could take you up to the stars and then—back down to the rocks just as quickly.

That a moment of deep connectedness could leave you feeling lonelier than you ever had before.

It made her despise him. More than she had before.

Because he had shown her pleasure.

And then he had taken this new, fragile thing he had built inside her and broken off pieces of it. He had stolen her protection. Stripped her bare and made her vulnerable. Nearly brought her to tears.

She was strong and knew how to protect herself against all manner of things.

But he was a storm. And against him she had no defence.

She would have rather he'd been cruel.

She would have rather he'd made it harsh and painful, and nothing more.

He had made her feel.

Sensations that were too big to be contained. That could not be shoved down inside her.

And it was then she realised that he had withdrawn from her in such a way that pregnancy would be prevented.

The darkness and a sense of isolation crushed down on her.

He had taken something from her. And he had given the possibility of nothing back.

She lay there with her eyes dry and her heart thudding a full, defeated rhythm.

And her last thought before going to sleep was that he had compromised her ability to lock her emotions down inside herself. And if that were true, she had no idea how she would survive her marriage to Lachlan.

No idea at all.

Chapter Five

He'd thought his conscience long destroyed, but the woman had made him feel like a brute. And his intentions to simply claim the wedding night quickly had been dissolved by that wide-eyed, delicate look. He had walked into the room and she had been standing there, like a woman lost to herself, and sensation he had not known he possessed the power to feel had turned inside him.

She was an instrument in his revenge and nothing more. But she seemed much more a woman, a person, separated from her father and all he represented, and he took no joy in her fear.

Grown men had trembled in his presence and he'd taken lives on the battlefield. He was not so small a man he needed to find strength in the fear of a woman.

He felt much more inclined towards giving her pleasure.

And why not? he'd asked himself. She was his wife. He had been long without a woman, between his last voyage, and his determination to take himself straight to Penny's father once he had decided his course. Why not take his pleasure with her as he chose and not simply dispense her of her virginity as quickly as possible?

He might be accustomed to treating sex as a transaction between a man and a woman, but in that sense he had always felt the transaction should be equal. Women were capable of feeling desire and satisfaction in the same way he was. He had always found it unsatisfying to leave them without it. It was true some whores were jaded and didn't wish to release themselves in that way, but then he felt that was a choice.

Still, he'd found many were happy to make it an indulgence and he was always more satisfied for it.

So why should he not afford the same courtesy to his wife? Why should she not feel pleasure? It was clear to him that the idea of physical pleasure between a man and a woman was foreign to her. That it was something she had not considered to be possible.

It was the shifting in his chest that had occurred after they'd come together that had sent him to the stables. Pacing around in the cold might do him some good.

One of his men, William, was sleeping on the floor, a blanket tugged up under his arms, his head lolled to the side. Lachlan nudged him with the toe of his boot.

'Captain?' the man asked, waking quickly.

They had been soldiers together. Neither of them slept very deeply. Wakefulness was instantaneous for those who had spent years on frozen battlefields littered with enemies and bodies.

'I need you to go back to the lass's house. You must collect some things for me. Meet us at the next inn.'

William stood, nodding grimly, and if he were exhausted or resentful of the order, he did not show it.

Lachlan had earned the loyalty of his men in battle, and, to those who had no home or family, he had offered them work after. Some remained on the ships, some were returning to Scotland with him.

They would be welcomed into the clan. He would make sure of it. It was an oath he'd sworn to those who had left the Highlands, as he had. Some of those men no longer had clans to return to, poverty and skirmishes destroying all that was left behind.

He would not leave them in England. They had become his men on the battlefield, united in fighting for a country they had no allegiance to. He would bring them back to where they belonged.

'Yes, Captain.'

'When we are back home,' he said to the other man, 'I will be Laird to you. Not captain.'

'Yes, Laird,' the other man said, inclining his head.

Lachlan gave his instructions, then spent more time than was strictly necessary evaluating his horse, the one who would carry him from here to Scotland. The carriage team they would change out at every coaching inn, but not his horse.

Perhaps his disquiet came from the fact he had never been with a woman who was innocent.

He preferred jaded women. Their souls matched.

Women who had experienced little good in the world, who had been given nothing in the way of comfort. And for a time, together, they could find a bit of warmth. A bit of pleasure.

Penny needed something more from him and he did not know quite what it was. Even more, he wasn't certain why he felt compelled to give it.

She was not a weeping, delicate female. She surprised him. Through all of this, she had never once dissolved.

But there had been something in the way she had responded to his touch. Her shock, her shame. She hadn't known her body could feel such things, that much had been apparent by the way she had responded.

It had done something to him. Had made something inside him feel as though it might be new, too. He didn't want that.

He hadn't asked for any of it.

He hadn't asked to pity his little wife.

Or care at all about her bird.

Or her box.

He busied himself with plans and strategies he did not require until he was ready to collapse from lack of sleep. Only then did he return to the room upstairs. Only then did he allow himself to lie on the bed beside her, staying atop the blankets rather than joining her beneath them.

She looked small and vulnerable. And one thing he determined then.

He would protect her. With his sword, if need be. He would protect her from any enemy that she might face. What he did not know was if he possessed the power to protect her from himself.

Penny awoke the next morning, feeling more exhausted than when she'd fallen asleep. Her body ached in strange places and, when the maid brought a bowl with warm water and a pitcher into the room, her face burned with shame. As if the other woman knew why she might feel the need to cleanse. Naturally, she likely would.

The burning in her face persisted as she washed herself—intimately—before she dressed.

There was a bit of blood on the cloth she used. Which led her to go and look at the sheets. A bit of blood there as well.

Emotion pushed against her throat. She felt very alone. And Lachlan wasn't there. She knew that he'd come back. She had felt him lie upon the bed and had waited for him to put his hands on her again, but he had not.

She had drifted in and out of sleep. When she had finally awoken when the sun pierced through the small window of the room, he wasn't there.

She went through the trunk he had brought up and found a blue dress, new stays and a new chemise as well.

With no small amount of contortion she managed to get herself buttoned into the garment. There was also a bonnet, with a navy ribbon that matched the dress, and a rich wool overcoat of the same shade.

She arranged her hair simply, reusing the pins he had removed last night, and she examined herself, trying to see if she looked as different as she felt. She could see no mark of what had passed between them last night, but her soul felt branded.

Scalded.

As if he had been attuned to her movements, the door opened then.

He appeared, large and intimidating as ever, and ready for the day.

If he was affected by last night's intimacy, he did not show it. She had no idea how she was meant to ride in a carriage with him having been close to his body the way she'd been. It was as if she could feel him now. Pressed against her. Even with all the space between them.

She felt the building pressure between her thighs and had never been angrier at her own body than she was now, for the way it responded to him. She reminded herself, grimly, of that pain and loneliness that had accompanied the act.

Her body could remember only the pleasure.

She was forced again to grudgingly admit that this was why women allowed themselves to be ruined.

She had been told of the innocence of women. That they bore children, that they were the fairer sex in all ways. That they possessed an innate purity that men never would. It was women's job to steady their urges.

What tripe. How could she steady his urges when she couldn't master her own?

'We should be on our way,' he said, the first words spoken to her since he had left her last night. She didn't know what she expected from him. She had no right to expect anything.

She didn't know why she felt gravely disappointed, why she felt restless and lonely and empty. She had never been told to expect more from marriage and her dreams regarding her union with the Duke of Kendal had centred around the female companionship she might find in his house. It was such a strange thing, because she had thought the Duke so beautiful. Because her heart had ached, but not after *him*, she realised now. After all that had come with him.

After what he had represented.

A softness and comfort she had never known. A warm house that was filled with people who cared for each other, rather than an old manor house that was always cold, containing two family members who did not know how to speak to each other.

Her sense of what her future might hold had been heavily influenced by those surrounding fantasies, but she had not known to dream of what her marriage itself might contain. A life living in that household, but not a life knowing a man as deeply as she realised one did know a husband.

Except, she didn't know him. She knew little about him, yet he had seen her in a state that no one else ever had. She knew next to nothing about him, yet she had touched his body in a fashion she couldn't fathom touching another. In a fashion she wouldn't have been able to fathom touching him had it not occurred.

It was disorientating to say the least.

When all her things were packed away she found herself being bundled into the carriage. He did not join her.

'What are you doing?' she asked, sticking her head out the window.

'I'm riding,' he said. 'Have no patience for sitting in a carriage that many hours.'

'I'm going to be alone for the duration?'

'You may occupy yourself with whatever you like.'

'I haven't got anything to occupy myself, if you will recall. I did not bring any of my things. I haven't a book.'

'I believe the woman who helped assemble your trunk included needlepoint.'

She quite liked needlepoint, but she didn't want to give him the satisfaction of knowing that. 'I would prefer nature writings on the flora and fauna of Scotland.'

'You won't be needing a book. I can instruct you.'

'But you won't be in the carriage with me.'

'And we'll not be in Scotland today.'

With that, the conversation ended.

They pushed themselves further that day than they had the first and, by the time they arrived at the inn, she was exhausted and her nerves were frayed. He did not help her get ready for bed, rather he sent a maid up to assist her, though Penny knew she could have done without.

She lowered all the lamps, save one by the door, and got into bed.

She couldn't sleep. She wondered if he would come to bed. She was angry, because she was so tired, but she found herself on edge, waiting for the man.

How could she sleep knowing that she might have an experience like she had the night before? Not being certain?

It had been altering and much as though someone had taken small scissors to the places where she was stitched together, snipped them all out and she was waiting to be made anew.

She didn't know if a reprieve was the answer, or if his touch might be.

She was resentful that he had suddenly become the largest thought in her head.

She hadn't chosen this. She hadn't chosen him.

And he consumed her all the same. Had burst through her

defences in a way that she hadn't foreseen and she hated it. She needed to find a way to remake herself.

And silence had only ever been her enemy.

The door opened then and there he was. She shivered. She couldn't help but react.

He began to strip off his clothes, the dim light from the single lantern playing tricks with light and shadow over that warrior's body.

She had been so overwhelmed by him last night that, while she had looked, she felt as if she hadn't been able to fully get a grasp of how he truly appeared. It had been like staring into the sun.

He had scars. Ridges of flesh that spoke of wounds sustained in battle. His chest was broad, his waist narrow, his thighs well muscled. And then there was… Well, the rest of him. Now that she didn't feel quite so intimidated she could see that he was, in totality, beautiful.

She had seen paintings of naked men, but their members were small and wilted. Not his. It was… In full bloom, by contrast to wilted, she supposed.

She wanted to ask him the words. For everything. That was what she really wanted. She needed a book, an encyclopaedia of his body, one that might come with labels and terms for each illustrated figure.

It was how she learned.

How she had learned everything that she knew so far. It seemed reasonable enough to wish that she might have a book for him. For this. For them.

He said nothing to her, came over to the bed and settled on top of it. Then she waited.

He didn't move. He didn't get beneath the blankets. She stole a glance at him and could see that he was lying on his back with his arm thrown up over his face.

He lay there brazen, uncovered, clearly not at all ashamed of his exposed form. She began to feel restless, for she could not sleep with such a great awareness of his presence. With him right there, not knowing what he intended to do. With that strange pressure building between her legs and creating a restlessness in the pit of her stomach.

'Lachlan,' she said.

'Don't,' was his response, clipped and short and angry.

'Don't what?'

'I'm not in the mood to be gentle tonight, lass. Just sleep.'

'I don't know what that means,' she said, feeling frustrated.

He growled and, suddenly, he was over her, his green eyes blazing into hers.

'You do that quite a lot,' she whispered. 'Growling like a beast.'

'You tempt me to it.'

'I don't know what that means either.'

'All the more reason you should have let me sleep.'

'I *can't* sleep,' she confessed.

He kissed her then and she wanted to weep. Because finally, finally she felt something. A surge of strength and power. She had felt so hollow and miserable and lonely all day, ever since he had left her bed last night. But now he was kissing her and every possibility he had raised the night before was there again. It was a magical thing, the way that his kiss burned away the anger she had felt. Her fear. Her trepidation.

He pushed the bedding down with no small amount of violence in his movement and pushed her nightdress up, settling himself between her legs, pressing his hardness to the cleft between her thighs and shifting his hips slowly. She was wet there again and the glide of his heat was smooth, stoking that desire inside her that she had felt the last time they were together.

He entered her much more quickly this time, but it didn't hurt. She felt slightly tender for a moment, but it receded quickly. His strokes were hard and fast, his grip bruising on her hips, and when his teeth closed down on her lower lip, the shock sent an arrow of even deeper pleasure through her body.

She was like spun glass and knew that he would shatter her soon. But this was so different than how she'd felt all day in the silence. There was a power in this because, as fragile as she was, he was right there with her. She tried to hold back, because she knew how undone it made her feel and it frightened her more than a little. But soon, she couldn't. His breath, his body, his kiss. The way his heart raged in his chest, the deep, masculine sounds of pleasure that were foreign and mystical to her ears, all combined to stoke the flame of her desire.

'Penny,' he said and, the moment his name fell from her lips, a plea she didn't quite understand, she broke.

She gasped her pleasure, clinging to his shoulders, and that was when he withdrew, spending his own pleasure on to the sheets.

She wanted to ask him why, but her thoughts and words were tangled, and he didn't leave tonight. Instead he settled himself on the blankets, keeping distance between them, and slept.

How...how could he? How could he sleep with all of this between them?

It forced her to conclude that he felt nothing. That somehow this had changed nothing in him.

That she was alone in feeling altered. That created a terrible loneliness indeed.

In the morning, he was gone again, just as he been the night before. Once again, he bundled her into the carriage and rode on his horse. And again, any closeness that she had felt evaporated.

Of all the concerns she had about marriage, she realised

now that they were foolish. She hadn't even known what concerns to have.

Right now, the deepest was all the feelings she had no names for. And a husband who made her feel both more whole than she'd ever felt in her life and lonelier, too.

This was not the life she had dreamed of.

'You're a fool for thinking you could have dreams in the first place.' And since she was alone in the carriage, she could say it out loud.

But then she rebelled against herself. No, she was not a fool. She was only a fool if she allowed it to stand.

If she wanted change, she would have to make it.

Chapter Six

She never turned him away. Over the next three nights she allowed him to lift her nightdress and take his pleasure in her.

Just looking at her filled him with a strange heaviness and he was grateful for the distance he could keep from her during the days they travelled. Her in the carriage, he on his horse. He did not understand the sense of growing connection to this wide-eyed Englishwoman.

By the time they were in their room at night, he was half-wild with a thing he couldn't name that made his body hard—but stranger still—made his heart beat too quickly.

As if somehow she had begun to set the pace for the blood in his veins.

He did not allow it.

He set the pace. He did not allow her to touch him. He kept control, at all times. But part of him ached to strip her completely bare and explore her body at length.

But she was a wife, not a prostitute. And the things he wanted to do to her were not indignities a man visited upon his wife. His education on carnal acts had been conducted in brothels. He had been a young soldier and it was the way of things. He'd been warned by one of the women there very early on that those who made a business of pleasure were different from delicate society women.

Especially if they were English.

And this he'd confirmed over the years listening to the men in his company talk. Even men who had wives at home, who found solace between battles in the arms of whores.

He'd thought of his own father and his reputation. The way he treated women. And how fragile his mother had been.

The only conclusion he could draw was that this was true. The line between wives and whores.

He gritted his teeth against his own hypocrisy. Because hadn't he only thought that if he were taking pleasure, the woman deserved it as well?

She had her pleasure. Every time he had his.

But there were certain acts that one did not sully a lady with.

A lady you forced into marriage.

Forced marriage was common enough. If not forced then arranged, based on little more than mutual need.

He had no reason to feel guilt for that.

On the morning of the fourth day, he set his delicate wife in the carriage and mounted his horse as he always did.

'I'm tired of the carriage,' she announced, her delicate face appearing in the window.

'You've a few more days of it yet,' he responded.

'I wish to ride today.'

'I haven't an extra horse for you.'

'I shall ride with you,' she persisted.

'You will be wanting the comfort of the carriage,' he said through gritted teeth.

'Then you can put me back in the carriage when you've tired of me. Or when I've tired of you. Whichever comes first.'

They had managed to exchange a few words since that

first day they'd ridden in the carriage together. Since then, only their bodies had shared communication. But he knew full well that if he put the woman on the front of his horse he would be forced to listen to her talk about toast or birds or any number of inane things.

That he found he could not deny her enraged him.

'Be quick about it,' he said, dismounting to help her alight from the carriage. He opened the door, lifted her out, then propelled her up on to the horse, nestling her in front of him, her round, glorious backside fitting snugly against his cock.

So it was to be torture for the next several hours.

She fit perfectly against him. He had never had occasion to put a woman on the front of his horse before and he had not appreciated the situation it might create.

And he had been correct about the chatter. For she did chatter.

'I do believe that is a Scots pine,' she said, the fifth tree she had named in as many minutes.

'Do you?'

'Yes,' she said. 'At least, it's what I recall reading in one of Gilbert White's papers.'

'You've truly spent that much of your time educating yourself on pines?'

'My father didn't have fiction in his library. So, I've spent a good deal of time collecting all types of information. On plants. Animals. Aqueducts.'

'An impressive array of subjects.'

'The Greek pantheon. Religion in general. But there was one area of my father's library that was sadly lacking.'

'Other than Scotland, you mean?'

'Yes,' she said. 'Other than Scotland.' She made a small sound that he couldn't quite interpret. A hum, as if she was considering whether or not she would carry on. Or pretending to consider it. In the short time he'd known Penny he'd never once got the sense she'd held back something she truly wanted to say. 'It was alarmingly lacking in the subject of human anatomy. As well as other…practicalities. I have some questions.'

The way she wiggled against him created a pull of desire in his body. 'Do you now?'

She paused for a moment, then turned her head to the side. He could see her elegant profile, her rosy cheeks partly concealed by the rounded curve of her bonnet. 'What do you call it?'

'My apologies, lass, I'm not sure what you mean.' He had a feeling he did know what she meant and that the intended target was stirring against her backside even as she manoeuvred around the topic like a battle strategist.

'Your…that is… I am actually aware of the biological… that is to say the Latin…'

'A cock,' he said, opting for bluntness.

Her shoulders twitched.

'Really?' she asked, her head whipping to the side again, the blue ribbon on her bonnet moving with her. 'Like a rooster?'

'Aye,' he returned.

He had the strangest urge to laugh. Not at her, so much as the situation itself. He could not remember the last time he'd laughed from humour. At least when not in his cups.

'Fascinating indeed.' It wasn't his imagination. She arched her back against him just then. 'A cock.' She tested the word and it was far too enticing, that sweet voice and the innocence wound through it, saying such a provoking thing.

'Be careful wielding that,' he said. 'That word on a woman's lips could cause the downfall of mankind. Or cause a scandal at the very least.'

'Is it? It's very difficult to know what's scandalous when you haven't the context. I've been so protected from scandal that I fear I'm not as shocked by some things as I ought to be. Ruination is such a broad term, don't you think? And, as far as I'm aware, a woman can be ruined by going into a closed carriage with a man, or a darkened path in a garden, as easily as she can be ruined by the actual... Well, by copulation.'

'Is that so?'

'Yes.' She paused for a moment. Then made that same humming noise she had before. 'What do you call *that*? Is it the same as it is with animals?'

Then he would have laughed if she wasn't sitting so close to him. Were he not pressed against her temptation of a backside. 'There are many things you can call it.'

'Tell me.' She sounded eager and bright and he wanted—badly—to drag her down from the horse, tell his men to occupy themselves, take her into the nearest copse of trees and spend his time naming the act while performing it with her in a variety of fashions.

It was the strength of the need that stopped him.

For where there was no control, there was chaos.

And Lachlan was not a man who indulged in chaos.

He shifted. 'Tup. *Screwing*. But then neither is a term you would use in polite company.'

She made a noise as if considering it.

'Don't go saying that,' he said.

'Why not?'

'Not fitting for a lady.'

'But the act is? For a married lady, at least. So why can't I say it?'

'You're not such an innocent, surely.' He knew fine ladies were sheltered from the world and he'd known she was untouched, but how could she know so little, yet respond to his touch so beautifully?

'I don't know. I feel as though I have gaps in my knowledge of the world. Of life. I didn't know that the act between a man and a woman would feel quite so good. Or quite so terrible.'

He stiffened. 'It's terrible?'

'Oh, it feels wonderful while you do it. But I don't understand why you won't...' She twitched her shoulders and for some reason he had the deep sense that she was frowning, though he couldn't see her face. 'I don't know the word for that either.'

'Orgasm,' he said. 'That's what the peak is called. The little death.'

'Oh,' she said. 'It does feel like that. As though your whole body might shutter to a stop at any moment. As if you're shattered and crushed back together all at once.'

He had nothing to say to that. He shouldn't feel...pleased.

He had never imagined that he might have such a forthright talk about such subjects with his wife. Not that he wasn't accustomed to speaking of it. The men of his acquaintance were quite bold about such things and whores certainly had no cause to blush about the subject.

He had not imagined that a woman of her breeding would engage in the discussion, but she seemed fascinated.

He remembered well the way that she had tackled saving the small bird. The tenacity of her. It was the same now.

'I know how one—or rather two—creates a child,' she said. 'I've read a great many books about farm animals. And I figure, as it is the same with all animals, it is the same with people. Also, I had a governess who presented quite a few stern warnings about men and their predation. Why do you not wish to create a child with me?'

'I'll not carry on my line,' he said. 'A decision I made long before I chose you as a wife.'

He didn't see the point in manoeuvring around the truth. He owed her nothing, it was true. He had married her only to take something from her father, not to give anything to her. It cost him nothing to tell her why he had no interest in fathering a child. 'My father was chief of the clan. By marriage to my mother. MacKenzie is her name. *Was* her name. My father earned his position through the trust of her father. The trust of the people. But he was weak. While the clan was diminished my father went to Edinburgh, and he spent his money, the money of the people, on frivolous things. On women, on houses about the city. He wanted to buy his way into being like them. Like a Sassenach.'

'What is that?'

'An outsider. English. That was what he became. He forsook his clan. The Highlands. After everything the English did to us.'

'But you fought for England. In the war.'

'Aye,' he said. 'I did. I would do it again, because the world has no place for bloodthirsty madmen and I would stand against that even if it meant standing with an enemy. Don't mistake me, my relationship with your country is complicated. But my allegiance first and foremost is to Scotland. Is to the clan. My father traded his allegiance for his own comfort. Charged outlandish rents to the farmers and spent their money. He used them poorly. I would see everything returned to the people. I will not carry on a weak bloodline.'

'You think your bloodline is weak because of your father's actions? If we're doomed to be our parents, then I'm fated to die very soon. Or become like my father, which I feel is only slightly preferable to early death.'

'My mother had many children,' he said. 'All of them are dead.'

'All of them?' she asked, her voice hushed. 'You lost all of your brothers and sisters?'

He dismissed the tenderness in her voice. 'I don't remember most of them.'

Only James had lived long enough to be given a name. Only he had lived long enough for Lachlan to remember his cries, his ruddy little face. His small, angry fists that he'd waved in the air as he wailed. Fever had taken him. And quickly.

'That's tragic, Lachlan. I'm very sorry.'

'The world is a harsh place. Life and happiness are guaranteed to no one. I survived. There must be a purpose to that.'

'And you don't think that that purpose is to have more children?'

'My purpose is to get the land back to the clan. To make sure that balance is restored.'

'So you've taken me from…from marriage to a duke, a household full of people and a life where I would have children to…to taking me up to a foreign land where I will have no one.'

No one but him.

But she didn't say that.

'Babies die, lass,' he said, his voice flat. 'If I remember anything from my youth, it's that.'

'I don't understand,' she said softly, 'why you would do this to me?'

'It's nothing to do with you.'

He felt her shrink against him. 'Of course it's not. Nothing is. I'm a pawn, aren't I? I don't get toast or my jewellery box. And none of it matters, because you are getting your revenge. And you're going to restore the Highlands the way that you see fit. You don't much care if I could marry the man that I loved. You don't much care if I wish you would…say something to me after you use my body. You don't care if I want to hold a baby in my arms some day. That is…a wife and mother is something I should be. It's…the way of things.'

'I don't have pity in my heart, Penny,' he said, feeling a strange tenderness there all the same. 'It's a wasted speech on me, bonnie girl.'

'What good is being beautiful? My father thought that beauty was my triumph. That it was what had got me into marriage with the Duke. But my beauty doesn't mean anything, because you would have married me even if I looked like a toadstool. All you wanted was his suffering.'

'Yes, but had you been ugly my marrying you would've

been a favour. Instead, it was an insult. That his beautiful daughter would be wasted on a barbarian.'

'So glad I could help with that,' she said, each word bitten off at its end.

'How is it you have such a tongue in your head? Such a sheltered girl, yet you don't seem to fear me.'

'Why should I? What else can you possibly take from me?'

The words scraped against something he hadn't known existed inside him.

'You will have a castle.'

'A castle?'

'Yes. The clan has a proper castle and it is no medieval fortress. My father used his money to make it quite modern. I think you'll appreciate it. All the comforts of home behind fortified stone walls.'

'Without a friend. Without children. I can go from one mausoleum to the other. A monument to sins that were not mine. I am truly a fortunate *lass*.'

He urged his horse forward, at a faster pace. 'There are always children running about the castle. I'm sure you'll find a bairn if it's what you desire.'

She said nothing to that and absurdly he found he wanted to go back to naming body parts and ecstasy for her education. For anything would be better than this. Knowing he had disappointed her and caring even the slightest bit.

What was it about this creature that called forth *feelings* in him? He knew drive. He knew how to chart a course and sail his ship to that destiny. He knew how to plan and wait and execute. He did not feel.

But she shifted things in his chest, like the rising and falling of a tide rearranged even the heaviest of boulders, and he could not see the reason for it.

'I swear to you this,' he said. 'Your life will not be a misery.'

Then he knew, for he was thinking of his mother. His

mother, who had been so badly disgraced by his father, who had lost all of her children but one. And though he knew his father deserved the largest share of the blame, he could not shake the guilt. It had followed him through life, following him on to the battlefield. All the women he'd failed to save. He might have married Penny for revenge, but he would never treat her cruelly. 'You will not fade away to misery. My mother took her own life, Penny. That was where her misery took her. That was where my father took her. I have seen things on a battlefield that would tear you right in two. I have seen what it does to men, the madness that overtakes them. Rather than protecting the vulnerable they...use their strength against them. They forget they are men and become like animals. I have seen men lose all hope and decide death is preferable to the life around them. The despair that takes you to get to that point is a tremendous pit. The pit my mother fell prey to. You may not understand my reasons, but you can take me at my word. That will not be your fate. But trust that my decisions are for the best.'

He had partly expected a quick rejoinder, but she said nothing. Not for a while.

'I'm sorry about your mother. I'm sorry if what my father did made it worse. Made it harder.'

'It did,' he said.

'Of course it did. If it hadn't, you wouldn't have been so bent on revenge, would you?'

'And what can you take from a man who has nothing?'

'His daughter,' she said, softly. 'And his chance to have a relation to a duke by marriage.'

'So you see that I had no choice.'

'You always have a choice,' she said. 'It's just that you might not like the results of some of those choices. And so you chose the one that suits you best. I could've run away from our marriage. I had a choice. Society would have made it very difficult for me to find a way to survive. The Duke's sister offered me help, but I couldn't in good conscience risk Beatrice's reputation. Or even the Duke of Kendal's. A duke he might be, but he is still beholden to society and they love nothing more than to watch a man of quality fall. He prizes his integrity and reputation. How could I be the one to damage all that he's built?'

'And so you fell on your sword for the sake of their reputation, then complained to me about my revenge?'

'And you have twisted my words and used them against me.' She sounded grudgingly impressed.

'I have experience in war. I'm trained to fight.'

'And I am trained to do needlepoint. So I am outmatched.'

'Somehow, I doubt it.'

For there was something about the woman that got beneath his skin and he could not figure out the where or why.

The road went on, wide and smooth, the fields on either side of them rolling and green, sharp rocks rising from the grass out in the distance, creating a shoddy patchwork that extended to the horizon line.

'What did you dream your life would look like?'

'Must you talk?'

'It's the reason that I'm riding on the horse with you,' she said. 'I don't like the quiet. It's heavy. I was tired of being alone.'

'I was not.'

'Was that your dream, then?' she asked. 'To be alone? In which case, choosing a wife as a pawn in your revenge game was poor planning.'

'Many men do not often see their wives.'

'Of course,' she said.

'Your dreams,' he said. 'Tell me of your dreams, Lady Penelope. If you want to know mine, surely you should tell me yours first.'

'When? My dreams recently consisted of a duke and his beautiful country home.'

'Somehow, I can't imagine you wished to marry him for his rank and title.'

He didn't know why he was so certain of that. Any person would be tempted by a title so lofty. Why should she be any different? Yet he sensed that she was. He sensed that it was not his title that had appealed to her at all.

'I'm tired of being alone,' she said. 'That's why I used to wander the estate the way that I did. Looking for small animals. I used to dream of being like the birds. I used to dream of flying away.'

He was not looking to fulfil this woman's dreams. He was not the husband she'd chosen. But her sadness bothered him and it made him want to offer her something.

'Well. The horse doesn't have wings, but it is carrying you away to Scotland.'

She took a sharp breath, her shoulders pitching upward. 'I suppose that's true. But I had been to Bybee House. I've spent so much time there. And I know the Duke's mother. His sister. She was one of my dearest friends, before her brother was told that I betrayed him. And his ward. Such lovely girls, and... They were the first real friends that I've ever had. I want to not hurt. To not have to...feel fear or grief.'

Her words, her face, mingled with images from the past. With a woman he couldn't save, whose last moment he knew had been spent in fear and despair.

'Aye, lass, wouldn't we all.'

'You can't tell me you feel fear.'

'I fought in a war for ten years and, no matter how grimly I told myself death was to be accepted, greeted like a friend, I fought to preserve myself as well as those around me. Death was commonplace, but one thing you learn is how strong the will to survive is.' A strange sensation tightened his chest. 'The very worst thing of all is to see that will stolen from another person. You must have some sense of the future. For me...it was restoring the clan.'

'And revenge,' she said, her tone filled with mock cheer. 'Aye.'

'I thought I knew what my life would be, then the Duke proposed. Suddenly I could dream of a whole new future. You took that from me.'

'Dreams, perhaps. But there is always adventure. Adventure often lies just far enough in front of us that we cannot see the destination,' he said. 'You cannot know to dream of what's on the other side of that.'

'Is that what you've had these last years? An adventure?'

He nodded slowly. 'Adventure is also not always good. I came to England to make my fortune and I did. But it was a circuitous route that took me over battlefields and brings me to a home where none of my clan may remember or accept me as chief. But make my fortune I did.'

'Was making your fortune your dream?'

'I was born with fortune. I did not need to dream of it.'

'Then what was your dream?'

'Nothing,' he said. 'I had everything until I had nothing. And then there was no purpose to dreams.'

'Only revenge?'

'A dream is nothing more than a wish. Revenge takes planning.'

'Well, then I suppose you planned well.'

'That I did.'

Yet, as he sat atop his horse with his wife clutched tightly against him and the carriage rolling behind them, he had the sense that his plan might not be going quite as he had expected.

It didn't matter. She didn't matter and neither did the feelings that she roused in his soul. What mattered was getting back to Scotland, not concerning himself with her feelings of loneliness or her thoughts of her own shattered dreams. Or giving names to the mysteries in her universe.

She was not a bland, English miss and he should have

given her more credit than that. But her failure to be boring hardly meant that he needed to recalibrate the way that he saw his life moving forward.

He was the husband, after all.

His wife was his property.

He protected what was his, kept it safe. He was not his father and he would not treat ill that which was his to protect. But she was his none the less.

He was returning home to the Highlands with much more property than he had when he left and that was a triumph.

It was all that mattered. He would concern himself with nothing else.

'That's an oak,' Penny said, though it lacked the spirit of her earlier proclamations.

For the rest of the day he contented himself with listening to her name the obvious, while the press of her arse kept him hard with wanting.

When they arrived at the next inn, he had his way with her as he had done every night before and, when he was finished, he did not concern himself with her loneliness.

Chapter Seven

The further north they'd gone, the more the landscape had changed. The greens became ethereal and she could easily imagine fairies hiding out behind the rocks, which grew to enormous proportions, jagged and sheer faced.

She wouldn't have known when they passed into Scotland, except that Lachlan told her.

She hadn't tried to talk to him again, not like that one day on the horse. She had kept things light.

She hadn't used the new vocabulary he'd given her either, but she had locked it away inside herself, for later use, because knowledge was power, after all, and she could use whatever she could lay hands on.

He had not changed his actions towards her at night. Still she found ecstasy in his arms, only to crash back down to earth when it was all finished.

Maybe that was just the way of things.

Maybe there was no answer. Maybe the intimacy between a husband and a wife created only questions, at least in the wife.

She felt startlingly vulnerable and didn't like it. She had spent her life working at ways to not be weak, to not be a potential victim to those around her. Her father was so volatile. Though he had not used his fists on her, his words had often cut deep grooves inside her soul. The games he played with isolation had tested her fortitude. If she had not found ways to layer protection over herself, if she had not found ways to please herself, ways to insulate herself, she would have been destroyed by now.

Lachlan had asked her how she had such a tongue in her head. She could only attribute it to her ability to protect herself, so why then did she find it so difficult to control that tongue around Lachlan and also to shield herself against the feelings that he created inside her?

It was distressing.

Today, they would arrive on the land of Clan MacKenzie. He had warned her that their reception might not be warm. He had sent his men ahead and, had the reception been deadly, he had assured her that he would have received word from a survivor. Unless there were none.

He'd given her a grim smile after that and she had not been able to discern if he were teasing.

She was not entirely sure if Scottish warriors engaged in teasing.

She found her husband extremely difficult to divine.

But then, she didn't find her own feelings any more clear.

Today, though, she kept her focus on what was ahead. She was seeing her new home. Her new home.

The words radiated inside her and she did not know what they meant. Not truly. For how could she make sense of calling this strange place home?

It was beautifully alien.

She could feel Lachlan's tension increase the closer they got to his home. The green went deeper as they went, the mountains higher, craggier. Penny felt like exactly what he'd told her she was.

An outsider.

They weren't the same. And this was not where she was from.

She understood now what he had meant. Understood now that this wasn't just a place a bit further to the north, but a stark, unforgiving landscape. Looking at Lachlan's face over her shoulder as they rode reminded her that he was from here. But he had lived in England for a great many years. If she found him uncompromising and forbidding…how much more so were the people who had been here all this time?

Some hours on, the path curved and she could see it. A great, great castle that stood against the sharp blue of the sky, the deep green fields rolling down below. It was high on a hill, overlooking a lake. There were houses dotting the landscape, rolling down to flatter green.

'Here it is, lass,' he said. 'These are the lands of Clan MacKenzie.'

'What are you doing?'

He stopped the horse and dismounted, taking her down to the ground with him. 'Get in the carriage,' he said.

'Why?' she asked.

'In case we are met with a volley of arrows.'

Fear gripped her. 'You don't think that will happen?'

His expression was grave. 'I don't know what will happen.'

She could see that it cost him to make such an admission, for her husband was a man who wanted to anticipate everything.

And if not even Lachlan Bain knew what might befall them here, then…

She was filled with disquiet and for the first time obeyed him without argument.

As they drew closer, she could see that there was a line of

men in tartan standing in front of the castle. They had swords and all other manner of weapons strapped to their bodies and held in their hands. They looked grim and forbidding, and not at all welcoming.

But no shots were fired.

That was a small comfort, at least.

'I'm Lachlan Bain,' he said. 'Son of Angus Bain. I've returned as promised. I have come to restore the land and make repayment for that which my father stole. I am here to take my rightful place as chief.'

A shiver went through Penny's body and something that felt a lot like pride. For he was the biggest, strongest man in a whole group of them, and his bearing was that of a leader. His words, his vows were true.

And in that moment...she trusted him. Trusted he was everything he'd said. It mattered to her. It was silly, maybe, that it mattered, that there was some measure of honour in what he'd done to her, even if she were a pawn.

He was driven by the need to protect his clan. To avenge the indignity visited on his family.

She might not have asked to be caught up in it but, looking at him now, she could see the full measure of the man he was and she found him...beautiful.

The line of men remained impassive, then one man stepped forward. 'Laird,' he said, inclining his head.

Penny didn't understand the protocol here, but she knew enough to understand the weight in that word. That at least one man was ready to acknowledge Lachlan's place.

'My father has ill used these lands and these people,' Lachlan continued. 'And you have my word that I will make right what he has done wrong.'

'With due respect,' the man who'd stepped forward said. He was tall, older than Lachlan, but it was impossible to tell by how many years for his face was brutally scarred. 'How do we know you will keep your word?'

'Execute me if I don't,' Lachlan said. 'You might remember me from when I was a boy. I went away to try to make my fortune and I have done so. My time in England was not what I planned for it to be. But I made more than I could have imagined. And I'm still learning. I have merchant ships and have left men in charge of my business in London. I am an asset to the clan.'

'Aye,' the man said. 'I swear that I will be the one to kill you if you don't keep your word. Laird.'

'I would expect nothing less. But I am not on trial. I am Laird here. And my word will be obeyed.' He tilted his head upwards and she could easily imagine the look on his face. Iron. Uncompromising. 'There can be no question. A house without a head will not know which way to turn. It will not stand. I will have no dissension in the ranks.'

She could see two men, on the end of the line, exchange a look, and her stomach went tight. Lachlan was hard and he was terrifying, but she could see loyalty would not be easily won, not even for him.

'It has been years, Cousin.' The man on the end moved forward and, as he spoke, Penny could see the resemblance between the two men, though this man was not as tall or broad or fearsome as Lachlan. 'I have been taking care in your stead.'

'And for that I am grateful, Callum,' Lachlan said. 'Your work here will never be forgotten. For I honour blood. I honour that which is mine. My family. My clan.'

He dismounted his horse and went back to the carriage, opening the door. Green eyes met hers and he extended his hand. She took it, trembling slightly as she exited the carriage. The dress she wore today was much finer than the one she had adorned herself in for the other days of travel. But she had known that they would arrive today. Had known she would stand before his people and it had seemed important that she looked the part of wife to the Highland chief.

Not that she had any idea what the appropriate dress was for that role. But her yellow dress with its gauzy white fichu would have to do.

She accepted Lachlan's hand, and allowed him to lift her down from the carriage. 'My wife,' he said. 'Lady Penelope Bain. She is to be treated with respect.'

Something swelled in her breast, joining the pride that was growing there. That he was presenting her in this way. That they were…together. United. The satisfaction she felt went deep beneath the surface of her skin.

She felt part of him. Bonded to him.

'You bring us a Sassenach wife and demand respect?' The tall man spoke.

'I demand the respect owed me by my birthright,' Lachlan said.

'Are you not just an Englishman?' the man spat. 'You have been away these many years. You fought for their army.'

'I'm not like my father. I've no love of the English aristocracy, nor do I feel the need to make merry with them. This woman is my payment. When I went to England I took work with her father, who promised me a ship. He lied. He sent me off with no wages, nowhere to go. And that delayed my return home. I became a war hero. A captain in the British Army.' His laugh was hollow. 'And with that I purchased my freedom. Our freedom. And when I had the money, when I had the power, I returned and took what was dearest to him. She is not evidence that England has conquered me, but that I have conquered England.'

Penelope felt stricken, as if her husband had reached out and slapped her. Presenting her as a token of war. She had no idea he'd intended to do so. She kept her head high, though her heart was hammering heavily.

'You'll find the castle ready for you,' said the first man who'd spoken. 'We began to discuss this when your coin first arrived, and made our final decision when your men arrived ahead of you.'

'An honour,' Lachlan said, inclining his head.

There was no emotion on his face. He betrayed nothing of what he felt.

Penny wondered if he felt anything.

It was the strangest thing she'd ever borne witness to. One moment they were standing opposite those men guarding the front of the castle like rabid dogs, the next they were moving to do Lachlan's bidding.

Lachlan barked orders, as if his position weren't new, as if there was nothing tenuous about it, as if there had been no doubt a few moments ago if the people would accept or kill him. Orders to have things arranged, to have rooms prepared. To have the horses put away. He took Penelope by the arm and led her towards the door of the castle.

It was so large, stone and imposing and mighty in its magnitude. A manifestation of her husband in many ways. Because there were castles in England and it was not demonstrably different from those that stood there, but there was a wildness to it all that made it feel like something separate altogether.

There were men in England. Warriors. Strong, brave men with height and breadth and strength. But they were still not Lachlan.

They entered the grand doors and she was struck by how different it was inside to what she had expected. For there was wallpaper, like in the great manor homes of England, and large, plush carpets. And it was nothing quite so cold or medieval as it had looked from the outside.

'I think you will feel at home. My father had a fascination with the English.' He said it with his lip curled, obvious disgust filling his being.

'I gathered as much,' she said.

The great hall was massive, most of the original stone

intact, with grand dining tables and other pieces of magnificence about the room. Grand portraiture hanging there, pictures of Lachlan's ancestors. Grand tributes to the clan. And at the head of a massive table hung a coat of arms.

As if she could forget that these were a different people. Their own nation in essence. The pride and fierceness seemed to reach from within the rocks. And she could feel injustice here.

Injustice that these people had been taken by England.

A proud people with a history that stretched back further than modern memory. They had been diminished by greed. The greed of Lachlan's father, yes. But more than that, the greed of England.

Penny couldn't blame them for being distrustful of her, not for one moment.

For they had been conquered and enslaved, their kilts outlawed for a time. Pieces of their national pride that made them what they were.

And it was only in fighting for a nation that had betrayed them and stolen from them that they had been given some of their national identity back.

She felt ashamed then, standing there, an Englishwoman in the centre of a Scottish hall.

Still, she didn't relish her husband presenting her as a prize.

There was unfairness in the world, but she didn't have enough power to cause it and her humiliation certainly wasn't going to diminish it.

Just a pawn...

All that hope that had been preparing to take flight in her chest had its wings ripped clean away. They were not one. She was little better than a prisoner. Him feeling loyalty to a clan, a castle, his family, had nothing to do with how he felt about her. She'd been an idiot to think it did.

She waited for him to make introductions of her to the

household staff, but he didn't. Rather, he ushered her up the stairs and down a long corridor. It was true that much of the castle had been modernised, but there were great portions that remained part of the Middle Ages. Cold and grey and stone.

'Our rooms,' he said. There were two doors, side by side. He pushed one open. 'I imagine you're tired from the journey. I will send a maid up to help you bathe.'

'Thank you,' she said, her voice sounding detached and not quite like her own. 'I… I could certainly use one.'

'The door there leads to my chamber. If you need anything. But it is likely that anyone on the staff can meet your needs should need arise.'

She nodded. 'All right.'

'I'm going down to the village.'

'Yes,' she said, as if she understood and agreed, but mostly she said it because she didn't think there was another option available to her.

Then he turned and left her there, standing in the chamber, quite alone.

She moved into the room cautiously. It was, as he promised, outfitted with every convenience she might have expected. Just as grand as the room she might have had in the Duke's country home. An intricately carved bed with swathes of fabric draped around the top of the wooden frame. The bedclothes were rich and velvet, plush and glorious looking.

The room possessed a grand fireplace that would ensure she was never cold. There was a *chaise*, a small table with chairs. Bookcases.

A large armoire and, when she opened it to look inside, she found dresses. More even than had been in the trunk for the journey. More than she ever owned in her life. He'd said he had things sent ahead. And he had not lied. But none of them were her things. Everything in the room was beautiful, rich and lovely, but none of it was familiar and it only added to that sense of being outside herself.

If she were to dissolve, there would be no one to see it.

She had no purpose or reasoning to push her fear or sadness or loneliness down into that place inside her, because there was no one to put a brave face on for.

She walked over to a vanity at the far end of the room, looked at the lovely, velvet-covered bench, then at the beautiful, marble-topped vanity to see something very familiar. That simple wooden jewellery box. The one left to her by her mother. The one that contained nothing more than pebbles collected at the estate, feathers. Things that mattered only to her. Things her father had not been able to sell. Things that were dear to her heart and only hers.

He had retrieved it. He'd said he wouldn't.

Lachlan had made sure she had her jewellery box.

If she were nothing more than a conquest, nothing more than a prisoner of war he had been fighting in his own heart for all these years, would he have done such a thing?

She didn't know.

She sat down at the vanity and wished she could cry. Her eyes hurt, pressure building behind them and growing in her chest. But she couldn't because she'd spent so long training herself to stay in one piece and, even when she was desperate to shatter, she didn't know how.

She hated this. In the moment, she hated him.

No. It wasn't his touch she feared, but the desperation it left behind. The need for something she could not put a name to. The desperate desire for something she had never expected her life would contain.

She sat in silence, her eyes filled with grit. And then she made a decision. She was not simply going to sit here and wait for a maid to come and bathe her. She was not simply going to be installed in a room.

It was up to her whether or not she was seen as a conquest.

It was her decision to make what her life became now.

Too long, men had controlled all that she was and all that she could be.

Yes, Lachlan was her husband. And, yes, there were decisions he had made for her life and her future that she could not control. But she was a woman and the household belonged to the wife. She would have been the Duchess at Bybee House and she would have made it her own. She would have had the responsibilities of running a household and she would have them here as well.

He would not simply relegate her to a bedroom and leave her here.

Something about that jewellery box, about its presence on the vanity, gave her the confidence that he would not wish that.

That he perhaps cared a small amount more than he pretended.

He could not possibly care to pretend less.

It was true. The only time she felt connected to him was when he came to her at night.

But this place was his. Part of him. And she had felt that the moment she had entered. The history in the stones. If she became part of this house, then she would be part of the history of Clan MacKenzie. Part of the history of Lachlan.

She was determined to see it so.

And one thing that was true of Penny was that once she made a determination towards something, then she would not be deterred.

And this would be no different.

Lachlan had stopped at every farm. His people were proud and they did not necessarily trust the new Laird. When he had presented the gifts of coin, he had to be careful to make sure he called it what it was: restitution. Not charity. Not mites being given to beggars, but property being returned, for the rents his father had charged during his life. For the cost it had had for the people.

By the time he was finished, his exhaustion was bone deep. They had travelled for hours today, then he'd had to make sure this bit of business was done and done right. He was a soldier and it was rare that anything took a physical toll on him. It was being back here. This place.

It was so familiar, yet he could not stop staring at it as if he had never seen it before. And he realised, as he stood there by the loch, the shadow of the castle looming over him, that he had never truly believed he would come back here.

He'd have thought it a dream misremembered by a desperate fourteen-year-old boy who wanted to believe there was a home that belonged to him somewhere in the world.

He had many homes. Had the money to instal himself wherever he chose in London. But it was not the same. For his blood flowed from here. The clan was his blood. His breath. His life.

For all the hatred he carried in his heart towards his father all these years since he'd been away, it was only intensified now. For how could he give allegiance to anything other than this place?

How could anything matter but the sacred earth that was enriched by the bones of their ancestors, down beneath the surface? How could anything bear more weight than the land? Their pride. Their strength. Their people. For you could purchase the title and you could dine in Edinburgh with the esteemed, make a play for being part of the peerage, but it would not change blood. Money could not purchase a home. A place of belonging.

It came from blood. The blood of his mother's family. Clan MacKenzie. And even if his mother's body was not in consecrated ground, she was here.

She was part of this earth.

He had brought his men with him—the men who had

fought with him in the war—and a few of the men who had set themselves up as protectors of the clan, the gentry and chieftains who had been holding the clan steady since the death of his father and prior to his return.

Though he did not have an easy camaraderie with the men, they'd all pledged their loyalty to him.

It was all that mattered.

They rode their horses down to the cottages that sat in the outlying areas. They were in disrepair here. The poverty pronounced. The fields around them fallow.

The door to one of the homes opened and a man came out, staggering. 'What is it ye're after?' he slurred.

'This is the Laird, McLaren,' a chieftain of the clan, Glenn, shouted at the drunk. 'Mind yourself.'

'Laird?' he said, his lip curled. 'Oh, we've all heard about you.'

'Then you've heard I've come to restore the clan.'

'Can't restore what's dead,' the man said. 'It's too late for us.' He swept his hand to the side, indicating the fields. 'While you were making merry in England your father destroyed us. Bankrupted us.' He spat on the ground. 'I'll have nothing from you. You and your Sassenach bitch.'

Lachlan drew his sword and got off his horse. The man stumbled back, fell to the ground. A woman appeared in the doorway behind him and screamed, 'Ye can't kill him!'

But Lachlan's vision was a red haze. He would not have his wife questioned. Would have no words spoken against her. Her honour, her safety, would be protected.

'I will have your allegiance,' Lachlan said. 'I am Laird here. My wife is the lady of the castle and you owe her respect.'

'Cut my throat,' the man said. 'I owe you nothing.'

'No!' the woman shouted. 'Ye cannae take him from me. We'll all die.'

He saw a child in the doorway then, staring up at him as if he were a devil.

'You will pledge your fealty to me,' Lachlan said. The man paled as Lachlan took a step closer. 'I am your Laird.'

'You have my allegiance.' The man's lip curled and it was clear in every line of his body he hadn't wanted to pledge it, but it was of no matter to Lachlan. The inhabitants of every house within sight were watching now.

He was a conqueror. This was what he knew. There was only one way to take respect and he would do it at the point of his sword if he had to.

'Are there any others who wish to voice dissent?' he asked, looking around at those who were gaping at the scene before them.

No one spoke.

'I have come to make restitution,' he said. 'But make no mistake. I am The MacKenzie. There is only one voice that matters here. Mine.'

There was nothing more to say than that.

They finished afterwards and, if his men disapproved of what had happened, they said nothing. He'd made it clear what he thought of those who questioned him.

He would not afford dissention in the ranks. Many clans had been destroyed. Farms abandoned. Castles left crumbling. He was fighting against a tide that would not turn unless he did it with his own hands.

He had to be in charge and unquestionably. One drunken fool would not undermine what he was. And he would not issue threats, however veiled, to Lachlan's wife. He would not call her honour into question. Lachlan would not allow it.

He made his way back into the castle, ravenous. He went back to his bedchamber and changed clothes, ignoring the hunger that flared inside him as he looked at the door that connected his room to his wife's.

When he went down the stairs and into the dining room,

he was surprised to hear an English voice rising above the familiar cadence of all the Scottish burrs around it. 'And what does the daily routine generally consist of?'

'You needn't worry about it.'

'Quite to the contrary,' Penny said. 'I do believe it is my position to worry about it.'

His wife was standing next to the dining table with the housekeeper and both women were regarding each other with deep suspicion.

'I'm hungry,' Lachlan said.

'Of course,' the housekeeper said, casting Penny a frosty glare before turning and making her way towards the kitchen.

'What is it you've got up to?'

'I need to know my duties,' Penny said.

She had bathed.

She had exchanged the heavier dress she had worn for travel for one that was white, light and ethereal and put him in the mind of the dress she had worn on their wedding day.

She wore a fichu which covered the swell of her glorious bosom, a pity, he thought, and her hair was arranged in an artful fashion, low on her neck, not quite to the English style.

He preferred it.

'You don't have duties.'

'I do. The duty of a wife is to see to the running of the household.'

'You're an outsider. You don't know our ways.'

'And I'm determined to learn them. You have not lived here as a man. I wouldn't imagine you know much more about the running of a household than I do.'

He went to issue a denial, then found that he couldn't. For, in many ways, she was correct. He had lived here until the household had become somewhat derelict. Ignored by his father. Only then had he even begun to consider what went into the maintaining of a household when the lack of it had become apparent.

'It is my job to organise the servants and oversee the menus.'

'The menu is my only concern at the moment. I'm ravenous.'

She looked up at him, her expression sharp. 'I did note that there is a bit more available than haggis and blood pudding.'

'Am I to look forward to a dinner of toast, then?'

Her lips twitched. 'It would serve you right.'

But when the meal appeared, it was rich and fast, with a great amount of variety. Pheasant and eggs and sturgeon. Root vegetables and a stew.

Fresh bread—he was extraordinarily thankful for the fresh bread. And the ale. The food felt like home. He felt home.

'You brought me my jewellery box?' she asked, looking up at him, something shining in her blue eyes that he couldn't read.

'I sent a man for it, aye.'

'You… After I asked you to?'

'Aye.'

'You said you wouldn't.'

Her gaze made something shift in his chest, made him feel as though he was reaching for something he couldn't put a name to. 'What is it you're asking for, lass?'

'Why did you do it?'

There was a feeling for it, but no words. He didn't like it. Didn't like the sense that there was something in him he couldn't identify.

He did not believe in such things. A man in his position had to know. There was no space for uncertainty.

But he could not put words to it and, more to the point, he did not want to. For there was a softness to the feeling and he could not allow for softness.

'It's not a matter of consequence,' he said, ignoring the itch beneath the surface of his skin.

'It is to me.'

'But not to me,' he said, his tone hard. 'And if it is of no consequence to me, it is of no consequence to anyone.'

'Of all the arrogant…'

'I am Laird of this castle. Chief of Clan MacKenzie. A lack of arrogance would not engender faith.'

'You didn't fetch the box to make me happy? Or to…be kind or…?'

'I wished to shut you up, even if just for a time, but it appears it hasn't worked.'

Colour flared in her cheeks and she looked away from him. He had done wrong by her. And that…he felt regret for that.

But to do right by his people meant he could not put her first. He had to guard against anything that might put the clan at risk.

He turned his focus back to his meal.

He didn't speak as he ate. And it took him a while to notice that she was sitting there quietly, much of her food untouched.

'You're not hungry?' he asked.

'I think I'm a bit more tired than I realised. I have lived a lifetime in less than a fortnight.'

He stared at her, quite unable to make sense of her words. This moment was the culmination of an actual lifetime for him.

These last days on the road had been simply that. Days. The woman knew nothing of the passage of time.

'You make no sense.'

'I fear we don't make sense to each other,' she said. 'For there is nothing terribly different about all of this for you, is there? You make a decisive move, claim what it is you want. And that's the way of it. It's nothing for you to use my body, because it could be myself or a woman who takes coin for such an act. It is nothing for you to travel, for you've been all around the Continent and I have never left England. I've scarcely been away from the estate. No man had ever put his hands on me, his mouth on me, until you. And you…

You just say how it is, how it will be, and trust that it will be done. You don't worry at all what that means for me. What it feels like for me. I lost the future I had planned. The hope of children. And you can't understand why it feels I've lived a lifetime in this span of days? You couldn't even give me a lie about my jewellery box. Some indication that you have a heart. I've had to replace any thoughts of what I had to what my lifetime might be with new ones. With yours. I'm glad it feels inconsequential to you.' She stood and moved away from the table. 'I'm tired. Don't come to my room.'

And with that she made a very decisive choice. She left him there with a full belly and less of a sense of triumph than he felt he ought to have.

He didn't know why in hell he'd felt he had to fight her about the damn box. Except it shouldn't matter.

And neither should the feelings of a woman who had been a small piece of what he'd planned to accomplish. His revenge was done and she was his. He had the clan to concern himself with now.

Yet he found himself concerned with her. And he did not know a way to banish those feelings now that they'd taken hold.

Chapter Eight

There was, Penny found, a strange sort of pleasure to be had in barring him from her room. For the first two nights, she was drunk on it. She'd ordered him not to come the first night. She'd locked the door the second. He'd tried it. Once.

She could practically feel his outraged pride through the heavy wood and she'd gloried in it. She didn't lock it the next night because she'd been hoping he might come through that door and she'd have an excuse to turn him away directly again.

Because all those nights he had come to her room while they had been traveling to the Highlands she had surrendered herself. All the pleasure that he had added to her body he had taken away again when he left.

When he finished and simply fell asleep.

Then it cost her when he took that small gesture, that beacon of hope represented in her jewellery box, and crushed it so callously.

The distance felt like a reclamation.

It was difficult for her to get the women in the household

to warm up to her. She did not experience open hostility, but the frosty nature of her interactions with Rona, the house-keeper, made it clear that she was not welcome as the lady of the house.

The kitchen maids, Margaret and Flora, were marginally better. Her personal maid, Isla, was quiet, but didn't seem to have any ill will towards her.

But she had heard whispers about Lachlan. The staff might ignore her, but there was an advantage to that. They often didn't notice when she was around and she was accomplished at listening in on other people's conversations. It was the only method of gleaning information that was as good as asking.

They said it was suspected he was no different than his father and that his English bride was evidence of this. Of his obsession with their oppressors.

Penny knew that wasn't true. Her husband was far from ob-sessed with her. In fact, he seemed quite happy to ignore her.

But she had concerns about the fact that his marriage to her was causing him trouble.

She gritted her teeth. She shouldn't care.

Except… This was her home. This was her home, whether she had chosen it or not. And she didn't want to spend her years here as an outsider. She could understand why they hated her. Her people had disrupted their way of life. While Lachlan might have a hope of restoring his clan, so much of the Highlands had been scarred beyond repair. The way of the clans was becoming near extinct and she did not expect that they would welcome her with open arms easily.

She had also heard that Lachlan had brought terror into the village. That a man had expressed his concerns about his return and Lachlan had drawn his sword.

She knew that he wasn't going to be violent without cause, but the fact he was trying to rule with iron over a people who were already inclined to distrust him… It wasn't going to work.

She had been victim of his remoteness. She already knew the way those green eyes could make a person feel.

Small.

He was not going to earn allegiance by terrifying everybody, by turning this place into an army, where he acted as captain as he had done during the war.

She was forming an idea, a plan. But she was going to need help.

It was not enough to simply plan menus. She was the lady of the castle and she was going to make that matter. But she had reached her limit here within the castle walls. She needed to get out. She hated the silence, the stillness.

She'd already taken a large chunk out of the library. She'd walked every bit of the gardens contained within the castle grounds. She'd retrieved her needlepoint supplies and had worked at stitching little flowers for hours on end. She'd begun inserting herself into the kitchen, learning to cook certain meals even though the maid protested. Gradually, in those things, she'd been reminded of who she was. It was like coming up out of a fog.

This life was still hers, even if Lachlan had put himself in position as Laird over her.

She could make the connections she craved. She could create a life she enjoyed out of what she had here. Lachlan didn't get to decide.

'Isla,' she said to her maid one day. 'I think I should like to meet more of the people. Lachlan spends his days working the land, working to restore his relationship to the people. It seems that as his wife I should do something.'

'The MacKenzie hasn't left any orders for you.'

The MacKenzie, she had learned, was what a man in his position was called. Like the King, but the highest of his clan. The most singular.

'I don't await his orders for everything,' she said. 'He thinks that he has full control, but he does not.'

'He must not be a cruel man, then.' Penny was surprised when Isla continued the conversation. Surprised and pleased. Her interactions with her maid had grown more cordial recently, but they still hadn't had much conversation. She was eager to get to know her better. They spent so much time near each other...why couldn't they be friends?

Penny frowned. 'No. Why do you say that, though?'

'Because it sounds to me that he hasn't got control of you simply because he won't exercise the right. And that means something stops him. A limit to his cruelty.'

Penny leaned towards Isla. 'Did the previous chief... The MacKenzie...did he not have a limit to his cruelty?'

'No. He wanted land. And he wanted money. He wanted to be part of the English peerage. It was a gift when he began spending so much time away from the Highlands.'

'I know as much from my husband.'

'His temper was a beast and one all the more easily roused when he was in his cups. He had many mistresses and beat them all.'

'He beat them?' Not even her father had ever sunk so low.

'Aye,' she said. 'One so badly she died.'

'He killed a woman?' She tried to imagine Lachlan losing his temper, tried to imagine him raging on her with his fists. She couldn't. And she had felt supremely wounded by the fact he had not fetched that jewellery box for her out of the kindness of his heart.

But he had been raised by a man who truly would harm a woman if he was of a mind to do so.

She had never felt protected. She had been sheltered in many ways. The cruelty she'd been exposed to had been a particular kind of neglect. It had shielded her from many of the other atrocities in the world. That a man could beat his lover to death...

'That's why he thinks there is something wrong with his blood,' she whispered.

'It's a silly thing,' Isla said. 'He's not a bad man.'

'You don't think so? I have… I've heard some of the household whispering. They think what he did in the village was a sign he might be violent.'

Isla shook her head. 'He didn't kill anyone.'

'That is a low standard for behaviour.' She paused. 'They also think…they also think his marrying me shows he's like his father. That he likes… English things. I don't know if they'll ever accept me.'

Isla made a tsking sound. 'You didn't personally slaughter our people. I understand the distrust. I don't fear you.'

'Well, I'm not very frightening. Lachlan, though…'

'If he were a bad man, you would know already. They would know already. Evil men don't take long to show it.'

'Don't they?'

'It's not been my experience. A drink or two and the alcohol ignites the temper on some brutes.'

Her maid could not be any older than she was. To think that she already had such experiences made Penny's heart squeeze.

'I hope you have a good man now,' Penny said.

Isla blushed. 'Aye. Though I know I shouldn't speak of it.'

'I don't mind,' Penny said. 'I've been very lonely. For… for ever. And I would like a friend.'

'I don't know if that's allowed.'

'Aren't I the lady of the manor?'

'I suppose you are.'

'Then it seems that I should get to make some rules. And I say that we should be allowed to be friends. But that isn't an order,' Penny said. 'You can't order someone to be your friend.'

'I will be your friend,' Isla said. 'It can be lonely in this house.'

'Then you'll come down to the village with me?'

'Yes,' Isla said. 'What is it you wish to do?'

'We can bring bread.' Penny brightened. 'We can bring bread and we can meet everyone. And you can show me who I should speak to.'

'I can do that.'

'Good.'

Perhaps she could help Lachlan find his place here. If she could balance his hardness with some of her softness.

As silly as it was, Penny felt triumphant because she truly felt that if she could make a difference here, if she could carve out a space for herself, then perhaps it might feel more like her life. And not simply a sentence that had been handed down to her by her father and his failures.

How strange. She had not thought of her father for some time. She didn't miss him or regret leaving home in the least.

For so many years her life had been consumed with him. And he hadn't loved her. He might not have used his fists on her the way that Lachlan's father used his fists, but his coldness had been an arrow through the heart.

The way that she had spent her life cut off, the way that she had spent it so lonely…

It ended here.

Her life was not where she had planned for it to be.

But she had been set on being a duchess. And there would've been responsibilities that went with that. There would've been this. This community of people that she bore responsibility for, and that she could have. She could make a full life.

With a heavy cloak settled over her shoulders, she and Isla ventured out into the village. Round rock houses were surrounded on all sides by sweeping mountains with sharp angles and curves that protected the dwellings from the harsh, cold winds. Grey stone broke through the blankets of green lichen, the only contrast to the deep colour, so vivid it nearly overwhelmed her vision.

It was wild, this place. The sky somehow higher here than in England. But great clouds reached down to touch the earth, wreath the mountains in mist.

Great meadows unfolded and rolled down towards the loch, while behind the village was a dark, imposing forest.

It was so vast it nearly overwhelmed her. This was adventure. Lachlan had spoken of adventure. And it was here. In this great monster of a place that felt as though it could consume her as easily as it could bring her to freedom.

She turned her focus back to the houses. Some were well kept, others in shambles.

Some had crops growing nearby, others looked as though they had a blight. When Penny knocked and offered food, some were kind. Some welcomed her and spoke of their hope for the future.

Others treated her with disdain.

Still more treated her less with open hostility and more with wary distrust. She was a reminder to them of why they struggled, of why they suffered.

But Penny was certain that kindness, softness, would help win the day here.

The path continued on down the hill and Penny charged in that direction, while Isla slowed.

'What's wrong?'

'It's bad down there,' Isla said.

'What do you mean?'

'Dugan McLaren and his wife. Their children… He's a drunk, and he spends all they have on alcohol.'

'Oh,' she said. 'Well, don't you think they'll need bread?'

'He's mean.' She hesitated. 'He's the man who spoke openly against The MacKenzie.'

A ripple of disquiet moved through Penny. 'Oh.'

'He will not welcome you.'

'Perhaps not,' Penny said, taking a sharp breath, 'but my husband is strong. Not cruel, as you said, and I don't think Lachlan would take kindly to knowing that there was a man in his clan buying drink rather than caring for his family.'

'It won't matter what The MacKenzie thinks if McLaren takes his fists to you now.'

'If he takes his fists to me, my husband will have him... Well, I don't know, but it would be something violent. I assume this man is well aware of that.'

She felt determined now. She carried on the path and then came to the most ramshackle of homes that she had encountered on this journey. The smell that emanated from it was rotted food, despair and drink. Filth.

She steeled herself, grateful they had quite a bit of bread left because she had a feeling that the children in this place would need it most of all.

Lachlan's father had been cruel. Her own father neglectful. And while it might not be the same as it was in this place, she knew what it was to have your life and your future dictated by the shortcomings of the man who had fathered you.

It wasn't fair. Not in any of those circumstances.

She went to the door and knocked. It opened a crack and a woman's face appeared. She was drawn and pale, exhausted looking. 'Hello,' Penny said. 'I'm Lady Penelope Bain. I'm the wife of the... The MacKenzie.'

'You're his fancy English lady?' The woman asked.

'Not fancy. But regrettably English.' She tried to smile, but the woman did not return it. 'I brought bread.'

'We are not beggars,' the woman said. 'And your husband has already terrorised my house.'

A high-pitched wail came from inside the house and she heard a chorus of small voices after.

'But maybe the children are hungry?' she asked.

A flash of something, not softness but not quite so brittle, came over the woman's face. 'If you have to force your charity on us, do it quickly and then be gone.'

The woman was stooped before her time, the house itself a hovel. The smell inside was nearly overwhelming.

'How many children are there?' Penny asked.

'Twelve living,' the woman said, her tone bitter.

'Oh, my,' Penny responded. 'Well, I doubt this will be enough bread.'

'They aren't all here. The Father knows where my whore of a daughter has gone off to.'

Penny drew back, shocked by the woman's words.

'If she's going to spread her legs so freely she ought to do it for pay. At least then we might eat better.'

'I...' Penny could not think past the intimacy of what the woman had said. She knew how overwhelming the act was. How wrecked she felt after. The other woman spoke of her daughter doing it as easily as breathing. 'There is bread.'

'Don't think we allow it,' the woman said. 'But if her father ever discovered it... He'd beat her to death.'

For the first time, Penny realised that the woman's face wasn't just haggard with lines of exhaustion. There were scars there.

'And does he...? Would he lay his hands on you?'

'I've made my bed. But if your Laird is anything like his father, you'll know the bite of his fists soon enough. Don't think your pretty manners will save you from it. Men are the beasts, they are.'

Penny didn't see the point in arguing with the woman. She didn't see the point of much of anything in the face of so much despair.

She had never seen anything like this. There were so many children. So much squalor, so little of anything that might help.

Yet again she was struck by how she had been protected even in her loneliness.

For her virtue had been shielded. She had always been full. Her father had never beaten her.

The world was such a harsh and unyielding place. And she had felt so hard done by in it.

But this... This was hardship.

She was angry about being lonely. Angry about the way her father had isolated her. But there wasn't a space to turn around in this house that didn't contain another person. At least back at her father's house she had had a place to escape. At least she had been safe.

'If ever you find yourself in danger...' Penny said. 'If you are ever in danger...come to the castle. He will not turn you away. If he knew of your husband's cruelty...'

'He's just a husband,' the woman said.

'Surely it doesn't have to be like this,' Penny said.

'Aye,' the woman said. 'But it does. I'm sure that women like yourself are treated like fine pieces. And in England I'm sure your rank and title protected you from all manner of things. But don't make the mistake of thinking it will be like that here in the Highlands. He is The MacKenzie and what he says is the law. If he decides to take his liquor and his rage out on you, then he will. And there will be nothing to stop him.'

Penny couldn't imagine why a woman she was bringing kindness to would speak to her in such a fashion. But that was when she realised: shame. Because nobody wanted to be in a position of pity.

And this woman was surely to be pitied. Penny spent some quiet moments talking to the children, and Isla joined in. They broke pieces of bread off and gave it to the *wee bairns*, as Isla called them.

When they left, her maid looked grim.

'It's a hell growing up that way.'

'You know?'

'It was a blessing to get work at the castle,' Isla said. 'Being in my father's house… But he drank himself to death.' Isla didn't sound regretful.

'A gift, surely,' Penny agreed.

'Aye,' Isla said. 'Until there wasn't money any more. Until my mother had to sell her own body to try to feed all the bairns. My wages weren't enough.'

'Where is your mother now?'

'Long dead,' Isla said. 'Women like her…women like my mother…they're not afforded a long life.'

'Your brothers and sisters?'

'Went to other family. Went to find work.'

They rounded to the back of the old house and there was a figure, cloaked in muddy brown, just walking up through the fields. She was a young girl. Maybe thirteen.

And when she shifted, moving the cloak to the side, something became very clear to Penny.

'She's got one in the basket,' Isla said, horror in her tone.

'Is that Mrs McLaren's daughter?' The girl was with child. It was clear from a distance. 'It must be. How she's hiding it… Her father must be more than a bit drunk to not have noticed.'

'She probably stays away. Stays hidden until he's too drunk to notice either way.'

'We will have to come and check on her,' Penny said.

She was suddenly overwhelmed by a strange sort of gratitude for life that she had never felt before.

She had long had the sense that her life was tragic. But it was nothing compared to a girl who was little more than a child herself, ready to bring a baby into the world, with no food, no money and a father who would no doubt harm her and the baby if he was in a black enough mood.

'That we will,' Isla said.

Chapter Nine

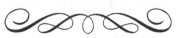

It was becoming an interesting battle with his wife. This fight for who might break first when it came to giving in to the need between them. A need he knew was mutual.

He could see it in the pitch of her breathing, the way she looked at him. The way her eyes shone bright when they sparred. Which was often.

It was a strange thing, though, to have cut off physical contact. For all of their desire had to find relief in their conversation and that had sharpened something inside him in new and fascinating ways.

He found her vexing still, of course. But it surprised him how much he enjoyed dodging her barbs at the door between their rooms. If he could not have satisfaction in her arms, he at least enjoyed her wit.

'Not tonight, I have developed a sensitivity to arrogance.'

'Ah,' he said. 'It must be difficult being so near to yourself then.'

'I sally forth.'

And another night…

'Tonight I have important needlepointing to finish.'

'Lass, I think we could accomplish your needlepointing and marital duties.'

'Lachlan, my fears of where the needle might end up... I am thinking only of you.'

Of course, this was amusing, but beneath it all...she was hurt and he could see it. He also didn't know how to heal the wound.

Now though, he had found out she was planning a party. A party.

Rona, the head housekeeper, informed him of this with great umbrage. 'She has also been going out into the village with regularity,' she said.

Anger that felt particularly sharp-edged lodged itself in his chest. Penny? In the village? With no protection?

'And what do they think of her there?' he asked.

'She's an outsider,' the woman said. 'But the people are grateful for bread.'

He was...in awe of her. He had been focused on exerting his authority. It was important that the people knew that he was here to rule. His father had shirked his duties and Lachlan would do no such thing. In his mind, a leader had a steady, iron hand.

But he had not considered this. Basic needs and comfort. These gestures of care.

'And what is my outsider bride planning exactly?'

'She claims it will bring a sense of...goodwill.'

'Does she now.'

He walked away from Rona and made his way up the stairs to their rooms.

He opened the door to Penny's bedchamber. He did not knock.

When he opened the door, she gasped, and her little maid drew back along with her.

'What is this I hear about you planning a celebration?'

'It seems only logical,' she fired back at him as if she had not just recoiled at the sight of him.

'Go,' he said, addressing the maid.

She scuttled out of the room, her head low, closing the door behind her.

'Are you going to draw your sword and hold it against my throat?' She had a bit more frost to her tone than she often did when they sparred.

'When have I ever threatened you, lass?'

She looked away. 'You haven't. But I have heard rumours about you terrorising the villagers.'

'I defended your honour. The man spoke against you.'

It did not matter if he was barred from her bed. She was his wife.

'I know,' she said softly. 'I went to visit the household. I spoke to his wife.'

'Foolish,' Lachlan said, that sharp-edged fear he'd felt earlier expanding inside him. 'You put yourself in danger.'

She had no idea the resentment, the anger that existed here. She had no idea of any of it. She had tripped out about the village like an unsteady lamb who had no idea predators might be near.

She was planning a party as if a merry time might heal deep scars in an evening.

'I was never in danger,' she said.

She had no idea. 'That you believe this is exactly why you are no longer permitted to wander the grounds.'

'And how will you stop me?'

'I am not above locking you in here, lass.'

'And I'm certain that I would find a way to escape.'

'You do not understand what you're playing with. These people do not all trust me and they will not all trust you. Some of them may see to use you against me. This is not your clan. These are not your people.'

'It is the life I have been given,' she retorted fiercely. 'I will not stand down. Not again. I have lived quietly for far too long. Was it not enough that I paid my father's debt with my body?'

'Not as often as you might.'

'Will you take it, then?'

It was a challenge. She was facing him down, daring him to be the beast that his father was.

He knew well that his father would have thought nothing of it and he would've beaten her for her insolence.

And he knew how that ended.

With a woman stepping out a tower window, down to the rocks below. To her demise. He would never crush Penny in such a way. That large, unnamed thing that lived inside him, that roared to life when she was near...

It would not allow it.

He would never hurt her.

And if anyone ever tried to harm his bride... It would be the end of them.

'I can take what I need elsewhere. I do not need to force myself on an unwilling woman. There are many that are more than willing.'

She tilted her chin up. 'Good.'

She refused to show him any sort of deference. And she made his body feel like not quite his own. It enraged him.

'Men tremble before me,' he said. 'Do you have any idea how many bodies I left littered on battlefields in France?'

'I don't,' she said. 'But are you saying you would kill me? Because I don't believe that. You could have done that as soon as we got into Scotland.'

'I've no wish to kill you.'

'A relief. You also have no wish to be a beloved leader to your people, do you?'

'Love is not the goal. Loyalty—that, I think you will find, is of greater importance.'

'They don't trust you.'

'Due to you, in part.'

'And I was a decision you made. In anger, I imagine. So, unless you decide to make a public spectacle of me, execute me in the courtyard, I expect I have work to do to prove to them that I am not simply evidence that you're like your father. Don't get angry with me for trying to fix what you might have broken with your revenge.'

He had nothing to say to that and was in a rage that she had struck him dumb. She had been a focus of his revenge. Repayment for years spent in England.

And she was correct. His marriage to her had only created more suspicion among the people.

'Tell me about your party,' he said.

'A celebration,' she said. 'Invite the other clans. Invite the people from the village. Fling open the doors. Food. So much food. Music, dancing. Make them happy. Yes, people want to know they are safe. They want to know that they have a leader who can protect them. No one who looks at you could be in any doubt that you could. That you could defend against any army. But life here has been bleak.' She let out a long, slow breath. 'And I know what it is to live a bleak life you cannot see any hope of having change.'

'You speak of your time with your father.'

'Yes. But my time here also if you don't allow me to find a place. And I believe that this will help. It is not enough to come in swinging a sword and making proclamations. There is pain here. They are wounded. The fields are scarred. So are their hearts. I've seen them. I've been talking to them.'

'I know,' he said.

'It is not enough to rule by making your subjects afraid of you.'

'I don't want them afraid. I want them to give me their respect. My father did nothing to earn it.'

'Terror is terror either way. You must show them something more.'

'I am not in need of the advice of a woman.'

Not even that caused her to back down. If anything, she bristled. 'You are. Very clearly you are. You are incapable of fixing this yourself. Rage at me if you want, but you know I'm right.'

He would admit no such thing. These sorts of things, this... this softness that she was talking about was outside his experience. He had never had a moment of softness. Not in his life.

He fought against images. Images of a woman long dead. Of babies who smelled sweet and felt so fragile, and died far too quickly.

'I don't understand,' he said.

'That's okay. You don't have to understand. But you could trust me on this.'

'And why would you know anything about this?'

'Because, as I said, I know what it is to live bleak. A moment of happiness can heal so many things. Just a glimmer of hope. An evening to dance, to have a full belly. Think of what it was like when you were at war. What would you have given for those things?'

He felt as if she had turned a key that was in a lock somewhere inside him. An understanding flooded him.

'It has been war here,' he said. 'Without violence, but no different.'

'Yes,' she said, the look of relief on her face doing something to that vulnerable place inside him that she had just discovered.

'If you see to the planning of this, then it will happen. I will... I will trust you.'

'Thank you.'

He moved towards her, but she shrank back. Rage filled him. He had the strongest desire to pull her against him anyway. To ignore her fear. Her reluctance.

But his father felt far too close to the surface of his veins and he'd meant what he said. There were many women who would have him. He'd no need to slake himself with her fear.

He did not know why it was different here. He didn't know why she had given herself to him willingly on the road, but in the castle she acted as if the idea disgusted her.

Perhaps she was afraid for her life, then?

He gritted his teeth. 'I don't want to be troubled with the details of this.'

'You have my word.'

'Good. At least there is some use for you.'

And with that, he left her as abruptly as he had come into the room. He raged down the hall, all the way out of the castle. He knew where he could find a lightskirt. That had, of course, been one of the first things his men had made sure to inform him of.

He could make merry with her. Give her that moment of hope that his wife was so entranced with.

But he thought of the way Penny had looked at him before she had shrunk back. When she had looked at him with hope that he might not disappoint her. That he might understand her. Do what she felt was right.

And he knew he was in no fit state to be with a woman.

'William,' he said, finding his man lounging in the courtyard. 'Pick up your sword.'

What he could not work out in the bedroom, he would work out on a created battlefield.

After a few hours of steel hitting steel, he felt exhausted.

But his desire was still not satisfied. There was only so much that talking could fix.

And he might feel a sense of pride that his wife had thought of dealing with the clan in a softer way…but he did not like having to participate in…levity.

Still, he would allow her to have her way here.

For whatever she thought, he had no wish to crush her.
None at all.

If anything gave him hope for his grim soul, it might
well be that.

Chapter Ten

The planning of the feast had been…interesting, to say the least. Mostly because it had forced her to lock horns with the indomitable Rona.

The other woman did not like her interfering with matters of the household, but Penny had a vision for what was to occur and she needed her help to accomplish it.

They had fought over the menu, over the acquisition of the food.

It had required sending men on a long journey to Edinburgh in order to acquire all that would be needed.

The land here would be restored, but as of now, anything that needed this sort of excess… There was no excess to be had. But her husband had money. A great deal of it.

When the men returned, they not only had what was required for the party, but had brought staples that they could store. So that there would be more bread, cakes even. There was flour and sugar, and butter.

And Rona'd had to admit that perhaps Penny wasn't so

bad, as she had convinced the Laird to open his purse to this extent.

But the next order of business was to inform the people in the village. Yet again, Penny selected herself as ambassador. They were, of course, wary. There had been nothing like this for longer than many of them could remember. No celebrations, for there had been little to celebrate. Anything extra had gone to Lachlan's father. To the lavish lifestyle he was bent on living in town. Just the mention of a celebration had gone a long way in proving to people that Lachlan might be different.

If he was willing to spend his riches on the people here, then perhaps that was a sign that things would continue to improve.

It made her feel useful. It made her feel...

This was what she'd needed. Lachlan made chaos reign in her heart and body and she'd hated that. The sense her emotions were no longer in her control.

Sitting in silence had always been the enemy. Her own thoughts. Her own heart.

But she could make a difference here. She didn't have to sit around and wait and feel.

She could act.

And so she did.

When she and Isla approached the McLaren residence, they both paused. 'They will be invited, too,' Penny said, feeling determined. She was nearing the door when she caught sight of the girl again.

Her heart jumped and she moved forward.

'You,' Penny said.

The girl stopped and met her gaze, wide-eyed. 'What's your name?' Penny asked.

'Nothing of consequence,' the girl said.

'But I've asked. And I'm sorry, I didn't tell you mine.'

'I know who you are. The MacKenzie's fancy piece.'

'His wife.' Penny refused to allow a child to offend her. 'Lady Penelope Bain. We're here to invite you and your family to the castle for celebration.'

The girl contorted her face. 'Why would we ever go there?'

'There will be dancing. Food.'

'I don't think my father will go.'

'Does he have to? It seems to me you're well capable of sneaking off when you wish.'

'I don't do anything of the sort.' The girl scowled even deeper.

Penny looked down meaningfully at the girl's rounded belly. The girl shifted, moving her dress.

'Don't be afraid of me. I want to help you. I... Does he know?'

The girl's eyes widened. 'I don't know what you mean.'

'You're with child. It's not well hidden.'

'Hidden well enough.'

'But you won't be able to hide a baby so easily.'

'I have time.'

'The father?'

The girl looked away. 'Not from here.'

'And you don't know him?'

'Well, he just took what he wanted. Didn't ask me.'

Anger and horror twisted inside Penelope. 'You were forced?'

'I'm not an idiot. I know what happens to women who say yes to men. Look at my mother and her twelve children.'

'Does your mother know you were forced?'

'She doesn't believe me. And if she does, she doesn't care. It only makes me more foolish that I put myself in such a position. Men are men. You cannae keep them from their nature.'

Penny's whole heart rebelled against that. But this wasn't the time for lectures. It was the time for action. 'What's going to happen to you?'

'Can't say as I know. I couldn't get rid of it.' The girl frowned. 'I tried. It didn't work. It's still there.'

Pity overwhelmed Penny. Along with fear. The girl was in danger. The baby was clearly in danger. And they had no one to protect them. And this, again, was something she could do. She was not helpless. She was Lady Bain.

She'd been a helpless girl locked in a room, once. And no one had possessed the authority to help her. No one but her father.

But this girl... Penny could help this girl.

'Listen to me. When the time comes, you can come to the castle. You'll be welcomed in. I'll bring a midwife to help you. We'll keep you safe.'

The girl looked shocked, then afraid. Penny could understand. Those closest to her were not offering help. Why wouldn't she be suspicious of a stranger offering it? 'I don't need help.'

'There's no shame in needing help.'

The sound of voices came from inside the house and the girl jumped slightly.

'Go,' she said.

'Will you tell your parents that they're invited?'

'Won't make a difference. You can't fix us. You can't fix me.'

The girl lowered her head and walked away, hunched over herself and the babe she carried.

'I'm beginning to recognise the expression on your face,' Isla said.

'What expression is that?' Penny asked, staring after the girl.

'That one that says you're ready to try to do the impossible.'

'Well, I've got Lachlan to agree to throw a party at the castle. I'd say I do quite well with the impossible.'

'Aye,' Isla said. 'I'd say that you do.'

Chapter Eleven

It was the day of the grand celebration and the amount of food was stunning. There were places to sit out in front of the castle. The door stood open. Tables and blankets were placed everywhere. There were musicians and dancers.

The great stone courtyard had a massive bonfire roaring at its centre. And food...there was such a feast laid out, for all. Not simply the chieftains and other gentry, but for the whole of the clan. Fish, game and fowl. Breads and cakes.

Everyone was dressed in their finest—whatever that might mean. From faded gowns that looked to have passed through several generations, to sweeping great kilts in different tartans.

It was quite unlike anything to ever grace the clan before. At least, not in Lachlan's memory.

And Penny was at the centre of the preparation. Her hair was a tangle, her eyes bright. She was wearing a dress that, if he was not mistaken, must've come from one of the maids.

She was working. And she looked...happy. Happier than he had ever seen her, certainly.

They had a few hours yet until the festivities began and she seemed bound and determined to have a hand in every last bit.

For his part, he had done nothing.

But this was her business. Her idea. He was still not convinced that it would have a bearing on anything. She was the one who seemed absolutely certain that it was necessary to the happiness of the clan.

The smell of meat roasting on spits was thick in the air, along with music, laughter and bawdy songs.

Inside the great hall, the setting was yet more grand. People filled the room, both from Clan MacKenzie and from other clans who had come from near and far. A mix of people and times. For this felt more like the stories of old, from when the clans had endless power and resources, and had not been touched by England.

The music was from an era gone by. The food—by virtue of the sheer, vast quantity—was as well.

This was the Highlands. The clan. Scotland. In a deep, essential way that stirred his blood.

One thing he had not considered was what a great demonstration of strength and power this was.

Because excess like this did nothing to dent his wealth, yet it was far beyond anything his people would have seen in more than a generation.

'You've done well,' he said.

She paused, looking startled. 'Well. Thank you. A surprise coming from you, considering that you've had little to do with the process.'

'You didn't need me.'

Something flashed in her blue eyes and, somehow, he felt an echo of it in his chest. He couldn't name it or hold on to it. But he felt it all the same.

'Well. It doesn't matter. Everything is in hand.'

'The clans will see how powerful Clan MacKenzie is. We are not on the brink of destruction. Not any more.'

'I did not have cakes made as an act of war. Please don't turn it into one.'

'Who said anything about war? But it is clear that we are the strongest.'

'That right there. Not everything has to be about strength.'

'It does. The reality of the world is that the winner will always be the strongest.'

'That's bleak. Why does there have to be a winner? Why can't people simply live and be happy?'

'Because there will always be a conqueror. Always. And if you are not a conqueror, you will be the conquered.'

'Truths learned in war?'

'Truth is learned here. In my whole life. Had I stayed here, this clan would have been conquered by my father's greed. I went to England to try to make my fortune. Your father bested me. I had to obtain power. I had to obtain strength. Had I not done so, these people would have fallen into ruin.'

'I can see that,' she said softly. 'But you're not at war any more.'

'There is always a war on the horizon. Even if it is not war as you think of it. You must always be prepared. You cannot show weakness.'

'What about kindness?'

He looked around. 'You have done that for the both of us.'

'They might like to see it from you.' Her words were soft, the touch of her fingertips on his arm softer still. But he felt it, like the blow from a weapon, so hard it radiated through him, settling low in his stomach.

'Do you intend to dance tonight? To show them that you have a bit of humour?'

'Why would I do that? I haven't got humour.'

'You don't think so? I thought sometimes it felt as though we found some together,' she said, looking sad. Why was she sad? She had got what she wanted. And as for the way things were between the two of them, it had been her decision.

If there was distance, it was not down to his choice.

The back of his teeth ached. She was lovely, even now, even in this scullery maid's costume. It was confounding. As was she.

'There has been no room for it in my life.'

'Well, show them that you're human tonight.'

'Why? I would show them that I am a king.'

'You don't have to struggle to show that, Lachlan. But you might have to work a bit to show them that you have a heart.'

'The people don't need to know their leader has a heart. They need to know I have a sword.'

And with that, he left her. But something about the conversation lingered with him. Made him feel disquiet.

He did prepare himself, putting on a great kilt, his sword at his hip. He was ready to make a display, both for his people and for the guests.

When it was time, he went between the connecting doors to his and Penny's room, again without knocking.

'It's time,' he said.

'You might knock,' she said.

'I don't have to do any such thing, lass,' he said. 'It is my castle. My domain.'

'How nice for you.'

She had transformed from when he had last seen her in the courtyard, overseeing the preparations.

And she was beautiful. Even angry at him. Her blonde hair was pinned low on her neck, her gown a delicate gold, the neckline low and wide revealing the creamy curves of breasts he had nearly forgotten the touch and taste of. She was a vixen, this woman.

She haunted his dreams and he couldn't pretend it wasn't so. She had bewitched him in some manner. He had had no answer for her when she had asked him about the jewellery box and he was convinced it was somehow related to his exile. But the only answer that he'd been able to find, there beneath the discomfort of his skin, had been that he had cared. Had cared about whether or not she was happy. And that did not seem real or possible in any regard. He was a man driven by revenge. A man driven by duty, honour and a sense of what was right. A man determined to be the very opposite of his father, Who had been hot-blooded and driven by such weaker devices as his feelings.

She looked up at him, an air of defiance in her blue eyes.

He took hold of her arm and it lit him up like the fire in the great hearth. 'It's time for us to meet our guests.'

'Of course,' she said. But her smile was cold. 'You must behave, Lachlan.'

'I am Laird here. I determine the behaviour.'

'Then don't turn this into a funeral. It is meant to be a happy occasion.'

'I will do my best not to frighten small children.'

'Please do.' She paused for a moment. 'That man…the one who challenged you. I invited his family to the celebration. He's consumed with drink and his wife and children live in fear of him. They don't have enough food…'

'There will be enough food,' he said, his voice grim. 'For everyone. As for the rest, it is a tragedy to be sure. And were I to ever witness a man harming his wife or children the consequence would be severe.'

'That isn't enough. We have to do something.'

'We are. This changes things. You have to have some trust in that. You cannot heal all the ills of the world, lass.'

'Isn't that what you're trying to do? Heal the ills of the world by pouring your money back into this clan? How is what I want any different?'

'There is a system here. A structure. The people here work the land and they should benefit from it. My father stole. Profited off the backs of his labourers in an unjust manner. That I can restore. That I can heal. The rest… That is up to them.'

That seemed to infuriate her, but she said no more because they were descending the stairs, and making their way towards the great hall. That was where they were announced by one of the chieftains. He as the Laird—and she as his lady.

The crowd of people let up a cheer as they made their way into the great hall. This was a hero's welcome.

This was the welcome Penny's actions had brought to him.

He had not truly understood what she was doing, planning this. But now that he stood here, surveying the people, the food, he understood. It was not only a demonstration for the people, but for him. Of what it meant to be here. Of what it truly was to be home.

And Penny was by his side.

She might not wish to take him into her bed, but she was here. And she was his.

The possessiveness he felt was strange. For while he understood the desire to possess, and to protect…

What he did not understand was his desire to see her smile. The pride he felt over this thing she had planned.

He took a seat at the head of the table, with her at his left. And as he sat, he spoke to the men there about the way the Highlands had been these last years. The way that things had changed. And the ways in which Lachlan was determined to see them restored.

All the while, Penelope sat, bearing the countenance of a real wife. A proper wife.

A lie.

When dinner was finished, the music began to play. And his men, deep in their cups by then, all began to shout for the Laird and lady to give them a dance.

Lachlan, for his part, hadn't danced without the aid of alcohol and outside a pub for more years than he could count. And before that, he did not think he ever danced.

This was necessary. The show of strength and unity. And if it was what the people wanted, he could not deny them. If part of him relished the idea that Penny would have to be close to his body again, that was inconsequential.

He was simply human.

Simply a man. A man who wanted to dance with his wife.

He pulled her to him, the dance much more at home in a tavern than here, but he didn't much care. The fiddle was moving fast and the other dancers were already drunk. Penny clearly didn't know how to dance a reel, but she followed as best she could.

When it was his turn to grab hold of his bride, he took her in his arms and didn't return her to the line, spinning her around with her crushed against his chest.

She laughed, her smile wide with her joy...

She was happy. Here with him.

In this moment she was happy.

It tangled itself around his heart, around his soul. He hadn't thought either of those things still existed inside him.

It was clear the display pleased his men, for they clapped along with the music, sending great shouts up into the air. And something shifted inside him. For this was what it meant to be home. This was what it meant to be in Scotland. To be in his clan. This hall. This castle. This music.

He was not an outsider here.

He was not an outsider for the first time in years. His accent was no different, his words not unique. The manners and dancing and food were familiar.

Penny smiled, her blonde hair twirling right along with her.

And he felt something...something he had not felt in years. Happiness.

It was an ache that bloomed in his chest and spread outward. And for a moment, he could not breathe past it.

She had been right. There was happiness here.

He thought it might be contained in her smile.

When the dance finished, his heart was thundering hard, his blood firing through his veins. And perhaps his head was a bit dizzy from drink, though he hadn't had overmuch, but he dragged her away from the dance floor, away from the party and into an alcove. He backed her against the wall then and finally did what he had wanted to do for days.

He crushed her mouth beneath his, claiming every stolen kiss that she'd taken from him. Every missed touch.

She wrapped her arms around him, her fingers spearing into his hair, kittenish sounds rising in her throat. Sounds of encouragement.

She had inflamed in him a desire that he did not understand. This creature who he had bedded in the most perfunctory of ways, but who had ignited in him a need that far surpassed any he had ever felt before.

He was not gentle. He did not give quarter to her innocence. He consumed her, his kisses deep and long and hard. He plundered her mouth with his tongue, taking all that she would give and then demanding yet more.

He was hard as steel and, if she were a whore, he would have demanded she take herself down to her knees and pleasure him with her mouth. The very image of his darling angel taking his cock between her lips created a fire in his veins.

They were so close to the party that anyone could see them. But it didn't matter, for he was chief. He was The MacKenzie. And this was his home. This was Scotland. It wasn't England. She belonged to him here. Him and no other. And whatever he desired, it might be his. Whatever he wanted.

He was not in shackles any more. He was not enslaved.

He had spent so many years labouring to find himself a free man. Fighting for a country he didn't owe allegiance to. Earning what should have been his twice over.

He had earned it with bravery on the battlefield, had seen

countless atrocities and more bloodshed then those who had not been to war could ever believe. He had toiled and clawed his way back to Scotland. And he had claimed her on his way. Payment for all those years of working for her father.

His payment.

Justification for his kisses, for risking her exposure, fuelled him.

He pulled the top of her dress down, exposing the rosy crests of her breasts. She was lovely. Far beyond anything he could've possibly dreamed.

So changed from the little creature who had brought him the bird.

How would he have ever known that he would have found such satisfaction in her arms? There was no thought now. Only a roaring in his veins. In his head.

Mine.

For he was a conqueror, his bloodline that of warriors.

And what his body understood was staking a claim.

Not wedding vows spoken in a church and recognised by soft English society, but an earthy, physical alliance. One that she had denied him these many days.

He would be denied no longer.

He kissed her. Kissed her until her lips were the colour of crushed rose petals, until she trembled beneath his touch.

'To your knees, lass,' he said, his voice rough.

She looked up at him, with wide, wild blue eyes. 'I don't understand.'

Suddenly, the world came back into focus.

Suddenly, realisation overtook him. He was no better than his father acting out of the fire in his blood. Acting like a man possessed. Like a man owed the bodies of everyone and everything around him.

Yes, it might be the law that a man owned his wife, but he had seen what happened when a man took that to heart. The ways in which it could destroy a woman. A good woman.

Of course she didn't understand. She was an innocent. Corrupted only by the few times he had taken her, quickly and without much finesse, in narrow, hard beds in coaching inns. And he was demanding she get on her knees like a seasoned piece in a near public alcove where anyone could walk in. This lady of a wife.

Wasn't that the point of her? To disgrace her?

No.

He had only ever wanted to disgrace her father. But tonight he had come close to disgracing her and that meant he'd dishonoured himself.

It could not be borne. Because that made him his father. The truth of his blood borne out in front of him.

'Go back to the celebrations,' he said.

'Lachlan...' Her voice was breathy, stunned.

'Go back, lass,' he said, his voice hard. 'If you know what's good for you.'

She left, backing away from him, her eyes on his the whole time. An accusation, he felt.

Back here so little time and the corruption of his own blood was beginning to seep through his veins.

He waited a moment. Waited until the evidence of his own arousal was no longer pressing against the front of his kilt.

When he rejoined the party, Penny was there, looking stunned.

But she didn't stay away from him. Rather, she crossed the space and joined him.

'Lachlan... Why did you tell me to leave?'

'You know perfectly well.'

'I don't.'

'There are things a man does not use his wife for, Penny.'

'What things?'

'I'm not going to speak to you of this.'

'Why not?'

'Enough,' he said, his voice hard.

'Why?' She pressed again. 'Why do you care how you use me?'

She asked the question without malice. And he had the feeling that she was asking it in much the same way she had asked why he had given her the jewellery box.

'It's nothing to do with you,' he said, keeping his tone deliberately uncompromising. 'It is simply the way of it.'

If he had failed the first time for answering in such a manner, then he had deliberately failed this time.

All the better.

For here, with all the power in the world he could want, he did not feel any more able to protect the weak than he had out in the world.

For he could not protect Penny from himself.

And that was a failure deeper than he could face.

Chapter Twelve

Penny had been brooding since his kiss at the party.

He had...he had made demands of her she didn't understand, then pushed her away, and she had never been more confused.

The touch of his mouth to hers had brought everything she'd spent the past few days avoiding roaring back to life inside her.

She hadn't banished loneliness by barring him from her bed. She'd simply built a wall between her emotions and the manner he used to reach them. But it couldn't hold for ever.

Because the silence between them was swollen. Large and filled with all manner of things Penny didn't want to navigate. She had been doing well. She'd spent more time in the village, had started a sewing circle with some of the ladies and had become more than competent at cooking. And she had been able to set Lachlan to one side. Or at least see him as a project rather than a husband.

Then he had kissed her.

With that kiss he had stirred up every deep, longing thing

inside her. There was that fire, that physical need. He aroused it in her so easily.

But there was more.

Deeper.

The way he'd danced with her in the great hall had felt like flying. His strength—whether quiet or on brute display—felt like a living force within her sometimes. As if his confidence and bravery had taken root inside her and grown, flourished and made her someone so different from what she'd been before.

She wanted to know him.

All those nights she'd refused him entry to her room and they talked. And in those quick moments he'd shown her so much. That humour he said he didn't have. Patience. Kindness.

She ached to be close to him in every way she could.

She hadn't allowed herself to think of it. But now she was consumed with it yet again. Along with his rejection.

It forced her to consider that he might not have pressed her, withholding because he didn't want her. That she hadn't ever had power over him as she'd imagined.

That second time they were together she'd felt his body tremble and she'd taken it to mean she could make him desperate, as he had made her.

But perhaps that wasn't so.

Because she was naive. Because apparently there were things men did not ask of wives. And he had wanted one of those things, but…but not from her.

And she didn't even have a clue what it might be.

It would have been better if she could hate him.

But the longer she saw him here, with his people, acting the part of chief, the more entranced she was by him. As she had been when she was a girl, trailing after him at the estate. How she hated that. That he seemed to have so much of a hold over her and she had none over him.

But he was so broad and brave, so willing to serve all of the people around him. Lachlan might not know how to show warmth, but she did. What he gave was strength, a steadiness that one could lean on. And while he had underestimated how much his people might need to have some joy... she thought she might not have understood how much they needed his strength.

As she talked to those who worked in the castle, it became clear just how badly scarred the clan was from the way his father had conducted his affairs.

Isla had told her horrible stories, worse even than about the mistress Lachlan's father had killed. Understanding more of where Lachlan came from, why he hated his father so much that he despised the blood in his own veins...

It made her care more for the strong, iron Highlander who didn't seem to have it in him to bend.

His uncompromising nature could be trying. And she'd seen it as an obstacle at first. Now she saw it as a gift.

She'd also discovered that Lachlan had been sending money back to his people from the moment he found out about his father's death. A great many things had been restored in the months it had taken him to gain order with his business and get himself back to the Highlands.

It was why the castle was so comfortable now. Why it was fully stocked with food and staff. It also led her to truly believe that what he'd said to her about his bloodline was a truth he held deep in his heart. Because if he felt it was the most honourable thing for him to produce an heir, then he would. She could not understand, though, because she did not know men who weren't utterly concerned with the carrying on of their line.

She had always assumed marriage would mean children. And she hadn't realised how deeply comforting she'd found that certainty until it had been taken from her. How much she'd wanted that.

To be a mother. To have someone to love and care for. To find that connection.

But as much as many men were driven to further their bloodline, he was opposed.

His father had damaged him. Everything she'd heard about the previous MacKenzie convinced her of that.

She wanted to find a path to connect the ways in which she knew him. The way that they had been intimate in the bedroom. The way that they had talked on the back of his horse on their journey to Scotland. The commanding, forbidding man that she saw prowling around the castle, who had kissed her as though she was the feast, then ordered her to leave him. The man who said her jewellery box had meant nothing to him, but had seen it fetched all the same.

She even wanted to understand the man who presented her to his people as a prisoner of war, more than his wife, but who had presented her to all the clans as his lady. Because she felt that the truth of Lachlan Bain was somewhere at the centre of all those things, whether she was particularly fond of each and every piece of him or not.

She had a feeling that some of her problems with him stemmed from the fact that she was so horrendously ignorant of men and all there was to know about their physical desires. For she felt there was a key in that. To the things that bothered her now. She wished that she knew more.

But she had got to know a few of the women who worked in the castle. Most especially the maid who attended her.

She found it strange that Penny enjoyed making conversation and Penny knew that. But she couldn't help herself. She was lonely. And she finally lived in a house filled with people. She was intent on taking advantage of that.

The head of the household found Penny's intrusions somewhat irritating and Penny could tell. But then, one thing she was very good at was ignoring when people found her irritating.

It was a gift.

* * *

She was in the kitchen, poring over the weekly menu, Isla next to her eating a midday meal of bread and cheese, the young scullery maids rushing about the kitchen. 'What do you know of men?'

Isla looked up from her bread. 'I'm not sure I understand.' But she could see that Isla did understand, only that she was hoping she might not have.

'Men,' Penny said. 'I find that I'm woefully ignorant on the subject.'

One of the maids—Margaret—laughed. 'You're a married woman.'

'It hasn't seemed to help.'

She waved a hand. 'Fine ladies who are married often know less than kitchen maids who are not.'

'Why is that?' Penny asked.

It suddenly seemed deeply unfair to her.

'Your lot protect you from the way of the world,' Margaret said. 'It's not a bad thing, mind you. Men can be...'

'Right rubbish,' Flora, the other scullery maid, finished.

'True,' Margaret agreed.

'Well, Lachlan is not. That is to say... The MacKenzie...'

'Yes. I know what you mean.'

'It just seems as though there must be *more* to pleasing men.'

The maids exchanged looks.

'Do you know?'

'I know a fair bit,' Flora said, looking sly.

'I was able to convince him to give me some proper terms.'

'Which ones?' Margaret asked, looking amused.

Penny knew that she was being mildly teased, but she didn't much care. 'Well, I know what a cock is.'

Margaret laughed, the sound a hoot, and Flora and Isla joined in. 'That is a good place to start. Men are fond of their cocks.'

'I'm not unfond of it myself.'

'Also a good thing,' Margaret said. 'Nothing worse than finding yourself in the position of having to please a man you don't find pleasing.'

'All I knew about men and women I had...pieced together from reading about nature. Then I was a wife. I expected to hate him. He stole me from my home, from an engagement to another man. I didn't know what to expect of a wedding night. But he can be so wonderful. And I find him beautiful.'

'That's a gift,' Flora said.

'It feels like a gift when we're together. But then it feels as though he's taken all the power away from me when it's over. And I just feel... I feel.'

Margaret just looked sad for her then. 'You have feelings for him.'

'Feelings?'

'Aye. I reckon you love him.'

Her words hit a strange place inside Penny.

Love.

She had never expected to love the man she'd married. She had felt, though, that she might love the Duke, and that had been such a wondrous and unexpected gift. With some distance she'd realised that it had never been him—she had not known him, how could she love him?—but the idea of him and all he represented.

Loving Lachlan could not be possible.

He had no softness. His manners were not lovely.

It wouldn't be easy to love him. And it made her feel as though the walls inside her heart were being stretched, stressed. In danger of crumbling.

'I don't. He kidnapped me. He forced me into marriage. I was supposed to marry a *duke*.'

'Lah,' Margaret said. 'But I still think you love him.'

She pushed that away. Firmly. 'I never expected love.'

So what then was all of this truly about? Why did she feel

an ache in herself that wouldn't go away? Why did she feel a deep pull towards *more*?

She thought of those nights in the coaching inns. 'I don't want him to be in control like he is. He pushes me away and it makes me…sad. He has let me keep him from my bed for over a week and I…there must be more than just him lifting my skirts and…and having done with it.'

Flora frowned. 'He doesn't see to your pleasure?'

'Oh, he does,' Penny said. 'But I never… He doesn't allow me to touch him. Or truly see him. And I feel like the key to him, to this… I've been holding him back from my room, but I don't want that any more. Are there books?'

'I don't know about books,' Flora said. 'The real truths come from women and far too many men are charged with the actual recording of things.'

'Well, I've never had any women to tell me such things. I made friends with the Duke's sister and his ward, but they know no more of men than I do. And his mother told me to simply think of household chores if I found the act over-whelming.'

Margaret wrinkled her nose. 'If you can think of chores, you might as well be off baking bread.'

'I can't think of chores when I'm with him. I don't want to. But I want…something else.'

'These men,' Margaret said, 'they spend all their time turn-ing their wives into little mice. Teaching you to be scared of a naked man. Why is that? Because a lady with some bold-ness is what truly tempts them. And they want all the control.'

'That's just it,' Penny said. 'He has all the control. He comes to me and I give him exactly what he wants, because he's made me want it. I have no fortitude. I absolutely give in. He makes my knees weak and he makes me…'

'He is a handsome man,' Isla said.

Penny felt a strange surge of possessiveness rise up inside her. He was her handsome man, infuriating though he was.

'He is. But I don't want him to have all the control. I want to have some.'

This, and the man himself, had become a problem she was desperate to solve. She didn't want to mope around being smothered by feelings.

'Then you need to take it,' Flora said.

'How?'

'Seduction.'

'I don't know how to seduce anything!' Penny said. 'I haven't any experience of men, I told you.'

'Well, what *do* you have experience with?' Margaret asked.

'I have nursed several small animals back to health.'

Flora coughed and Margaret smothered a fit of giggles with her hand. Isla, for her part, looked away.

'Right,' Flora said. 'That is not the same. And it won't help you.' She tapped her chin. 'You're very beautiful. Use your body.'

'How?'

'Go to him naked.'

'I couldn't do that.'

'Why not?'

'It's obscene.'

'It is,' Flora said. 'What you'll be doing with him is more obscene still.'

This was true. Everything that took place between them was shocking. And the fact of the matter was...she wanted to know more.

'There is a book,' Isla said. 'It's hidden. But I know it belonged to the previous Laird and it is...informative.'

'Where is it hidden?' she asked.

'There is a box in the library. It has a lock, but the key is in a tableside drawer by the chair at the far wall.'

'Well, that's...thorough.'

Isla looked very serious. 'The book is quite...thorough.'

'Take me to it.'

And that was how she ended up making her way to the library with a trail of housemaids giggling behind her. But Isla, true to her word, led her straight to the key and box, and placed the key in her palm. 'Use it well.'

Penny opened it slowly to find a slim volume with a nondescript cover. She opened it and her eyes widened at the sight.

The art was quite lavish and very detailed. On some pages there was a man and a woman. On many…a man with several women.

She could not look away, the scenes so shocking and entrancing, the descriptions frank and bold.

It would seem that what she and Lachlan had engaged in was an incredibly basic version of all the various things a man and woman could do with each other's bodies.

She was not interested in the scenes containing a crowd, not in a personal sense. Though she did spend a good while turning the book in various different ways to try to fully grasp the mechanics of the situation.

She'd have thought she might be shocked to look at such graphic instruction. But the primary thing she felt was…hurt. She put her fingertips over a particularly salacious drawing of a woman using her mouth on a man's most intimate part. Did he not want these things from her? Or was this the same as him not wanting to give her a baby? The same as him treating her like a prisoner?

Was he doing all of these things with females elsewhere? Because if all of these things were possible, and surely a man like Lachlan would know about them, then he could not be satisfied with the brisk actions they committed under the cover of darkness. Those acts had been altering for her, but she had no experience. So of course it was the absolute heights for her. But for a man such as him? Would he want more?

She did not find herself disgusted, not by any of it. There was no reason to be, after all. Every touch that she had received from his hands had been pleasurable. And the idea of exploring him more only excited her.

Ruin.

The word whispered inside her and echoed off all the tender, hurt places in her heart, an excitement threading itself through her soul and making her feel renewed.

She was a married woman now and could not be ruined. She had been brought here and, as with the running of a household, her relationship with Lachlan was something she had to find a way to control.

Her heart thundered heavily and she took a large volume of Shakespeare off the shelf, held it against her chest, in front of that forbidden book, and made her way to her bedroom. The book bordered on vulgar in places, but it inflamed her imagination.

It seemed that there were very few borders when it came to relations. But this, she supposed, was the difference between copulation—in that reproductive sense that she knew from scientific texts in regards to roosters—and screwing.

He'd said she shouldn't say that word. But then, she felt that she didn't have the knowledge to understand what it had meant.

In the text, various activities were referred to as bed sport and she could see why. It looked all very athletic and like something quite sporting. A fox hunt. That took place in the nude.

And the fox might want to be caught, because the consequences seemed…delicious.

She closed the book and sat on the edge of the bed, feeling…bright. As though she had been lit up from the inside. All those possibilities swirled in her head. And there in the centre was her own pain. At the way he had treated her. At the fact he had not come to her.

And she wondered if he was going to, or if she was going to have to be the one to bridge the gap, with all of this. With her newfound knowledge on the subject of what was possible between a husband and a wife.

Part of her wanted to protect herself.

She crossed the room and went back over to her vanity, to the jewellery box.

Yes. Part of her wanted to protect herself and badly. But there was this jewellery box. Evidence that perhaps she was more than simply a prisoner to him. That she was more than simply the satisfaction of a decade-long quest for revenge. He might not understand the way that he had shaped her life. The way that he had changed it. But he never would as long as she didn't force him to reckon with who she was.

She could fade into the woodwork. She could become that prisoner.

Or she could continue to create the life that she wanted. To take the raw material that she had and build for herself something happy.

But she couldn't do it as long as the sadness existed inside her. This deep loneliness that she felt when she thought of the man.

She felt certain that there was happiness to be had here, but it was not apart from her relationship with her husband. How nice it would be if it were.

You have feelings for him.

He was the one who had rearranged her existence. How could she feel nothing? She felt a great many things for Lachlan Bain. It was impossible for her to not.

He had awakened her passion. Had inflamed her senses.

He had stolen her from the only life she had ever known.

The man had to reckon with her and her curiosity. Her feelings, whatever they were. Because who else would?

Determined, she pressed her fingers against the jewellery box. This time, when her emotions rose up inside her she did not push them down. This time, she held them close to her breast and let them burn into a flame of determination.

Lachlan Bain might be accustomed to being a conqueror. But tonight, he was going to learn what it meant to be claimed by his prisoner. And maybe, in the end, she would be free.

Chapter Thirteen

Lachlan was bone tired by the time he settled into his bed. And what he did not expect was for the door between the rooms to open.

He had not tried to go to her room since the party. And he had missed talking to her. As much as he missed the scent of her. The feel of her softness beneath his hands. He'd got another taste of her and it had been fire.

He'd done his best to ignore it.

But now the door was open. And there stood Penny, wearing nothing but her nightdress, her hair loose and curling, falling down over her shoulders in great golden waves.

Other than that first night, they'd made love in the dark, so he had not seen her in such a state of undress often enough to be immune to it. There was a determined glint in her blue eyes, her full mouth set into a firm line.

'What is it you're doing, lass?' The words came out rougher than he would've liked. 'I'm tired. I'm not in the mood to demonstrate restraint. And I'm certainly not in the frame of mind to talk.'

'I didn't come to talk,' she said.

And with a fluid motion she let her nightdress fall in a diaphanous puddle, away from her body. There she stood, naked, her body glowing in the candlelight. The flames licked and danced over her skin and he was transfixed.

'I told you,' he said, his voice rough, 'to leave me.'

'Yes. For the first time you came to me and then you sent me away when I faltered.'

'It is not you who faltered,' he said.

'It doesn't matter.' She licked her lips and he felt the action in his cock. 'I have spent some time in your father's library. And I've found something...that I believe was meant to be hidden.'

She made her way towards the bed, each step decisive, her hips swaying with the motion. She was like one of the fae folk. Otherworldly and magical. Potentially dangerous to a foolish mortal. She was nothing like the prim English miss she'd been that first time he'd seen her in her father's house. Except...

Even then, there had been a glint of something in her eyes. She'd always had spirit. The spirit that had carried her through their marriage, the trip to Scotland. That had seen her planning banquets for the entire village. Delivering bread to places she was not welcome.

She was a most unexpected woman. Certainly not the pale pawn he had imagined he was manoeuvring about the board when he had first met her.

She had proven herself to be not a pawn, but an ally. She saw manoeuvres he did not. She was quick and warm, and had an ease with people that he had certainly never had.

She was something quite a bit more than he'd anticipated.

She came to the foot of the bed and he went tense. It was against his every instinct to lie there still. He was naked beneath the bedclothes and what he wanted to do was reach out and take hold of her, bring her down over his body and impale her with his aching stiffness. He had been denied for far too long and for the life of him he couldn't say why he had allowed it.

Except something inside him whispered, *For this*.

Because it had been a challenge and one he had been determined not to lose.

He was not a slave to this Englishwoman whom he had brought with him to Scotland. He was not his father. And it would've been a blow to his pride to be unable to keep away from her when she was not willing.

Any man would have a woman who came naked into his bedchamber.

She did not control him.

So he lay still and allowed her to spin her plan out and see where it might take them both. 'I understand now,' she said softly. 'I understand what you intended me to do when you asked me to get down on my knees. I didn't.' She licked her lips again.

Provocative tart.

'I spent the afternoon looking at pictures. They made me feel so very strange.'

She was a lady. And he could imagine her feeling nothing beyond disgust for the kinds of things she would have found in a book of that nature.

'Here,' she said, pressing her hand low against her stomach. 'And lower still.' Her gaze was earnest and forthright, and he found himself wondering why it was he'd thought this lady would do anything but face the challenge head on.

This lady who had asked him what his cock was called. Who had asked for the frank names of all they'd done and who had dared to defy him whenever he laid out an expectation.

Her eager innocence meant that she did not play games when it came to matters of intimacy. Though, withholding had been a game in and of itself. But when it came to the actual act her curiosity overrode any sort of coquettishness.

'Often when I was alone at my father's house, there was only my imagination for company. And I realise now there was such a gap in my education that my imagination suffered. Realising what I could have occupied myself with... If I would've known to dream of a man's body... I would have. If I would have known to think of a kiss as deep and wonderful as the ones I've had from you... I would have thought of nothing more.' She reached out and drew back the blanket that was covering him at his waist. She revealed his aroused state and her eyes went round. 'If I would have known...'

'What?' he asked, his voice rough. 'Would you have lain in your bed and put your hand between your legs? Would you have tried to do something to satisfy the restless need that you found there?'

Colour flooded her cheeks. 'I'm sure that's a very wicked sin.'

'Aye. But I'm a wicked sinner. It's far too late for my soul. So I wouldn't have wanted you to abstain from such things on my account.'

'I would have,' she said, her voice soft.

'Have you done so at night? When you thought of me.'

He didn't know why it might matter, not in ways beyond the physical. But it did. For this moment brought together all that time spent talking at their bedroom doors, rather than screwing. And all the times he'd desired her, too. It all bled into this moment.

Made it sharper. Keener somehow.

'I didn't know you could do such a thing. I squeezed my thighs together tight when I felt restless.'

'A lesson to you, then. You can find pleasure from your own hand. But you can be sure it will never be as keen as the pleasure you find with me.'

'I see.'

She looked obscenely intrigued by the idea. She curled her fingers around his length. 'I did see that men could find satisfaction from a woman putting her hand on him.'

'Aye,' he said, his voice rough.

'You feel… You're so hot.'

'You put a fire in my blood,' he said.

'Good. Because there's a fire in mine as well.'

'And why have you not come to me these last nights? Why have you closed your door to me?'

'Why did you not walk through it?'

An impasse. Perhaps they were both too stubborn to allow the other to see any sort of weakness. Weakness in the form of wanting.

'There was one act in the book that I was curious about above all others,' she said.

But she didn't tell him. Rather she lowered herself over his body, pressing her lips lightly to his shaft.

His hips bucked upwards and she startled. He put his hand on the back of her head and urged her back to him.

'Take me in your mouth,' he growled.

He had thought this a bad idea only days ago, but he had lost sight of why with her naked and soft and glorious above him. With her on her knees ready to worship in this way, why should he stop her, why should he not take what she was offering?

He was a man of battle. A man who sought to control all that was around him. A man who'd failed to change the tide when it counted. A man who felt awash at times in those failures. And this…this was like a baptism.

He needed it. He could not turn her away.

Her pink lips parted and she took in the head of him slowly, working her mouth up and down over his shaft. He moved his fingers deep into that thick, silky hair and guided her as she tried to take him deeper, and deeper still.

This was far beyond what he had ever envisioned. An

angel, fallen to her knees, fallen from heaven, taking part in pagan delights here in his bed.

And this was why he had not been able to bring himself to lay down with a doxy. Because this was what he wanted. Penny. On her knees before him. Pleasuring him, not with skill, but with all the bright-eyed determination she put into everything that she did.

The slick heat of her mouth took him nearly to the brink. It had been far too long since he'd been inside her and his hold on his control was tenuous. She created magic with her tongue and set fire to his reason. There was nothing except for the wet, deep suction of her mouth. There was nothing but them. He had been a man of base needs for as long as he could remember. When he was hungry, he wanted food. When his lust was inflamed, he wanted sex. When his anger was stoked, he wanted satisfaction. When wrong was done to him, he wanted revenge.

He did not care about the manner in which he received those things. But she created in him an appetite that could only be filled by her.

And she created in him a yawning ache for more. But as quickly as she created that need, she fulfilled it, the glide of her tongue over his body a sort of witchcraft.

Pleasure built behind his eyes, his whole body tensed. While he wouldn't mind spending himself down her lovely throat, he felt that was a step too advanced in her education.

And he wanted to be inside her. Properly.

He pulled her away from him, then lay down on his back, bringing her over the top of him, her slick entrance resting against his hard shaft.

'Now, lass,' he said. 'You wanted control? It's your turn to ride me.'

Penny was trembling, both with arousal and with shock over what she was doing.

She had done it. She had steeled up her resolve and gone into his room. She had done exactly what Isla and the others had described.

And it had been wonderful. She had never, ever once thought that perhaps the act might disgust her. No. She had known that everything about his body was pleasing to her. Absolutely everything. And if it made her a wanton, then so be it.

Now, as she sat astride him, his big, hard body pulsing beneath hers, she had different thoughts about ruination.

She was not going to be ruined in this bed. She was being remade. Reclaimed.

Or perhaps claimed for the first time.

For all of her life she had been an oversight. A creature that no one much cared about except what she might do for them. Her isolation and her position in society as a gently bred lady meant that she was not only ignorant of the world around her, but of her own body. Of the magic that it contained. Of the true beauty of being a woman. Heat bloomed low in her belly and in that place where she was slick and hollow, waiting for him.

She had felt conquered by him on their wedding night, and every night after. But she saw it differently now all of a sudden. After the way that he had trembled as she taken him into her mouth. After the way that she had found her own power as she lavished pleasure upon him.

He was not taking from her by being inside her. Rather, he was demolishing walls built up high and thick inside her, around all that she was and all that she expected to be. She felt strong, because she knew these things now. Because she knew of her own power. And men—men like him, gentlemen, even—they already knew. They knew what it was to have the sort of passion between men and women, and they deliberately kept it from ladies. Deliberately kept secrets about their own bodies from them. And by laying with Lachlan, she had discovered truths. By being with a man who shared and shared freely, she had found that there could be more.

Not for wives, Lachlan had said. No, for some mythical class of woman, prostitutes, harlots. Women who were disdained in fine circles, but valued in the bedroom, by men who desired acts that they could never teach the women they married, because then they might understand, fully, the power that they wielded.

But she understood. She understood it now.

And she had meant to come back together with him so that she might find closeness with this man, but she had found a closeness with her own self that she had not anticipated.

She had been locked in a prison for weeping when she'd been a girl. She'd been locked in herself for years since. Expectation and carefully concealed knowledge, and the weight of the fact she had no true control over her destiny.

But here…

She felt free.

She manoeuvred herself so that the head of his cock was pressing against the entrance of her body, then she lowered herself over him, inch by tantalising inch. She looked down at him, at her brawny captive, who filled her with his hardness to the hilt. He was so handsome it made her ache. And that was the other side of this power.

She was not unaffected.

For he was utterly and incredibly captivating. The hard lines of his face, the sculpted angles and planes of his chest. The cords in his neck stood out, his biceps straining as he moved his hands to grip her hips and hold her down over his pulsing manhood.

She could feel how much he wanted her and that drove her on. Made her feel a power unlike anything else. But it also heightened her own need. Made her slick and desperate for satisfaction.

It had been so long for her.

She didn't know if it had been for him.

Her stomach soured at the thought of him laying with a prostitute.

And whatever other women there might have been, they weren't here now.

It was something that ladies were supposed to accept. That their husbands would seek entertainment elsewhere.

She did not share. And after tonight she would make that clear.

He had taught her what it was to feel pleasure in that first week of their marriage. And now she would teach him what it was to be hers.

She began to move, arching her hips up and down, shuddering with satisfaction as she felt the length of him sliding inside her.

She had missed him. She had missed this.

Yet it had never been like this. Because here, with the candles flickering over his face, she could see that he was in the grips of a pleasure that looked nearly like pain. That he was utterly hers. In this moment.

Inside her.

She rode him until waves of need made her internal muscles pulse, until ripples of desire radiated out from low in her stomach further down. Until her head fell back and she cried out her pleasure, crashing down over her. In her. Then on a growl she found their positions reversed, found herself lying on her back, her great warrior looming over her.

He was fierce and he was strong, and was terrifying in the most thrilling of ways.

He had told her that a show of strength was always necessary. That it always benefited a man for those around him to know he was strong.

Tonight she thrilled in that. In his strength. And how very much a man he was.

It had been so foreign to her at first. But now suddenly she understood. She was soft. She was female. And her body had the power to make him shake. He was man. He had killed countless men in battle, hadn't he told her so?

He could easily kill her. With one large hand wrapped around her throat, he could end her before she ever had the chance to scream. But he chose instead to give pleasure with those hands. To hold her in all of that strength and not crush her with it. The strength of a woman. The tenderness in a man.

Though he was not tender now, his powerful thrusts pushing her back against the headboard, making her cry out in pleasure. The ridges of wood bit into her skull. She didn't care. She was so desperate for all that he could give her. For what she wanted. She was desperate for everything.

And suddenly she understood. She understood that great well of emptiness that had opened up inside her after the other times they had come together. For their bodies had connected, but this time their souls had entwined.

This was unleashed. And it was what she wanted. The warrior. The man. The one who was frightening and beautiful all at once.

She wanted to see not only what his lovers had seen, but what men on the battlefield had seen before them at the end of their life. She wanted every piece of Lachlan.

She didn't understand it. Didn't think she ever could.

But it didn't matter, because there was no room for thought now. She was a creature made entirely of sensation, when for most of her life she had been stitched together by too many thoughts and a great hollow pit of loneliness.

But not now.

Now, she was bursting with sensation. With pleasure like she had never known.

She had come to seduce him and had been thoroughly seduced in return.

And she was glad.

'Lachlan,' she whispered his name.

'Penny.'

Her name on his lips made her soar.

She hadn't imagined that she might find her peak again after she had already done that so quickly before. But when she did, it was earthy. Deeper. Her second climax shaking her, rocking the very centre of what she was. Then he growled and did not withdraw from her body. Instead, he poured himself into her as he shuddered out his own orgasm.

Little aftershocks of pleasure made her quake and she clung to those brawny shoulders.

When she fell asleep, she tangled her body around his. And she did not allow for distance.

In the morning, Penny was woken up by, not Isla, but Lachlan.

The night before came flooding back to her in great, co-lourful images.

Her face burned.

He was standing there at the centre of the room, gloriously naked. His broad chest bare, chiselled and covered with hair. His waist was lean, his hips narrow. And his manhood…was very definitely interested in exploring yet more pleasure between them.

It took her a moment to realise he was holding a tray. With a tea service, and a plate that seemed to have…

A piece of toast.

'I had thought you might wish to take breakfast in bed.'

He set the tray down in front of her.

'Did you fetch that naked?' She was trying to imagine the kitchen maids handling all that rampant virility in their midst.

And while she was only teasing, even in her own thoughts, she found that the idea made her burn with jealousy. Because she didn't want to share the glorious sight of Lachlan's body. It was hers. Hers alone.

She picked up the piece of toast and bit into it fiercely.

'I don't get thanks for that?'

'Oh, of course you do. But you didn't go into the kitchen naked, did you?'

'I did not. It might surprise you to learn that I do possess some manners.'

'Good. I feel that it has not been established between us, but I would like it very much if you did not go to see whores.'

She successfully shocked him into making a sound somewhere between a laugh and choking. 'You would appreciate that?'

'I find I don't relish the idea of sharing your body.'

'Well now, lass, you denied me your body.'

'I did,' she said. 'Though I sort of expected you to take your husbandly rights without my leave.'

'Is that what you would have preferred?'

'No,' she said, her face feeling hot, her throat scratchy.

'And so now you're concerned about my taste for doxies?'

'It is a concern.'

'There haven't been any,' he said.

She blinked. 'None?'

'Oh, no, lass, many. But all before you.'

'Oh.'

'I found I didn't have the taste for it.'

'Why not?'

'The hell if I know. All I know is that when craving the touch of my innocent wife, it did not appeal to me to go to a lightskirt to find my pleasure.'

'Well, I would like for that to be... I would like for you to not.'

'I promise,' he said. 'I vow. Only you.'

She hadn't expected that. She hadn't expected for him to promise, to vow. And he had. Easily.

'Good. And if there any more...tricks that you wish for me

to learn that are not becoming of a lady... I find that I quite enjoyed learning those others.'

'Vixen.'

'Perhaps I am. I would've done quite well as a duke's wife. The peerage are notoriously unfaithful to one another. Perhaps I would've enjoyed exploring my many options.'

'You have one option.'

'And that is?'

'My cock. And with it, you may unveil the mysteries of the universe.'

'That is quite a lot of confidence in one cock.'

'Confidence has never been my issue.'

'Thank you,' she said finally. 'For the toast.'

'You're welcome.'

A warmth spread in her chest. This was what had been missing. This. He held her all night long, then he had brought her toast. In that, he had shown just a small bit of caring. And she found that she had desperately needed it. Just something to show that he was...changed.

Because she was changed. And there was no denying it.

'And thank you for the fidelity.'

'There is a cost to that,' he said.

'What is that?'

'You no longer have your own bedchamber.'

A delicious, forbidden shiver raced through her. 'If I can have toast, then it will be a small price to pay.'

'I believe you've just sold your body for toast.'

'And yet I find myself unashamed.'

It was true. With him, there was no shame.

She had made friends here and they were a balm for her loneliness. But this was something more. The fulfilment of a need she hadn't realised she'd had.

Such a strange thing to have moved into a life so far away from the one she had imagined, only to find exactly what she had been searching for.

Chapter Fourteen

Lachlan's men had convened for a meeting. They had been issued an invitation to visit the Laird of Clan Darrach and he felt it only right to consult his men. Though he would decide how to proceed as he saw fit.

That was the easy part of the meeting. They would be gone at least three nights, between travel and the acceptance of hospitality. Some would remain behind to protect the people, but Lachlan and a select group would go.

He had been back for over a month now, and he felt it was time to get a sense for the way things had progressed.

Penny was the biggest surprise. Lachlan saw her strengths easily, but when he introduced her as a topic among his men he was surprised to see they saw them as well. That they gave full credit for her planning of the party, which had brought the clans together and felt like the start of a new era. That they saw her caring for the people in the village, building relationships and community.

Of course, not everyone was accepting of the Sassenach bride, but he felt that more were than were not.

Tensions remained, however, most disturbingly within the men who acted as warriors for the clan. The biggest opposition came from his cousin, Callum, and the men who served under him. But he was blood and Lachlan felt a particular loyalty to him out of that connection.

Callum was from Lachlan's mother's line. And he owed loyalty to that. To the MacKenzies.

'The feast was excessive,' Callum said. 'There is concern that, while you shared this time, your English wife will beckon you to behaviour more like that of the English aristocracy. Such unrestrained displays of craven wealth are not welcome here.'

'It was a gift,' Lachlan said, protective of his wife and of the celebration she had planned.

'Aye, and the people loved it.' Lachlan was surprised when Paden, one who was loyal to Callum, spoke out against him. 'Though there is unrest still regarding your wife.'

Rage ignited in Lachlan's gut. 'And many of the people love her. She has gone out daily into the village to share food. To offer aid. She is the one who brings back the needs of the people to me. I have no interest. Were it not for her, they would find their bellies much less full.'

'You must be firmer,' Callum said. 'What we need is a Laird with a fist of iron. We have no need for parties.'

'Yet it seemed as if the people *did* need a party.'

'This is not a London ballroom,' Callum said. 'This is Scotland. Clan MacKenzie is proud. We are warriors.'

'You need not speak to me of war,' Lachlan said. 'I know war. It was my world for nearly ten years. All of life cannot be a war. I fought tirelessly. And it was that fighting that gave me what I needed to return here. To restore our people and our land. I know war. Not the petty skirmishes that happen here, but devastation on muddy battlefields. Young men filled with lead. Their bodies destroyed by cannon fire. I have no desire to be at war for all of my lifetime. And perhaps the people of the clan deserve better.'

'Austerity with survival is better than luxury for a time, only to have it end in death,' Callum said.

'Where is death?' Lachlan asked. 'There is no enemy at the gate.'

'But there could be an enemy at the gate, any day. At any moment. And we must be prepared.'

'There is a difference between being prepared and living under siege when it is not necessary.'

'You would be better off divorcing your wife. Sending her back to England. Picking a Scottish girl from the village,' Paden said.

'I have married Penelope.' He thought of last night, of the brilliant fire that had burned between them. It had been like that ever since the night she had come to him a fortnight before.

The distance and coolness that had existed between them in those first weeks since their return to Scotland had melted away. Whatever reason she had for keeping her body back from him, she had banished it. She came to him joyfully. Freely.

And he received everything she gave. And took more.

There was disquiet, in the back of his mind, a concern that perhaps he was allowing himself to become far too consumed with her. It didn't help that one of these trusted warriors seemed to agree. But there was something far too English and foreign about her. He was in danger of being infected by it.

'I could've stayed in England. I have great wealth there. A thriving shipping company. But I'm Scottish. I am the clan. And I came here as quickly as I could because this is what kept me going when there was nothing else. Knowing that my responsibility lay here. An English wife should not concern the people. If I wanted to be English, I would've stayed there.'

'That's enough,' Graham said. 'Your wife is your wife. It

is done. There is no reason to pretend it could be otherwise. Any mutterings from the people... They will be silent once they see the prosperity that's to come.'

'They had better.'

'A threat against your own people to protect a Sassenach?' Callum asked.

'To protect my wife.'

He had vowed that the day he'd taken her from England. He had always known that, physically, he would defend her. He was a man who did not tolerate the mistreatment of the vulnerable. And to him, women and children were vulnerable.

But that had been a vow in keeping with his sense of honour.

This wasn't about the vulnerable or the weak. This was about Penny.

She was good, better than he deserved. Better, he thought, than these men deserved and that was certain.

And as he stormed out of the great hall, he realised it was true. Protecting Penny had become important, for she had become more than a pawn. She had become more than he had ever intended.

She was his queen.

She was, like the rest of his clan, *his*.

And that meant he would protect her. With all that he was.

The weather was truly vile. Rain poured down, creating boggy soup out of the mud all around the castle. Penny felt as though she was going to go insane from being cooped up as she was. But when she had suggested going out, Isla had clucked her tongue and made proclamations about all the ways in which Penny might catch her death.

There was little movement outside. Those in the village who could hunkered down to escape the storm. Lachlan and most of his men had gone to a neighbouring clan and they weren't expected back before morning.

She could only hope that he was safe. It was such a strange thing, to worry about the man. He had survived years of war. Violence she couldn't fathom. And she was concerned about rain being his undoing.

But her worries were shoved aside when Rona came racing into Penny's bedchamber.

'There is a girl here,' she said. 'She said that you told her to come to you if she had a need to.'

'Yes,' Penny said, standing before she could even think of what she might be doing. She didn't need to know who it was. She didn't need to be told. She already knew.

The girl whose name she didn't even know.

And there she was, standing in the core door, looking wild eyed and frightened. 'It's too soon,' the girl said.

And to Penny, she truly looked like a child in that moment. Pale and frightened. Not a woman ready to give birth.

'How soon?'

'I don't know,' the girl said. 'I don't know enough about such things. But my mother… She's had twelve children, and I have some idea of… It's too soon.'

'We need a midwife,' Penny said.

'I'll fetch one,' Isla said. She turned to the girl. 'Do you want your mother?'

'She said she wouldn't help me,' the girl said, hysteria colouring her voice. 'She said I had to leave. She said my father would kill me and it was better if I died out in the rain than to force him to sin in such a way.'

'I'll have his head,' Penny said. 'I won't need Lachlan to do it. I'll take his sword and I'll have his head myself.'

Perhaps that was the influence of her brawny, Scottish husband, but she felt terribly bloodthirsty in this moment. She wanted to lay steel into all the men who had harmed this girl and into the woman who protected a man above her child.

What a deadly weapon, this thing that took place between men and women. What a horrendous way it could be twisted.

Penny was again stunned by all she had been protected from.

The girl doubled over, writhing as a pain racked her small body.

'You must come to my bed,' Penny said. 'We will make you comfortable until the midwife comes. I promise you will be cared for. And so will the babe.'

The girl braced herself on the wall. 'I feel as though I might die.'

'You won't die,' Penny said.

She vowed it. It wasn't fair. This girl going through such a terrifying thing. And Penny's husband didn't want children.

He had only made a mistake that first night they'd come back together. Every night since he had spent himself on the sheets. Penny would love a child and yet that wasn't to be.

This girl… This girl's body and life was being torn away from her because she was with child.

It was wrong. It wasn't fair. Not to either of them.

Most especially not to the girl.

'Perhaps you'll give me your name now,' Penny said, helping the girl into the bed.

'Mary,' she said. She closed her eyes, a tear running down her cheek.

All the anger and bravado that had been with her the other times Penny had met her was gone.

Penny sat with the girl, as her pains became greater, closer together. She stepped out into the corridor with Rona as the hours advanced. 'How early do you suppose she is?'

Rona shook her head. 'I don't have bairns of my own. I don't know. I can't tell by looking at the girl.'

'I'm worried for them both.'

Rona looked at Penny, her expression softer than Penny had

ever seen it. Things were never easy with the prickly house-keeper, but she seemed united with Penny, in this at least.

'It would probably be a gift to the girl if the bairn died,' Rona said, looking regretful as she spoke the words.

But Penny had a feeling the woman was right. For where would this girl go back to, with a baby in her arms? How would she be able to face her family? Her father?

It was such a terrifying thing.

But Penny wanted the baby to live.

Penny wanted life for them both.

Watching another human being experience such physical distress made Penny's stomach churn.

By the time the midwife arrived, the girl was in extreme pain, gripping the bedclothes and thrashing back and forth.

Her hands gripped the sheets so tightly that Penny feared she might harm herself.

'Is there anything that can be done?' Penny asked the mid-wife.

'It's just the way of things. And she's a bairn herself,' the woman said, disdain in her tone. 'She's not prepared.'

'No,' Penny agreed. 'She's not.'

'The man who did this to her should be thrashed.'

'He should be killed,' Penny said. 'If The MacKenzie had any idea where he was his life would be forfeit.'

She knew that. In her blood.

For Lachlan was not an abuser of women. Far from it.

'Ah, lass,' the midwife said, shaking her head sadly. 'Men don't often see this as a terrible crime unless it happens to their own wife or daughter. Even then.'

'He would,' Penny said, conviction burning in her chest.

'A welcome difference to the previous Laird, then,' the woman said, her mouth in a grim line.

'So I've heard.'

* * *

The hours went by in a slow, tense fashion, until the girl's pain seemed to be utterly unbearable.

'It's time, lass,' the midwife said. 'Time to push.'

The girl was wild-eyed and it was clear she didn't understand, but then nature seemed to take over and she grunted, her eyes wild.

Penny grabbed hold of her face and looked at her. 'You're not alone,' she said. 'We will not let harm come to you.'

Calling from a strength inside herself that left Penny in awe, Mary pushed with all her might.

And then she continued like that, without making any progress for what seemed like hours.

Penny was exhausted, she could not imagine how the girl felt.

'Is it always like this?' she whispered to the midwife.

'There is sometimes more trouble than others,' the woman said. 'This babe doesn't want to come. I'm going to have to try to help.'

Penny didn't quite understand, but she soon learned. The midwife positioned her hand in such a fashion that she tried to ease Mary's pushing as the girl bore down with all her might.

'I can feel the baby's head,' the woman said.

Penny could offer no help there, but she could hold Mary. As her own mother should have done. Could be there for her. Could show compassion.

Could offer something other than blame and scorn.

'Good lass,' the midwife said.

Another push and Penny could see the baby's head.

Then it was suddenly over. The babe out in the world and Mary sagging with exhaustion.

There was no cry and a deep sadness expanded in Penny's chest.

It had taken so long. And it was early.

Penny wanted to weep for the injustice of it, but she couldn't.

Instead, she simply sat holding on to Mary's hand.

And then there was a sound. A whimper, more than a cry, but it soon grew, thin and tenuous, filling the room.

She looked at the baby and saw that, though it was dusky, it was moving.

'There we are,' the midwife said. 'There we are.'

'Does it live?' Mary asked.

'Yes,' the midwife said.

Mary let her head fall back against the pillow, a tear tracking down her cheek.

'I'm glad,' she said.

'Please hold the babe,' the midwife said to Penny.

Penny took the babe, wrapped it in her shawl. The midwife began to give care to Mary. She finished with the rest of the delivery, worry etched in her face.

'What can I do?' Penny asked.

'Nothing,' the woman said. 'She's bleeding. There are herbs I can give to try to slow it. But... Sometimes...'

'No,' Penny said. 'I won't let her die. She's been given nothing. No help at all. No kindness. She cannot die without ever...'

'These herbs should cause contractions in her womb. It helps slow the bleeding.'

The midwife made tea on the fireplace in the room and Penny did her best to guide Mary in drinking it.

The bleeding lasted through the night. By the time it was slowed, Penny knew her bed could not be saved. But as long as Mary could be, it didn't matter.

She heard a voice out in the corridor. Her husband's.

He'd returned.

Penny's body was stiff from being held in unnatural positions for too long and her eyes were gritty.

She stood, making sure the babe was secured in his little nest upon the bed. And then she went to the door.

'The village girl, Mary McLaren. She's had her baby.'

Lachlan looked as though he was gazing at the horror of battle. Penny looked down at herself and realised that she bore the marks of the particularly difficult medical event.

'I'm not hurt,' Penny said. 'It's not... I don't know if she will survive. Mary or the babe.' Emotion caught hold of her chest and it heaved on a dry sob. 'No one has slept and it's been so many hours...the girl doesn't deserve this.'

She felt herself sway and then suddenly found herself being lifted up off of the ground, held close to her Highlander's chest.

He began to walk back towards his bedchamber, where he closed the door behind him. Then he stripped her of her dress, all her bloody garments going to the floor. She shivered. But she found that she was not embarrassed, because she was far too focused on the exhaustion of her body.

He called for a tub to be brought in and for hot water, and wrapped her in a blanket to conceal her modesty as the staff went about doing his bidding.

'But Mary...'

'She will be seen to,' he said. 'Don't worry. You look as if you're about to fall over dead.'

She felt as if she were. But she also felt guilty for abandoning the girl in such an uncertain moment.

'You will not be able to help if you cannot see straight,' he said.

When the bath and water were produced, Isla offered to stay, but Lachlan sent her away. 'I will care for my wife,' he said.

He picked her up and deposited her naked body into the tub of warm water.

His hands were gentle as they skimmed over her skin and an ache of loneliness opened up inside her.

Sadness.

For she had adored this man's hands. When they gave her

pleasure, she could find power in it. Could find a way to make a balance so that she wasn't left trembling and wrecked. But today had compromised her defences in a way that frightened her. She was small and reduced. She had never felt so much fear, not even when she'd discovered she'd been sold to Lachlan in the first place.

Now he was touching her and his hands were tender, rather than arousing, though they still created sparks over her skin. He was large and she was tempted to lean against his strength.

'I just want to help,' she said.

'You may not be able to,' he said, but there was no cruelty in his voice.

'The baby is so small.'

'I've seen what happens with small bairns. It is just the way of things.'

'It's not fair,' Penny said. 'That all they should know is suffering.'

'Lass,' he said, his voice tender, scraping against raw places inside her. 'The world is harsh and cruel. It doesn't care if bairns get a chance to live. Or if girls get a chance at happiness.'

She knew he meant that. Down to his soul. Down to his very bones.

'I don't want to believe it,' she said.

She felt emotion rising up inside her. Emotion that reminded her of the day her mother had died. But there was… there was hope still. For Mary and the babe lived. And while they lived there could still be hope. Hope.

She closed her eyes and let Lachlan's rough hands smooth away some of the pain inside her. Let the warm water soothe the ache that had taken over her muscles, for it had been a day that was long and painful, and it was not over.

She cared for the both of them and couldn't simply stop because she was exhausted.

She didn't like it, for there was no place to put emotions like this. There was no way to stop them and Lachlan being kind was only making it worse.

But she was too tired to fight it. She could only surrender to the warm water, surrender to his hands. Surrender to this. To them.

'You are a soft thing,' he said, his voice rolling over her, even more soothing than the water. 'I forget that you haven't seen quite so many hard things of the world.'

'My mother died,' she said softly. 'I know about death.'

'You're supposed to bury your parents,' he said, his voice rough.

She did not normally press him. Their conversations stayed carefully around the edges of the deep, sad things that had hurt him in the past.

But she wanted to press now.

'It doesn't matter,' she said. 'Didn't your mother's death hurt you?'

'The manner of it, aye.'

'I was five. I was five when she died. It felt a lot like this. Confusing. Unfair. And I felt helpless. I didn't know what to do. And there was nothing to do. It was such a stark and horrible thing. I couldn't fix it. She was gone. I just wanted to save her and it was too late.'

She thought of every little animal, of every plan she had spearheaded since. All the way down to this. To trying so hard to save Mary and the baby.

It was the lack of hope she had never been able to accept. That she might never be able to do something to fix the situation. That she truly was helpless. That she truly was a pawn.

And had she been fighting against that from the moment Lachlan had stood in the great hall of her father's house? Hadn't she been trying to find a way to be active, to fix, to repair, to do something about this yawning void inside her?

The one that she had contained inside a shiny jewellery box. But that could not be.

It could not be. And she had tried. She had tried so hard. But she was failing by inches. For her heart was bruised and battered and she knew that she must never cry.

But Lachlan hadn't locked her in a room by herself. He had drawn her a bath. He was here. And he was holding her.

What would he do if she wept?

And why did she want to see? She had found answers to her loneliness over the years. Had made friends by following people around and chattering at them. But this was something different. This desire to sit here and share silence. To allow his hands to create emotions, to soothe and to arouse. And why was it that the man who had brought her the jewellery box, that symbol of her own survival, why was it he who challenged that very way of living?

Why did he make her wish there was more?

This.

This tenderness.

Being held while her heart was sore…

It was as if she had been waiting for this all of her life.

And she hadn't known that. Hadn't wanted to know. For with the comfort came vulnerability. And with that vulnerability came fear.

How could she trust this part of herself to a warrior? To the barbarian who had bought her for revenge?

But this didn't feel like revenge.

It felt like nothing ever had and she wanted to bask in it. In him.

All while her soul trembled with fear over what might become of Mary and her child.

'When my mother died,' she said, speaking slowly, 'I wept. I cried from the very depths of my soul. Each sob was painful, because they came from somewhere so impossibly deep. My father hated the sound of my grief. He said not to cry because she was in heaven and if I did that I was a heathen with no hope. But I missed my mother. I missed her. And I couldn't stop crying. In his anger he took me to my room and he locked the door. Locked me inside. I couldn't come out until I learned how to lock away every last one of my tears. I know about death. It still isn't fair.'

Her throat went thick, her eyes filling with tears. Shameful tears. Tears that she was supposed to be able to keep inside. But she was so tired. She was so afraid. And weary with the lack of justice in the world.

She wasn't alone.

She could talk and someone was here to listen. And maybe…maybe she could cry. Just maybe.

A tear slipped down her cheek and she shuddered. Shivered.

'Lachlan,' she whispered. 'Kiss me.'

Because anything was better than feeling this. Anything was better than surrendering to this. And she found herself being lifted out of the water by her strong, wonderful Highlander, and he held her against his chest as he kissed her and kissed her. As he took her deeper into the carnal, sensual world that he had created inside her. One that existed apart from that place where she locked her feelings away.

Because this was theirs. She wasn't alone here.

But it wasn't about power, not this time.

Not about skill.

This was about being in that room with someone else. Crying and having a person there who would listen.

He laid her out on the bed, looking down at her as if she was a sumptuous feast.

And she shuddered. Shivered.

He slowly divested himself of his clothes, revealing his beautiful body to her. She would never tire of him.

There was something in the moment that felt like a surrender. There was something in the look on his face, in the tender paths his hands had just traced over her body, that made her feel safe in the surrender.

It didn't make her feel weak.

Rather, it made her feel brave. Strong.

She could surrender. She could choose to surrender, she didn't have to hide. She didn't have to push her feelings down deep. She didn't have to lock them away.

Because she was not a child.

And she had not been put in a wooden box with her mother that day. No matter that the room had felt like a coffin, it wasn't. Because she was alive, no part of her dead. Yet she had let part of herself be buried because of fear. A need to protect herself. A need to make sure she was never alone with her pain the way she had been that day.

But she wasn't alone here. She was with Lachlan. And so she wept as he trailed kisses over her naked skin. As his head moved down between her thighs and made a feast of her, creating a helpless, swirling sensation inside her that she didn't turn away from. No. She embraced it. Embraced him. Let his tongue and mouth push her higher, further, than she had ever imagined she could go.

It was like flying.

You helped me save the bird.

That injured bird. The injured bird with the crippled wing who had been grounded, his injuries preventing him from soaring high. But he had been restored.

And now, so was she.

Like a bird who had found flight once again.

It was magic.

They were magic.

He licked her until she shattered and in the pieces of herself she found beauty. Brilliant, sparkling glory in that shattering.

And when he thrust into her body, she gasped. It wasn't an invasion this time, though, and it wasn't a power play. It was a joining. A coming together in answer to the hollowness inside her.

And all it had taken was for her protection to be down. For her walls to have cracked and crumbled.

Then she could feel it. Could feel him.

Each glorious inch of him reaching places inside her that transcended reason.

And where those walls had once stood he rebuilt something different.

The woman she might have been.

Not just a woman who had escaped from her father, not just a woman who had learned how to survive.

But a woman untouched.

A woman who didn't have to fear laughter or tears.

A woman who had gone so far past the concept of innocence and ruin.

A woman who feared no pleasure or pain as long as her warrior was with her.

And it wasn't only his strength, but the strength he had found in her.

All through showing care. For it was the softness in his battle-battered hands that had created this.

The tenderness in his touch, in his voice, that had allowed her to open up.

When it was over, he lay with her, tracing shapes over her bare skin.

'If I had known that your father locked you in your room that way… I would've killed him before I took you.'

'No one needs to die,' she said softly. 'I survived.'

'A person can survive many things,' he said. 'It doesn't mean they should have to.'

'Neglect can't kill you,' she said softly.

'No, lass. It can. I know you've heard how my father used his fists on his mistresses. About how he killed one. It's true.

He did. He never raised a fist against my mother. He never did, because she was the Laird's daughter. But his neglect, his transgressions against the clan, they contributed to her despair. That despair caused her death.'

'I had to live,' she said softly.

'Why?'

'I don't know. But something in me always believed… When I took care of the animals that I found, I believe that I was making enough of a difference. I know that it was a small thing, a silly thing, but it felt as though it mattered. It made me feel as though I mattered. And when you would walk with me, when I spoke to you, I felt real.' She closed her eyes. 'I grieved when you left. As though you were dead. I didn't cry. I haven't cried since I was five years old. Not until today.'

He pulled her into his arms, held her against his chest. And she listened to the ragged beat of his heart beneath her ear. 'I will tell you this,' he said. 'You were the only person who spoke to me like an equal for those years. And perhaps that's the real reason I came for you. You felt as though you might be mine.'

She said nothing to that. Exhaustion began to take hold and she found her eyes fluttering closed.

But the last thought on her mind was that he felt an awful lot like he might be hers.

Sealed with tenderness, kisses and tears.

She had dreamed of a different life. In a stately, civilised manner home with a man who put propriety above all else.

Lachlan rarely seemed to have a concept of propriety.

But he had a fierce, deep sense of protecting what was his.

And right then, she was very glad to be counted as his.

Chapter Fifteen

Lachlan had expected to hear of the bairn's death by morning. But it lived.

As did the girl.

He didn't care for the worry that it put on Penny's face. Not in the least.

His wife was too soft. Too hopeful in the face of something Lachlan had seen all too many times.

The babe was... It was far too small.

And he knew full well that good intentions would not keep a child alive. Nor hopes or prayers or dreams. For if they could, his mother would have kept all of her children, and perhaps she would have lived.

If she would've but had more to live for.

She'd had one son and that son had failed her.

And he had tried...

He saw that soft, cherubic face in his mind again.

Not one of his brothers or sisters.

The bairn that he'd found near a battlefield while in the army, badly injured near his dead mother, a peasant girl, from the look of things, who had been brutalised by French soldiers.

He had tried.

And Lachlan had profited from saving a peer, but he had to ask God, had to ask whoever might listen, with a quiet rage in his heart, why a dissolute, titled man might survive grave injuries, but an innocent child hadn't been able to overcome them. He could still remember the little boy's whole body being bright with heat. When he had been certain the injuries would not take him, and the fever had.

He had been at war for six years by then. And he had seen atrocities that left scars on his soul.

But he understood why Penny had saved all those small creatures at her estate.

Because sometimes it was those small things that made you hope. They made the world feel bearable. That little boy…

Saving him had become the most important thing in the world to Lachlan.

And he had failed.

That failure stayed with him. And it also taught him better than to hope when there was little to hope in.

The world didn't care.

Perhaps God was too busy to trouble himself with the very small, even when they were innocent.

But this morning in the castle, the bairn lived.

Still, he knew better than to trust in it.

He could understand why it was a necessity for the girl and child to stay here. They could not be moved. Not in their state.

'Her father will kill her,' Penny said when they took breakfast.

'I will not allow it,' Lachlan said.

'I thought you could not control what a man did in his own home.'

She brought his own words back to him and they shamed him. Her blue eyes were level and unyielding. He had known his wife was strong, but she'd demonstrated that strength in new ways every day. She was becoming Scottish. Part of the clan.

'I will not allow harm to come to them,' he repeated.

The days passed and the babe continued to live. Mary grew in strength.

It was time to decide what to do about them.

But along with Mary's healing, his wife had changed.

She was quiet more often. Sometimes she simply sat near him. She would touch him, her head on his shoulder, her hand on his thigh.

He did not know what to make of the change. Neither did he dislike it.

She was doing a great deal of caring for the babe. It seemed to him the mother only took him for feedings, otherwise Penny had taken to carrying the child around.

Yes, it was time to discuss finding a permanent home for the girl and her child.

He understood that she couldn't go home—the issue of Dugan McLaren was one he was going to have to solve. But first Mary needed to be cared for.

She would be protected in the castle, that was true. But perhaps he could find placement for her in another clan, though the matter of her attacker troubled him.

She had said she didn't know him, which made him suspect it had been someone from a different clan.

He believed that to be the case, right up until she was beginning to move about the castle and she passed into the great hall while his men were present.

Her eyes locked with Callum's and he saw fear there. Utter terror. Her face went white and she stumbled back.

Then she collected herself and walked quickly back towards the stairs that would take her to her bedroom.

Lachlan said nothing. But he watched the face of the man

for a good while, trying to read it. Trying to see evidence of what he suspected written there. Guilt. Fear. Something.

The man remained blank. That began to arouse suspicion in Lachlan above all else.

For what man would pretend the woman had not fled from him in fear?

One who did not want it noticed.

One who wanted to be able to deny that he was the reason why.

When Lachlan saw Penny later, he approached the subject directly.

'Has she said to you who her attacker might be? Or has she stuck with the story that it was a stranger?'

'She's never mentioned it again.'

'I suspect Callum.'

'But Callum is… He's your cousin.'

'He is. And one of my detractors. Certainly no supporter of yours. The way his eyes follow women around the room troubled me. And I find I've a concern about what he's done to Mary.'

'Lachlan…'

'I will not allow it.'

'Perhaps we should help her escape.'

'No,' he said, his voice hard. 'He will face justice. If it is true, then he will face justice.'

Accompanied by Penny, he went into the bedroom that Mary and the babe occupied. She was holding the child, her expression blank.

'The man,' Lachlan said without preamble. 'The one who got you with child. Was it Callum MacKenzie?'

'I told you,' she said, looking away, 'I didn't know him.'

'The fear on your face when that man was in the great hall says otherwise, lass.'

Mary's face went mulish. 'It is best for myself and the bairn if it's a secret.'

'Why?'

'I do not have to explain to you how it is for a woman,' she said, looking every inch a child and not a woman at all. 'There is no help for me. My own father would kill me. My mother blames my own actions.'

'And I do not,' Lachlan said. 'You and the bairn are under my protection. And I do not allow rape to happen within my clan.'

'He's too powerful...'

'I am The MacKenzie,' Lachlan said. 'There is none more powerful than I. Was my cousin, Callum MacKenzie, the man?'

'I...'

'He was,' Lachlan said.

'He will kill me,' she said, her voice hushed. 'And the baby.'

'He will not,' Lachlan said. 'For dead men can do nothing.'

There was no justice in the world, none but that which Lachlan would bring about himself. There was a snake in the midst of his men and he would not allow that to continue. He would not allow it to go on. He would allow for none of this.

He was Laird. And he would see justice done.

Penny was frozen with terror for all the hours that Lachlan was away.

She had no idea what her husband intended to do. But she feared, not only for his safety, but for his soul.

When he returned, a great shout was heard out in the courtyard.

All of his men were assembled and he had Callum MacKenzie walking in front of him.

Penny ran outside. 'Lachlan,' she said. 'What is it you intend to do?'

'I will make an example of this man,' Lachlan said.

It was then she realised that half the village had trailed into the courtyard.

'This man,' he said, pointing at Callum with his broadsword. 'This man used his strength against a woman. A *child*. He forced himself on her. I will not allow this to continue. This will not be tolerated. Not while I am The MacKenzie. For this is not the reign of Angus Bain. Your pleasure is not your master. *I* am your master.'

'You cannot do this,' Callum said.

'My word is law,' Lachlan said. 'I can do what I please.'

'A trial...' Graham said.

'It is not necessary. Especially among my men, among the gentry, I will discipline as I see fit.'

'You bastard,' Callum spat. 'You prize the life of some bitch over a man who shares your own blood?'

'I prize justice.'

'This isn't justice,' Paden said. 'It is an execution.'

'Laird, surely...' Even William, the boy Lachlan had brought back with him from war, looked at Lachlan with uncertainty.

That seemed to spur Lachlan on. 'Surely an example will be set and you will all know—I do not grant mercy. Not in these matters. If a woman or child is harmed here, the man responsible will be held accountable.'

'Lachlan,' Penny said, rushing forward. 'What do you intend to do?'

'Listen to your Sassenach. Even she doesn't want you to do this,' Callum said. 'This is not the way of things.'

'The way of things is wrong,' Lachlan said. 'At least under the hand of my father.'

'Lachlan,' Penny said.

He turned to her, his expression fierce. And he lowered his voice. 'You would have him live? He would do the same to you as soon as look at you, all men like him would. You would have this dog continue to use women as he sees fit?'

'No,' she said softly. 'But surely...'

'We keep him in the dungeon for the rest of his life?'

'I don't know,' she said. 'But your soul...'

Something flashed in his eyes. Shock. 'No one has ever paid a care for my soul, Penny. I was a soldier for ten years, there is more blood on my hands and blackness in my heart than you could fathom. It is too late for me.'

'Someone else...'

'This is my clan. Why would I pass the spilling of blood on to another man? You would have me put this on someone else's head?' Penny stood back, her heart hammering.

She knew she couldn't stop him.

Callum had raped Mary. Got her with child. The girl had nearly died. And even now she had nowhere to go because of what he'd done. But it pained her, this heavy weight that her husband must carry.

And she didn't want it. Not for him.

She wanted to spare *him*.

That horrible look in his eye, dead and determined, all emotion gone... It was much like the way she had trained herself to be before she had found a way to open herself up. Before she had found a way to weep.

His heart was scarred over and it was carrying him now. This man who understood this concept of justice, but never mercy.

And where was the mercy deserved for a man like him?

It wasn't Callum that she worried for.

It was Lachlan.

For Lachlan was the one who had to live with all this blood, all this pain. But the man had been at war for ten years and she knew he saw this differently.

'Go inside,' he said.

'No,' she said.

'There is no reason to expose you to this. Go inside.'

'Lachlan...'

And she felt that if it were his duty to rid the world of the man, then she must bear witness to it as his wife.

'I said leave,' he said.

Callum was down on the ground, his position that of a man defeated. But then, when he looked up at Lachlan, there was spite in his eyes. 'It's that Sassenach that you've brought to us. She's made you soft. For what is a woman for but a man's cock? If a woman's going to wander around offering it, why shouldn't I take it?'

'She did not offer,' Lachlan said. 'Do you deny that?'

'Since when does it matter?'

'Since I am Laird.'

'An Englishwoman's dog,' he spat.

Then he moved towards Penny. Penny tried to move back, but Callum had retrieved a sword from the ground and was barrelling towards her.

The rest happened in the space of a breath.

Lachlan moved faster and raised his broadsword. Brought it down in one fluid movement.

Penny looked away, her heart nearly exploding through her chest as she heard the sickening slice of blade through flesh. The sound of the man's head separating from his shoulders.

Her heart was thundering so hard she could scarcely breathe. Lachlan's strong arms were around her then, holding her from falling on to the ground. Keeping her from collapse.

'William,' he barked. 'Deal with the body.'

'Yes, Laird,' William said.

Penny was shaking, trembling.

'I told you to go inside,' Lachlan said. Holding her arm, he propelled her on with him, into the castle.

Her heart was throbbing in her chest, her emotions tangled together. She didn't know what she felt. She touched his shoulder and he turned to face her when they were inside the great hall.

Blood was splattered over his bare chest, up to his neck. It reminded her then of when he'd come back and found her in the castle after delivering the baby. Stained with the evidence of life. Of what…of what had to happen whether it was easy or good or not.

He had protected her. Saved her.

He had been determined to protect Mary. He had not been intent on executing Callum to prove his strength or might. It had been to put a stop to harm because the man was unrepentant. Saw no sin in his actions.

She was perversely grateful, however, that he had made a move for her. For it made Lachlan's actions those of a soldier in battle and not an executioner.

'I would have felt no guilt for it,' he said, his tone hard.

'I know,' she said, her chest squeezing tight. 'But I would have cared that you'd had to do it. I would have wept for you.'

'No one weeps for me.'

'I will.'

'There is no justice but what you make, lass. The world doesn't right these injustices. You must do it yourself with steel. My father did not protect this clan. He did not protect his wife. And I… I have seen things end badly. I have no great faith in the world to right its wrongs on its own. Nor do I labour under the delusion that I can always prevent it with my own strength. This, this I could do. Do not waste your sadness on me.'

Something twisted inside her then. And she felt…new. Looking at him, she didn't worry for his soul, not at that moment, because this was a man who knew his conviction. He was a man who would give his all to protect those who were weaker than himself.

A man who would protect her with everything he was.

He was not a man who would lock her away because she

cried. He was not a man who would ever harm the innocent. The vulnerable.

A man with all the strength in the world, all the power, and he would use it justly.

She trusted that. Deep within herself she trusted it.

'You need to wash,' she said.

She took his hand in hers and he followed. Which she knew was a choice, because he did not have to be led anywhere by her. 'The Laird needs to bathe,' she said.

With great speed, the staff had seen to preparing the water for him.

It was set out in the centre of their room and she took care in taking his clothes off his body, washing him clean of any blood.

'Thank you,' she said softly, as she sat next to the tub. 'Thank you for protecting us.'

''Tis justice,' he said.

'You know many men would not see it as such. They would not consider what he'd done a great crime.'

He looked at her. 'My mother despaired of her life. There was no escape. There was nothing for her. I would not have my people live in such desperation. Men...physically we are stronger than women. Where is the victory in overpowering one who could never fight back? It is a coward who takes joy in oppressing those weaker than himself. If a man wants to fight, if he craves violence, then he should find an opponent who might just as easily kill him.'

'When you were at war...'

'The brutality we saw, committed not just on the battle-field. There was a woman...' He hesitated slightly before pressing on. 'She was long gone from this world by the time my men found her. I will not tell you what she looked like.' His voice was rough, laden with the horror of what he'd seen and she could understand, then, why the death of a man who'd committed crimes against a woman would never linger in him for a moment. For this…this ate away at his soul. 'I have seen a great many atrocities, lass, and very few things are grim enough to cause me to lose sleep. But that… My dreams are haunted by that.'

She moved her hand slowly over his chest, to soothe. He put his hand over hers and she looked down at his scarred knuckles. 'It is not the bodies of dead men I see in my mind. It will not be Callum's lifeless body that lingers with me in my dying day. It will be the pain of girls like Mary. Of my mother. Of that nameless woman. It will be the weakness of men who should have been strong. And all the ways in which I was too late to stop it.'

'But you stopped it,' Penny said. 'You did.'

'The gesture coming a bit too late as we have a sickly girl in the room next to ours, with a bairn that may or may not survive.'

'He gets stronger every day.'

'You can never put your trust in these things, lass. Trust me. Now I do not wish to speak of these things any more.'

'Would you like supper?' she asked.

'Aye,' he said.

There was some great satisfaction in taking care of him this way and she wasn't certain where it came from.

But maybe it was just that same thing that had driven her to care for wounded creatures. It made her feel as though she mattered.

She might not be able to mete out justice in quite the way Lachlan did. But she was his wife. The Laird's lady. She was part of the clan. And she felt that, deeply, for the first time. In full support of her husband and the decision he had made today, hard and unyielding though it had been.

It was a statement. And they had come back to the clan under grave circumstances. And it meant that they could not tread lightly. He could not.

Even against his own blood.

She had supper brought up to their room and they ate together. They didn't need to talk.

But her connection with him felt strong. They didn't need to be touching. He didn't need to be inside her. She didn't need to chatter endlessly. She could simply sit and be near him.

A revelation.

She felt very suddenly inside herself. In a life that was hers.

A castle that felt like hers.

With a man who felt like hers.

This place was harsh. And it was different than anything she had ever been exposed to. It forced her to be stronger. It forced her to be different.

At the same time, time with Lachlan forced her to be fragile as well. To open up deep, compassionate places within her own heart.

Her interactions with Mary and her baby touched her in that way as well.

For the first time in her life, her world felt big. More than that, she felt powerful within it.

It was a gift, a change that she had never expected.

'Are you quite ready for bed, my Laird?'

'Past ready.'

And she went to him gladly.

Chapter Sixteen

There were grumblings among his people. While many supported the action he had taken against Callum, there were factions, even within his own men, who were bitterly angry. They did not think that a woman's chastity should be prized over the life of a man. Particularly when a woman's chastity had not even been proven.

He was beginning to feel concern for Mary's safety. She was ensconced in the castle, and growing healthier by the day. But they would need to find a position for her and he knew it could not be back in the village.

It had become customary for he and Penny to take their late meal alone in their room.

'Have you spoken to Mary about where she might want to go?'

'I think she'd like a domestic position somewhere,' Penny said. The place between her brows pleaded. 'I've written a letter to Lady Beatrice Ashforth. The Duke's sister.'

'Yes,' Lachlan said. 'The Duke. It has been a while since I've heard you speak of him.'

'It has been a while since I've thought of him,' she said.

He did not know why, but that gripped him with a fierce, possessive pleasure.

'And what did you ask this friend of yours?'

'Initially, I had intended to ask her about household positions. If she might be able to provide a reference, or give me names of those who might be willing to hire a girl from Scotland. But then… Instead I asked about school.'

'School?'

'She's young. She could go to a school that might train her, give her an education that she could use to take a position as a governess. She could have more options available to herself than simply being a scullery maid. Perhaps she'll choose that life. But when I thought she might die the thing that grieved me most was that she didn't have a chance. She didn't have a chance at a better life. She didn't have a chance to know what it was to be loved. To choose anything beyond this… This position she was born into.'

'That is the life most people must contend with,' he said softly. 'Not everyone is spirited off to the Highlands, after a broken engagement to a duke, a duke who would have vastly increased her circumstances. Whichever path you'd taken, your life would have changed. You have experienced extraordinary events.'

'It does not surprise me that you consider yourself an extraordinary event,' she said, a sly smile touching her lips.

'It is the way of things, lass. Most do not escape fate.'

'You did. A destitute Scottish boy who made his fortune, who survived nearly a decade at war. You're allowing this clan to escape the fate that your father consigned them to. Shouldn't Mary have a chance?'

'You're forgetting the bairn.'

'I haven't forgotten,' she said softly. 'But that is… Have you noticed she does not hold him?'

'I have not noticed the girl or the babe more than necessary.' It wasn't true. For he had seen how pale and weak Mary was and had watched her increase in strength, but had also seen that her interest in her child did not grow. The child still did not have a name. Not uncommon, for life was harsh and the chances of a baby dying were great enough that often the naming of them was delayed.

'I want her to choose. Because she had no choice in any of the things that brought her to where she is. I want her to be able to choose.'

'Do you expect word from your friend soon?'

She nodded. 'I hope.'

Word came early the next day. With Beatrice writing to say that she could find a position for Mary at a school, thanks to the influence and generous donations of her brother.

His wife began to weep.

'Always caring for wounded birds,' he said, dashing a tear away from her cheek.

She went immediately to Mary's room.

'Mary,' Penny said. 'I've had a letter from a friend of mine. She's sister to a duke. In England.'

Mary's eyes went round. 'A duke.'

'Yes. She has found… There is a position available to you at a school in London.'

'A school? What school would take me? No school wants a fallen woman who can't read or write…who has a child.'

'That you cannot read or write is not a concern. We can find you a position in a household with your baby if that is what you wish. But if you don't want the baby to stay with you…'

The look on the girl's face was one of such deep, pure emotion Lachlan had to look away. It was anguish, but it was hope.

'I can't leave him…'

'How old are you, lass?'

'Thirteen,' she said.

Everything in him turned. He didn't regret the death of Callum, not in the least. The man was worse than a devil, and he could burn in hell as far as Lachlan was concerned. Burn in hell for touching a child.

'I had to become a man when I was thirteen,' he said. 'When it became clear my father was not one. Eventually, I made my way to England and I made my fortune. You have been forced to a burden you should not have been. But what you do now...it is your choice.'

'The baby...'

'He'll be cared for,' Penny said.

'My parents won't. And, I wouldn't want him with them, even if they were willing, I wouldn't want them to have him.'

'If it was what you wanted,' Penny said, her tone careful, 'I would care for him.'

Lachlan took a step back. But Mary's eyes filled with tears. 'You would take care of him?'

'I would.'

'Would he be yours?' The girl's voice was filled with so much hope, it was nearly as sharp as any sword, as gutting as any bullet could have ever been.

'Only if that's what you wanted.'

'I tried to get rid of him,' Mary said. 'I felt terribly guilty about that, after he was born and I saw him. But... I can't take care of him. I don't know how. And I never imagined that I might be able to go to school. That I might be able to learn something...'

'You can,' Penny said. 'And if you really want, if you work at your studies, you might be able to find work as a governess.'

He could see a whole world of possibility in Mary's face. 'Not live in a house full of children like my mother. Not getting beat for the rest of my life by my husband. Learning to... to read and write and to get a real job. In London...'

'I just want you to be able to choose,' Penny said.

'I never knew I could choose. Not anything. I've never been able to.'

'You can now. And whatever it is you choose…'

'I want to go to school. If he can be taken care of… I don't know how to do it. I've been here, with no work to do, and I don't know how to soothe him when he cries and I don't know how to hold him right. And it is not his fault, but his father… His father hurt me. When I look at him I think of that.'

'You shouldn't live that way,' Penny said.

'Thank you,' Mary said.

'All I want is for you to make the best that you can with that choice,' Penny said. 'And don't look back. Don't wonder if you made the wrong choice.'

Dread built in his chest. The thought of this tiny, vulnerable child being in his care. Of Penny loving him. Of Penny…

If she lost this bairn, what would it do to her?

Lachlan waited until they left the room to turn to his wife. 'You do not mean to keep the child?'

'Why not?'

'You did not ask me.'

'You said to me, while we were on the way here from England, that I would likely be able to find myself a baby.'

'I did not say that.'

'You did.'

'If I did, then it was because I was simply thinking you might hold a child on occasion. Not because you were going to take in a foundling.'

'If your issue with children is your bloodline, then why can't I have someone else's baby?'

'So, is this what it is? You're offering her this position so that you can take the child?'

She looked stricken. 'No. How could you ask me that?'

'It seems to me a reasonable enough question, lass.'

'I do want the baby. I love him. And I'm much more prepared to take care of him than a girl of thirteen. I have a husband with all the money and power in the realm.'

'And you did not ask that husband what he might think of it.'

'It's a baby. And you made it perfectly clear you want nothing to do with them. But you told me that you were withholding a child from me because you didn't want to carry on your bloodline.'

'Do what you will, Penny,' he said, anger rolling through him. 'But this is not my responsibility. I have plenty enough to see to without taking on an abandoned child.'

'He's not abandoned. She's making the best choice that she can, for both of them. If you could have seen the desperation on her face when I first spoke to her. She didn't want this. And even now, it's clear that she has struggled to bond with him. That she hasn't. It isn't fair what she's been through.'

'Do what you will,' he repeated. 'But I'll have none of it. I have nothing to do with it.'

'I didn't think you were an unreasonable tyrant. I knew how badly your father had hurt you. How badly he hurt all the people here. And even though I don't believe your blood is tainted, Lachlan Bain, I could understand why you do. But what I don't understand is why you...why you're angry with me about taking this child in.'

She didn't understand. For she had not seen the things he had. The way the loss of her babies had destroyed his mother, year after year. The vow he'd made to that wounded child, on a battlefield years ago, that he could not keep.

That strength, love and power could not keep a bairn on this earth. No matter how deep it was.

She said she knew. She didn't.

'If you wish to take this on, I cannot stop you. I won't. But you're sheltered, Penelope, and you still believe that everything will work out right for you in the end because it has.

But I know how quickly fever can take something that small. And when your heart is shattered over the death of a child...'

'Lachlan, you can't... We cannot guarantee that things in life won't hurt. Just like you could not know for sure if you would succeed here. But it doesn't mean you didn't try. I cannot guarantee that the child will live two years, ten years, thirty years. But... This kind of closing off yourself...that's what my father did. And he couldn't stand my emotions. He couldn't stand them, so he shut me away. And then I ended up shutting away pieces of myself for most of my life. And I missed them. But here... Here I have found myself, and I will not go back. I won't stop love simply because it might harm me. I cannot do that.'

'On your head be it.'

And he turned and left his wife standing there. If he were a man who could feel guilt, he might have felt it now.

But he couldn't.

His wife was still the woman who had saved that bird.

But he was not the man who had helped her.

And he never could be again.

Chapter Seventeen

The closeness that she had felt to Lachlan began to splinter. It made her whole body feel splintered with it. But she had made Mary a promise and the duty she felt for the baby required action.

After Mary was bundled up and sent tearfully away to England with one of Lachlan's men, and also with Flora, who had found a position in London, it only got worse.

Because then Penny began to take over the care of the baby in earnest. It was up to her to name him. But she was having difficulty thinking of a name. Her father certainly didn't deserve a namesake. Lachlan wouldn't want one. And his father...

Well. There was no chance of that.

She had spent the past two days walking the halls, holding him and repeating different names.

The midwife had helped her find a wet nurse and they had got the woman situated in the castle. Penny was sorry that she couldn't feed the little boy, if only because she was desperate to find some way to let him know that she was his mother.

His mother.

She had lost her own mother so young she could barely remember her, and the word *mother* was tied to beautiful, soft feelings, which often gave way to the sharpness of grief.

But the gift of being able to be a mother, to be able to find a way to reconnect with that word, with that relationship as the mother herself... It was a gift she had not realised she wanted.

She had wanted to be a mother because she had simply assumed it was something she would do. Because it was a given that a lady of her standing would become a wife and mother.

When Lachlan had told her she wouldn't be, she'd been forced to contend with why that hurt.

And the reason became bright and brilliant while holding the baby one afternoon.

Because it brought her closer to her own mother. Because it made her understand the way she had looked at Penny. And made her feel as if she might have been loved once in the way a parent ought to love a child.

It was a week into her being the child's mother, when she finally thought of a name. And right at that same moment, she realised that she had not thought of the little box inside herself where she used to keep her feelings in all that time. She had simply felt them. She had felt love and concern and worry and despair, so deep and real over these past days.

She had felt happiness, joy, deeper than she had ever known it.

It astounded her that with that joy she could also feel some of the deepest pain she'd ever contended with. Over the fact she wanted Lachlan by her side for this. Wanted him to be united with her. For they had become family. Clan. And now this child was part of it and there was a wedge between them. She wanted all of them to be family.

She wanted Lachlan. By her side, always.

But she felt it. She didn't hide from it. And she wasn't confused by it.

He was not withholding his body from her. He was as ravenous for her every night as he had always been. But she could feel a distance there. And he didn't speak to her the way that he often did. Their silence no longer had that sweet sense of the companionable.

She was part of him enough to feel the distance and to know that it was real. She didn't have to know why.

There was a particular torture in having his body and knowing she no longer had his soul with it, for she'd experienced the difference. And now that she knew...now that she knew, it was devastating.

'I've named him,' she said, as she held him during supper that night.

'Have you?' He could not have sounded less interested if he'd made an effort to.

'Yes. Camden. It's Scottish.'

His expression was dry. 'Thank you. I didn't realise.'

She narrowed her eyes. 'It means winding valley. I wanted to give him a name that was connected to this place. To the clan.'

And one that felt like the true journey of her heart. Through a winding valley that was sometimes dark and frightening, fraught with peril, but was beautiful and worth the journey, no matter the cost.

'Not an English name?'

'He's not English,' she said. 'And neither am I.'

He paused, his broad shoulders shifting. 'You still sound English enough.'

'I'm part of this place. I'm part of you. Even if you're not very happy with me for the moment.'

He arched a brow. 'I'm not unhappy with you.'

'You are.'

'What have I done to make you think so?'

'You know.'

'Am I not sitting with you and having a meal?' He made a broad gesture over the food as if to suggest his grandness.

'You are. But it's not the same.'

'Do I not give you my body every night?'

'For all I know you give your body freely to whores as well. It used to be different between us. And you know that.'

His face turned to stone. 'Do you give your body to whores?' she asked. 'Even though I asked... I told you not to?'

'No,' he said.

She let out a sigh of relief, and looked down at Camden, brushing her thumb over his downy soft head. 'You like me a great deal more than you pretend. And right now, you're a great deal angrier with me then you're admitting.'

'It's just I've nothing to discuss when it comes to the lad.'

'So he'll grow up without a father?'

'I cut his father's head off and did us all a favour. I would have done well to grow up without a father.'

'Is that the problem? Do you not think you'll be a good father? Because you will. I know you will. The way that you take care of the clan, the way that you defended Mary... You're a leader, Lachlan, in a way your father never could've been. And his blood is in your veins. So I don't believe that blood is weak. Because in you...in you it has become something entirely different. You believe in honour. And you believe in what's right.'

'Aye,' he said. 'I do. I believe in taking that which my father corrupted and restoring it. And giving it, along with the burden of leadership, to the people. I had intended for it to be Callum, now not so. But there are men among the chieftains and I will choose one of them, and their descendants, when I see who is worthy of it.'

'Honourable,' she said. 'But that's only relinquishing responsibility in the end. It's just fear of what you can't control, isn't it? And I understand that. I came here with my feelings locked away tight. And can you blame me? For nobody in my world ever treated me with any care. The only one who ever did… It was you, Lachlan. And then you were gone and I was left devastated yet again. But there is no good that comes from living that way.'

'There is plenty of good that comes from it,' he said. 'See the good that I've done here? That's what comes from it.'

There was something strange behind his eyes, though, and if she didn't know her hardened husband quite so well she would've thought that it was fear.

Fear. Was it possible the man was afraid?

Camden had a particularly difficult night and she chose to sit in her bedroom, which was now the nursery, holding him close, rather than allowing Rona or one of the other maids to see to him. The wet nurse came when he was hungry, but otherwise, Penny sat with the baby.

Perhaps Lachlan was afraid of being like his father. Or perhaps it was something deeper, yet more simple. She looked down at the tiny delicate baby and thought of what Lachlan had told her.

That babies died.

And she wondered if that was what truly frightened him. Loving something only to lose it.

For Lachlan did withhold his love.

He might care for her, but he didn't…

What a foolish thought.

Love.

She had never imagined she would have a husband who loved her. It was such an uncommon thing that you might find a person you could marry who might also love you. Whom you might also love.

A whisper of something went through her heart. Like an arrow. She chose to ignore it.

She simply continued rocking Camden. But it was Lachlan whom she thought of. And all the great distance between them.

And while she didn't push her feelings away, she refused to give names to them.

To do otherwise would cause far too much pain.

Chapter Eighteen

He could hear screaming. *Wailing.*

It pierced through his sleep. His dreams shifted, morphed half into memory. And he saw him. A tiny, helpless boy lying next to the body of his mother.

Crying and crying. Blood all over him. No way to tell if it was his or hers.

And he held him close. That tiny, fragile thing. He held him close to his chest.

'I promise,' he whispered. 'I promise to protect you.'

He woke with a start. His eyes open in the darkness of the room, but there was still wailing.

It was coming from the room next door.

And his wife wasn't in bed.

He got up, stumbled to the door that connected the two spaces and opened it.

This room was empty, too, of everything except for the bairn.

Camden.

Camden, she had named him. For the valley. For the land

that belonged to his clan. For this new place that she claimed to have adopted. As she had done this child.

The image of Penny, devastated and grieving, tore at him. But he was still in a strange fog. A place somewhere between sleep and awake. That was where these memories came for him.

And they were all mixed together with the baby that was screaming in front of him.

He approached the cradle, which held the child, and stared down at his angry, red face.

He reached down and one flailing fist connected with his finger. He stilled. The child's fist rested there and he didn't know what led him to shift, but he did, and the tiny fingers wrapped around his own.

A strange, primal surge of possessiveness ran through him and he took a step back, uncertain of where it had come from.

The child started to cry again.

The crying only reminded him of that boy.

He had not held a child since…since one had died in his arms.

Slowly, he picked the tiny body up out of the cradle, held it in the crook of one arm.

The baby turned his head back and forth, making small routing sounds, like a pig. 'You'll be disappointed,' Lachlan whispered. 'I've nothing for you. I don't know where your nurse is. Or your mother.'

His mother. If Penny was the boy's mother, he supposed that made him a father.

He had never wanted to be a father.

For reasons that had built one on top of the other over the years. For reasons that echoed inside his heart and never seemed to get any quieter.

For reasons that screamed at him even now, as he looked down at the tiny, improbably fragile being.

He had made promises before. That all would be well.

He had made promises to save a life he had not been able to save.

Babies died.

It was the way of things. He had learned that early. He had grown up in a house filled with such death. This very castle. So much loss within the walls of it. He had come to accept that. To expect it.

But the useless brutality of what he had come upon on that battlefield…

He had promised. And he had failed.

What promises could he make his own children? What promise could he make to his own son?

He knew he could not prevent disease or sickness any more than he could prevent a clear day from turning into a storm.

He would not be able to protect this child, any more than he would be able to protect Penny from the grief that would drown her if she were to lose the child.

He had never wanted to be a father.

The door to the chamber opened, and in came Penny.

'Oh,' she said. 'I'm sorry. I went to the kitchen to see if I could find something to eat. I didn't realise he would be so upset. He was fine when I left.'

Her eyes were round and she was staring at him with a mix of fear and scepticism.

'Take him,' Lachlan said. He offered the child to her.

'Just a moment,' she said softly. She began to move around the room, setting her tray of food down on the table by the bed. 'I've been with him all evening.'

'Did you leave after I went to sleep?'

'Yes,' she said. 'I'm afraid I haven't been getting much sleep. I might have to call the wet nurse.'

'Why is it that you tend to him quite so much?'

'I don't know how else he will know I'm his mother. I didn't give birth to him. I can't feed him. I wasn't with him from the beginning in quite the way I am now. I just want him to know.'

'I'm sure that he does,' Lachlan said. He was not certain of any such thing. He knew nothing of babies and even less of what one might know or think.

'Why do you not want him?'

'Penny…'

'I want to know. I want to understand. Because you're a good man, Lachlan Bain. You care for all the people in the clan, yet you don't want to care for this child. And look at how easily you hold him.'

'All I know of small children is death,' he said. 'Loss.'

He went to her and handed the child to her. 'To me, that is what this means.'

'But some children live. Or you and I would not be standing here.'

'Aye, some do. But many do not.'

'Lachlan…tell me. What is it?'

His lip curled. 'Is it not enough my mother lost every bairn save me?'

'There's something else, I can feel it.'

So could he. Pain like a wounded, clawing beast.

A darkness that went somewhere past rage.

It wasn't the rage that bothered him. It was the grief. Useless and soft. As pointless as mercy. But if Penny wanted to know, if she wanted to take part in this…on her head be it.

'The woman I found. Raped and murdered by the French. They left her baby for dead as well. He'd been grazed by a bullet. A deep wound, but nothing vital hit. They left him by his mother's body to die. I picked him up and wrapped him in my shirt. I made a promise to save him. For days we marched on and I carried that child. Until he became hot with fever. He died, Penny. There was nothing I could do. My promises were empty. I cannot promise you this bairn will live, nor any. I could not stop it if sickness took him. Nor can you.'

He never spoke of this. It had happened before young William had joined the company. He didn't know where any of the men who'd witnessed it were. It was a failure he carried alone. The one that rested heaviest of all.

For while he felt guilt over his mother's death, he'd had no way to return. He felt anger over that, most of all, for it was Penny's father who had prevented his return.

But he'd been able to take his revenge against that enemy. Nameless French soldiers…

He'd slain many on the battlefield and somehow it had done nothing to make that boy and his mother feel avenged. The stain was on his hands, no matter how much he tried to make it otherwise.

'Lachlan, you tried.'

Three more useless words he could not fathom.

'And it did nothing. It would do nothing to protect you either.'

'I'm not your mother,' she said quietly. 'More importantly, you're not your father, so you could never push me to be.'

That hooked into something deep inside him and he realised that he did worry about that. About her sinking into a state of despair should she encounter such loss. His mother had been left with nothing to live for. Nothing.

He didn't want Penny to experience the same.

And when had he begun to care about her feelings?

Perhaps because it was much easier to consider her a pawn when he had not known the whole woman. And he did now. Courageous, fierce and beautiful. He had found her silly. He found her pursuits of saving creatures to be a mark of that silliness. But he could see now that it spoke to something deeper. And he had not asked for that. Had not asked for any manner of insight into who she was.

Because it didn't matter. It shouldn't. A man in his position was most definitely in want of a wife, but he did not need to know that wife. He did not need to care about that wife.

There was a lot of ground between that and the abuses his father had dealt out. And no need to cover it. He could not afford softness, but that did not mean cruelty.

Because there was enough cruelty in the world as it was and if a man was soft he could hardly keep it out of the walls of his castle.

He knew that to be so.

For what had softness ever gained him?

It could not bring that boy back from the dead. Any more than it could protect the one here now.

He turned sharply and walked back into his bedchamber. His blood was stirred from being woken from sleep and he should never have gone into the bairn's room. That was her domain, not his. It was not up to him to care for a wee babe.

Women's work. And if the woman needed a child to keep herself occupied, that was her concern.

His was with the safety and protection of them, of the clan. She was his. And they would both do well to remember it.

He could not sleep. He prowled the room for the better part of an hour and could hear Penny and the wet nurse moving about the room.

Then, she finally came back in.

'You could have stayed,' she said, 'if you weren't going to sleep.'

'I don't want you caring for the babe at night any more. You must move him in the room with the wet nurse.'

'I want to take care of him.'

'It is impractical. There is a reason a woman is here to see to his needs. You are the wife of the Laird. It is not your responsibility.'

'He's my baby.'

'He is a foundling.'

'He's mine,' she said. 'As if he came from my own body. As you will not dictate to me how I care for him.'

'Aw, but, lass, I *will* dictate it to you. Because I am your Laird.'

'You are my *husband*,' she said. 'And I don't know what has you in a state.'

'I am The MacKenzie. I create the state.'

She frowned ferociously. '*You* are an arrogant sod. And it is well past time you slept.'

'I'm not a bairn that you can put down to sleep,' he said.

'Then don't behave like one.'

Anger fired through his blood, for she had no right to speak to him in such a manner. And there was no reason for her words to feel as pointed as a dagger. No call for it to feel as if she was speaking directly to his soul. This clan was his. This castle was his. She did not determine the rules.

'You do not dictate to me, Penny.'

'And you don't seem to understand that this is not simply about a child. You hold yourself back. Not just from him. From me.'

'Perhaps you have forgotten,' he said, 'as you have grown so comfortable here in my care, but you are my captive.'

'Am I? I rather thought that you were mine.'

'You mistake me,' he said, 'because I have not been cruel to you. And I will not be. But do not mistake that for care.'

She drew back, as though he had struck her. And that only made him all the more angry because, if he had struck her, she would not be able to stay standing. And he would not. He didn't think she understood just how well she had been treated. He owed her nothing. She was an Englishwoman with a father who was barely better than his own. She was defying him with the child and he was allowing it, to an extent.

'You would be a good father,' she said softly. 'You would be a good husband. I know you think you've been a husband to me and you have. But not all of you. You're fighting it. You're fighting your feelings and you're fighting me.'

'I'm fighting nothing. It's you who are fighting the way of things. The truth of things. You do not wish to live with the true state of the world, with the state of this life. I'll allow you the babe, but do not push me further.'

'I think that perhaps the real problem is that you do care. And you want more.'

Penny could see the moment that she had pushed her husband one too far. The banked fury in his green gaze would've been terrifying if she had not known that he would never harm her.

Physically.

Emotionally, however, he had the power to devastate. And she knew it. He had the power to destroy her with a few carefully placed words and she knew that he would not hesitate to do so if it came down to it.

Then, he closed the distance between them, all that fury like a green fire.

'You forget,' he said. 'You forget what you're here for. You forget what a wife is for.'

He wrapped his arms around her, his hold rough.

He had never treated her like this, not even in the beginning. For in the beginning he'd had a care for her innocence. Now that was gone.

She could see that he had been tested past his limit.

But she… She had not been.

She was not the innocent that had first been taken by Lachlan Bain, she was not that girl. She was not the girl who had been locked away, weeping and wailing in her bedroom, unaided by her father or his staff.

She was not even the girl who had mourned the loss of a servant boy who had been her only window into humanity. Because that boy was before her, buried beneath this mountain of a man, but she knew he was there. Because she had seen a glimpse of it when he'd held the baby.

He could pretend that he had no connection to the child. He could pretend he didn't want one. But she had seen it.

He was not made of stone.

He might wish that he were and she had the feeling that he did.

When he spoke of the woman who died on the battle-field, of the baby, the baby he'd held in his shirt, she could see his pain.

She could see that it wasn't a lack of love that he possessed. It was too much. A deep well of caring that was far too great for him to contend with.

The boy who had come all the way to England to try to save his clan. Who had been too late to save his mother.

The boy who had—like her—tried to find hope in small things.

It was why he had let her trail around after him, she was convinced of that.

It had not been an accident and had not simply been be-cause he was trying to patronise his master's daughter. No. It had been more. It always had been. And at every turn the trust he had tried to have in humanity had been abused.

The way that her father had cheated him.

It was only on a battlefield covered in blood that he had found any sort of salvation.

It was no wonder he could not find faith enough to allow himself to care.

And this was where her strength was tested. This was where she proved that she had been changed by all of this.

Because as he held her against his chest, all his fury pour-ing down over her, it would be easy to shove her love, to shove her fear, down deep, to not let him see any of it.

But she would not turn away from her feelings.

Oh, she had thought she loved the Duke. Because of his manners. Because of his family.

Because he represented a soft, gentle life which had felt like the stuff of dreams after her hollow, cold upbringing.

But she had not needed gentility. She had not needed safety.

She had needed wildness and adventure, and all of the things that she had never imagined she would be strong enough to endure. She needed his ferocity.

Because only this, only this hardness, only the strength, could have demolished the walls inside her.

She could have lived a quiet life with the Duke. Protected, cosseted.

But in the end, it would have been little different than the neglect.

A slightly softer prison, perhaps.

But she would've never found herself.

For she was strong and she was fierce. She was enough to be the bride of a warrior. To be the lady of this castle.

To stand and defend her child. And to fight for her husband.

For his heart. To fight for the battle of all that he was.

Because they both deserved to be whole.

She had seen marriage only as an entry to a new life.

Because as a lady her destiny was to be with her father until she was with a husband. And so to leave her father… There had to be a husband. She had known only that she wanted different. She had not known that she wanted everything. But she did. Everything.

Love.

Not that sweet sort of pleasantness she had imagined finding at Bybee House. Days spent needlepointing with a cat. But this wild, untamed ruggedness that cut swathes of tenderness through her heart. That made her exposed and vulnerable as much as it made her strong.

Love.

This bright, brilliant, terrifying thing that made her strong enough to stand against the Highlander.

This man had been to war. And he had never truly left. For he was fighting. Fighting against himself.

Against what he sought to destroy, a weakness in his blood that she knew wasn't there.

Not in this man.

And she would show him. She would show him not only her strength, but his own.

He kissed her, hard and punishing, and she knew that he was trying to take this thing that had built so much closeness between them and force a wedge. But she wouldn't allow it. She didn't need books any more. She knew his body. And she knew all the ways that she could make it hers just as well as he knew how to make her body his.

And so she met him. She thrust her tongue deep into his mouth, wrapping her arms around him, pushing her fingers through his hair. She bit his lower lip and he growled. She found herself being propelled backwards on to the bed, his large body covering hers. He tore at her dress, her stays, her chemise, shoving it all down her body and throwing it down the foot of the bed like insubstantial gauze.

He had only been half-dressed, so it took her less time to divest him of his garments, leaving him as naked as she was. His arm was like a steel band around her waist, and he pinned her to the soft mattress, her breasts crushed to his broad chest as he continued to kiss her as though it might save them both.

Or damn them both.

He seemed to be on a path to hell and wanting to drag her along with him so he could prove the point.

Perhaps that they were too different. Perhaps that this was not sacred after all.

But it was.

In all of its forms. For between them, this passion could not be corrupted.

He kissed her, deep and hard, then, with his arm still wrapped around her, he turned her, wedging his cock against her bottom, moving her half-ruined hair out of the way and kissing a hot trail down the back of her neck. He pushed his hand between her thighs, teasing her swollen flesh with his fingertips.

'Still you're wet for me,' he murmured against her ear. 'Wet for a monster. How does that make you feel?'

She drew her head back and met his gaze. 'Strong.'

He growled again, manoeuvring her on to her stomach before drawing her up to her knees, his chest over her back. 'Let us see how strong you are, then.'

He positioned his hardness at the entrance to her body, slick and ready for him. But she had not taken him like this before.

This was what she had read about. This was what she knew.

The way animals came together. Not face to face, or with the female riding astride, but this base coupling, which between the two of them she knew was designed to make her feel as if they were distant.

She arched her back, moving herself against him, urging him to thrust inside.

He gripped her hips, hard, and then slammed himself home. He controlled the pace, the depth, and it was punishing.

She turned to look back at him and their eyes met. The desperation that she saw there told her that his dominance was only a façade, for he was no more in control of this than she. He might be the one with the physical strength to control the movements, but he was just as captive to it as she was.

Hope bloomed inside her. Bright and brilliant.

For she was not a captive now.

She had been a captive in her life with her father, hoping to move to a life of more acceptable captivity beneath the rule of her husband.

But the Duke had wanted her only because he had seen her as easy. She had helped his sister and his sister liked her. It would create peace in his house and it removed him from having to engage in the marriage mart.

She would only ever have been a pawn to him, though he never would have said that to her.

Those manners, after all.

But Lachlan...

He wanted her.

He needed her.

He was wounded and needed to be healed, and she could see that she was the one who would be able to accomplish it.

He could not minimise her power. Not with his strength, not with his control. Because it was too late. The bond had been created between them and he needed her.

And she had seen it.

As if he could read her realisation, as if he could read her thoughts, he grabbed hold of her hair, pulling her head so that she could no longer look at him. Pin prickles of pain broke out on her scalp, but it only reminded her of how powerful the desire between them was. For even that pain twisted and became need.

For even that made her slicker, made her hotter, brought her closer to the edge.

Ruin.

No. This was not ruin.

It was salvation. For them both.

'Lachlan,' she said, whispering his name like a prayer.

And he fractured. His movements became harder, more intense, and the depth of his hardness moving inside her body combined with the pressure built a deep, aching spiral of pleasure that built and built, so deep inside her she thought she would never be able to withstand it when it broke.

Then it did, her body pulsing around his, drawing from him his pleasure, making it her own.

They shattered together. And, somehow, it made her feel whole.

He moved away from her, breathing hard, and she knew that he had reached his completion inside her. She was happy for it. Pleased with the loss of control. She knew he would not be.

He swore a vile oath.

'Don't you know by now?' she asked.

'What?'

'Don't you know by now that the blood in your veins is not tainted by your father? The blood in your veins is infused with everything you've done. With everything you are.'

'Do not tell me the way of the world, lass. You are a child. A child who never left your estate until recently. You know nothing of the world.'

'I know about grief. I know about hope in the face of hopelessness. I know about staying strong when everything crumbles around you. I have seen sadness, despair. I have felt it. I know what it is to live small, you're right about that. But I know what it is to live big, too. I have done that. Here. With you. And I... Lachlan, I didn't know that I can have so much. I thought that I would count myself fortunate if I could find a way to survive in comfort. But here I have learned to live. And I... I never expected love, Lachlan. Ever. And when you stole me away from the life that I had planned for myself... You told me you would even deny me children and I was in despair. But it is the strangest thing, because it is through that that I found the deepest, most true part of my heart. I love you. I love you, and I had no expectation that I might love a husband. I do. Different than any sort of love I've ever felt. Different than I thought love could be.'

'No,' he said, his voice hard. 'There is no place for love here.'

'There is every place for love here. This is such a vast, untamed place. A winding valley. It is the perfect place for it.'

'But I am not the man for it. I'm not the man for your love. I don't want it. I can't return it.'

'Why do you think that?'

'Because it is the way of things, lass. I am The MacKenzie.

I have to be strong. I have nothing in my heart. I have fire in my belly, and that is the best that can be asked.'

'Lachlan,' she said. 'You love your people. You loved your mother. And I believe you loved that child you tried to save...'

'Love is useless,' he said. 'It only turns you into a grieving sack of pain. My mother loved. She loved my father for his sins. She loved every one of her children who died and she loved me, who failed to return to her in time. What did love give to my mother?'

'I'm sorry,' she said. 'I'm sorry about your mother. I think love made my father grieve in a way that hurt me, too. He loved my mother, for if he did not, I don't know that he would've minded if I cried. I think it reminded him of his own pain and he didn't want to feel it. But isn't that the real problem? That we don't let ourselves bleed? That we don't let ourselves feel? That is a prison. It's a prison that feels hopeless. At least pain is something. I think the real problem is when we feel nothing.'

'No,' he said. 'The problem is when we forget our purpose. Feelings cloud purpose.'

'And what of your anger? What of your revenge?'

'Perhaps it did cloud my purpose,' he said. 'Because I brought you here. And perhaps this is no place for you.'

'Lachlan...'

'You are my wife and will continue to be the lady of this manner. But we do not need to share a bedchamber. We do not need to share a life.'

'So that's it. I challenge you and I'm sentenced to a life living beside you and not with you?'

'It is better,' he said. 'You have your purpose. You have your child.'

'It isn't enough.'

'How can it not be enough?' he raged. 'How can it not be enough? You were content to go and live with your Duke and you would've had no more from him. Is it the title you miss? The balls?'

'You're right. I would've had nothing more with him and I wouldn't have minded because I wouldn't have wanted more. I wouldn't have expected more. Not for myself. Not from myself. But with you...'

'How?' he asked. 'How have you discovered this with me?'

'Because you brushed my hair. Because you got the jewellery box. Because you tried to rescue that boy when many men would've left him as a casualty of war. Because I see who you are and you can tell me that man is dead, but I know he is not.'

He only stood for a moment, looking like stone. And she let tears fall from her eyes. Let them spill down her cheeks. 'Because I have all these tears for you,' she whispered. 'For us.'

'Do not waste your tears on me,' he said. 'I neither want nor need them.'

He didn't leave the room. He didn't tell her to go. Instead, he laid down on the bed, as if he was going to sleep, as if he was going to ignore everything that had just happened between them. And she realised she had no escape. No reprieve. If the man wanted to retreat inside himself, there was nothing she could do. She could not leave the castle. She could not leave him. And she didn't want to, because she loved him. But while he had done enough to reach her, while this thing between them had broken down the walls inside her, she had not done enough to breach the walls in him.

And that was a kind of despair that she feared might be all-consuming.

She dressed herself and, refusing to be moved from her bed, laid down on the other side of the mattress. But the space between them might as well have been furlongs apart.

For his roughness and their passion had not succeeded in putting distance between them.

But his denial of their love had.

And she did not know how she would ever find a way to repair it.

Chapter Nineteen

They had neither spoken nor touched for two days. Every night, she would lay down in her nightdress beside him and turn away.

But what had been said needed to be said. Love.

He had no wish for her love.

Love.

He could think of nothing he wanted less.

The distance between them was so great he was not terribly surprised when she did not join him for supper. But when he found the baby wailing in his room and Penny did not come, he began to feel concerned.

The wet nurse came and looked from Camden to Lachlan.

'Where is the lady?'

'I've not seen her.'

'It's unusual,' the wet nurse said, picking up the babe and putting him to her breast.

It was more than unusual. He could not imagine his wife leaving when the baby might need her.

'See to the babe,' he said.

He walked out of the room, and made his way down the great, long corridor, searching for Rona. 'Where is Lady Bain?' he asked.

'I've not seen her. Not since mid-morning.'

He continued to search. Not only was there no sign of her, there was no sign of Isla, her maid. Of course, they could have gone down to the village, but Penny had not been doing so, not since the birth of the baby. And certainly not since the execution of Callum.

Something felt wrong.

Had she left him?

No. She might leave him, but she would never leave her bairn. For all that he'd said to her the child was a foundling, he did believe her when she said he was like a son of her own body. He had seen it in the way she had taken care of him. He continued to search the castle and the grounds. And he was about to carry on to the village, when he noticed a flash of blue in a thicket in the courtyard.

He made his way to the blue and what he saw made his stomach tight with dread.

Isla.

Crumpled on the ground, blood on her head.

He knelt down and could see the girl was breathing, but only just. She was unconscious. He picked her up, holding her to his chest as he carried her towards the castle. The girl was small, insubstantial, and it was no effort for him to carry her. Still, his heart was hammering, because he knew. He knew that if Isla was in such a state, then Penny was worse, or...

A great, wrenching pain nearly cleaved his chest in two.

No. He would not think of it.

He could not.

He set Isla down in the great hall. 'Rona,' he said. 'We need a healer. Someone. Anyone.'

The housekeeper's face contorted in horror and she went to her knees by Isla's still form. 'What happened?'

'I don't know.'

'Where is Lady Bain?'

'I don't know that either. I'm going to trust you to make sure Isla is taken care of. But I have to go and find my wife.'

Lachlan's sword was already strapped to his hip and he went outside, ready to give orders for his horse to be readied.

But there were men who were not present.

And his suspicions were deeply roused.

'William,' he said. 'Ready my horse.'

'Aye,' the lad said.

He put his hand on the lad's shoulder. 'Where is Paden?'

'I saw him earlier,' he said. 'Going into the wood.'

'Was he alone?' Lachlan asked.

'Aye. But he had…he had something large concealed in a cloak. On his horse.'

Lachlan bit back a curse. 'Be my eyes here. You report back to me anything you hear. Do not make your loyalty to me explicitly known.'

'I think there is no chance they wouldn't guess it,' William said. 'I wouldn't be here, I wouldn't be part of this clan if not for you.'

'And I trust in your loyalty. But make it seem as if you might move with the wind. If it be changing.'

'What is it you think is happening?'

'My wife is gone. I found her maid unconscious. And Paden has vanished. I have my suspicions. But I will see them confirmed. And if I am correct, I will turn all the flowers in the courtyard red with the blood of those who dared touch my wife.'

Penny's head ached. She could not remember what had happened. She couldn't remember where she was. It was difficult for her to open her eyes, but when she did, she found that she couldn't have remembered where she was, because…she had no idea. And she was certain she had not been brought here awake.

Dimly, she became aware that her feet and hands were numb. That they were tied.

She couldn't move.

She shifted and that was when she saw him.

Paden.

'What have you done with me?'

'You're awake,' he said.

Her only response was to blink.

He made a dismissive sound. 'You won't be for long.'

'What are you doing?'

'I'll give you no explanation. You have your part to play in it.'

And here she was, being treated like a pawn again. Bound and lying on the ground in the middle of a forest and not being told why.

Of all the things to anger her, it was a strange thing.

But that was perfect. For if he did not think that she mattered, if he did not think that she mattered or could accomplish anything, then he might let his guard down and underestimate her.

It was the look of hatred on his face that rattled her. It was savage and much more intense than anything she had seen before.

Dimly, she could remember that she and Isla had been attacked, ambushed, outside the castle. Isla...

'What did you do to my maid?'

'She might live,' he said. 'You, though, you probably won't.'

Her heart felt torn in two. And it wasn't even so much fear of losing her own life as it was leaving the life that she had at the castle. Camden. Lachlan.

She *loved*.

Whole and bright and brilliant for the first time in her life.

And it didn't matter if Lachlan loved her back, she loved him. And she had spent the last two days withholding that from him because she was wounded. And what good had it done her? It hadn't done her any. It was foolish. So utterly foolish.

Two days wasted when she could've loved him. And what had her spite been for? Trying to protect herself. Again.

Yes, he had hurt her. But he'd been trying to hurt her. He'd been trying to drive her away because it was all he knew how to do. Because he was a man who had experienced terrible pain and he hadn't been able to break through that yet.

Apparently her own breakthrough was imperfect.

It didn't matter. Now none of it mattered and, if she could go back and do it differently, she would. If she could go back and simply love him, with everything she had, with no thought to her own protection, then she would. Because he was the conqueror of her heart.

Joyfully. Intentionally. She had allowed him to claim her and was happier for it. Or she would've been, if she hadn't been so determined to make his rejection about her.

Yes, he had tried to make it so. But he was protecting himself.

For he was not so endlessly brave as all that.

He was afraid of all that he could not control. And all the evils of the world that he could not keep at bay.

Then she had been kidnapped.

Who knew what would happen?

'You're using me as bait, aren't you?'

Because if he had wanted to kill her, it would've been easy. But, no, he wanted to kill Lachlan. And there would be no way he could accomplish that cleanly.

'Bait. The start of a revolution. The start of a war. If the clan believes that you have been murdered by Clan Darrach, all the better.' A grin lifted his lips. 'I couldn't challenge him at the castle now, could I? And a man who has survived a decade of war would make for a terrible challenge. But if he sees his woman bound with a sword at her throat, he'll be forced to surrender. And then, when the clan hears of your murder, of Lachlan's...we will blame it on Clan Darrach and my path to Laird will be clear. It's what Callum would've done if he could think of anyone but himself and his own prick. But, no. He was angry, but he didn't act. If a man doesn't like the direction his clan is going, then he should take action for himself.'

'You're a coward,' she spat. 'Not even brave enough to challenge Lachlan in a real fight. But Lachlan cares about the clan.' Her chest went tight. 'Above all. You've misjudged him.'

'Nay, lass, I don't think I have. And his weakness, like Callum's, will be his end. I will take the power. And all the Laird's money is to go to the clan. He's willed it so.'

And then he would have it all. Lachlan's money and power and both of them out of the way.

'I'll kill that bairn of yours as well,' Paden said. A chill went down her spine. 'Callum's whelp. There need not be any more blood MacKenzies in the castle. No one who might challenge my claim.'

'My husband sought to take care of the clan. And nothing else. My husband has spent his life working to get here so that he might do right for his people. *You* are nothing more than a self-seeking bastard.'

'Some fine English lady you are.'

A surge of rage went through her, of power. 'No, I'm no fine English lady. I'm Lady Penelope Bain. Of Clan MacKenzie.'

And as she lay there, her body aching, she didn't even know what to hope for. Because if Lachlan came, then he might be killed.

But if he didn't...then she certainly would be.

She whispered a silent prayer.

Please, if you love me, stay away.

For if he loved her…he might sacrifice for her.

He had to live. Because if he didn't live, Camden wouldn't live.

She needed them both to live. And this was why people feared love.

Because loving someone as much as she loved them hurt. Even while she was facing her own end, her worry was for them.

'Don't bother to pray for deliverance,' Paden said. 'It isn't going to come.'

Despair rolled through her. But then she looked up and saw a bird on the branch of a tree, bobbing his head, hopping back and forth. An absurdly cheerful thing in the face of all this.

But it meant something.

Because it was the bird that had made her sure that Lachlan was good all those years ago. And it was the memory of that that had given her faith in him in the present.

He would come. He would come for her.

And they would triumph.

Because there was no point of the world where it could be otherwise.

Lachlan might not be able to believe in hope.

But she believed in him.

And now, that would have to be enough.

Chapter Twenty

Lachlan's blood was fire and he didn't know who among his own men he could trust. So he rode out into the woods with his horse and his sword and the rage that fuelled him.

There was a sign, easy enough for even a casual tracker to follow. Evidence that a horse had gone this way recently. And it could be from any number of men, it was true. But he had to trust that it was leading him to Penny.

Penny.

And what if she died? What then?

He had told her, revenge was not a dream, it was a plan. And that was what he had tried to fashion out of his life. A plan.

A goal divorced from feelings so that he did not become his father.

So that he did not become his mother.

There was too much at stake.

But it did not insulate him now. Because somewhere along the line Penny had become a dream. She had slipped beneath his skin, beneath his defences. And though he hadn't wanted it, it was so.

He followed the path that William had set him on. When he came to the end of the trail he stopped and saw the broken branches just off there. He knew that he'd found them.

He drew his sword and rode into the clearing.

And there she was. Bound.

Suddenly Paden was behind her, his sword at her throat.

The smile on the man's face was savage. 'There you are. I was expecting you.'

'I will gut you like the treasonous dog you are,' Lachlan said.

'I don't think you will.' Disquiet filled Lachlan's gut. 'I'm not sad to be found by you, Lachlan. I have men in wait. Did young William send you this way? Your man. It may shock you to learn that your own man betrayed you.'

That hit him with the force of a bullet.

'No,' Lachlan said.

'Oh, yes. Young William is from Clan MacConnell. His mother left home when there was nothing left, went to Clan MacKenzie for protection. Your father killed her.'

Fire swept through his veins. 'I've nothing to do with what that bastard did.'

'It doesn't matter. William wanted revenge. I do have it. At my hand.'

'Leave Penny be.'

'I have no quarrel with your woman. If it weren't for you, she would be nothing. She wouldn't be here. But I also have no fear over cutting her neck.'

He pressed the blade against her throat, drawing blood. Penny's eyes were wide and fury rose up in Lachlan's veins.

'Drop your sword, my Laird.'

He tightened his grip on the weapon. 'You play a dangerous game.'

'You can let me kill her. And while I finish you could easily kill me. It is only a problem if the lass is worth your life.'

And here it was.

Weakness.

Because he could not let them harm Penny. Because he should care about the clan, only the clan. And his own life mattered only as far as it benefitted the well-being of his people.

But *she* mattered. She was the sun and the stars. The way he could guide himself. Without her, he was only a blade. Nothing more. Without her, he could not be the leader that he needed to be. Without her...

It didn't matter. None of it did.

Without her it was lost. Whatever he'd been trying to win. What did the clan matter—rock and dirt and tradition—if there was no heart?

And Paden was right. He had identified his weakness. For his weakness was this woman.

This was love.

And love was exactly what he'd feared.

Still, in the face of it, in the face of the very reason he'd sought to keep his heart free of love, mercy and forgiveness...

He dropped his sword.

Penny let out a short scream, a tear trailing down her cheek.

Two of his men came out from behind the trees, wielding their swords.

Lachlan held his hands out. 'Release her.'

'No,' Paden said. He kept his sword at her throat and the men began to advance on Lachlan. In a flash, he knew exactly what he must do. The blade bit deeper into Penny's throat and blood trickled down her beautiful skin.

He saw red.

He would have only a breath, then he would lose her.

But he would not allow her to be lost.

He roared and charged at Paden and the man froze, clearly unwilling to kill her quite yet as she was his only means of controlling Lachlan.

A mistake.

Lachlan wrapped his fist around the blade, ignoring it as it sliced into his palm, and wrenched it away from her throat, pulling it from the man's grip. Bloody, he pushed his fist into Paden's gut. And when the man fell back he took up his sword by the handle and separated his head from his shoulders in one fluid movement.

By then, his men were on him, but Lachlan rounded on them. One blade went through his shoulder and he let out a vicious yell as he turned and drove his sword first through one man, then the other.

And he waited. Waited to see if there were more.

And through the clearing, he saw him.

William.

The lad standing there, holding his own sword. He did not have the posture of a warrior, in spite of having been a soldier. He looked like what he was: a boy. Narrow in the shoulders and fearful in the eyes.

Lachlan felt not one moment of regret for ending Paden, or the other two. But running William through did give him pause.

'Don't,' Penny said. 'He's a boy.'

'I was a man when I was his age. And he nearly cost us your life.'

'Lachlan…this is what revenge does.'

Those words caught him in his chest. 'Aye,' he said. 'And he will learn what happens when your revenge does not go as planned.'

'He can't do anything to you.'

He ground his teeth together. 'I don't show mercy.'

He approached the lad and William began to tremble.

'My mother…' he said.

'I did not lay a hand on your mother, lad. And if you wish to quarrel with me, then you will quarrel with me. But my wife's blood has been spilled and if you think that I will give forgiveness for you trying to avenge your mother by spilling the blood of my wife...'

'I'm sorry,' William said and dropped his sword.

'I cannot abide a coward,' Lachlan said. 'You should at least fight me. Stand in your convictions.'

'Lachlan, please,' Penny said.

'*Why?*' Lachlan asked. 'Why should I spare him?'

'Because he doesn't know another way. That's all this is. Vengeance in fighting and violence. He was never given another way.'

'I saved his arse. I brought him back home. If it weren't for me he wouldn't be here. He was given another way. He chose vengeance.'

'So did you. You used me for your vengeance. Don't be so prideful that you don't see that.'

Mercy.

He looked down at his sword, red with the blood of men he could not allow to live. He had lived his life without mercy.

Except for the babe he'd tried to save.

Except for the bird.

And the bird and the babe had given him more than killing ever had. He could not explain it, only that he felt changed.

For he had stared down the worst of what it might mean to have a heart and he'd chosen to love.

And in his weakness, he'd been most powerful of all.

Lachlan lowered his sword. 'Where is your clan?'

'I didn't lie to you in England,' William said. 'They're gone.'

'Then you've nowhere to go. Because if you come back to Clan MacKenzie, it's a cell that will be awaiting you.'

'Laird...'

'I'm sparing your life. But you will not show your face

in Clan MacKenzie. And do not even think about spreading poison to the other clans, because I will make it known what has happened.'

The boy looked as though he might weep.

'I didn't want her to be hurt,' he said.

'You only wanted me killed.'

'Paden said there would be money and power enough for everyone. And you keep all the power to yourself.'

'Look what you've done with a small amount of it. Ask yourself if every man ought to have power. Or if some of you do not possess the fortitude to wield it.'

The boy lowered his head. 'I'm sorry. I've nowhere else to go...'

All of a sudden he saw the boy differently. He saw himself. Reckless and angry and willing to make sacrifices of the innocent in order to see his vengeance played out.

For had he not done so with Penny?

She had not transgressed against him, but he was happy to catch her up in his revenge against her father. For anger was a sword being swept broadly across a battlefield, catching all in its path as enemies.

And there was only one cure for it.

He had seen it in Penny. The way she treated the members of the clan, those who lived in their household. The way she had given so much to Mary. The way she loved Camden as her own.

The way she was with him. For she had no reason to be a wife to him, no reason to show him care when he had swept her up in his vengeance.

Love.

Mercy.

He had been bound and determined to show none, but more punishment, more anger...would not heal this boy. And he might have set out a consequence, but what would he gain? What would the world gain?

This was what Penny had shown him, from the beginning, only he'd been too stubborn to take it in.

Sometimes you saved the bird. Because whether it lived or not, you had tried. Because whether it got you anything in return, it was good for your soul.

And only Penny had ever worried for his soul.

'Return to the castle,' Lachlan said.

'Laird...'

'Tell Rona you've need of food and sleep.'

Tears filled the boy's eyes. 'I betrayed you...'

'And we are not dead. None of us. So we have a chance to change course. William, I have never been a man to show mercy. I have seen the world as a merciless place. It can be. But if I am not willing to show mercy in it, how can it ever be more?'

The boy nodded, his expression grave. 'Go back, lad,' Lachlan said.

The boy did not have to be asked twice.

Then Lachlan turned to Penny and ran. He knelt down on the ground beside her, gathering her up against him as he undid her bindings.

'Lachlan,' she said, weeping against his chest.

'You're safe, lass,' he said.

He looked at the bodies around them. Safe. She was safe. 'William sent me here,' he said, grimly. 'Knowing that they were waiting.'

'He knew that he could use me to make you drop your weapon.'

'Because even Paden saw what I did not,' Lachlan said.

'What is that?'

'How much I love you, lass.'

'Love?'

'Aye,' Lachlan said, his heart feeling as though it had nearly been ripped in two. 'I do love you. And I realised just how much when I had to face the fact that he could use you to get to me. There is no denying it. There is no protecting my heart. It would be better for The MacKenzie to have no vulnerability. It would be better for him to feel nothing. For I should've thought of the clan and nothing more. But I didn't. I couldn't. I love you. And right when I realised what a grave mistake it was, I accepted it.'

'Lachlan…'

'I sent William back to the clan.'

'You did?'

'Yes. I have never shown mercy, not in all my life. But you have shown me that…lass, I cannot make a world that is safe. One that will shield you or me or the bairn from all harm. But I can create a world around us that is better. I thought only the sword, anger and revenge could bring about change, for I thought they were the strongest forces. But that is not true. You have shown me this. Change comes in small ways. In giving chances and choices. Mercy. In loving when it is too much to bear. I love you in that way. It is too much to bear.'

'I love you, too,' she said, the words coming out on a sob.

He brought her into his arms, lifted her up off the ground.

'You can't carry me all the way back.'

'Aye,' he said. 'But I can.'

'You were stabbed in the shoulder!'

He shifted, feeling the sting and tear of the wound. 'Aye,' he said. 'It doesn't much matter. Not when you're all right.'

'How did you know you could do that? How did you know you could defeat all those men?'

'I didn't. But I survived ten years battling the French. And while a Scot was always going to be a greater challenge… I've done well surviving to this point.'

'I suppose so.'

'And I had nothing to live for then. Nothing but a vague idea of revenge and honour. Now I have you. I have you to live for, Penny. And I had your life to save. So there was no choice.'

'I knew you would come. I was also afraid.'

'I wonder if it would've been kinder for me to leave you. You would've never had to be afraid with your Duke.'

'No. But I would never have loved him either.'

He stopped walking for a moment. 'Penny,' he said. 'I didn't have a lot of faith in the world to begin with. But what little I had the war did a good job of taking away. And I thought…if I could save that bairn…'

'But not even that.'

'Not even. And somehow I got it in my head that not having feelings would protect me. That it would protect everyone. But my father loved nothing. He loved nothing but power. And that's what allowed him to act as he did.'

He kissed her lips, softly. 'But I love you. And it's what allowed me to do what I did tonight. I love you and it makes me stronger. It makes me weaker. It makes me vulnerable, but you've shown me that perhaps a leader must be vulnerable sometimes in order to truly lead.'

'You let William return to the clan.'

'Aye. And if not for you, I wouldn't have even let him live.'

'He's only a boy.'

'And I wouldn't have cared.' He cleared his throat. 'And truth be told, what I said to him echoes in my own heart. That the woman I used…the woman I used for my own dark revenge loves me and wants my life saved. That counts for something.'

'You're a good man, Lachlan Bain. And I always knew that part of you was still there.'

'It wasn't,' he said, taking hold of her hand and putting it over his chest. 'It wasn't there. It was with you. All this time. I'm starting to wonder if I came back to your father's house to collect my heart. For I think I left it there a long time ago. And you took care of it in my absence. I want you to continue to care for it because you have it.'

'I love you,' she said. 'And I never even knew that I wanted love.'

'I knew that I didn't. But you've changed me. And you've shown me that love is what makes the world matter. Because without it…there is revenge and there is honour. But there is no joy.'

'No.'

'Do you want to go back to England? I don't want you to go, but I feel as though I have to give you a choice. Because I took it. Now I need to give it back.'

'No,' she said. 'I choose you. I choose this. I choose the clan.'

'And I choose you,' he said. 'Not for revenge. For love.'

And as they walked back to the castle, the anger and pain of the last years began to fall away. For all that hurt, all the loss, had made him. And love had never been part of the future he planned for himself. But now he knew that it was what he needed.

Penny was what he needed.

Lachlan Bain was a patient man. But he had no real idea of what he'd been waiting for.

It had taken a chattering Englishwoman to show him.

He could only hope she had the patience to continue showing him.

'We must get back,' he said. 'To our son.'

Her blue eyes filled with tears. 'Yes. We must.'

Epilogue

Lady Penelope Bain was eating toast when she suddenly had the urge to cast up her accounts and, upon doing some counting, discovered that she was pregnant with the barbarian's child.

'Are you upset?'

Over the past months much had changed about Lachlan in the way that he was with her. The way that he was with Camden.

Life at the castle was different, bright. Isla was back in her position and healthy as ever. They'd had letters from both Flora and Mary, who were happy in their new positions. Mary's letters had been written for her, at first, by other girls at the school. But the most recent had been done in her own hand.

Her life was changing. One word at a time. One lesson at a time.

Her life was changing because of love.

As Penny's had. And Lachlan's.

Love had overtaken fear and he no longer held himself

back. But…she wasn't entirely sure if he had banished reservations about the two of them having their own child, though he no longer took extreme precaution to prevent it.

'It has taken time,' he said. 'But you know, it was never my blood I feared. I feared losing something I loved. For I did, as a boy. Time and time again. And when I failed to save that bairn…'

'You didn't fail to save him. You were the only chance he had. Without you… No one would've held him in his last moments.'

She watched as something in her mountain of a husband cracked.

'I had never thought of that,' he said, his voice rough.

'You didn't fail. You tried. You cared. That's hope, Lachlan. And it is the most powerful thing in the world.'

'Ah, lass,' he said. 'You give me so many more reasons to hope. Reasons to love. And I'm grateful.'

And hope they did, for years to come.

They had five children after Camden, all grew into boisterous, spirited men and women.

It was Camden Lachlan asked to one day be Laird.

'But my blood,' he said. 'It isn't yours. Or my mother's.'

'Aye,' Lachlan said. 'But the love inside you is. And I have learned that that is the only thing that matters.'

And that night, when he lay down beside his wife, he set about proving that very thing, again and again.

'How strange,' he said after, as he held her, 'that the one thing I thought I should not have has been the only thing I needed.'

'What is that?'

'Your love.'

'I love you, too,' she said, then she made a thoughtful face. 'The Duke really did have lovely manners.'

'You don't like lovely manners,' he growled.

'You're right. I don't. But I *love* you.'

* * * * *

Historical Note

One of my favourite pieces of research for this book was on the role of the Scottish soldier in the Napoleonic Wars. As the Wars are an important piece of Lachlan's back story, I wanted to dig into what it might have been like for him.

Highlanders were associated only with rebellion at the beginning of the Wars, but eventually their bravery and fierce fighting style—particularly that of the Forty-Second and Ninety-Second Regiments—earned them respect within the military. Bagpipes and kilts had been banned by the Dress Act of 1746, but the ban was lifted and, while kilts were not everyday dress at that point, they became a symbol of Scottish pride and were worn by Scottish soldiers during the Wars.

It is said that they rode into Waterloo to the sound of bagpipes, shouting, 'Scotland for ever!'

I knew that would be exactly Lachlan's sentiment—so, although kilts were not in fashion during Lachlan and Penny's time, I felt it was reasonable that Lachlan would wear one, as any man wears his military uniform even when he's finished his service.

Marriage Deal With The Devilish Duke

Author Note

Beatrice and Briggs's story has been in my head in some form or another for quite a long time. I loved the idea of a woman setting out to ruin herself—only to be ruined by the wrong man...who turns out to be the right one. But further to that, the idea of a sheltered young lady and a rather dominant duke fitting together just perfectly is something that's been sitting there in my imagination for a while, waiting for the right moment. Bea and Briggs were definitely the right moment.

I have always loved dukes. I don't know what it is about them. Perhaps it's the same reason I love a billionaire hero in a contemporary. I love a man with seemingly endless power brought down by the love of a woman who might—for all the world—seem so much less powerful. Yet, in the end, his heart beats for her. And that makes her the most powerful of all. Because love is the most powerful of all. More powerful than dukes, or society, or scandal.

I hope you enjoy this story as much as I enjoyed writing it.

Chapter One

1818

There were not many things a woman could control in the world. Her life determined not so much by the winds of fate as the whims of men.

But there was a point where Lady Beatrice Ashforth decided that while she could not be the ultimate queen of her own existence, she could be the architect of her own ruin.

And in the end it would amount to very much the same thing.

Her brother, Hugh Ashforth, the Duke of Kendal, might have control over many things, but only so long as she behaved.

She was through with behaving. The life that Hugh wanted her to live stretched out as grey and unending as a mist on the fields of the Bybee House grounds, the house she would never leave if her brother had his say.

She would never have a Season. She would never...

Marriage, he had decreed, was not something she need concern herself with.

For she was taken care of.

Her brother had consulted a physician—the one who had cared for her in her childhood—on her continued good health, and it had been the opinion of the doctor that childbearing would be the death of her.

That had been all her brother had needed to hear to decree that she should stay beneath his protection.

Beatrice was concerned with her freedom.

She had spent her childhood shut up in the walls of Bybee House. Everything from fresh air to rain to too much sunlight was deemed the enemy of her health.

When her father had died, the responsibility for her health had fallen to Hugh. Hugh did nothing by half measures.

He cared a great deal for her happiness. He brought her sweets from London whenever she wished, new dresses, beautiful bobbles for her hair.

That was precisely why she'd come up with her scheme. One she had told no one—not even Eleanor, her brother's ward—about.

Well, she had told one person. Her accomplice in the plan.

But she trusted James. His family had purchased a country manor within proximity to Bybee House four years earlier and the two of them had fallen into a strange sort of friendship.

She had never expected to befriend a man. She knew it was somewhat unseemly for a young lady. But Beatrice was accomplished at sneaking out. It had been the only way she could ever have fun as a child. The only way she could leave her bedchamber.

More than that, she had sensed that…it was where she might find her strength. Lying in bed, endlessly bled by physicians, confined to rooms with low light. She felt as if she were withering away. A flower starved for the earth, the rain and the sun.

Out there she had found strength she hadn't known she'd

possessed. It was how she had met Penny, who had once been destined to be her sister-in-law, until the engagement to Beatrice's brother had been broken. And ultimately, she had found James, and a deep friendship with him.

That friendship had led to conversations about marriage. He was having issues around the subject as well. He did not want a wife, in truth, and though he had not been able to explain it all to her—he had stumbled over his words and in the end asked if she could simply believe him—they had discussed a potential solution for them both.

She would have freedom. She would have a life, a real life. A life as a woman, rather than simply as her brother's shut-in sister for the rest of her life.

At least tonight the party was at the house, which meant she would be permitted to be in attendance. Though, she was not treated as a real guest. She did not dance. Or have a dance card. Had not made her debut in society.

For after all, what was the purpose?

Hugh did not wish her to marry. And so, he did not have any plans to bring her out. It all made her feel so desperately sad. So desperately lonely. As a married woman she would be permitted to attend balls. She knew she was playing a very dangerous game. That her reputation would be poised on the edge of a knife, and the wrong interpretation of the moment, the wrong strain of gossip, the wrong timing, could damage her in a way that made things quite difficult. But she was invisible as it was, and she would rather be ruined than non-existent.

'You look beautiful,' Eleanor said.

Her friend was lounging on the settee in the corner, dressed in a delicate silver gown covered in glittering stars. Eleanor was to debut this Season. She would not be formally presented in court, as her father had not been part of the aristocracy. Bea didn't know the full circumstances surrounding

Hugh's connection with Eleanor's family, only that he had been named her guardian and she was now his responsibility.

Well, Beatrice was his responsibility as well, and he had made decisions about her life that were far too high-handed for her to endure.

'Thank you,' Beatrice said, looking at herself in the mirror. She liked the dress that she was wearing, but she did not look beautiful in the way that Eleanor did. For Eleanor was allowed to look like a woman.

And Beatrice still... She was not in a sophisticated ball gown, not in the way that Eleanor was. Her hair was not pinned up in the same fashion. But it did not matter. For Beatrice was going to make her own way. Her brother was a duke, and he was powerful. And he prized propriety above all else.

He had been engaged a year prior to the daughter of an earl. And when he had heard rumours of her affair with a Scottish soldier he had broken the engagement off swiftly. Coldly. Her brother was a good man, and she knew it. His care of Eleanor was evidence of that. But he had absolutely no tolerance for impropriety. Not after the way their father had treated their mother. He had made a mockery of honour, and Hugh despised it.

Which made the game she was about to play tonight all the more dangerous. Hugh would see her married to James after this. But he would be... He would be deeply disappointed in her. He would not understand. As far as he was concerned he was the head of the household, the head of the family, and what he deemed to be right and true and necessary was so. Her brother was arrogant, all the way down to the soles of his boots.

He was a duke. No one dared question him. No one except for his best friend, the Duke of Brigham, whom they all called Briggs.

They were as different as two men could possibly be. They

might have the same title, but their behaviour, their outlook on life, was quite different.

He would understand. When she explained to him. If she was allowed to explain it to him. Ever. If her brother didn't actually kill her.

Though, she doubted he would, considering he was pushing her to this place out of his concern for her untimely death.

'You seem distracted,' Eleanor said.

'I am rather,' Beatrice said. 'I only hope that tonight is...' She could not find a word for it. 'Fun.'

What a silly, nonsensical word for planning to upend your whole life.

Eleanor smiled, but the smile seemed sad. 'I am sure that it will be. Your brother is intent on finding a husband for me.'

'You don't sound happy about it.'

She smiled and it did not reach her eyes. 'What I want is impossible, Beatrice.'

Beatrice's heart crunched slightly. On behalf of her friend. If there was one thing that she knew about Eleanor it was that... Well, she knew that Eleanor was in love with her brother. It had been clear when Hugh had become engaged to Penny last year.

Oh, Eleanor had been lovely to Penny. And she had said nothing. But the devastation was evident behind her eyes.

Beatrice had never felt it was at all appropriate to mention it. For no matter how true her feelings were, no matter how real, they were doomed. Hugh would no more return her affections than... Well he would not. For many reasons. Propriety, the title... He would have in mind a very particular sort of woman to be his Duchess. She knew that about her brother. He had very particular ideas. And they would not include Eleanor or her feelings.

But then, her brother's plans never did. They did not take into account the feelings of others, only what he assumed to be right. When his former fiancée, Penny, had explained to Beatrice the truth of the situation—that she had not had an affair with a Scottish soldier, but that her father had sold her to him to pay off his debts—Beatrice had believed her. Whether or not her brother had... It hadn't mattered. The damage had been done. And there was nothing that could have been done about her marriage. In the end, Penny had agreed to marry the Scot and go with him back to the Highlands. But the truth didn't matter. Not to Hugh, whose opinion of Penny had been altered forever.

Once Hugh determined someone had fallen short, they could never again be held in the same esteem they had been before.

That could be her after tonight.

Yes. It could be.

But she had two options. She could either go along with what her brother wanted for the rest of her life, or she could attempt to claim something for herself.

And so she had decided on this endeavour, dangerous though it was.

She knew that the reputation of a woman was a perilous thing. And that becoming ruined was actually much easier than remaining beyond reproach.

'Shall we go downstairs?'

'Yes,' Beatrice said. 'Let's.'

It was just time for guests to begin arriving. Beatrice wanted to make sure that she was tucked away in an advantageous corner of the ballroom so that she could watch for the arrival of James. And from there, she would decide the best course of action. Because she would have to figure out exactly where she had to be seen with James. And what exactly they needed to be doing.

She was not entirely certain how tonight would unfold, and she needed to...think. Needed to get a sense for what was happening.

She took a sharp breath and steeled herself, as she and Eleanor walked down the stairs. Their feet didn't make a sound on the rich, burgundy carpet that covered the stairway. Marble from Italy gleamed bright on the floor of the entry, reflecting the lights of the elegant chandelier that hung above. Intricate scrollwork carved into the crown mouldings.

But it paled in comparison to the opulent ballroom. The marble there was gilded at the seams, frescoes painted on the walls and the ceilings of angels and demons locked in heavenly battle.

They moved from the entry into the ballroom, and Beatrice immediately set upon the punchbowl. She was quite pleased to see that there were already refreshments placed out, and that there were a few people in attendance. Her brother would arrive on time. Not a moment sooner or later. What was fashionable did not matter to him. It was a matter of being a man of his word.

When the ball truly did start, Beatrice was relegated to the back by her own sense of propriety. She was a guest without truly being a guest. In many ways it was actually shocking that Hugh allowed her to come downstairs and attend in any measure at all. He could have just as easily kept her shut up in her room. But he did not.

It was quite the break with tradition. By Hugh's standards.

James was not here yet, but she knew that he would be. And soon. Her brother arrived, made greetings to his guests. And eventually made his way to the back of the room.

'How are you finding this evening?' Hugh asked.

'Lovely. As ever,' she said, fighting the urge to twist her hands with nervousness. He would ask what was wrong if she displayed a hint of nerves. He was far too perceptive. It was not part of his charm.

His eyes darted behind her. 'Where's Eleanor?'

'I do believe that she was asked to dance,' Beatrice said.

'Was she indeed?'

'Yes.'

Her brother's gaze was sharp.

And she could see that his concerns would be transferred elsewhere. She did wonder sometimes, if he believed so strongly in the force of his own will that he did not worry about her defying him, or if he simply did not believe her to be a woman. If he did not believe that anyone would ever see her that way. It was entirely possible that he believed he did not have to guard her against suitors because he did not believe that she was capable of having any.

He saw her as a *sickly child*.

The thought made her very sad. Deeply so. And sometimes when that despair welled up inside her she...

Her chest felt heavy. And she ached. That clawing feeling that she couldn't breathe overtook her and she worked hard at her trick. One she had cultivated on those long days spent ill. Was it her body denying her breath through restricted airways or fear making her think it was? If she slowed the moment, the world, she could find the truth. And so she did, relaxing her shoulders and breathing in deep. Then she dug her fingernails into her palm, the slight pain soothing.

Pain was an interesting thing.

At least, in Beatrice's opinion. Some avoided it, and she supposed that was its purpose. To tell you to turn away from a path, to warn you of harm.

But she hadn't had that choice. Pain was part of saving her life, part of the regimen doctors used on her body.

She'd had to forge a different way of relating to it.

It marked so many steps taken in her life. Good and bad. She had been bled as a child. Frequently. It had been excruciatingly painful. Many of the treatments she'd been subjected to had been. And then, as her health had begun to improve, she had taken what opportunity she could to sneak out and roam the estate. That was how she had met Penny. She had found her lost on the estate, having wandered too far from home.

Beatrice had been loath to let anyone know that she had been out, as she hated to reveal her secrets. But she had found a great deal of freedom and pain out in the world, when she had finally been able to explore nature. Bee stings and the sharp pain of falling and scraping your knee. Falling out of a tree.

All things that she never wanted her brother to know had occurred. But she had begun to associate it with her liberation.

And sometimes... There was a familiarity to it that hurt. It was not something she spoke of. Not ever. For it made little sense, even to herself. Yet as her nerves began to fray she found balance in the pain in her palm. A sort of grounding sensation.

A sense of strength.

A sense that she knew herself and that she could withstand far more than anyone believed. It was that sense that gave her confidence now.

She felt a strange prickle at the back of her neck, and she looked up, just in time to see Briggs walk in.

The Duke of Brigham.

When he walked in, a ripple went through the room. Briggs was the sort of man who attracted attention wherever he went. It was undeniable.

He was magnetic in a black coat, black waistcoat and white cravat. He wore buckskin breeches and black Hessians. In a room full of men dressed in similar fashion he should not be notable. But whether it was the fit of the clothing, or simply the quality of the man beneath, he was more than notable.

He was outstanding.

He was the most beautiful man Beatrice had ever seen. She was certain he was the most beautiful man anyone in this room had ever seen. And the reaction to him indicated that. But it was not just his appearance—though his dark hair, kept just long enough to carry a slight wave, and his piercing blue eyes were certainly the pinnacle of masculine attractiveness.

No. It was his bearing.

He carried an air of authority that was unquestionable. He was an entirely different man to her brother. Not one bound quite so tightly by honour. And yet. And yet there was never any doubt that he was in absolute control. Of himself.

The *ton* had an obsession with him, as did every marriage-minded mother. If he had a fault, it was that he was already in possession of an heir. But his marriage had been brief, and many years ago, so much so his bachelorhood was firmly re-established.

As was his reputation as a rake.

But he was also…kind. And she had always found him easy. Easy to talk to. Easy to befriend. She knew he did not think of her as a friend. She would be little more than a child to him, for as long as he'd known her. But she carried a deep well of affection inside herself for Briggs, and whether or not it was sensible or reasonable, it remained.

It was…

She felt sometimes as if the stars hung on his every word. And that the sun shone because of his every breath. She would not say that she carried a flame for him, not in the way that Eleanor did for Hugh. No. It wasn't that. Briggs was beyond her. It was simply that she… That she could not imagine her life without him. And in that way, yet again he was like the sun or the stars. Unreachable, but it was unfathomable to imagine life without that warmth. That presence.

He did not acknowledge her. Not formally. In fact, he crossed the room and made his way to a group of ladies. Not debutantes.

Widows.

Men of his sort preferred widows. They did not have to observe the same strictures as young ladies. Beatrice could not pretend that she understood the nuance of that. She felt a strange prickling sensation though, watching him as he spoke to those women. And then he turned, only slightly, and his eyes met hers from across the room.

And he winked.

Her heart jumped in her breast, and she turned away. She did not want him to look at her for too long. She had the fear that he might be able to suss out that she was up to something, and the last thing she needed was to be caught out by Briggs.

She nearly fainted from relief when she saw James arrive. He was wearing a smart grey coat with a blue waistcoat, the effect overall much softer compared to Briggs's much more severe attire.

He was sweet and handsome, angelically so. With blonde hair that curled at the base of his neck, and pale blue eyes.

She did not feel... What she did not feel was as if a magnet drew her to him. As if she could not look away from him. She felt comforted by him.

Friendship.

Theirs was a deep and real friendship. One that—were it known about by the *ton*—would see her ruined anyway as she had been alone with him without a chaperon before. Now they would simply need to court public ruin.

In the absence of her brother's blessing, she would have to force his hand. Because he hated scandal above all else. Which meant... She would have to create one.

And he would never see it coming, because he did not believe her capable.

James came to her, a second glass of punch in his hand.

'Are you thirsty?' He handed it to her.

She appreciated it. The care it demonstrated. He was like that. He was kind.

'Thank you,' she said.

'Have you devised a scheme for the evening?'

'I have to figure out where I think we might be seen and

by whom. Logic indicates that it should be Hugh who catches us out.'

'I see. And are we to simply wait in his bedchamber?'

For some reason those words made her stomach tighten. 'His bedchamber? I do not think we need a bedchamber.'

The look on James's face was almost…pitying. 'Perhaps you're right.'

'A lady can be ruined by walking along the wrong garden path,' Beatrice pointed out. 'I could have been ruined long ago if it was known I went calling at your residence and took tea in your drawing room without the presence of a chaperon.'

'I rather think that for the scheme you're devising there was going to have to be a measure more than *walking* involved. Or taking tea. There can be no doubt as to what is being witnessed.' He looked down. 'I fear your brother enough to know he must think the only option is for us to marry, lest I find myself called to account, and on the wrong end of his pistol.'

She looked up at him, feeling helpless. Because she did not know *what* he was alluding to.

She was… She was terribly sheltered. And she had seen pictures in some of the books left in the library that depicted nude nymphs running away from male suitors, and it always made her feel uncomfortable. For some reason, those images came back to her now, and she had a feeling… Well, she had always had a feeling that something to do with those images related to *ruin*. It was only she could not connect them.

'I should like… I…'

He smiled, and it was kind. 'I do not wish to force you into anything, Beatrice. Please, if you wish to turn back, it will never be too late.'

'This is for you as well,' she said. 'You also must feel… you also must have the life you desire, James. And I care for you. If I could help you, I wish to.'

And she might never be able to understand exactly why

he didn't want a real marriage. And perhaps the two of them would be giving up certain things. But they would have friendship. And all the freedom marriage afforded.

And she… She had felt for him. Because while he was a man, he was a second son, and he did not have anywhere near the power that her brother had in his position in society. He was facing enormous pressure from his family, and it was a pressure he did not want. Beatrice didn't have to have experienced the exact same thing to understand what it was to be presented with a life you did not want to live.

'I know,' she said. 'I know what to do. It would be best to have the largest audience as possible, while seeming to believably seek isolation. I know where to go. We will be found, not only by my brother, but by his associates.' Briggs would be among them. The very idea made her skin feel scorched. Shame. She felt a deep sense of shame.

'He often retires to his library at some point during an evening such as this,' she continued. 'If we could contrive to be in present…and…'

'We should only have to be locked in an embrace,' James said. 'That should be enough.'

She felt somewhat mollified by that. A simple embrace did not seem so ruinous. But she knew that to the broader society it would be seen as such.

'Yes,' she said. 'I believe that is so.'

'We shall meet there.'

'Yes. And in the meantime, endeavour not to draw suspicion.'

She waited. Waited until the hour drew closer for her brother to begin to make his way from the ballroom. They would have to get there before him. With a bit of time.

James was already gone.

She swept from the room, taking care not to be seen, and tiptoed up the stairs, towards her brother's library.

The only light in the room was that cast by the fire in

the hearth. She hoped that the staff would not precede her brother to light candles for those who would soon occupy the room. The staff might offer her discretion. She did not want discretion.

She wanted to be ruined.

She sensed movement in the corner, and she turned, her stomach tight with nerves, her entire body nearly surging with unnatural amounts of energy. And then she heard footsteps. Just at the same time. And before she could think, before she could do anything but act, she did so. She flung herself at the figure in the corner, wrapping her arms around him. But he was so much taller than she had expected him to feel.

So much more solid.

The figure…the man…moved against her, and she nearly fell backwards. And then he lowered his hand, cupping the rounded globe of her buttocks. And she knew that hand was *much too large* to be James's.

Terror streaked through her, but just then, the door flung open wide, and along with the open door, came the light.

'What in the devil is happening?'

She looked towards the open study door and felt…everything shatter. It was not merely her brother and a few colleagues; it was a house tour. Complete with some of the sharper-tongued gossips of the *ton*.

And then she looked up, up at the man who held her in his arms, to see familiar blue eyes. Far too familiar.

The stars. The sun.

Briggs.

His hand was still planted firmly on her buttocks, and suddenly the warmth of his body became an inferno, the strength of his hold a revelation.

She could not breathe.

You can breathe. No man is allowed to steal your breath.

Even so, the fact remained…

She had flung herself at Briggs. And her brother had walked in just in time to see it.

'I demand an explanation now. Or I will have no choice but to call you out.' She could see murder in her brother's eyes, and she knew that he was not speaking in jest.

'There is nothing untoward here.' Briggs released his hold on her slowly, ensuring that she did not fall.

'And yet, we have all witnessed something quite untoward, sir.'

'It's my fault. It's my…'

'There is no question. There is no question of what must be done.'

She looked back at Briggs, who was gazing at her brother with fury in his eyes. 'Of course.'

'What's it to be. Pistols at dawn?'

'No,' Briggs said, his voice firm. Decisive. 'It is to be marriage.'

Chapter Two

〰〰〰

Philip Byron, the Duke of Brigham, was not a man to be trifled with. He was not a man easily bested, nor was he a man to back down from a challenge. But at the moment he felt thoroughly bested, by a chit barely out of the nursery. And were there reasonable challenge to be had in the current situation, he would gladly undertake it. But the only man in the world that he considered a true friend was currently glaring at him with clear murder in his eyes, and Briggs was well aware that when it came to the honour of his sister, Kendal would follow through with that murder.

Kendal was hardly a prude. The man took his pleasure when he wished. Briggs knew that better than most. They frequented clubs, gaming halls and brothels often enough. But that was just it. When it came to pleasures of the flesh, Kendal kept it separate from his family. And he certainly did not go about despoiling ladies. Neither did Briggs, for that matter. And he would never, ever have touched his friend's sister. It was she who had flung herself at him. But at the current moment, there was no space to say so.

He regarded Kendal closely. 'Might we see that your sister is safely ensconced in her chamber and continue this conversation in private?'

'No,' Beatrice said, scrambling even further away from him. 'I don't need to be ensconced. I wish to speak to you, Hugh, we must...'

'Do not speak to me,' Kendal said. 'Neither shall you speak to me,' he said to Briggs. 'Not until I have had a chance to...'

'I'm sorry,' Kendal said to the group of waiting guests. 'I must adjourn the tour. I bid you please make use of my hospitality further. But I would also ask that you refrain from speaking on the matter that you think you have witnessed here until we are able to set it to rights.'

The entire group dissipated at Kendal's command, for he was, after all, the Duke. But Briggs knew that there would be gossip. That it was unavoidable. The damage was done. And it did not matter what had truly happened.

'Hugh...'

'Go,' Kendal said. 'Go to your bedchamber, and we will speak later.'

'I wish to speak now.'

'I will not hear you now.'

'But please I...'

Kendal held up his hand, and he could see that Beatrice was weighing her options. She could persist. She could say what she had to say between his denials. Or she could wait until he was in a better frame of mind. And when she demurred to Kendal's commands, Briggs did think it was likely the better of her options.

She left the room, and Kendal closed the door behind him.

'Explain this to me.'

'I was simply standing there. I do not know who your sister thought I was, but I swear to you, that I have never, and I would never...'

'Good,' Kendal said. 'I know exactly what manner of man

you are in your relationships. I should not like my sister exposed to any such thing.'

'Have no worries, Your Grace. I have not exposed your sister to my appetites.'

The air seemed less deadly in the aftermath of that admission.

'You have an heir already,' Kendal said, looking at him closely.

Briggs felt a stab of discomfort over the mention of his son. It was true. He had already achieved the highest purpose of his life. He had sired an heir. The line would continue. It did not matter that he had been ill-suited to marriage, always and ever. That he had no idea what to do with the child, particularly not one with the difficulties his own had. But he was receiving good care and a fine education.

What else could be asked of him?

'You must marry my sister,' Kendal said.

'You believe that I did not touch her.' That was important. Briggs had very few people in his life he considered friends.

He had not been allowed at school until he was fourteen. So ashamed had his father been of his behaviour and so intent had he been on crushing Briggs, to remake him into something he could control, something he could understand.

When he finally had been allowed at school it had been after his father had died.

His mother had sent him.

'You're the Duke now,' she'd said, her voice still soft from years of tiptoeing around his father. *'You are no longer simply Philip.'*

And he had not been Philip. Not once since.

He'd become the Duke of Brigham, wholly and completely. He had made a new man of himself. Briggs.

Ironically, that was what his father had wanted all along and it had taken the bastard dying for Briggs to accomplish it.

Still, he had not found school easy and the process hadn't occurred overnight. When it came to friends...

In truth, he had precisely one.

And it was Hugh.

Hugh sighed and turned away from him, as if gathering his thoughts. Or just perhaps reining in his desire to punch Briggs in the face.

He imagined, had he been anyone else, Hugh would have attacked him on sight. It was only the strength of the connection between them that he didn't. Hugh had been Briggs's first friend, and in the end, he felt that Hugh was the only true friend he had even now.

While he might understand the rules to society now, while he did not require Hugh to act as a guide any longer, he did not feel a connection to anyone else.

In truth, he knew Hugh felt the same. They'd both had the full weight of their titles thrust upon them far younger than they should have. They had navigated those dark waters where boys became men. And the rarer passages of boys becoming dukes. And they had done so together.

It was that history now which kept Briggs from certain death and he knew it.

Also what kept him back from challenging Hugh in return, a defence of his own honour justifiable under the circumstances.

It was not his fault Beatrice had thrown her body against his.

A body that was quite a bit softer than he had ever allowed himself to imagine...

'Yes. Because I do believe that you are man of honour, and you would at least confess your sins, even if you had sinned in such a manner.'

'If you will not believe that I would never compromise your sister, then please do believe that virgins have no interest for me. If you will recall, I have already had a lady wife who could not bear me.' He did not speak of Serena. Ever. It was a mark of just how exceptional the situation was that he did so now.

'What happened with Serena was not…'

'I do not need your reassurance, Kendal, particularly not when I stand before you with the choice of marrying your sister or taking your bullet. It is rather duplicitous, do you not think?'

'You're my friend, even if I would like to shoot you at the moment.

'Honour is everything,' Kendal said.

'I know. And you know I share your feeling. I understand why you must see the world as you do, given the way your father set about salting the earth of morality while he drew breath. But you must not think it would be a good thing for your sister to…'

'A marriage in name only,' Kendal said. 'Society will never have to know of your arrangement. You have always been good to her. Protect her, as I wished to do.'

'Do you not think your sister might have something to say about that? You consigning her to a marriage only in name?'

The alternative…well, Briggs could not see it. His father had died when Briggs was so young, he had been resolute in his need to marry and produce an heir as quickly as possible. He had married Serena when he was twenty-one. And had lost her at twenty-three.

He had been infatuated with Serena and he had been so certain…

He had been so certain love would grow between them. If not love, at least a friendship.

He had been naive.

He had interpreted her mercurial nature as something exciting. The scope and change of her moods like a tide. So stark was the ebb and flow of them that he could read them easily.

But they became erratic. The high of them often as un-settling as the low, which could last months. And eventually became all that remained.

It was only after his marriage with Serena had deteriorated to the point she no longer spoke to him that he realised he'd been…a romantic. He'd believed that she would be the one person he could be himself with.

He had met Beatrice when she was a girl, and had felt instantly drawn to the child who was nearly a prisoner in her bedchamber. He so rarely felt compelled to reach out to people around him. And truly, he did not often need to. He was a duke. People were desperate to reach out to him, and it made his life all the easier for it.

But she…

He had wanted to make her smile. In a world that seemed very determined to give her nothing to smile about.

If there was one thing he had understood, it was what it was like to be born into a life you had not chosen, and that felt ill-suited to your nature. And so he had always paid her visits when he'd come to call. Had always brought her sweets from London.

He had recognised a rebellion in her eyes, and he had felt a kinship to her. For he had been much the same. In the wrong life, the wrong family. Perhaps the wrong bloodline. Never meant to be the heir.

She had been placed in the wrong body. One that could not contain the wildness in her spirit. One he wholeheart-edly supported.

Until, of course, it ensnared him.

Still, he would never have sentenced the poor creature to a marriage with him.

One of the many, many ways in which he was wrong in-cluded what he desired from women. He had been young and foolish and he had believed that his wife would…that as she was a virgin when she came to his bed he might—in time—introduce her to his preferences and she would share them.

Nothing could have been further from their reality.

In the years since his wife's death, many women had enjoyed their time in his bed. But those women were not *ladies*.

Ladies, marriage…

All of that was supposed to be behind him.

'You can continue to do whatever you like,' Kendal continued, as if a wife was an incidental hardly worth overthinking. 'You already have your heir. And Beatrice will have…a child to care for should she wish it. She… She desperately wants that. I know when the doctor told her that it was not advisable that she bear children she was deeply upset.'

'She cannot have children?' Briggs had not been aware of that.

'She *should* not. That is my concern. She very *likely* can. But you know how her health was in her childhood, and it is the opinion of those in the medical profession that she would take a great risk to bear children. It was why she was not to make her debut this Season.'

'That's what you told her?' Briggs asked.

'Yes.'

'What *exactly* did you tell her, Kendal?'

'That she would not need to marry. That she would not marry. Because I would take care of her. And of course I will. She is my responsibility. It is my responsibility to keep her safe.'

He could see his friend had no real idea of what he'd done, and further that he…did not know his own sister.

Beatrice was sweet, it was true. But she was also quietly determined. And she was not half as biddable as she appeared. Over the years he'd stayed at Bybee House on many occasions and he knew Beatrice was often *not* where Kendal assumed her to be. He had seen her appear at dinner out of breath, with red cheeks from being in the cold, and occasionally a leaf somewhere in her tangle of brown hair.

But of course, his friend's largest shortcoming centred around the idea everyone took his authority as seriously as he did.

His little ward, Eleanor, she hung on his every word.

His own sister on the other hand…

'I see,' Briggs said. 'So, what you've done is create this situation we find ourselves in, while laying blame everywhere else.'

'*How* have I created the situation?' Kendal asked, clearly outraged.

'You offered your sister a life sentence. Living here at Bybee House in the country, away from society, from friends, from freedom. I don't know why she chose to target me as her means of escape, but she has found it, hasn't she?'

'What exactly are you saying, Briggs?'

'You sent the lady from the room, so we cannot *ask* her. But do you not suppose that she was taking matters into her own hands? Now she is ruined. If I don't marry her my honour will be worth nothing. If you don't call me out as a result of this ruination, your honour will be nothing. If Beatrice does not marry, she will be… Well, she will never be received in society, will she? Not that you were to allow her out. She is, of the three of us, the one who stood to lose the least.'

'You do not think…'

'I am telling you that I have never laid a hand on your sister. And somehow, she came to be in my embrace in this study, which, I believe she knows you make use of in the evenings following such gatherings.'

Briggs could see the wheels turning behind Kendal's eyes.

'Shocking though I know you find it,' Briggs said. 'Not everyone agrees that you know best. Clearly, Beatrice is among that number.'

'*Beatrice,*' Kendal said.

And this time it was her name that held the tinge of murder. Kendal turned and tore from the room, and Briggs went after him, because after all, why should he not? He had already ruined the lady, why not accompany her brother to her bedchamber?

They wound down the labyrinthine halls of the massive estate, Kendal's footsteps announcing his outrage against the marble floor. He flung her doors open, and a maid, who had been kneeling by the fireplace, immediately scurried away.

Beatrice was laying on a chaise, looking collapsed, which gave Briggs a strange sort of squeeze in his chest. He had come to know Beatrice when she was aged fourteen or so, and had not known her in the worst part of her illness. And he had to wonder if this was how she had looked then. Pale, drawn, and not infused with the sort of life he had come to associate with her.

She sat up, her face swollen, her eyes red. She looked distraught, so much so that it would nearly be comical were it not for…everything.

'Briggs,' she said. 'Please know that I did not mean…'

'You did not *mean* to entrap Briggs?' Kendal asked. 'Then who, my sister, did you intend to be caught with tonight?'

'Hugh…'

'Do not think me a fool, Bea, I know that this was a plot of yours.'

Of course, Briggs had been the one to tell him that. But it was not the time to comment on such a thing, he was certain.

Kendal continued, 'Who did you intend to be trapped in a marriage with, Beatrice?'

'Had I been caught with James rather than Briggs you would never have known it was a plot…'

He curled his lip. '*James.* James. That friend of yours from the country estate next door?'

Beatrice tilted her chin up, intending to look imperious,

clearly. It was not terribly effective, given the tip of her nose was red. 'Yes.'

'His father is a *merchant*,' Kendal said.

'His father is an *earl*. The same as Penny's, and you were going to marry her.'

At the mention of his former intended, Kendal's face went to stone. 'That is of no import. That is enough for me. It is not enough for you.'

Beatrice swung her legs over the edge of the chaise, the motion sudden and not at all ladylike. 'You were not even going to allow me to marry, so what concern is it of yours the title of the man that I choose?'

'I feel we are perhaps having the wrong fight,' Briggs said. 'As he was not going to allow you to marry, and now you cannot marry this…this *boy* anyway.'

'I'm sorry,' she said, turning her focus back to him. 'I did not know that you would be there. I expected for James to be there already. But he was not and… It was you.'

'This is dangerous,' Kendal said. 'And foolish. You were playing with things that you knew nothing about. What you have done… You have potentially damaged yourself beyond saving. You *have* to marry Briggs, but that does not mean that society is going to be kind to you. You were caught in his embrace. Unfortunately for you, the wrong sort of people, the worst sort of gossips, saw. And from where I was standing the embrace had the mark of the obscene.'

Briggs snorted. Because, honestly, it was becoming theatrical. 'I dare say that it looked nothing like obscene to *you*, Kendal. You might be playing the prig in front of your sister, but you and I both know that you have seen and participated in more decadent pursuits of a common afternoon, let alone a night in an empty drawing room.'

And yet, the impression of her luscious roundness remained in his hands, and he had to confess if only to himself that it felt a bit like *obscene* where the sensation lingered.

'Not,' Kendal bit out, 'with a lady.'

'Beatrice is more than suitable to be my Duchess,' Briggs said. 'And I will not tolerate a bad word spoken about her, in society or this room.'

He did not know why he defended her. Not in light of everything.

Perhaps it was *because* of what she had done.

It was foolish. Ridiculous. And exceedingly brave. She had risked much to defy her brother.

Had she done it for love? The love of this... James?

He looked at her, at the misery on her face.

He did not think she had. She was not *heartbroken* now, but furious.

She had done it to kick against Kendal, and for that he could only feel a grudging sort of respect.

From infancy, there had been a clear path laid out for Briggs. All he had to do was marry and produce an heir, and the rest... It was his choice.

Beatrice was beneath Kendal's authority. And she had limited options when it came to opposing it. None of what her brother had was hers. Nothing would ever pass into her ownership. She would have to acquire a husband to ever change her circumstances, and Kendal had taken steps to ensure she could not do so.

So she had defied him in the only way she could.

Forced his hand.

In truth, he was angrier at his friend than he was at her. In this, he understood her. The desire to have one's own life. To make one's own choices. All while being thoroughly misunderstood by those around you.

In his case, actively despised.

'A duchess?' she said. 'I don't want to be a duchess. I just want to marry James. I want to be free. And I want to have a life of my own. I didn't want to stay here forever. I already made an entire life of these walls. And I could not take any more of it. You took everything from me, Hugh, when you said that you would not allow me to marry. When you withheld presenting me to court, having my Season. I… I did not have a choice. I told you then that I could not bear it and you did not listen. And now you cannot simply hand me off to Briggs…'

'What I *offer* you is an honour,' Briggs said, the reality of the situation not quite yet settling in. For it was too much to fathom. Beatrice. Beatrice as his wife. Him taking a wife a second time…

He had never intended such a thing.

Perhaps William needs a mother.

William had a governess. William…

Was the angriest, most difficult child he had ever known. He had terrors in the night, and destroyed all of his toys. He did not speak fluently, and he was volatile at the best of times. It was only because he had managed to secure a very esteemed governess that anything went as well as it was currently. She was a sturdy woman with a capable manner, and years of experience. She had informed him that she had known children like William before. It was her opinion that he would grow well enough, though would potentially always have a different sort of manner about him.

The boy had support. He did not need a mother.

William had had a mother, who had not cared enough about him to stay.

Just as Briggs had had a father who had hated him.

At least he loved his son.

You leave him to his governess more often than not…

But he did not scorn him.

Surely that had to count for something.

'I am preserving your reputation the best I possibly can,' Briggs said. 'And my own. You have given me no choice in the matter, Beatrice.'

'I will secure a special licence,' Kendal said.

Briggs snorted. 'I am more than capable of securing my own special licence, Kendal. Or do you forget that you do not outrank me?'

He caught his friend's gaze, and held it for a moment.

He did wonder sometimes, if Hugh forgot. That they were not now schoolboys. That Briggs no longer required his protection, his guidance.

'I have *not* agreed to marry you,' Beatrice said.

Briggs looked down at her, and saw that her eyes were filled with tears. Perhaps he had misread her.

'Did you fancy yourself in love with James?' Briggs asked. She said nothing, though her misery seemed to increase. He felt almost sorry for her. 'You will recover.'

'Get some sleep,' Kendal said. 'There will be a wedding to plan on the morrow. And we will have to inform Mother.'

Chapter Three

Beatrice was desolate. Everything was wrong. And worst of all, she didn't even know who to speak to about it. Or if she could speak to anyone about it. That was how she found herself slumped in the morning room with nothing but cold meats and eggs for comfort.

It was then that her mother came in.

'Beatrice,' she said softly.

It was the softness that nearly broke her.

But everyone was soft with her. Always. Except for Hugh last night. And Briggs had not looked particularly soft either.

Her heart gave a great thud.

Briggs. She was to marry Briggs. In three days' time. And suddenly, she felt overwhelmed by all she did not know.

About him. About the world. About what was to be between a husband and a wife.

'You're crying,' her mother said.

Beatrice touched her face. There were indeed tears on her cheeks. She had not realised.

'Did he hurt you?' her mother said, drawing close to her.

She reached out and put her hand on Beatrice's. 'Has he... forced you into anything? I will not consign you to an unhappy union, Beatrice. I know that your brother thinks that it's best but if he...'

Beatrice shook her head. 'He did not hurt me.' Hurt? Being held by Briggs had been the furthest thing from hurt. She had avoided thinking of that moment, but now it loomed large in her mind. 'I am the one that ruined everything. I am the one that caused this.'

Her mother looked at her closely. 'How exactly did you cause it?'

She explained her plan to her mother. Her ultimate rebellion against Hugh. 'And I could not tell anyone because you would stop me. But I... I am not as weak as everyone thinks I am. I have... I have dreams. There is a purpose to why I survived my childhood. I nearly died so many times, but I did not. And if I'm simply to live out all my days here at Bybee House, I don't know...'

'Oh, Beatrice.' Her mother put her hand over hers. 'Hugh does not mean to hurt you in any way. It's just that he worries for you.'

Her mother loved her, and she knew that. She also knew her mother had spent years deep in the throes of a relationship with Beatrice's father that had been anything but easy.

In those years, her mother had often been withdrawn. When her father had flaunted his many infidelities, her mother disappeared into her chamber and did not emerge. Or worse, into laudanum.

She had overheard her mother say to a visiting friend once that being married to the Duke would not have been so awful if she did not loathe him and desire him in equal measure.

Beatrice had not understood what it meant. She still did not.

But in the years since her father's death, her mother had

emerged much stronger. Much happier, and Beatrice had never wanted to do anything to disturb that.

'I know it. But this was more than protection. And I had to do something about it.'

'It is a good match,' her mother said. 'He is a duke. He is well liked in society...'

'Yes.'

She didn't know why, but he also frightened her. On some deep level. As much as he drew her to him. And she had not intended to embroil him in this.

'He deserves better. Than me.'

He had lost a wife already. Beatrice did not know what ailment had taken his first Duchess, but to be married to a woman who had been told she might not... Be strong. She had not intended to steal any chances from him and a happy life. She and James had an agreement. An understanding. Briggs had not been part of it, and he did not deserve this.

'His honour will not allow him to let this all fall upon you, dear.'

'But it *should*,' Beatrice said. Then angrily disagreed with herself. '*No*. It should fall on Hugh. Because he is the one who forced me into this position. He is the one who made this untenable. And I... I'm just so sorry. I care quite a lot too much about Briggs for this to... For this to be his fate.'

'Beatrice, we must speak. And you are getting married in three days and...'

'Yes?'

'There are things that a married woman must do. There is... A duty in being a man's wife.'

Beatrice tried to imagine what duties that might entail when one was married to a duke who surely had a full household staff. Well, her mother saw to a great many domestic activities.

'I must help run the household,' Beatrice said.

'Beatrice,' her mother said. 'I mean there is more than that. It is only that you will be expected to...'

'Yes?'

'There is the marriage bed.' For a moment her mother's face took on a distant quality, the expression in her eyes something fond and sad and angry all at once.

And just when it became too sharp to bear, it eased.

'What happens between a husband and wife in the bed-chamber,' her mother continued.

Bedchambers. James had said they ought to be caught in a bedchamber. And then she thought of nymphs again.

And of her governesses. All young and pretty and fluttery and more interested in her father than in her.

'Oh.'

'It is not so unpleasant. Your husband will...know what to do and he will take the lead.'

'Like dancing?' she asked.

Though she had been given lessons in dance.

Her mother looked relieved. 'Yes. Like dancing. He will lead you, and he will ensure that all is well. As you said, he is a good man.'

'What... What am I to *do*?'

She wished she knew...anything. She felt like a great blank space was stretched before her and all she had were scattered images and ideas, and what she wanted to do was demand answers.

What made a true marriage?

What happened in bedchambers?

Why were women so easily ruined?

Why had she felt like she had when he'd held her?

She had the sense these things connected, but she did not know how. And it was an endless frustration at what was denied her.

She had been so protected here at Bybee House. She was never permitted to go to London. Her father had died when she was a girl and her brother remained unmarried. She had seen interactions between unrelated men and women only at the handful of balls her brother had given and even then it was like…

Watching a pantomime.

It gave only hints and ideas and just enough to be maddening.

'You can think of other things,' her mother said. 'Pleasant things.'

Think of *other* things. That was what she did when she was forced to engage in needlework. She thought of anything but the project she was currently involved in, as it was untenably boring.

It simply did not sound like anything she might want a part in. And was another resounding point in favour of the facade marriage she had been planning with James.

James.

She would have to speak to James. He undoubtedly had heard.

The door to the morning room opened, and their butler appeared. 'His Grace the Duke of Brigham is here to call upon the Lady Beatrice.'

Beatrice's heart gave a start.

'I suppose I should stay and offer to be your chaperon. But I feel it is a trifle too late. I will let you speak with him.'

Beatrice wanted to call her mother back. Tell her no. Because she was terrified of being alone with Briggs at this current moment. Which was silly, because she had never been terrified before. But she doubted that today he would be bringing her sweets. She doubted it very much.

He had been in her bedchamber last night, and apparently there was something scandalous in that. Last night she had been too upset to truly consider that.

He swept into the room, somehow she could tell he was wearing a different coat than the night before, though this too was black. He looked like a storm. And everything in her went still. She couldn't breathe.

Her mother dipped her head. 'Your Grace.'

'Your Grace,' he returned.

And then she left them in there. Alone. And the doors closed firmly behind her.

'Briggs...'

'We must speak. About the reality of the situation that we find ourselves in.'

'Of course,' she said. 'I know that we do. I know that...'

'You need not fear anything from me. I am aware of your condition.'

'My condition?'

'Your brother has informed me that you were not to bear children.'

'I...'

'I have an heir. Already. That will not be an issue.'

That made her desperately sad, and she didn't even know why. Presumably, she and James would not have had children. After all, theirs was to be a presumptive marriage in name only. Not a true marriage, he had said. She did not know exactly what that meant, but she did imagine that it precluded offspring.

'You look distressed.'

'James...'

'Yes. Are you going to try to tell me that you loved him?'

'And if I did?'

'I would not believe you. For you threw yourself into my arms easily enough. You let me hold you. You did not seem to realise I wasn't your beloved.' He fixed her with his dark gaze. 'You would know the arms of the man that you loved, Beatrice.'

And she remembered the way he had held her again. The way his hand had slid down over her rear, and she felt horrible, scalding heat go through her body.

Another clue, she felt.

But he was not asking for a true marriage. He had an heir.

It is not different than James, then.

And yet it felt as if it was.

'James is my friend,' she said. 'And the idea of marrying for convenient reasons suited him.'

'Marriage is only ever convenience, if it is not, it is an inconvenience.'

'Some people fall in love,' she said.

Except she had never known anyone who had. She was quite certain that Eleanor loved Hugh, but there was no reciprocation. And there would be no marriage.

'That is very rare, Beatrice, and even if they do... It does not last.'

She wondered, then, if he was speaking of his wife. Of course, it hadn't lasted. She'd died. Beatrice had never known her. She had not seen Briggs at all during his brief marriage. They had been mainly in London. She had never met his son either.

A strange, twisting sensation assaulted her stomach. His son.

Would she be his mother?

Everything was changing so quickly. She had an idea in her mind of what it would be like to marry James. He had said that he wished to travel abroad, and she was quite amenable to that. She had looked forward to seeing Paris, and Italy. To spending time in London. All things that she had never done. She had been cosseted. She had been kept to herself. With him, she knew that she would go to more social engagements. And together they would enjoy themselves. For she did enjoy his company very much. She liked Briggs. She always had. But it was different. It was simply different.

Everything about him was different.

One of the many things she had no name for.

'Your brother wishes us to marry here. In the church.'

She nodded. 'Yes. That… That would be fine.' She had not thought about where her wedding would take place. Not even when she had concocted all of this with James. She had not given further consideration to any of this. Not really. She had pictures in her mind of a life. But she had not truly thought about what all this might entail. Yes, she had thought that she had been prepared to face Hugh's ire, and that was something. But there were so many other things along the way that she had not fully considered.

She curled her fingers into fists, stabbing at her palms, as she bit the inside of her cheek, looking for that sort of grounding that occurred when she was able to overcome pain.

But then, there was a strong grip on her chin and she found her face being tilted upwards. She met his eyes. Those dark, shockingly blue eyes, and she felt…

Calm. Quiet.

As if the storm inside her had been halted by the touch of his hand.

'You have nothing to fear from me.'

'I know,' she said.

Her breath was at a standstill, her heart suspended in her chest. And then he moved away, and the world began to move again.

'You look frightened.'

'I'm not,' she said.

A lie.

His gaze was cool, and filled with reproach. Unfamiliar. For she had seen Briggs largely in good humour throughout her acquaintance with him. But then, when would she have had occasion to see him otherwise? But she had not seen him look like this. She had known it was there, though. She had sensed it. For had she not seen the way that he drew people to him? That he commanded all the attention in the room.

Authority. He wore it like other men wore overcoats.

'You are lying to me,' he said.

And she wondered if he had been able to read her mind.

'Sorry,' she said, lowering her head. 'I did not mean to lie.'

She looked up at him from beneath her lashes, and she saw something flash in his eyes. Something she had no name for, but that created a strange sensation low in her stomach. 'You must tell me,' he said. 'You must tell me the truth, Beatrice. It is important.'

'I promise. I am frightened. Because I don't know...' She searched for the right word. But there really was only one. 'Anything.'

He chuckled. 'You need not concern yourself with anything.'

'Why aren't you angry with me?'

Of all the things, that made the least sense. Why he was not filled with rage. For she had forced his hand into something that he gave no indication he wanted.

'Because it makes no difference to me, Beatrice. I have the resources to care for you.'

'But if you wished to marry...'

'I did not,' he said, clipped. 'As it has been previously stated, I have my heir. There is no reason for me to ever marry again, and I had no intention of doing so. However, you shall be as my ward.'

'Your... Your ward?'

'Yes. As I said, your brother has explained everything to me.'

'I'm not free.'

This was the second time in the space of very few hours that he'd looked at her as though she was an object of pity. 'Darling girl, there was never a question of you being free. You would belong either to your brother or to your husband. That is the way of things.'

And then he turned and left her standing there, feeling as if he had poured cold water over her head. Because he was right. She had been seeking freedom... But she could not own anything. She could not make her own way. She had been seeking freedom by means of tying herself to another and...

And that meant there would never truly be freedom.

That was how she found herself running blindly through the estate, making her way to James.

When she arrived at the house, her hands were muddy, and she was in a state. But she did not care. His housekeeper admitted her quickly and ushered her into the sitting room to await him. She had been Beatrice's accomplice from the beginning. Supporting and encouraging their friendship, though she was not sure why.

It was only moments later that James came into the room.

'Are you hurt?' he asked.

'No,' she said. 'I'm engaged. Which at the moment feels tantamount to the same thing.'

'Dammit, Beatrice...'

'I'm sorry,' she said. 'I've made a mess of this for everyone.'

'Don't be foolish, you daft girl. I don't care about myself. I care about you. I'm not being forced into marriage. And I never was. It was an opportunity to help you and to deal with my father, but it was never a necessity. Not in the way it was for you.'

'I feel so terrible...'

'Beatrice,' he said. 'Sit down with me.'

'I will.' She sat. But then she immediately wanted to stand back up. So she did. 'I cannot,' she said. 'I have too much energy.'

'All right. Then we will both stand. Beatrice, my problem is not that... I can trust you. Yes?'

'Of course you can. I was going to marry you.'

'Yes,' he said. 'I know. And I should have told you this

before you were committed to that. But I did not want you to change your mind. I did not wish to lose your friendship.'

'You cannot lose my friendship.'

'I might yet. But I will... Beatrice, I do not wish to have a true marriage with any woman. Because I do not have... I do not have the ability to love a woman.'

'Why do you think that?'

'Because I wish... When I think of my life. When I imagine who I might find happiness with... It could only ever be a man, Beatrice.'

She felt... She did not know what to think of that. She did not know what to make of it at all.

'Oh. But you cannot do that,' she said.

'No. It is against the laws of the King. And I could be imprisoned for it. Or killed.'

'Oh.' Yet again she felt as if there was something she was missing. What did anyone care who James wished to give his heart to? Why should there be laws? It made absolutely no sense. 'I do not see why it should matter. Should we not all be able to find our own happiness? Why can we not? Briggs told me today that I would never find freedom. And he was not being cruel. He was correct. I cannot find freedom because as a woman I can never own anything. All money that is given to me is charity. The houses I live in belong only to men. And when I marry Briggs... He said I will be his ward. Not his wife. And that is his determination to make because... He is a man. But you're a man also,' she said. 'You cannot be free either, can you?'

'Beatrice...'

'Why is it that only certain people are allowed to have happiness?'

'Beatrice, I cannot begin to understand why the world works in this way. What I do know is, as long as people like you, and people like me, are determined to be happy, we will find ways. We do not need the permission of others. I'm thankful that you are my friend. That you look at me, and you feel no judgement. But you were willing to be my wife as you were.'

'I wish I still could be,' she said.

'You care for Briggs,' James said. 'I think perhaps more than you know.'

'What do you mean?'

'You watch him. Whenever he's in any room, and it cannot be held against you, mind, as he is a handsome bastard.' James smiled, and his cheeks turned slightly pink. 'But it's more than that. You like him a great deal.'

'Of course I do. He's always been kind to me.'

'I think you are drawn to him.'

'I don't understand.'

His smile was full of sympathy and she hated it. She was extremely tired of being surrounded by men who understood more of her own future than she did. 'You will. When you go to live with him. I think it is possible that with Briggs you will find more than you could have with me.'

'I cannot. For he's set on honouring my brother's wishes.'

'That is if he does not find it difficult.'

'I am very tired of not understanding what it is people are saying. Or not saying. Or trying to say.'

'I'm sorry,' he said. 'Please stay my friend. I think I'm going to go away to London. Without you here... There is little reason to stay.'

'James...'

'I love you, Beatrice.' He smiled again. 'Not as a husband.'

'I love you a great deal as well,' she said. She nearly said not as a wife, but then, she still did not know exactly what that meant. And yet somehow... She knew she didn't.

'I will be there for you. As a friend.'

'Thank you,' she said.

And whatever else might happen, she knew that she had

him. And that mattered. But she was left to turn over what he had said about Briggs. About her feelings for him.

And there was no satisfactory answer anywhere inside her.

Chapter Four

It was the eve before his wedding and Briggs found that he
could not sleep. Not that a wedding was overly consequential to him.

Particularly not one to Beatrice.

Beatrice...

She was sweet. But what an insipid word it was for her.

An image of her face, her expression fiery, filled his mind.
And it was more than just the image of her. It was the feel
of her.

When she had thrown herself into his arms as a woman
flinging herself off a cliffside. Heedless, determined.

Fearless.

Soft...round in all the places a woman should be.

He tightened his jaw, his hand clenched into a fist.

She was not sweet. Look what she had done in the name
of gaining her freedom.

Poor girl.

She had got herself tied to him, and while he saw no purpose in altering the course of his life over her misstep...

Her life would change.

Or perhaps it wouldn't. Perhaps it would be much the same. But her dreams might be just slightly crushed.

For she had sought a life she would not find with him.

He stood from the chair he was seated in and walked over to the window, looking out over the estate. It was dark, the tops of the trees rustling. And in the shadows, he could see a flash of movement.

Something white fluttering in the wind.

He watched the strange, haunting movement for a moment.

Then, found himself walking out of the bedchamber, and down the stairs. He did his best to minimise the echo of his footsteps on the hard floor. He walked out through the front door, and turned to the right, following the walls of the great estate home, out towards where he had been facing. It was a clear night, and the air had a bite to it. And he did not know why he was compelled to chase ghosts outside his bedchamber window.

Perhaps he preferred them to the company of the ghosts that he found inside it.

He stopped there, at the edge of a grove of trees, and he could still see the fluttering white. Moving forward and backwards. Closer and further away. He took a step forward, then another. And suddenly realised.

'You could catch your death out here,' he said.

'Briggs?'

He had been right. It was Beatrice. He could not mistake her bright, starlit voice. It was like silver.

As he got closer, he understood what he'd seen from the window. She was suspended on a swing that hung in the centre of the grove of trees.

'Lucky for you. Not a highwayman. Or anything else intent on stealing whatever fortune you have on your person or your virtue.'

Her virtue.

He should not think of her virtue.

And yet, it was difficult to avoid thinking of it altogether. Her brother had concerns about her bearing a child, but there were many ways to find pleasure...

It was far too easy in that moment to imagine her as the virgin sacrifice in her white nightgown. Far too easy to imagine her sinking to her knees before him...

You will not be teaching her the ways you find pleasure.

She would be disgusted. Likely go screaming right back to her brother, who would ensure Briggs lived out the rest of his days as a eunuch.

'What are you doing out here?'

'I thought I saw an apparition outside my window.'

'I am not an apparition,' she said. 'I am just Beatrice.'

'A relief.'

Her hair was loose; he had never seen it so. Falling over her shoulders in thick, heavy curls. She was pale and wide-eyed in the moonlight. Like a virgin sacrifice to be taken by the gods.

But not by him.

'I am... I am considering my life in your servitude, Your Grace.'

'Servitude?'

'I'm not free. Was that not the discussion we had mere days ago?'

'You will be freer with me than you ever have been before,' he said, and at the same time he wondered if that were strictly true. 'You will have the protection of being a married lady. Scandal will not be able to touch you quite so easily.'

Though because of her health... She would not have all the freedoms that she might've had otherwise. But he would not say something. Not now. Not when he was trying to comfort her. A task he was unequal to. For he was not one to offer comfort to anyone.

'And what sort of freedoms will I have?'

'What do you wish, Beatrice?'

She closed her eyes. 'I wish to see things. More than this place. I did not ask for this,' she said. 'I did not ask to be ill. To be fragile. It is an insult, I feel, that my spirit does not match my body. For I have always felt that I...' She closed her eyes and tilted her head back, a shaft of moonlight illuminating her skin. And he could see that her nightgown was...

Transparent.

Even in the dimness of the moonlight he could see the shadow of her nipples, the faint impression of dark curls between her thighs.

She was like a goddess. Beautiful. Untouchable.

Absolutely untouchable, no matter that he was to be her husband.

He had married a woman so like her. Serena had been fragile. Beautiful. Virginal. And utterly unprepared for him. Their life together had not been happy. In fact, he felt, unavoidably, that he was part of her being driven to such despair that she could no longer live.

The one person on earth he had attempted to connect with. The one person he had attempted to find a real relationship with and it had...

He had not loved her. But he had thought that he might one day. He had been ready to fight for that. To make it his aim.

But in the end, he had disgusted her. He had told her he would change. That he did not need to indulge himself.

She'd said now that she knew, she could not see him the same again.

She'd barely tolerated intimacy as it was.

'When I read stories, I imagine myself as the heroine. I can see myself slaying dragons and defeating armies, riding a horse through the fields as fast as possible, and... Falling in love. But then to be told that my body cannot do those things... How is that fair? Why could I have not been given a sweet, retiring nature? There are many women who are happy to be home. Who are happy...' She shook her head.

'Of course, I don't suppose any woman wishes to be told she cannot have children.'

'Some might see it as a path of ultimate freedom, in many ways,' he said.

'What do you mean?'

The sadness of Beatrice, the thwarting of her plans, the realisation that he was…

That he was the master in her life now, that all compelled him to offer her something. To speak, even when it hit against sharp places in his soul.

'When you have a child, your cares will be with them always. Your life will never fully be your own. To have another person placed in your care like that is to never truly have your heart beat for itself ever again.' He swallowed. 'At least that is my experience of it.' He did not speak much of fatherhood. But for him it was… A painful reminder of his childhood, and he could not escape the feeling of shortcoming that he had now either. He did not know sometimes how to reach his son.

'It must be wonderful to love like that,' she said.

'I don't know that *wonderful* is the word I would use.'

'Well, I will never have the chance, will I? Except… I will care for your child, Briggs. I will. I promise. I will be his mother, if… I'm sorry, I do not wish to bring up memories of your late wife. And I do not wish to cause any hurt. But…'

'I do not hold in my heart a deep grief for Serena. Do not concern yourself with my feelings.'

'I just should not wish to erase her memory.'

'If William cannot remember her then it is her own fault.'

He could see that she was confused by that, but she did not ask, and he did not offer explanation. Of course, the fact that the late Duchess had taken her own life was something that was rumoured among the *ton*, and it did not surprise him that it had not trickled down to Beatrice.

She had cut her wrists in the bath. Her maid had found her, the screams alerting the entire house to the tragedy.

He remembered lifting her from the water still…being covered in water and in her blood.

And the sorrow.

The sorrow of having failed someone so very deeply.

Serena, but also William.

Her family had gone to great lengths to pay to have her buried in the church graveyard. He could admit he would not have done so. His grief had been nearly as intense as his anger, and his concern had not been in where she might be laid to rest, but on what he might tell his son.

Her family had worried only about the disgrace.

They had paid handsomely for her death to be called a drowning. An accident.

Though there were enough rumours in the *ton* about the truth of it. They only wished to whisper behind their hands and fans, about the Duchess burning in hell.

They did not behave in a way so bold as to speak of it openly.

It was the cowardice in that which bothered him most of all. That those people had no such principles as to allow themselves to expose their meanness so boldly and loudly.

It was, he thought, the greatest tragedy of their society.

The way certain things were hidden. It did not make them less prolific for all their concealing of such vices. All manner of bad behaviour flourished in the world. It was only those who should be protected from it who were left ignorant of its existence, and therefore susceptible to brutality.

'Then I shall do my best for him,' Beatrice said, determined.

'He is a… He is a wilful boy,' Briggs said. 'He is not terribly affectionate. You may find him difficult.'

He felt disloyal saying such a thing, but it was true. If she was expecting an easy path to dealing with the void she felt over not being able to have children of her own, she was likely not going to find it filled in his house.

'I do not have a perfect idea in my head of what it means to have a child,' she said. 'I was warned against fantasising about such things, and so I didn't. I will not find it difficult to love who he is. There is no idea of him built up in my head as to what I feel he *should* be.'

Her words, just then, were a revelation. For wasn't that the true enemy of happiness? Expectation that could not be met.

He was well familiar with it. Far too familiar.

He moved closer to her, and then behind, grabbing hold of the swing and pulling it back. His knuckles brushed her hair, soft and silken. And he could smell her skin. Rose water and something delicately feminine that he could not place.

Perhaps it was simply Beatrice.

He released the swing, and she floated gently forward, her hair streaming behind her. And when she came back, he caught her, holding her steady, lowering his head and whispering in her ear, 'I think we will find a way, don't you?'

He released his hold on her again. He could not decide if prior to this he would never have put himself in this position with his friend's sister, never would've been alone with her, or if it would not have felt...weighted.

Because he had been somewhat isolated with Beatrice on any number of occasions. Here at the house, they had not been so formal. Kendal had trusted him, and he had never once moved to violate that trust. And would not have. But he was marrying her now, and whether or not it was to be a real marriage, it had shifted the positioning of their relationship. Had shifted the way he saw her.

Forced him to realise that she was a woman.

On that thought, she returned to him.

'Will we?' She turned to face him, and it brought her mouth perilously close to his. It was plump, and soft looking. In that moment, he felt an undeniable sense of the tragic.

For it was possible that for her protection, no man would ever taste that mouth.

No man would ever be able to tap into that passion that existed beneath the surface of her skin, for it did. And that he had always known. It was perhaps why he had always favoured her. Why he had brought her sweets from London.

Why he had taken the extra time to talk to her. Because she was trapped here at the estate, and there was so much more to her than she would ever be able to express. She was right. Right then he could feel it. The storm beneath her skin that she was not allowed to let out. She was staring at him, her eyes filled with questions that were not his place to answer.

He could feel her fury. Her fury in the inability to get those answers.

Poor Beatrice.

'I do not intend to make you miserable,' he said.

'But you will not take me to storm armies either, will you?'

'The primary problem with that,' he said, releasing hold of her again and letting her fly through the air, before bringing her back to him, 'is that I do not know at present where there are any enemy armies, on my life.'

'Surely you can find some, Briggs. I have great confidence in your abilities.'

'In my ability to start a war?'

'Yes.'

'Should you like to be my Helen of Troy, Beatrice?' he whispered, far too close to her ear, as he brought her back to his chest, her scent toying with him now. 'Shall I launch a thousand ships for you?'

He pushed her forward again. 'But I do not wish to sit at home,' she said, looking back as she drew away from him. 'I wish to fight.'

'It is still the same result, is it not? A war, all for a woman.'

'I imagine I nearly started a war between you and my brother.'

He continued to push her on the swing, allowing her to fly free before bringing her back. Only ever letting her so far. So high.

'He believed me easily enough.'

'Because he does not think me capable of anything truly shocking,' she said.

'Because he trusts *me*,' he said, wondering right then if he was worthy of his friend's trust. For as he brought her back, through the swing back, he ended up pressing the warmth of her body against his.

And he could feel the softness of her hair against his chin. And he knew that he was going to have to visit a brothel when they returned to London.

As a newly married man, he would be visiting a brothel.

He nearly curled his lip. Disgusted with himself.

But then, that was the state of things. He was not necessarily proud of the man he had become. But he was not waging a war against his nature either.

And in this instance it was a kindness to his wife.

For many reasons.

'I'm sorry,' Beatrice said. 'Of course that is true. I did not think of it that way.' She let out a slow breath, and he could feel it shift her frame. Then she leaned her head back, and it came to rest upon his chest. She jumped, but did not move. And he simply held her there, his hands gripping the ropes on the swing so tightly he thought he might cut his skin open. 'Am I unbearably selfish?'

His chest felt tight. The rest of him felt...hard.

'You are selfish, perhaps,' he said, his voice rough. 'But we all are. And the world favours the selfishness of men. You did what you thought you had to.'

'I would feel better if you were angry with me,' she said.

He laughed. 'I apologise for not being able to accommodate.'

He released his hold on her and she made a small sound

of surprise as she went careening forward. But his heart was thundering too hard, and he should not hold her against his body that way.

'Why can't you be angry with me?'

'Because my freedom is not in question. I will continue to do exactly as I please. As I have always done.'

She laughed softly. 'You've already told me that isn't true. You have a child. Your heart does not beat simply for you.'

He had nothing to say to that, so he pushed her again on the swing.

Beatrice felt breathless. She did not know why. Not breathless in the way that had marked her childhood. Breathless in a way that frightened her.

This breathlessness was not unpleasant. Being close to him was not unpleasant. He had a solid presence that made her feel... Quieted. She had always liked being around him, but this was different. Leaning her head on his chest had felt natural, though she knew it was not proper. She was past proper. She had failed at being proper; she had gone and ruined herself, hadn't she?

He pulled the swing near him again, and she could feel the heat from his body. She felt warm herself.

Her heart thundered almost painfully. He moved his hands, his fingertips brushing against her shoulders, and she shivered. She could sense his strength, and she wanted to lean into it. To test it. In a way that she was never allowed to test her own.

Tears stung her eyes. Because she felt like she was on the verge of something that she would never fully be able to immerse herself in.

Never fully be able to understand.

She turned her head again to look at him, and most of all to chase that strange prickling feeling she had felt before. When she had turned to face him on the swing and their faces had been so close. She was closer to Briggs than she had ever been to a man before. Well, with the exception of that moment in the library when he had put his hand on her hindquarters.

'I would give anything to taste that sort of freedom,' she whispered. 'To know what it's like.'

'People do things… To find that,' he said, his voice low, shivering over her skin in a way that left her feeling shaken. 'To find that sense of pushing against the edges. They take themselves to extremes. But it is not always advisable.'

'Who gets to decide?' she whispered.

'I suppose whoever has the greatest interest in keeping you safe.'

'I sometimes wonder, though, at what point you must abandon safety in order to live. I feel like men are so rarely asked to make these choices. Or at least, if they must, they are the ones in charge of those decisions.'

'Sometimes you have to trust that those who care for you might choose a better path for you than you would choose for yourself.'

He meant him. He meant choosing for her. 'Why must I trust that?'

'I do not have a good answer for you, Beatrice.'

'That is disappointing. You have no anger for me, and you have no answers for me.'

'No,' he said. 'I do not.'

'We are to be married tomorrow.'

'Yes,' he said.

'I do not know what it means to be a wife.'

'You do not have to know what it means to be a wife,' he said. 'You will be a wife to me, and there will be a specific way that can play out. But I will make sure you know everything to do.'

And amid all the uncertainty she found that promise supremely comforting. It was all she had to cling to. And cling to it, she would.

Chapter Five

Briggs had managed to procure the licence easily enough. And he had gone back to Bybee House, though his house-keeper had asked him if he wished William to come to the wedding.

'I should not like to disrupt his schedule.'

'You do not think he might wish to see you married?'

The only reason that Mrs Brown could get away with speaking to him in such a way was that she had been with the house since he was a boy. And she had certainly spent more time with him than his own parents.

'I do not think that,' he said. 'He would find it dull, and the trip would only be taxing.'

And so he was now at the church, prepared to do what he must.

There would be few people in attendance. Beatrice's mother, he assumed Kendal's ward, as she was good friends with Beatrice. And Kendal himself, of course. But other than the minister, he did not imagine there would be another.

No one was in attendance. Not yet. He walked out of the

sanctuary, and through to the back, where there was a small garden, and a stone bench. And upon it sat his bride.

He had last seen her on that swing, with the night drawing a protective veil around them.

It was bright and clear out this morning.

He could see her perfectly well, too well. And the vision mingled with the intimacy of the night before. The way she smelled. The warmth of her body pressed to his.

She was dressed in blush, the gown cut low, as was the fashion. But he had never seen Beatrice in *such* a fashion. She was...

She was a stunning picture there, her elegant neck curved, wisps of dark curls falling down over her pale skin. And her breasts...

She looked up, eyes wide. 'Briggs.'

'What are you doing here?'

'Oh, I escaped. I thought I might come early and...'

'Thank you for telling me the truth.'

He had not been imagining it. The same thing he had seen in her eyes in the library... He could see it again now. She liked to please him. She liked being told what was expected of her.

And that should not intrigue him.

He knew better than to visit his inclinations on a lady. These were things he had attempted in his first marriage, and he had since learned the marriage bed was not the place for such activities. There were brothels that catered to men of his tastes specifically. And everyone involved knew exactly what to expect. And even, enjoyed it. That was the thing about his particular desires. They might be hard, uncompromising.

He might enjoy being in charge, and doling out punishment where it was due. But a woman's submission was only enjoyable if it was given willingly.

And if she received pleasure from the act.

Beatrice would never understand.

He would be very surprised if she understood much of anything about the dynamic between men and women. Ladies were so sheltered. He had experience of such a thing with his first wife. But Beatrice… It was likely she was even more so. Off the country as she was, and with a family that had no intention of ever marrying her off.

'You told me that you wanted the truth. And so I am committed to offering it to you.'

'Good.'

She blushed. And he would be lying to himself if he did not admit that it was an incredibly pretty blush.

'Where will we go?' she asked.

'To Maynard Park. My family home.'

'Oh.'

'We will go to London for the Season. I must see to my duties at the House of Lords.'

For him, the Season typically marked a month-long period of work and excess. As he was not participating in the marriage market, he did not play games unless he was required to attend balls out of deference to a political pursuit. He took his duties relatively seriously. After all, a man had to possess some purpose in his life, or what was the point of it? It was far too easy to be a man in his position and do nothing, care for nothing. To simply exist, as he had much power and wealth, and it was easy for him to do so.

But that was not the way that he saw the world. He would not say that he was an extraordinarily good man, but he did not see the purpose in occupying his space if he did not try to do something to improve the state of others.

'Oh,' she said, immediately looking pleased. 'I do so wish to spend the Season in London. I have not been… But one time. And never for an entire Season.'

'I have a home there that I feel you will find comfortable.'

'That's wonderful.' She smiled slightly. 'I am… Is it wrong that I'm pleased?'

'It is a life sentence, Beatrice. You can either look at it as if you're going to the gallows or... Enjoy your time in the dungeon, I suppose.'

Badly chosen words on his part.

'I must do my best to enjoy it.'

But she looked a bit pale and uncertain.

He felt rather than heard the approach of his friend, and he turned and saw Kendal standing there. He looked disapproving.

'Shall we begin the proceedings?'

'Are you ready?' Briggs asked, somewhat mocking. As if his marriage was one on the time schedule of a man other than him.

His marriage that was not to be a marriage.

He looked at the lovely lines of the woman who would be his wife.

Not his wife in truth.

And then he looked back at Kendal. 'Yes. Let us hasten the imprisonment.'

Beatrice looked slightly wounded by that, but he did not see the purpose in soothing her. He was not going to be hard on her. Not in the end of all things. But he also did not see the purpose in making this any easier on her than it need be.

She had been the architect of this particular sort of destruction.

It does not matter to you.

It did not. It did not and would not matter to him. It could not.

The brothels would receive him whether or not he was newly wed.

And with thoughts of brothels lingering in his mind they entered the church again. The minister was standing there looking reproving, and Briggs had a strange sensation of guilt, which was not something he carried with him often. The minister must be very good.

Briggs could almost feel the hellfire against his heels as he stood there.

Sadly, he was a man who enjoyed the flames. He never had been properly able to feel shame.

Not over certain things.

He had been correct, the only other souls in attendance were Beatrice's mother, and Eleanor, the ward.

Eleanor, for her part, looked quite large-eyed and upset. On behalf of her friend no doubt. Being married off to the big bad Duke.

The minister read from the Book of Common Prayer, and Briggs's most dominant thought was how strange it was to be here again.

With yet another young, sweet miss.

But he was not the man that he'd been. Going into marriage with expectations of something entirely different.

He had been certain that he could make a friendship with his wife. At the very least.

Be something other than his parents' frosty union.

He had not managed it. If anything, he had failed.

He had failed at forging connections with all of the most important people in his life. With the exception of course of Kendal. Though that was likely somewhat compromised now.

It was a short ceremony. Quick and traditional. Legal. And that was all that mattered. They were married in the eyes of the church. And society would have to be appeased by the quick union.

It was incredible how decisive it was. A spare few words exchanged between two people who had been little more than acquaintances to each other a few days prior and they were now bound together for life.

And then they were bundled up into their carriage, making the three-hour journey to Maynard Park. And they had not exchanged a single word to each other since that moment in the garden.

'You will tell me, if you have need of anything,' he said.

'Such as?' she asked.

'Clothing. We are to go for the Season, I assume you will wish to go to... Balls.'

She blinked. 'I did not think that you would wish to attend them.'

'I do not,' he said. 'But you are my ward. Not my prisoner, for all that I may have alluded otherwise.'

'I'm not your ward,' she said softly.

'It is best if we think of it that way.'

And that he not think of last night, and the temptation he'd felt.

'I see.' She looked away from him. 'Well. I shall need some dresses. It is not that my brother has not been generous, but this gown was taken from Eleanor. She had gowns made for the Season. I do not.'

'We shall remedy this.'

'Thank you.'

'It is nothing.'

'I cannot tell if you're angry with me,' she said. 'Am only I held to the standard of being perfectly honest, or does that apply to you as well?'

'Only you,' he said. She clearly did not see the amusement in this. 'It is for your protection,' he said further. 'I must know what you need, what you want, for if I do not, how can I care for you to the extent that you must be cared for?'

'How will I know anything if we do not speak with some level of honesty?'

'I imagine we shall continue on together as we began.'

'You are my brother's friend. We do not often speak. Occasionally, you have brought me sweets.'

'I do not see why that needs to change.'

She sighed. 'Well...should I call you Philip?'

Something rang out, sharp and hard in his chest. He did not know how many years it had been since he'd heard that name spoken out loud.

'No,' he said.

'We are married and...'

'Briggs will do just fine. When it is not Your Grace.' And how easy it was to imagine her calling him that from a position of supplication. On her knees.

Her pale breasts exposed completely...

He clenched his teeth.

'And you will call me...'

'Bea,' he said. 'Beatrice. As I always have. And I will bring you sweets and we can...'

'And I can go on as I ever was, but with a new lord and master? You rather than Hugh?'

He did not wish to think of being her lord and master.

It heated his blood. Brought back that image he'd had of her in that virginal nightgown. His sacrificial virgin.

His disgust with himself in that moment went so deep as to be in his bones.

Was he quite so perverse that even knowing how he'd disgusted Serena he could still desire to take Beatrice in hand this way?

There was a reason he consorted only with prostitutes.

'It is up to you, Beatrice, what you intend to make of this union.'

'No,' she said, 'it is not. It is not up to me, it is more up to my brother than it will ever be to me.'

'You were not to have a real marriage with your friend,' he said, looking at her and ignoring the crackling between them, and it was there. Real. Like a banked flame.

He did not like it.

'I know,' she said.

He knew why it was different. He did not have to ask.

'How old is your son?' she asked, sighing heavily, as if

she'd accepted a subject change would be the only way to move forward.

He did not know why he didn't wish to speak of William with her.

She would be in the same residence as William in only a few hours. But he was… He was protective of the boy.

There were people who would not understand.

He wanted only to protect him from those who would… who would see his vulnerabilities and use them against him.

He did not wish for anyone to think unkindly of William. It was a fierce impulse, one that he could not quite make sense of. That, he supposed, was…being a father.

It was not the way his own had been. His own had seen his weaknesses and stabbed at them without mercy.

Had used them to devastate and torment.

'He is seven,' he said.

'I don't have any experience with children,' she said. 'I have always… I thought it should be nice to have my own.'

'I'm sorry for your disappointment.' He did mean it.

Being a father rooted him to the earth. Without William he wasn't sure what he would do. Spend his days and nights in brothels likely. Without a wife, a need to earn income or anyone on earth to answer to he would…

Stop trying.

He would sink into debauchery and obsession as deep as he could go and never surface.

William prevented that.

William was his reason for being a decent man. He had never felt a sense of pride or affection for his own father. He wanted William to feel both for him.

Whether or not he did was another matter.

'I should think it would be nice to have a child to care for,' she mused. 'In that way, I suppose you are preferable to James.'

'That is the only reason?' He looked at her, trying to ascertain if she truly did not have feelings for the man that went beyond friendship.

She'd said, but it seemed reasonable to him that she'd been harbouring finer feelings for him in some hidden chamber of her heart.

'No, he...he is easy and kind and I enjoy his company.'

'And I am...?' Briggs asked, because he could not help himself.

'You are occasionally kind when brandishing sweets, but no one would call you easy.'

He kicked his legs out forward and leaned back. 'Is that so?'

'You are too... You are you, Briggs, and I do not know how else to say it.'

'And James,' he said, ignoring that. 'Is he in love with you?'

'No,' she said. 'He...he has his reasons for wishing to marry me, but none of them include the kind of love you mean.'

There were not many reasons that a man would wish to enter into a sham marriage, but Briggs could think of one quite obvious reason. He wished for her sake she could have married her friend. They could've likely had a companionable union.

More's the pity for all involved.

'I do not know what I'm supposed to feel,' she said. 'For I am a married woman now, but not a married woman. And I am angry, because I think there are many mysteries in the world that will be withheld from me because of this. Because you are intent on treating me as a ward and not a wife.'

She was edging into dangerous territory, and he knew that she had no real knowledge of that. No real concept.

It had always been thus with her. She was forceful in her speech and he often wondered if it was due to how she had been treated in her illness. As if she was trying to prove she was not fragile.

'There are some mysteries that you might find are best left that way.'

'So you say,' she prodded, her cheeks turning a deep shade of rose. From embarrassment or anger he could not say. Though he was nearly certain it was both. 'Because you are a man and nothing is barred from you. I cannot tell you how infuriating it has been to attempt to divine how to orchestrate my own ruin when I am not entirely certain what it is that ruins a woman. It is being found alone with a man certainly. And being in your embrace. But I do not know what further there is to such an embrace. Or children. I am aware that one must be married to have children. But I'm not aware of what occurs to make it so. Clearly it is something beyond vows, or my brother would not have been so quick to allow me to marry you, no matter how tenuous a state my reputation was in.'

'I will provide you with reading material,' he said. He had no intention of doing such a thing. If she wished to comb through his library...

Of course, his library contained reading material of a more graphic nature, rather than informational.

'You are infuriating. The whole of mankind is infuriating.'

He chuckled. 'Oh, I do not disagree with you.'

She leaned back in the seat across from him, and he found he could not take his eyes off her. Her skin was light cream, her curves so much more ample than he had realised. There was something sweet and sulky about her mouth. He had never noticed that before. And the way that she looked at him. It was a particular sort of look. Demure, when he knew she was not. Not really.

She straightened, and her eyes sharpened. He did not like it. 'We have all this time. Why not give me an education yourself, rather than referring me to your library?'

And those words hit him with the strength of a gunpowder keg going off.

He knew she did not mean to be provocative, for she did not even understand provocation. Did not know why a woman had to take care not to rouse a man's appetites. Did not understand why men and women could not be alone together without a chaperon.

Truly.

She was appallingly uninformed. And somehow, was managing to inflame him almost more because of it.

'You've spent most of your life in the country,' he said.

'Yes.'

He would regret this. But she was his now. That made a strange sensation crystallise inside him.

A lock turning in a key.

She was his. Under his care. And he would care for her. She would have the finest of gowns. He would ensure that she wanted for nothing. She would be happier with him. Happier than she had been back at Bybee House.

And as she belonged to him, it was his decision just how in depth her education was or was not. She wanted freedom. She was a married woman now, whether or not they ever consummated that union.

He locked his jaw together at the thought.

Beatrice.

She was beautiful. But there was much more to sex than beauty.

Many women were beautiful.

He preferred his beauties bought and paid for. A transaction that required no exchange of self, just bodies.

Yes, Beatrice was beautiful, but that did not mean he could not control himself with her.

He had always *liked* Beatrice. Had always felt a measure of pity for her, to be sure. She had been a cloistered girl, and when he'd first met her she had never ventured out of the family drawing room.

'What have you seen of animals?'

Dear God, he was pushing things where he ought not. And yet, the realisation did not stop him.

Impulse control had always been a problem.

Unless he was with a woman or focused on his orchids. Both were singular pursuits that required an intensity of focus he otherwise found impossible.

'Animals?'

'Have you never seen animals engaged in…procreation?'

She blinked. Rapidly. 'No,' she said.

He was counting on that. He was counting on an amorous hedgehog to have made this easier for him.

Currently, he felt enraged with the whole of the species.

'Never mind.'

'I was kept inside most of my childhood. Yes, I did grow up in the country. But in truth, I mostly grew up *in* Bybee House. I spent a great deal of my childhood in bed in my room.'

An orchid.

The thought bloomed in his head and took root.

Beautiful. Fragile.

Needing a firm, guiding hand.

He gritted his teeth. 'What were your ailments?'

He had never truly discussed this with Kendal, as it was not his concern. Or, hadn't been before. 'I need to know,' he said. 'I need to know, so that I understand how best to care for you.'

'I have been just fine these many years, Your Grace.'

'You are in my care,' he said. 'And that matters to me. I take care of what is mine.'

'I do not…belong to you.'

'The Church of England would see it differently.'

'My breathing. My throat would become very tight, and it

would become nearly impossible to take a breath. And any illness of the lungs always… Progressed. Badly. I would get very hot and… They would have to bleed me.'

'And now?'

'It is not so frequent. I have not had a true attack of it in years.'

'That is a terrible way to spend a childhood,' he said.

'I learned to find ways to appreciate it,' she said, her expression deathly serious and hard as stone. 'I hated the bleeding at first. But I would imagine that it was making me stronger. That it was draining away the bad, and that the pain was fortifying me in some way.' She got a strange, faraway look in her eyes. 'And I remember the first time I escaped from the house. And I exerted myself in ways I was not permitted to. I ran through a field. My breathing did become quite hard, but I hid it. I enjoyed it, even. For it was a mark of freedom. And while I was running I fell. But the pain that I felt then was the most real thing. The ground biting into my skin. It was my consequence. Mine. And it was… Somehow wonderful.'

He felt frozen in the moment, not because he was uncertain, no. In these matters Briggs did not traffic in uncertainty.

No, he wanted to stop and linger in it. In the spark it ignited beneath his skin.

The way she spoke of pain. As if it transformed her.

Gave her power.

He knew that feeling. He was not the one who received, but the one who gave. The feeling of absolute control—so unlike how he'd always felt otherwise.

The world had felt wrong for him. Everything in it insensible. He'd had little control over his moods. He'd found solace in his obsession with botany, then in growing flowers himself. Cultivating something with his hands that was both delicate and difficult.

When he'd got older he'd begun to fantasise about women. Controlling their pleasure in the way he controlled the bloom of an orchid.

He had never considered that Beatrice might be the one who understood, but there she was, explaining the piece of pain she experienced in a way not even he had ever heard.

And he was held transfixed.

Of the strange expression on her face, and of the deep, yawning hunger that he could feel it open up inside him.

'And your breathing now?' he asked, doing his best to move past this moment. 'How is it?'

'Mostly manageable. I rarely have incidents now. I have not been sick for many years. The doctor does fear that my lungs are weak. Because of that he feels…carrying a child, giving birth…is something I likely cannot survive. That is why. My lungs.'

'And your susceptibility to other illnesses, I imagine.'

'Yes,' she said, her voice sounding distant. 'I imagine.'

'And that is why you've never seen hedgehogs rut,' he said.

She wrinkled her nose. '*Rut.* That does not sound pleasant.'

'It is not. To watch hedgehogs do it.'

He was walking a thin line. And he knew it.

Like when he'd held her to him last night.

'It is oversimplified,' he said. 'To reduce it all to the creation of the child.'

'But they are connected,' she said, pressing. 'That does make me feel better as it makes me sense that there are perhaps *less* things that I do not know about.'

She had no idea.

'Or so much *more*,' he said.

'That is *not* cheering.'

'You may find none of this cheering in the end. Have you ever kissed a man?' He sensed that she had not.

'No,' she said, her cheeks turning pink.

'Not your friend James?'

She looked away. 'I told him I was not in love with him.'

'Love does not always matter when it comes to issues of attraction, I'm afraid.'

'All of this is confusing.'

'It is,' he said. 'Sometimes deliciously so. There are times when you want a person you may despise. When you might want someone who is utterly forbidden to you.' *Treading on the line now, Briggs.* 'Does he make you feel warm?'

Her eyes went round. 'Warm?'

He cursed himself even as he moved to the seat beside her in the carriage. 'When he is close to you,' he said, lowering his voice. 'Do you feel warm? Flushed?'

She drew back, her eyes getting wide. 'No.'

He was meanly satisfied by that. 'He is your friend, then.'

'I said,' she responded, her voice breathless.

And it was not fair. For he was a terrible rake and he was pressing the limits of it here with her, and of his own self-control.

Were his tastes in shagging more mainstream he would be an even more incorrigible one. As it was, he had to be selective about his partners. He knew how to make a woman want him. He could make her understand. But what was the purpose of it? What was the purpose when…? This was not what he had been tasked with. Not at all.

'I feel warm sometimes when you're near me,' she said.

Dammit.

'Now?' he asked.

'Always,' she whispered, as if it were a revelation.

And he tried not to think of when he'd had a handful of her buttock. How round and supple it was. How perfectly it fitted his palm.

How she'd felt leaning against him on the swing.

How that dress lovingly showed the curve of her bosom.

'If I were to kiss you,' he said. 'It would increase. Quite exponentially. And you would understand. You would want to be closer to me. I to you. And it would feel the most natural thing in all the world to remove anything that stood between us.'

'I don't...'

'Clothes.' He was torturing himself, and he could not say why.

He preferred to mete out pain, not be on the receiving end of it.

'I *knew* that naked nymphs had something to do with it,' she said, looking up at him, as if in a daze.

'Naked nymphs?'

'I saw a book. In my father's library. In his collection. There were...' Her cheeks turned pink. 'Naked women. Nymphs. Running from men.'

He bit his own tongue. To remind himself why he needed control. 'Yes. They were running to preserve their virtue, I have a feeling. For if the men caught them, had their way with them...'

'You speak in more veiled metaphor. *Have their way with them.* I wish to understand. What it means.'

'You are familiar with the ways in which men and women are different?'

His wife had been given a basic bit of education from her own mother before they wed. He had not had to explain everything to her. Beatrice... Beatrice would have to have everything explained to her were they to have a true wedding night. And they were not.

But he had always liked to tease flames. He didn't know why he was suddenly taking the torture, rather than giving it.

Though, Beatrice was not untortured.

'I have seen anatomy,' she said, sniffing. 'Drawings. In science books. And, of course…statuary.'

Ah, the naked limp statuary. Which would give her no real idea of men at all. At least, not of him.

She does not need an idea of you.

'The purpose of the difference is that we fit together,' he said. 'And that is the way in which you create a child. But it is more than that. It can be much more than that.'

Her eyes rounded, her lips going slack. 'What more?'

She sounded dazed, and she sounded fascinated, and he truly wished she were neither.

'Pleasure.' He looked at her, and he did not break her gaze. 'Pain. Which for some is quite near to the same thing.'

Her blue eyes glistened with something then, a keen interest he wished to turn away from. But could not. 'Is it?'

'Yes.'

'Briggs…'

They were saved by the fact that the carriage arrived at Maynard Park. He did not much believe in divine intervention, but he was going to have to give serious consideration to it at this moment.

The old place was grand, he had to admit, but he had no real fond feelings for it. He had not had the happiest of childhoods, and then he had not had the happiest of beginnings as a man. He'd had the interior renewed, and had ensured the gardens were revamped as well, and had seen to the installation of a greenhouse.

It didn't completely erase the memories of what it had been like to grow up here.

And you keep your son there. Locked up like the prisoner you once were.

He pushed that thought away.

It was different.

The driver manoeuvred the carriage to the front of the

grand entrance hall. It was all stately pillars in marble. Not to his taste. And yet it was his. And it felt in many ways as if it spoke to a great many things that he was. A great many of the wrong things.

He assisted his wife from the carriage, unwilling to allow the footman to place a finger on her. His possessiveness was unfamiliar. He was accustomed to it in the context of an interlude with a woman. After all, that was a hallmark of the dynamic. But he was not accustomed to it when he was fully clothed. And he wondered… He wondered if he might find a strange sort of fulfilment from this. From caring for her. Having her.

Even if only in this regard.

He escorted her to the front of the house, and the door opened, his butler a firm and imposing presence.

Mrs Brown the housekeeper was standing just there, smiling warmly. 'Your Grace,' she said. And she made her way to Beatrice and clasped her hand. 'Your Grace.'

'Hello,' Beatrice said, suddenly looking awestruck and shy.

'Do not worry,' he said.

And he could feel her calm next to him.

'I am Mrs Brown. I'm the housekeeper.'

'I'm pleased to meet you,' Beatrice said.

And then he heard a great howl echoing through the halls. Beatrice startled.

'No need for alarm,' Mrs Brown said, smiling. 'It is only that he's having to change for dinner. He did not wish to stop what he was doing.'

'William,' he said. 'That's my son.'

'Is he well?'

'Yes,' Mrs Brown said. 'He is quite all right. I assure you.'

But there was something worried behind her eyes, and he hated to see that.

As much as this…discontentment in his son chafed against something inside him.

'Welcome to Maynard Park.'

Chapter Six

Beatrice woke up, her heart thundering. It took her several moments to realise where she was. She was in Briggs's house. She was Briggs's wife.

She was sleeping alone. In an unfamiliar bedchamber. And she could hear a sound that was like howling.

She turned over and put her pillow over her head, trying to drown out the haunting sound, sleep tangling with reality until she was on the moors running from a ghost, rather than safe beneath the bedclothes.

When she woke her eyes felt swollen and she felt gritty and bruised.

She took breakfast in the morning room, and did not see Briggs.

She had a small meeting with Mrs Brown, standing in the hall nearest the entry, and made arrangements to plan the menu for the week.

Beatrice had to admit she found that cheering, and hoped that she found the food at Maynard to be to her liking. It was not as if she was fussy, but she enjoyed nice foods rather a lot.

Her pleasures in life had been small, always, but very deeply enjoyed.

She went into the library and found a copy of *Emma*, which she had read before but had quite enjoyed. She tucked it under her arm and there was an attractive illustrated compendium of birds, and she added that too.

She took them back to her room and looked around the space. It was elegant, the walls a blue silk, with matching blue silk on the bed, trimmed with gold. The ornate canopy had heavy curtains, though she couldn't see why she should need to draw curtains back in this isolated room that only ever contained herself or her maid.

She deposited the books at the foot of her bed and went back out into the hall.

And that was when she saw him for the first time.

The boy.

He had unruly brown hair and slim shoulders. He was very slight, his expression sulky.

William.

This must be William.

The boy turned and went back down the hall. Towards the sound of the late-night howling, she realised.

Over the next few days she spotted the boy in the house a few times, but never Briggs, who seemed to ensconce himself in his study at the early morning and not...un-ensconce himself until well after she was ready to retire for the evening.

And sometimes at night, she heard that howling.

One word came to her each time she saw that child.

Loneliness.

She knew it well. She was living it now.

When she crawled into bed on her fourth night at Maynard, her fourth night as a wife, she tried to read *Emma*. And could not.

Because in those words she looked for any...anything she

might be able to recognise. Longings, feelings. She could not...find herself in those pages.

Briggs did not want her. Not really. He did not care if she was here or at Bybee House.

She felt no giddy joy over marriage and could not care at all about the marital prospects of the silly girls in the novel.

She set it aside and stared at the ornate ceiling of the canopy, her eyes tracing the lines of the gold crest there.

Was this to be her life? Not any better or altered than that life at Bybee House?

No. She would...she would not allow it.

And that was when the howling started.

She got up from the bed without thinking and raced to the door. She cracked it open and held herself still there, waiting. The howling grew louder. And she walked out of the room, making her way down the cavernous hall. It was a huge home. Not unlike Bybee House. Though less Grecian in style. She had noted the frescoes painted on the walls; they were a bit more vivid than the ones to be found there.

But it wasn't the frescoes that had her full attention now. It was that sound. Like a wounded animal.

William. She knew it was William.

She raced towards it, not thinking. And pushed the door open. It was another bedchamber. A child's room. And the child was on the floor, dressed in his bed clothes, weeping and thrashing.

He had not met her, not yet. They had only seen each other from a distance, and she hesitated to make a move, for she would be a stranger to him. But no one else was here.

So she raced towards him and dropped to her knees. 'William,' she said.

But he said nothing in response. He only kept screaming and crying, twisting to get away from her. It took her a moment to realise that he was sleeping. Sleeping, and lost to reason. Lost to any sort of reach.

'William,' she said softly, reaching her hand towards him, her heart contracting painfully.

She had never experienced anything like this. But when she was a child her body had been in agony sometimes. And she had felt as if no one in the room could truly reach her. As if she was living in her own space, where there was only pain. And she had learned to place herself there firmly, to find a way to endure it. But it was always lonely. There was never connection there. There was never a space to be comforted.

There was only enduring.

And she broke, for this boy. For this boy who was experiencing that now.

This boy she saw alone.

She lurched forward, just as he retreated to the wall, hitting himself against it. She grabbed hold of him and pulled him against her body, holding his arms down, holding him still.

'Be still,' she said, making a shushing noise. 'Be still.' She held on to him tightly. 'You are well. You are safe.'

It took a time, but eventually the screams quieted. Eventually, he surrendered to the way that she held him.

He was not alone now.

'Be at peace, William,' she whispered.

Silence descended, finally. He was damp with sweat and breathing hard, his exhaustion palpable.

She held him against her breast, swaying back and forth, some instinct guiding her.

The door opened, and she could see it was Mrs Brown.

'Your Grace,' she said. 'I apologise. You should not have been disturbed. It took me a wee while to rouse myself...'

'Does this happen often?' she asked, already knowing it did, for this was not the first time she'd heard him.

'Yes. He has nightmares.'

'I have heard him...upset like this during the day as well.'

'It is not the same. He is easily...angered by changes in his routine.'

'I see.'

'This should not have fallen to you. It is my responsibility to see to him at night. His governess needs rest. She is in a room far from him for that reason, after her day she is tired.'

'I do not mind,' she said.

'Often, when he is here, His Grace sees to him. He must be in his study still.'

As far as she could tell, His Grace was only ever in his study.

She was relieved to hear he did see to his son. She had yet to see the two of them together.

'It is all right,' she said, stroking the boy's head. She picked him up, his form limp. And she returned him to his bed. 'Does he usually sleep after this?'

'Yes. There may be another episode, but typically one is all he will have on a difficult night.'

'I'm glad to hear that. But I will listen for him.'

'If you insist, Your Grace,' Mrs Brown said, clearly at her limit with how much she was willing to argue with the new Duchess.

'Yes.'

She was filled with a sense of purpose. For she had comforted the boy. And she could comfort the boy. She might not ever be a wife to Briggs, not truly. But she could be a mother to this boy. Because she had understood him in that moment. It might be an entirely different circumstance, and entirely different...everything, but she understood. On a deep, profound level. For he lived in a space that people could not reach him in, and she had spent much of her childhood doing the same.

Being ill. Being shut up inside.

Tonight had been like witnessing a person who was shut up inside themselves. She knew what that was like as well.

As she had said. A spirit that was held back by the body she was in.

She waited a while, and then she returned to her room, her heart rate slowing. And as she drifted off to sleep, she made a plan. A plan for the next day. She would not simply be a ward. She was going to take charge of her life. She was going to find out what she could do. What she wanted.

And she would begin with William.

The next morning at breakfast time, she went in search of the child.

She found him in the nursery with his governess, sitting at a small table and looking furious.

'William…' The woman was saying his name in a cajoling manner.

'Good morning,' Beatrice said, coming into the room.

The boy did not look at her. 'William,' she said, saying his name purposefully. 'Good morning.'

He looked up in her direction. Though his eyes did not meet hers. 'Hello,' he said.

'You had a difficult sleep last night,' she said.

His expression went black and he turned his head away. 'Who are you?'

'Did your father speak to you about the fact he was getting married?'

The boy did not answer.

'Did your father tell you that he was getting married?' She restated the question.

The boy nodded, his head still angled away from her.

'I'm his wife. I am your stepmother. You may call me Beatrice,' she said.

He lowered his head, his focus back on his breakfast.

Beatrice moved to him, and sat down. He looked up, startled by her presence. His eyes connected with hers for a moment before darting away. It was as if it was difficult for him to look straight at her.

'I like to swing,' she said, feeling as if there had to be a way to capture his interest. 'I like to read. And I like to hide in the garden. What do you like?'

He didn't say a thing. But he stood up and went to his bedside table and opened a drawer, pulling out a small box. He opened it and held it out to her.

Inside was a small collection of cards, with pictures on them.

'This is the Colosseum,' he said. 'It is in Rome. It was inaugurated in AD 80. This is the Pantheon,' he said, showing her the next card.

He continued showing her sites from all over Europe, with a special focus on those found in Italy. His knowledge was breathtaking. He knew dates and locations, precise details. And he seemed perfectly happy to give her each and every one.

'Do you wish to go to these places?' she asked.

'Yes,' the boy answered.

'So, this is a box of your dreams,' she said, smiling.

His brow creased. 'It is a box of cards.'

He looked so like his father then. And the realisation sent a strange sort of twist through Beatrice's midsection. He was part of Briggs. It was undeniable. She could see it so clearly now.

'Well, they are very nice cards,' she said.

She sat with the boy, who said nothing more voluntarily throughout his breakfast. His governess stood in the corner, watching her with hard interest. It was not entirely accepting, but she had a feeling that the woman was protective of the boy. Beatrice herself had no real experience with children, so she did not know what she should expect of the child. He seemed different, though. That much she knew.

She wondered if she did. For she had certainly not spent much time in the company of those who were not her family. She had her few very close friends, and that was all. She did not spend time out in broader society.

'William,' she said. 'I should like to see the grounds today. Remember how I told you I like gardens?'

'To hide,' he said.

'Yes. But, also to walk in them. Is there a spot in the garden here that you favour best?'

'No,' he said.

'I see.' She tried to think of another way to say it. 'Is there a place that is interesting? Where you can tell me about the flowers?'

Something in his expression changed. 'Yes. There is a garden and it has statues. I like that spot best. It reminds me of Rome.'

'Excellent. Shall you and I take a picnic for our lunch this afternoon?'

'I do not eat outside,' he said.

'Well, perhaps you might try?'

'I do not eat outside.'

'Should you like to eat outside?'

'I don't know.'

'All right. Then we shall try it. And if you don't like it, we don't have to do it.'

He looked thoughtful about this. 'All right.'

'Then you and I shall see each other this afternoon.'

She stood and walked out of the nursery, and heard the footsteps of his governess behind.

'Master William does not like interruptions to his schedule,' she said.

'No, I imagine he does not. But I would like to begin a new schedule. I would like to spend time with him.'

Beatrice had no experience of running a household, but she had watched her brother and her mother do it in decent fashion for a number of years. She did not feel fully confident in her position, but one thing she did feel confident in was her connection to the boy. It was loneliness. It echoed inside her, and she knew that it echoed inside him as well.

She knew that he felt the same sort of isolation that she did. It did not matter if they were the same, or different, those feelings she knew.

And she would not rattle around this house doing nothing. She could not do that.

'Perhaps we should speak to His Grace.'

'You are welcome to speak to His Grace,' Beatrice said. 'I am not sure where he is. I am not sure what his routine is. I only know that I must make my own. And I should like it to include William.'

The governess was wary. 'William can be a difficult child,' she said.

'I'm continually warned of this,' she said. 'I held him last night when he was overtaken by terror in his sleep. I understand. When I arrived he was quite upset. But I do not think that makes him difficult.'

'I love him,' his governess said. 'That is not what I mean.'

'I believe you,' she said. 'And I wish for you to believe me. I do not wish to toy with this child. But I have married His Grace, and I... I must find a reason to be here.' She had not meant to say that. Had not meant to expose herself in such a fashion. Or their marriage. For it was nobody's business that it was not a true union.

Though they had forgone the traditional honeymoon trip. And indeed any sort of honeymoon phase.

She did not know how they might express that, but she had a feeling it was not as they had been these past days.

'I want to be a mother to this boy.'

'Forgive me, Your Grace,' the governess said. 'His own mother did not care for him, and I am quite protective.'

Her stomach went tight. 'My father did not care for me,' she said. 'I was blessed to have a wonderful mother, however. But even so, I know what it is to have a parent who does not care. And to lose that parent quite early. I do not wish to cause him harm. And I promise you that should he become upset, I will bring him to you.'

'Thank you, Your Grace. What am I to do with my time?'

'Whatever you wish,' Beatrice said. 'Take some time to rest. Or read.'

'Oh, I don't...'

'Do not worry.'

Beatrice went to the kitchen and asked about having a picnic compiled for herself and Master William. She was met with slightly quizzical expressions, but nobody openly questioned her. And she spent the next hour considering what she might wear out in the garden.

While she was being dressed, she took a moment to ponder the absurdity of it all.

She had been a spectator in her own life for a great many years. Subject to the commands or the whims of those in authority over her. Even if they did love her. And here she was, taking part in running a household, caring for a child. She was deeply surprised and pleased by all of it and she might be confused about everything with Briggs, but it didn't matter. She had not had any of this a week ago. Not this home, not this child. Not the sense of purpose. Husband was inconsequential. And she did not have unlimited freedom, it was true. But she had more freedom. Or rather... A different sort of freedom. A different sort of life. It might not be an adventure around Europe, no grand tour. But she had taken a small one sitting on the floor with William this morning.

And it was not mouldering away in the country. Well, she supposed she was mouldering away in the country, but it was a different part of the country. So, there was that to be cheerful about.

In the end, she was deeply satisfied by the blue dress that her lady's maid put her in. It was a light airy fabric, and she attired herself in a fichu to cover the swells of her bosom. It was not ballroom, after all.

But she looked... Entirely like the Duchess of the house, and not like the child she had felt like only a week before. She was a woman. As close to making her own decisions as she possibly could be, at least, to the best of her knowledge.

Time had passed quickly, and before she knew it was time to collect William.

The boy that she found stubbornly sitting in the corner of his room, was not quite the amiable chap she had met this morning.

His dark head was lowered, and his face was fixed into a comical scowl. He had dark-looking circles under his eyes.

'Are you tired?' she asked.

'No,' he said.

'He has had a bit of difficulty with lessons today.'

'I sometimes had difficulty with lessons too,' she said, trying her best to relate to him. She reached down, and tried to take hold of his hand, but he would not rise, and instead, leaned backwards, rooting himself even more firmly to the ground.

'William, I have very nice food in this basket.'

He did not say anything.

'Shall we put your shoes on?'

'No,' he said.

'And why not?'

'I don't want them.'

'You must have shoes.'

He only lay down on the floor, not answering her at all.

'I will see to him, Your Grace,' the governess said.

'No,' Beatrice said, confused, but determined. 'William,' she said, trying to sound stout. 'I'm going to have a picnic. I will have one here if I must. But I am intent upon eating with you.'

He rolled to the side, not looking at her.

She took the blanket that was draped over her arm and spread it out over the floor of the nursery. Right atop the beautiful rug. Then she sat determinedly, placing the basket beside her and beginning to place the food all around them. 'I am quite hungry.'

'No,' he said.

'Well I am.'

'I don't like it. I don't want shoes.'

'If we eat here you don't have to put on shoes.'

'I don't want shoes,' he said.

'I said you did not have to have them.'

'I do not want shoes.'

She did not know what to make of it. He seemed upset, though not inconsolable. He made his statement about shoes at least four more times before going quiet. As if the idea was firmly rooted in his mind and he required extra time to ensure it had been dealt with.

Beatrice decided to change her tactics.

'Do you like cheese?'

The boy did not answer. He was involved in examining a spot on the wallpaper.

'I quite like it,' she said, firmly, cheerfully.

She stared at him for a moment and wondered if she had miscalculated, in a fit of arrogance, imagining that she understood him. His loneliness seemed to be something he chose. For he did not look at her. And he did not seem interested in her overtures.

But maybe he simply didn't know how.

'William, do you know it is polite to look at someone when they are talking?'

He turned his head, sharply and only for a moment. And then he went back to staring at the wall. 'I don't like it.'

'You don't like to look at people?'

'No.'

She searched herself, trying to sort out the best way forward. 'What do you like to look at?'

'I already showed you my cards.'

'You did.'

For her part, she ate some cheese, because it made her feel soothed.

She heard heavy footsteps coming down the hall, and stilled. It could be a manservant, but it made her think of...

The door pushed open, and there he was.

His eyes connected with hers, and he looked momentarily surprised. And then... Angry.

'What are you doing in here?' he asked.

She expected William to scramble upwards at his father's presence. But he did not. Instead, he remained as he was, laying with his back to her, facing the wall.

'I'm having a picnic with William,' she said, smiling determinedly. 'Would you like to join us, Your Grace?'

He frowned. Which was a feat as he'd been frowning already, but he managed to do it again. 'Would I care to join you...in a picnic?'

'Yes,' she said brightly. 'I have not seen you these many days.'

She looked at William, who was kicking his feet idly, but still not looking.

'Good afternoon, William,' Briggs said. 'How are you?'

He didn't respond to his father.

Briggs, for his part, did not look perturbed by this at all.

'Don't you want to say hello to your father?' Beatrice prompted.

'It is no matter,' Briggs said. 'Sometimes William does not feel like saying hello.'

She was surprised by the easy way that he accepted this.

Confused, she shuffled over, making more room on the blanket. 'You want to join us. Surely you've not taken your lunch yet?'

'I have not. But I do not sit on the ground.'

'That is very interesting as William informed me earlier that he does not eat outside.' She adjusted her seating position on the floor and it made her dress go tight around her hips, which caught his attention more than it should.

'And you told him what?'

'I asked him to try.' She looked like steel just then.

His brows lifted. 'And here you are, eating indoors.'

'Far easier to accomplish than the moving of a large dining table up to this room, don't you think?'

'You think that you will win with me where you have not won with my son?'

'Yes,' she said.

'Have a picnic.' It was William's first acknowledgement of Briggs.

They both stared at the child. Who looked serious.

'Have a picnic,' he repeated.

'There,' she said, smiling up at Briggs. 'William wishes you to have a picnic.'

Chapter Seven

Briggs was… He didn't know what he was. Of all the things he had expected when he had walked into his son's room, it had not been to see Beatrice sitting with a determinedly cheerful expression on her face in the middle of a blanket on the floor, eating a picnic.

Nor did he expect to see William laying on his side, staring at the wall.

Beatrice might interpret this as insolence, but Briggs knew that it was not. He also knew that if William were unhappy with Beatrice's presence, he would've made it known. He would not simply lie there quietly.

He had been avoiding her.

That was the truth. And now that he acknowledged it to himself he felt replete with cowardice, and cowardice was not something he trafficked in. He had told himself that it was for her own good. After all, the conversation in the carriage ride had steered far too close to intimate for what he had decided their marriage would be. But he had also decided that she was his. And he fundamentally could not excuse his neglect of her. Not when her care and keeping was his responsibility.

What he had not expected was for her to be with William. And he felt... Oddly exposed, and angry about it. At war with the emotions that Beatrice created inside him.

And he found himself sitting down. On the floor. He hated that she was right. But he could not deny William. And he had asked him to have a picnic.

'William has shown me his collection of cards.'

'Has he?'

'Yes. I quite enjoyed hearing about everything he knows.'

'Unless you've spent a considerable amount of hours with him, you have not scratched the surface of what he knows,' Briggs said, marvelling slightly at the pride that he felt when he said it. William was in possession of a great deal of information. And while he might not be able to carry on a fluid conversation about whatever you wanted him to, he could certainly give you all of the information there was to have on the Roman Colosseum.

'I don't doubt that,' Beatrice said.

William rolled over then, as if he was intrigued by the direction of the conversation. Briggs couldn't help but smile.

'You know quite a lot, don't you, William?'

'I know everything about the Colosseum,' William said.

'William, are you interested in London?'

'London is interesting,' he said. 'Westminster and St James's Palace.'

'You're very clever,' she said. 'Do you look forward to joining us in London?'

'He won't be joining us,' Briggs said.

William did not react to that.

'Why not?' Beatrice asked.

'He will not be joining us because he does not like to travel. He finds carriage rides to be interminable, and the disruption to his routine makes him fractious.'

'Oh, it all makes me fractious as well,' Beatrice said. 'I am quite upended, and a bit fussy. But that does not mean we should not do things.'

'He will not wish to go to London.'

'London has Westminster Abbey, St James's Palace. Grosvenor Square.'

He recited facts rather than stating his feelings on the matter, and that did not surprise Briggs. Sometimes he seemed to be making a conversation, and other times, you couldn't force one out of him. Briggs didn't see the point in trying.

He let him speak his piece, though.

But he found that he did not necessarily want Beatrice to see, for he was afraid on behalf of William that she would offer judgement, but she did not.

'You should've spoken to me, before you involved yourself with William.'

'She is my friend,' William said.

Briggs was absolutely stunned by that. He did not know what to say. 'She is?'

'I've never had a friend,' he said.

'You have your governess.'

'She is a governess. This lady is my friend.'

'I cannot argue with that.'

Beatrice, for her part, looked exceedingly pleased.

They continued eating in silence, and when they were through, William's governess came and made it clear that it was time for him to continue on with his lessons.

They walked out of the nursery, and Beatrice left behind him.

'Why can we not take him to London?'

'Why have you inserted yourself into my son's life?' he asked.

'I had nothing else to do,' she said. 'I felt that I had something in common with Master William. I am lonely. And I can assure you that he is as well.'

'Did he look lonely to you?' His son barely glanced at people when they were in the same room as he, not when he was engrossed in something else.

'I somehow have the feeling that he does not necessarily look the way you or I might when we are feeling something. But it does not mean he does not feel it.'

He was stunned by the insight, as he had known that was true for some time. Even if no one, including William himself, could confirm it.

'You are correct about that, but that does not mean that he is lonely. Or that he wishes to go to London. You have spent some time with him, and that is very nice of you. A kindness. However, that does not give you a complete view of all of his struggles.'

'I went into his room last night. When he was having one of his terrors.'

Guilt ate at him. He ought to have heard William, but he had been in his study. He had spent much time there since bringing Beatrice to Maynard Park. Anything to keep her distant from him in the night when his vision was invaded by thoughts of beautiful virgin sacrifices, on their knees before him...

'Yes, that is one of his difficulties. He sometimes does that during the day as well, though, when he is not asleep. His moods can be incredibly capricious. I do not always know what will cause... There is a disconnect. He loses himself. In his rage. He has never harmed anyone. I do not think he ever would. I cannot explain it better than that. But I do not think he would enjoy London. I think you would find it noisy, I think you would find it confusing, I think you would find the journey arduous. And I am his father. You might think that I have made this edict out of a sense of my own convenience, but I assure you it is not for my convenience. It is not so simple. Would that it were for my own convenience. Then

I might not feel so much guilt. I might not feel torn. By my duties to him, and my duties to the House of Lords.'

He felt a stab of guilt, because there was also the duty to his libido, which he had faithfully attended these past years. But that was part of quitting to London. At least for him. The opportunity to see to his baser needs. And he had a great need to deal with them now.

Of course, he would already have Beatrice in tow.

Beatrice likely had no idea what a brothel was, let alone the particular delights he saw in them.

She looked at him in a fury. 'Your Grace, I did not seek to question your commitment to your son, but I do have a differing opinion. He dreams of seeing things. He dreams of seeing the world. I think perhaps in part the trip will be upsetting for him, but it seems as if you find sleep upsetting at times, and he cannot be utterly and completely shielded from every bad feeling.'

'Why not? Why do you think that is not something that should be done? You had the benefit of having it done for you. And you discarded it. You discarded your brother's protection, and now you are under mine. And you must do as I say.'

He had not asked for this. For her intervention with his son, his most private, painful relationship. The one he would die for, kill for.

He had not asked for her to be here, bewitching him and making him long to touch her. Taste her.

Receive her submission.

This was her fault, and not his.

If she did not like the way it was in his household, she should not have flung herself into his arms.

'Is that how it's to be, Your Grace?'

'And when is it that I became Your Grace, and not Briggs?'

'The moment you stopped being my friend. Maybe you never started. I believed that we were friends, Your Grace,

I did. I had a great deal of affection for you. But since all of this, all you have done is stay in your study.'

'This is what I do with my life, Beatrice. You have always seen me when I was away from my duties and responsibilities. You only ever see me away from Maynard Park. *This* is my life. I have a duty to my tenants to manage things to the best of my ability. I have a son, and my duty is to make sure that his life… I wish for him to be happy, Beatrice, and I do not know how to accomplish this. There is no road map. There is no map for parents, not in the general sense, but when you have a child like mine, who is not like any other child I have ever met, how is it that I'm supposed to ensure his happiness? When cards with pictures of buildings on them make him happier than toys, and when he does not always smile even when he is happy. How am I to ever know what to do?

'Do not speak to me with such authority and confidence. Do not tell me what I have denied you, when you are the one that put yourself in the situation. You wanted my anger, and now you may have it. You might have got your way. You might have escaped from your house, but you have stepped into my life. And I warned you that I would not disrupt it for you.'

She looked wounded, and he regretted it. But she had no right to speak to him on such matters. She might be a woman in figure, but she was a child in so many ways. Desperately sheltered.

'I was a child like that. It might not have been for the same reasons,' she said, her voice filled with conviction, 'but I was that child. My parents did not know what to do. Hugh has never known what to do with me. I have been isolated and alone because of the differences in me. Because of the fear that my family has always felt for me. And it might come from a place of love, but the result is the same. I have been lonely. And isolated. Controlled. And at the same time… Do you know what it is to be a child who has accepted that you will likely die? Because all of that fear that surrounded me all the time, I knew what it meant. I knew that it meant I was dying. I was surprised to wake up some days. Many days. I endured pain that would make grown men weep. And I learned to do so without fear. Having a different set of circumstances does not make you weak. I am not weak. Your son is not weak.'

'I did not say that either of you was weak.'

'When you deny him the chance to fail, it reveals that is what you think.'

'Beatrice, you have spent your life cloistered in the house. You do not have a child. You do not know what I have endured, what it has cost me to try to be the best father that I can be to him.'

'I do not deny it,' she said. 'I am certain that you have... endured a great many difficult and painful things trying to parent him, but that does not... Maybe it is helpful for me to challenge you.'

'You have spent a few hours of my son, you do not know him.' And he felt guilt. Because he was not listening to her. And he did know it.

He was denying the strength he knew was in her, choosing instead to focus on her weakness, which was a petty and small thing to do.

But he had not asked for Beatrice to uproot his life, any more than he had asked for any of this. What he had done, he had done for her.

For her, or for yourself?

He pushed that to the side. It made no difference debating this with himself. She was here, she was his wife. And he would conduct their marriage, and raise his child in the way that he saw fit, and it was not for her to tell him otherwise.

'You mean well, Beatrice,' he said. 'I know you do. You are a kind, sweet girl...'

'You make it sound as though you are speaking of a kitten. Kind and sweet and well meaning. But you forget, Your Grace, that kittens have claws, and you have vastly underestimated mine.'

She turned to begin storming away from him, and he caught her by the arm.

The action shocked her, clearly it did; her eyes went wide, her cheeks pink. That was what he noticed first. Then after that, he noticed the way that her skin felt beneath his touch. Soft. Warm. And he was transported back to that garden. To that moment when he had realised just what a lovely woman she had become. And perhaps that was why it was so easy to dismiss her now. To turn all of this into a treatise on her inexperience. To write her off as a child, because as long as he could think of her as such, he had an easier time keeping his hands off her.

'You may have claws, kitten,' he said, his voice soft and stern. 'But do not forget that I could pick you up with one hand if I so chose. I do not deny that you possess a certain amount of ferocity, but I have an iron hand, and you would do well to remember that.'

'Threats?'

'Not deadly threats,' he said, pushing hard at the bonds of propriety that he had laid out for himself. 'But perhaps you do require a punishment. For all that he has kept you hemmed in your entire life, Hugh is quite indulgent towards you.'

Her lips parted, her breasts quickening. 'You do not know of what you speak.'

'Perhaps not. But I know more about you than you might think.'

'If you knew anything about me, you would not treat me as you do. You would not ignore me for days on end. I am little more than an antiquity to you, set up on a shelf in this house and left to gather dust.'

She jerked away from him. 'You do not have the authority to punish an object.'

'I have the authority to do whatever I wish.'

'Perhaps. But where is the glory to be had in unchecked authority? Authority that must be taken.'

And her words tugged at his gut, because she had hit right against the very thing he knew deeply to be true. There was no joy in wielding authority when the supplicant was not willing. But this was not a game to be played in a bedroom. This was...

What was it? He didn't seem to know.

Neither did she. That much was clear. Her eyes burned bright, with both rage and excitement. And he knew, he absolutely knew that she had no idea why this battle excited her. He knew all too well that it fired his blood. And he felt nothing but contempt for himself. Over his lack of control. Because he had attempted it at this moment. Brought it to this place. Not because it was an accident, because he was actually threatening to punish her, but because he wanted to tease the fire inside her. Because he wanted to push that limit and see how far it might go. She was not a simpering miss. He didn't mind a simpering miss, particularly when she was playing a role. But he found he responded to the wilfulness in her. She liked to fight, did Beatrice. And that said more about her than she knew.

But she moved away from him, effectively placing herself in a safer spot. Smart girl. It was better that way. Better that she end this now.

'You're right,' she said. 'This is the first time I have seen you in your real life. And I thought that I knew you based on what I saw when you were in the presence of my brother. But I do not know you. I will not make commentary on you. However, I feel strongly about William.'

'Why is that?'

'Because I see myself in him. And you might find that silly, or you may not believe it, but I do. But it is true. Protection at what cost, Briggs?'

'He does not...'

'As you said, he does not always show it. I understand that everyone around me, everyone in my life, was simply trying to make things better for me. Perhaps not my father, but my mother and Hugh wanted only that I should be safe. But they wanted my safety so very much that they did not consider risk is part of living. But it must be. Because there is so much that I have not tasted, so much that I feel I have not done. Survival, *breathing*, cannot be the end of it. I am certain of that fact.'

'But without at least that there is nothing,' he said.

'William isn't going to die of a trip to London. He just might find it difficult.'

'I only meant if we were speaking of you, Beatrice.'

'Thank you for thinking of me,' she said. 'But I'm tired of it. I wish to think of more.'

And as he watched her leave, he could not escape the sensation that he was failing yet again. That he was not... It was not any better off with Beatrice than he had been with Serena. And worse, he wondered if Beatrice would be any happier.

Chapter Eight

Beatrice wondered if she would ever have a peaceful night's sleep. She worried about William and listened for his cries while she should be sleeping.

She rarely saw Briggs.

And as each lonely day stretched on—with Alice the governess not warming to her, with most meals eaten alone and nights stretching on endlessly, she realised this was truly no different than Bybee House.

Except she did not have her mother. She had no one here who cared about her at all.

Except perhaps William, but it was very difficult to say. Some days with him were lovely. Others...

He often became angry and lashed out. Afternoons seemed very hard for him. Beatrice could understand why Briggs wanted to protect him, but he was so bright and brilliant, and seeing him sequestered in isolation—as she was—felt wrong.

When she had lived at Bybee House she had cocooned herself in her innocence. She had not wished to look too deeply at the world around her.

Choosing to look at the bright colours of the frescoes and not too closely at the chips and cracks in the paint.

Not searching herself deeply for the truths of her parents' lives or their actions. She had instead focused on her own world. The one she created in the gardens alone. In her secret friendships.

In fantasy.

Yet her decision to fling herself into James's arms had been the first step away from that and into reality.

She had landed somewhere much…harder with Briggs.

In all the ways that could be taken.

Her foray into the real world was difficult and she felt as if she was shedding layers of down, her insulation against the harsher truths of life falling away.

She was not sure if she liked it.

But she could not help William if she turned away.

She was trying to sort out exactly how to broach the topic with Briggs, over a buttered roll with preserves, when Gates the butler walked into the room.

'Your Grace, Sir James Prescott to see you. Shall I tell him you're at home?'

Her heart lifted.

James.

The idea of seeing her friend made her almost giddy.

If Gates thought less of her because a man had come to call on her he did not show it. She had a feeling that had more to do with his sense of propriety regarding his position than it did with whether or not he actually judged her.

When James entered the room, it was as if the sun shone twice as bright on the pale blue and gold. And he was golden. Like the sun. She'd forgotten what it was like to have someone smile at her.

Gates nodded and left the room, leaving the doors open wide.

'James,' she said, 'I am so, so pleased you've called. Sit and I'll ring for tea.'

'Thank you, Bea,' he said, sitting and looking at her, his expression intent, and there was something about having her friend there, having someone who truly knew her and understood her look at her, when Briggs had been ignoring her, that made her eyes fill with tears. James's expression became alarmed. 'Are you well? He isn't being an ogre?'

She blinked heavily, annoyed at herself. 'He being my *husband*?' She dashed at one rogue tear that had slid down her cheek.

'Yes.'

'Why would he be an ogre?'

'You seem distressed.'

'Yes, but why would it make you think he is...unkind to me?'

James hesitated. 'There is a lot of talk about the Duke of Brigham. And his...proclivities. Though, I should not pay heed to gossip of that nature for clear reasons.'

Beatrice blinked, feeling as if she were missing a piece of the conversation again.

'To be as delicate as possible, he is a man of exotic tastes. Some might say perverse, though I never would.'

Briggs? Perverse?

She did not have a clear idea of what that might mean, except it called to mind someone who was twisted and warped in some way. One thing she could not imagine was her brother being friends with someone that were true of.

Much less allow her to marry him.

You are a ward, not a wife...

'I've seen no proof of anything of the kind,' she said, trying to smile.

'Probably a good thing.'

'What is that supposed to mean?'

James sighed and sat in the chair opposite her. 'That you are sweet. And men like him are not.'

'People keep saying I am sweet. Why is that? What have I done to suggest that I am?'

'You...'

'I am stupid, is what I am. I do not know enough people, I have not been educated broadly on enough topics, I have not done enough.'

'You are not stupid,' James said. 'You are innocent.'

'Well, I am tired of it.'

'Do you wish for him to take your innocence?'

She suddenly felt that same warmth she'd felt in the carriage. She was embarrassed, but...but James had told her his secrets. Secrets that could see him jailed. What did she have to fear with her friend? This dear, lovely friend who had put his faith in her in such a real way. 'I... It would be better if I knew what that meant.'

'There is nothing to know. Beatrice, I knew what I was, what I wanted, before I knew details or specifics. You do not need to know the full list of things one might do, to know you wish them.' She still felt confused, but she couldn't be angry because his smile was so gentle. 'The question is, do you want to be closer to him?'

'I...'

'Do you want to kiss him?'

Her face went hot. 'I do... I...'

'Then kiss him, Beatrice.'

'He said...'

'That has nothing to do with what he *wants*.'

Bea's breathing became short, harsh, and she could feel her heart beating in her temples. 'James, I cannot...'

'Whatever he says, Beatrice, you are his wife.'

She let out a long breath. 'Enough about me. Please. What are you doing?'

'I came to tell you I'm leaving.'

'Leaving?'

'Yes, I...am travelling to Rome with a friend.' The way he said friend was heavy.

'Will you stay there?'

'For a while at least.' He smiled. 'I'm happy, Beatrice.'

'I am very glad for you, I...'

She felt him before she saw him and when she looked up, her husband was in the doorway with all the subtlety of a storm. 'Your Grace,' James said, standing quickly. 'I came to say goodbye to your wife. I'm leaving the country.'

Briggs's eyes flickered over him. 'You must be James.'

He did not sound friendly, or impressed.

'Yes,' he said.

'In the future if you wish to call on my wife, you will ensure I am present.'

'He's my friend,' Beatrice said.

'He is the man you intended to marry. And I'll not be made a cuckold in my own home.'

'If you cannot give any credit to my honour, at least give it to hers,' James said.

Briggs looked at him, hard. 'I have nothing to fear from you, do I?'

The side of James's mouth kicked up. 'No. I am leaving, though, so if you wish to have me arrested it will have to be quick.'

'I am the last person on earth to have a man arrested for his inclinations.'

'Ah. I did wonder.' James turned to her. 'Remember what we talked about. Be you, Beatrice. And if that's not sweet, then don't be sweet.' He leaned in and kissed her cheek, and the feeling of affection that overwhelmed her nearly brought her to tears.

So few and far between were connections in her life.

'I will see you again, when I return.'

'Yes,' she said. 'Come to dinner. Bring your friend.'

He left her there with a squeeze of her hand and when she turned to face Briggs, his eyes were like ice.

'What were you thinking?'

Briggs couldn't account for the rage that was currently pouring through his veins.

'I was thinking that I would take tea with my friend, who came to sit with me. Which is more than you have done, Your Grace.'

He knew this side of her. He had seen it when she'd pushed at Hugh in her bedchamber. He had often admired her spirit, but he admired it much less now that she chose to use it against him.

'If my household were not so loyal to me, the scandal you might have caused...'

She laughed. 'Here I thought married women entertaining other men was de rigueur.'

The rage in his blood threatened to boil over. 'Not in my house.'

His tone was hard, uncompromising, and he could see the way she responded to it. The way her cheeks lit up like a beacon on a hill, a signal to a man like him that she would melt like butter if he were to place his hand on the back of her neck now...

She would go to her knees willingly.

He shut that thought down with ruthless precision.

'We are leaving for London in the morning,' he said, ready for a change of subject.

He had been enraged seeing her in here with another man, regardless of the fact he was not a man who would be interested in her. Regardless of the fact he was not supposed to want her.

He was eager to get out of this house.

He had grown to see Maynard Park as his own. For some reason, though, the demons of his childhood felt close now.

Perhaps because it was the very beginning of summer, with flowers beginning to bloom.

A reminder.

His father had died this time of year.

His father had also destroyed everything Briggs had cared about in June, and humiliated him while he did it.

'Briggs, I do wish you'd reconsider about William.'

The mention of William on the heels of the thoughts about his father brought him up short.

'No,' he said, his voice sharper than intended.

'Didn't your parents…?'

'I went nowhere. I stayed here.'

'Were you happy with that?'

Sometimes. Because it had meant living as he chose. Only doing what he enjoyed. Losing himself in his own world.

'You want to make everything simple,' he said, his voice rough. 'It is not simple. You are angry that you've been protected all your life, but you can't know whether or not that protection was necessary. You cannot know if you would have died without the intervention you were given.'

'I…no. I don't suppose I can know that.'

'You resent it but it might be the very thing that saved you. William may be lonely, but being exposed to other children might not be the best thing for him. It would not have been for me. I…am angry at my father. But on that he might have been right.' It cost him to say it, and to the end of his life he would not know why he had.

Except Beatrice was honest.

In all things.

And there was something about that honesty that seemed to demand it in return.

If there was one thing a man such as himself valued, it was the necessary balances in life.

She looked at him, her gaze far too insightful. 'Why are you angry at your father?'

'It is not important,' he said, his jaw going tense.

'It must be. For you to be angry after all this time.'

She was so guileless in her questions. As if she merely wished to know.

And it compelled him to answer.

'My father was cruel. He enjoyed that. Enjoyed making others feel small. He wielded power and control over those weaker than himself. And do you know what that makes him?'

'What?' she asked, her voice shrunken to a whisper.

'A coward. A real man, a man of honour, does not use his power in that way.'

'You don't use your power that way,' she said.

He looked at her and he wanted to…he wanted to cup her chin and hold her steady, hold her gaze until she had to look away.

He could use his power, his strength, to make her feel good.

And just then he felt desperate to do that. It would ease the ache in him as well, this restless fury that had been building since he had brought her here.

Perhaps it is her.

Another reminder of all you once hoped for.

All you can never have.

He pushed that aside.

He could not have her. Not like that. And he would not allow lingering memories of Serena, or of his father, to push him to violate his friendship with Hugh.

To put Beatrice at risk.

'No,' he said, finally. 'I do not.'

'What did your father…?'

'My father liked to humiliate. He liked those around him to feel small. Undone. And he could do so with a few well-placed words.' And actions. His father had not hesitated to take away whatever Briggs had found himself obsessed with.

He would wait, though.

Until he had invested time and himself into it. Would wait until the loss of it had an exacting, heavy cost.

'Briggs, I...'

'I am not an object to be pitied. My father is rotting in the ground and I am the Duke of Brigham.' He smiled, and he knew it did not reach his eyes. 'I may not be perfect in regard to William but what I want is for him to avoid shame.'

'I believe you. I do know that you only have his best interests at heart. I...'

'You just don't trust me. Because you're a foolish girl who has seen nothing of the world and yet is convinced she knows the right way of it.'

He successfully cowed her then. But she rallied, and quickly. 'Perhaps that is true. But my innocence has been forced upon me. I can learn. But what I see in William is not the product of inexperience. Quite the opposite. I recognise myself and it pains me.'

'You see loneliness. Because it is what you felt. I did not feel lonely here.'

'What did you feel?'

He felt a slow smile spread over his face. 'Rage.'

Chapter Nine

Beatrice knew that she should be excited. They were headed to London just before the Season started, and Briggs had promised her new dresses.

She was not feeling excited.

Not after the way everything had happened between the two of them. She was still upset about William, and Briggs's refusal to bring him. She was still upset about what had happened with James the day before, and still...

Deeply confused by the conversation they'd had after.

She was a jumble of feelings. None of which were sweet or strictly innocent.

Kiss him.

Her heart jolted. She did not wish to kiss him. She was angry at him.

For his heavy-handed behaviour. For the way he made her feel.

For what he made her want.

She was still ruminating on that, standing at the entry of the home, when William, Alice, and several more bags came down the stairs. 'What is this?' she asked Briggs, as he appeared alongside her.

'I thought about what you said,' he returned, his voice clipped.

'You thought about what I said?'

'Yes,' he said.

'And you changed your mind.'

'Yes,' he said. 'I changed my mind. William shall accompany us to London for the Season.'

It was difficult to tell if the boy was pleased or not. But she very much hoped that he was. She hoped that he would enjoy his trip, and she even hoped that she could be the one to take him to some of those places he was so interested in. Places she had never been either.

It was a five-hour carriage ride to London, and William was alternatively fidgety, fussy, quiet, and extremely talkative. He spent a good hour of the trip telling Beatrice each and every fact he possessed about Italian architecture. And there were quite a lot of them. Later she realised that it was the same time in the afternoon that she had first arrived at Maynard Park. When William had been screaming inconsolably.

They had to stop so that the little boy could relieve himself, and they paused the carriage, and rather than his governess accompanying him, it was Briggs who got out of the carriage.

Alice made a study out of avoiding any sort of eye contact with Beatrice. Which she supposed was probably common enough, but she didn't have anyone to talk to. She was older than governesses often were. She reminded Bea nothing of the little frothy blonde creatures her father had favoured putting her in the care of.

Though she had a feeling her governesses had not been selected because of the care they might give *her*. A thought that made her skin feel coated in oil.

She squirmed in her seat and thought about getting out simply to stretch her legs and get some distance between herself and the unfriendly woman.

But a moment later she heard a great wail, and the governess immediately departed the carriage. Beatrice wasn't far behind. William was on the ground, refusing to be moved. Briggs looked...grim, stone-faced, but determined.

'William,' he said, not raising his voice at all. 'We must get back in the carriage now.'

'I'm tired.' William was flopped, utterly, limply across the ground.

'It doesn't matter if you're tired. You cannot sleep here. You may sleep in the carriage.'

'I can't sleep in the carriage. It's too noisy.'

'William.'

'I can't. I can't. I can't.'

And that began a period of long repetition. Denials and recriminations. The young boy thrashed on the ground like a fish, and refused to be settled. He ground his heels into the soft mud, kicking and flinging rocks into the air.

Beatrice was frozen. She had no idea what to do, what to say. She felt useless.

And for the first time she wished she were back at Bybee House. Where she was safe. Where she could not cause the harm that she had clearly caused here by begging Briggs to bring William.

Finally, Briggs plucked him up from the ground and held him as close to his chest as possible while the boy squirmed.

'Back in the carriage,' he bit out to both Beatrice and the governess.

The governess obeyed quickly, but Beatrice stood and stared at him.

'Do you find there is something to gawk at?' he said.

'No,' Beatrice said. 'I'm not gawking.'

'You do rather a good imitation of someone who is.'

He moved past her, opening the carriage door and depositing William inside. William continued to howl unhappily.

'Get inside,' he said.

And she obeyed.

'William,' she said, trying to keep her tone placating. 'Didn't you want to see things in London?'

But he was simply screaming now, and there was nothing, seemingly nothing at all that could reach him. She did not know what to do, or how to proceed. And Briggs was only sitting there grim-faced, staring straight ahead.

'William,' she tried again, moving forward.

And was met with a short slap on the hand, directly from William, who screamed again, 'I can't.'

It didn't hurt, his slap, but it shocked her, and she drew back, clutching her hand.

Briggs leaned forward, plucked William up and held him in his arms, his hold firm, but not harming him in any way. 'William,' he said. 'You may not hit. Ever.'

'I can't. *I can't.*'

'William,' Briggs said.

'I'm not William.'

And neither of them said anything after that. They simply let him scream. Until he tired himself out, with only thirty minutes to spare before they arrived in London. The town house was lovely. But she could barely take it in. Or the excitement of being in London. She was too enervated by everything that had occurred on the ride. By how badly she had miscalculated. No wonder Briggs was so protective of William. No wonder he had been concerned about taking this journey. It was not because he hadn't wanted to take it on board. It was because it was devastating to watch William unravel in that fashion. And she hadn't realised it. Of course she hadn't. She had not listened.

Not really.

She had been so certain that she knew best, and she had been wrong.

William had drifted to sleep by the time they got inside, and it was Briggs who carried the limp little boy up the stairs. He said nothing to Beatrice, and she could hardly blame him.

'Your Grace.' The housekeeper in London, Mrs Dinsdale, put her hand on Beatrice's shoulder, as if sensing her distress.

'Oh, yes,' she said.

'You will find a lady's maid waiting for you. You may go and get freshened up for dinner.'

She dreaded it. Dreaded sharing a meal with Briggs. Of course he never shared meals with her out at Maynard Park. So perhaps, he would not do so here.

She was escorted to her room and introduced to the maid, and a collection of dresses she had never seen before. She was wrapped in something lovely and soft, a beautiful mint-green gown that scooped low, with no fichu to provide coverage for her bosom.

Her hair was arranged in a complicated fashion, with a string of pearls draped around her head like a crown.

How lovely she looked to take dinner by herself.

She went downstairs, her heart thundering madly, and predictably found the dining room... Empty.

'Might I take dinner in my bedchamber?' she asked one of the attending servants.

'Of course, Your Grace,' the man said.

She went back upstairs, and there she sat, looking quite the prettiest she ever had, in solitude.

Dinner was beautiful. And far too extensive for only her, but she ate her way through each course all the same. Mackerel with fennel and mint, roasted game, and pickled vegetables. Followed by a lovely tray of colourful marzipan, which she found she overindulged in.

She did not stop eating until her stomach turned.

And then she had her maid undress her, take her hair down,

and put the pearls back in their box. And she looked in the mirror and found that she had become Beatrice again. Just her usual self, with nothing of any great interest about her at all. And she felt exceedingly sorry for herself.

You should feel sorry for William.

She did not understand. But then, he was a child. It was likely he did not have the ability to connect the fact that the journey was what was going to take him to those places that he longed so to see. If he could not endure a journey such as this, how did he ever hope to reach Italy? But these were all things a seven-year-old could likely not reason, she told herself. But it did not make her less frustrated.

Nor did it help her sleep. Long after she should have extinguished her candle, she tried to read.

She tried to read *Emma*, but found she was too furious at the contents to enjoy it. And the illustrated compendium of birds was not compelling enough to hold her interest.

She paced the length of the room, practically wearing a hole in the floor. She looked out of the window, and felt compelled to escape. As she had done so many times at Bybee House.

If she could've crawled out of her own skin she would have done so, but failing that, she simply contented herself with fleeing the house.

And so, she did so here.

She opened the door to the bedchamber and quietly made her way down the stairs.

She did not know if there was a back garden, but she assumed so. And she was not disappointed. It was a lovely space, bathed in moonlight, with a massive fountain, surrounded by several statues.

Nude statues.

It was *very* Roman. William, she thought with grim humour, would likely find it quite interesting.

She found herself staring at a naked warrior, clothed only in a helmet, which she felt left him vulnerable in many other ways.

Briggs had asked her if she knew what made a man and a woman different.

Of course she knew. She was not an idiot.

He had said it was so they could... Fit together. Make a child. The idea made her flush all over. For imagining such an intimate part of herself fitted against...

Kiss him.

She swallowed hard.

Who gets to decide?

She circled the statue, examining the powerful thighs, the rather muscular-looking derrière. At least, this took her mind off the disastrous carriage ride. Yes. It was a very different sort of body. Though it was made of stone. Perhaps that was why it appeared so hard. She knew Briggs was solid though. Not like her at all.

A sound made her turn, and she saw Briggs, standing in the doorway. He was not dressed for bed, rather, he was dressed to go out. He was standing there, looking through the glass. And she felt inexplicably quite caught out.

She moved away from the statue, and waited to see what he might do. If he would turn away and continue on as he had intended to do, or if he would come out to her.

She did not have to wait long for her answer.

The door opened.

'And are you trying to tempt brigands to scale my garden wall and kidnap you?' he asked. The words were like the Briggs she'd known for much of her life. The tone was not.

'I had no aspirations of such,' she said, turning away from him.

'You only wished to leer at my statuary?'

'I was not leering. I was admiring the artistry.'

'Of course,' he said. 'How could I be so foolish? A lady such as yourself would never do anything half so…interesting.'

'Briggs…'

'I only came to check that you were well.'

'I am not well,' she said. 'I fear that I made things incredibly difficult by pushing you to bring William on the trip, and I… I am deeply… Deeply sorry, and so very… I did not mean to upset him. Or you.'

'But the end result is that you have,' Briggs said. 'And there is nothing to be done for that.'

'I am sorry,' she said.

'It doesn't matter,' he said.

'It clearly does.'

'No. It does not. I made the decision in the end to bring him. It is done.' He looked past her, into the darkness, then back at her. 'Do not stray from the garden.'

'I would not.'

'You are in London, now, and you must take care. You will not leave the house without accompaniment. This garden being the exception.'

'Yes. Sorry, I had quite forgotten that I was your ward, and in no way your equal.'

'Even if you were my wife, you would not be my equal.'

She sucked in a sharp breath at the barb, that she had a feeling did not reflect what he thought about anything, but rather was designed to harm her. And it had. Why was she so fragile where he was concerned? It made no sense. And yet, he made her feel as if she was made of broken glass.

Why did he have this power over her?

It was something beyond friendship, for theirs was no easy companionship. She resented the way he avoided her when she should not care about it at all. His disdain hurt. She did not understand how they had got here.

It had changed since he had touched her by the fire in her brother's study.

And again after he'd pushed her on the swing.

And most of all after they had married, after the carriage ride.

It should have worked, this arrangement. And yet nothing about it did.

'Of course not.'

He turned away from her.

'And where is it you are going?' she asked.

'I do not have to answer to you.'

'That in and of itself is an answer. And *such* an answer,' she said. 'Why you do not simply wish to tell me…'

'I am going to a brothel, Beatrice, are you familiar with the term?'

His face looked cruel now, and she hated this. This was not the man who had brought her sweets. This was a dark and furious stranger, the man who had compelled her to stare across the ballroom on that night, the man who captured her breath.

She knew that he was angry, but there was something in his cold, quiet fury that made her feel sick.

'No,' she said. 'I… I don't know what that means.'

Perhaps it pertained to his duties at the House of Lords. But judging by the expression on his face she knew that it did not.

For that would not hurt her. And right now, he wished to hurt her. She could feel it.

'It is where a man goes when he wishes to purchase the company of a woman.'

That immediately brought to mind an image of Briggs sitting down to tea with a lady, and she was absolutely certain that was the wrong image to be in the middle of her head, and yet there it was.

'Still confused?' he asked, and his tone was unkind.

'Stop it,' she said, feeling angry now. 'You are aware of the gap in my knowledge on certain things, given the cloistered life that I had led, and it is one thing to acknowledge them, but it is quite another to cruelly take pleasure in them.'

'I cannot help what I cruelly take pleasure in, Beatrice. Perhaps I am a much crueller man than you have any idea of.'

'I should hope not. For I am your ward. And what ward should like a cruel guardian?'

His lips curved. Beautiful. Painful. 'I suspect you might enjoy my cruelty.'

'I am *not currently*,' she bit out. 'As it happens.'

'When I speak of female company, I mean shagging, Beatrice.'

She wanted to howl at him in frustration. 'I don't know what shagging is.'

'It is what men and women do. And it is not for procreation. It is for pleasure. A man and his wife might engage in such acts for procreation, but there are a great many things that a person can do to pursue pleasure.'

Her head was pounding, her temples aching.

'And you are... You are off to seek them with other women.'

'I will not seek them with you.'

'And so you go to a brothel to seek them out with other women. And you would throw it in my face while not giving me information on exactly what it entails. So if you wish to harm me, do so by speaking plainly, rather than speaking around the truth of the matter.'

'I am off to screw my way to oblivion. To forget everything that happened this day. To forget that you are my wife. To forget that my son is here. That is what I intend to do. And if you should like a more graphic description of all that I shall do, I am sorry to disappoint you. I can see that you are quite interested in a man's cock, judging by how closely you were studying the statue. Mine will be inside another woman tonight.'

It was so cool it took her breath away, and she still could not quite sort out why, except the idea of him sharing intimacies she was barely able to wrap her mind around made her want to vomit in the nearest shrub. And she knew that he wanted her to be hurt. That was the clearest and most obvious piece. What he was saying was designed to be harmful.

And he well knew it.

And before she could gather a response, he turned and walked away. She stood there, stunned for a moment, breathing in the sharp night air. And then she ran after him. Just in time to watch him walk out through the front door.

She stood there, feeling tender, hurt. She did not want him to touch another woman. She was beginning to piece it all together, of course. For these were all the mysterious acts that must follow kissing. She had never even partaken in such a thing, and…

Of course he would seek out other company. Even if she were his wife in truth he would likely find her boring, and her ignorance tiring.

She was tired of her ignorance.

She was tired. Tired of everyone else deciding what was best for her. Tired of her own limitations.

She was tired.

And still, she could not sleep.

She decided that she would wait up for him to arrive home. Even if it destroyed her to do it.

Usually, a visit to Madame Lissanne's was like a visit to an old friend. The velvet brocade and access typically felt like a homecoming. But not tonight. Tonight, his stomach was acid. He was angry, and he had taken it out quite unfairly on Beatrice. Beyond that, he had been intentionally as crass and mean as possible, and it was not what he had promised Hugh that he would do as husband to his sister. Truly, the only piece of his word that he had kept was that he had not visited his desires upon her. No. He would do that here. If Pamela was available, he would see her. She was curvy and lush, and excelled in her submission. Her demure manner would be a welcome change to Beatrice's sulky mouth.

Here, he was treated like a king. Here, he was given a glass of his preferred whisky, and ushered to a bedchamber to wait for a woman who suited his desires and was available. And indeed, it was Pamela. She offered him a shy smile, her eyes not meeting his.

And he waited. For a rising feeling of excitement. For desire. For something. He waited to feel what he should for a woman this beautiful. A woman he knew performed exceedingly well.

She made her way across the room, to where he sat, then dropped to her knees before him. She reached forward, making for the buttons on his trousers.

'No,' he said. 'I did not tell you to touch me.'

Colour swept across her cheeks, and she looked away. 'I'm sorry, Your Grace.'

And for some reason, when she said those words, he thought only of Beatrice. And how the words sounded on her lips. And he felt... Guilt. Guilt that he was here when he had married Beatrice. Most of all, over the way that he had treated her prior to coming to the brothel.

'Stand. Take your dress off.'

She complied, removing her gown, and revealing that she had nothing on underneath.

Her body was lovely, her mons waxed clean, and normally, he would be feeling some sense of desire or excitement. He felt nothing. And perversely, she looked absolutely aroused by his complete uninterest. If only his uninterest were feigned. But it was not.

He could obviously proceed. But he was too furious. And the woman he needed to be dealing with was not here.

'I'm sorry.' He stood, walked forward and grabbed hold of her chin. 'I'm not in need of your services tonight. I will still issue payment.'

'Have I done something wrong?' Whether or not hers was a desire to truly please, or concern she was losing a valuable client, he did not know. But it didn't matter either.

That she made it impossible to tell was why she was so good at what she did.

'The problem is with me. And I must go and sort it out.' The money would be put on his ledger, and he would settle the account later. There was no need for anything quite so common as for money to change hands then and there. He walked out of the den of iniquity and on to the far too busy streets. Then he began the journey home. And he called himself every foul name he could think of.

He tore through the front door of the town house, intent on taking himself up to his bedchamber. And he saw that she was still outside.

He could see that sweet, white nightgown, which she had been wearing the night that he had come upon her in the swing.

She turned, eyes wide. 'Seems a rather short visit to a brothel,' she said, but her face betrayed her shock.

'You have no idea how long such matters should take.'

'Perhaps not. But given the severity of your manner when you left, I expected it to be a rather long night.'

'And here you are.'

'Do not flatter yourself. If you are suggesting that you think I was waiting for you...'

'I would never suggest such a thing,' he said.

'Why are you here?'

'Because,' he said, taking a step towards her, 'of you.'

'What have I done?'

His blood was boiling now. And he knew that he should not move even one fraction of an inch towards her. But he did. He did, and as he did, his desire drew up tight inside him like a bow. And he was on the edge of control. Which did not happen to him. He was a man who prized control above all else.

It was his linchpin. The most important thing to a man such as him. He could never afford to be out of control. Not ever.

'Ask me your questions.'

'I have no more questions for you. Except perhaps why you insist on treating me so poorly?'

'You wish to know the secrets of the universe. You wish to insert yourself into my life. Do you wish for me to stop protecting you?'

He could see her running quick mental calculations. He could also see that she had no idea what he was asking. And it was not a kindness that he was doing it.

'You wish to step into this role in William's life. You wish to understand the world. You wish to be trusted to go to war. Then you tell me now. What is it you wish to learn?'

'Everything,' she said, the words exiting her mouth in a rush.

And then he reached the end of it. The end of everything.

And he took a step forward, wrapping his arm around her waist and drawing her up to his chest. He could feel her breasts pressed against him, lush and supple. And the way she looked up at him, her eyes full of wonder, did something to him that he could not adequately describe.

He could kiss her. But instead, he gave in to a much darker temptation. He put his hand on the back of her head, grabbed hold of the thick braid that hung down the centre of her back, and tugged, hard.

Chapter Ten

Beatrice's heart was thundering like a galloping horse. The sharp pain that started at the base of her neck spread out over her skull, delightful prickles of sensation cascading over her, and uncomfortable warmth.

And she felt... Fortified. Strong. Held tight there in Briggs's hold. And she could not understand why this was happening. Why he was now standing so close to her, why he was making her feel this way. And why he had the power to do so.

He had told her that for some pleasure and pain was one in the same. And the deep, curling sensation at her midsection made her feel he had been right. And more unsettling, she had a feeling he had known he would be right about her.

He was looking at her with a blazing heat that spoke only of confidence. He had known that he could do this. That she would not cry out or pull away from him. He had known that she would want to press herself more closely to him.

It was his certainty that rooted her to the spot.

It was his certainty that intrigued her.

That infuriated her.

The certainty of this... This man who was infinitely harder than the stone statues all around them.

He pulled again, and forced her chin to tilt upwards. Tears gathered at the corners of her eyes, and she withstood. She felt proud. Infinitely so. For she was strong. And free.

Here, in this moment, she felt as if she was proving it. Not just to him, but to herself. To anyone who had ever found her weak.

This was her moment, to step into the role of warrior. Prove she could withstand.

And that thought alone brought her an infinite sense of satisfaction.

And then his mouth, oh, his mouth. It was on hers, and it was not the stuff of romance and softness. It was a hard sort of heat that she had never imagined. It was devastation. Each movement of his lips was expert and, combined with the intense tug on her hair, made her feel as if she were drowning.

Oh, she felt she was drowning.

And then, he slid his tongue between the seam of her lips, and her legs folded. But he caught her. By her hair. And the resulting tug drew a scream from her lips that he swallowed. His hold was firm, and he did not let her collapse completely. Briggs would never let her collapse completely, and in spite of everything, she felt that to be true. In spite of all the anger that had just passed between them, she trusted that.

She trusted him.

She found herself being pushed backwards, right up against that naked male statue. Because she had been right. Briggs was just as hard. But he was hot. The marble was cold beneath her back, and it dawned on her slowly, as she shifted her gaze for a moment to stare at the statue, that the very hard thing she could feel pressed against her stomach was...

Well, if she was correct, the statue paled in comparison to Briggs.

He was kissing her. She could not quite believe it. Did that mean that he... Did that mean that he wanted her?

She was so new to this. To the idea of desire. Of want. But he had said that people did this for reasons other than procreation. He had said that it was about pleasure. And pain.

And then she found the top of her gown, the chemise beneath, being pushed away, revealing her breasts.

He took a step away, only for a moment, and stared down at her, his expression hungry.

She was confident in that. His expression held hunger. She did not know how, but it was as if some ancient wisdom inside her body had materialised for this moment.

And she did not feel confused. Somehow, the absurdity of her lips meeting his, of his tongue sliding against hers, crystallised these mysteries, and if anyone had asked her how it would do that, she would have said she did not know. She would've said it was impossible. She would have said that she did not wish to be licked by Briggs, and yet now she knew she did. And that she wished to lick him in return.

He moved forward, holding her breast with one large hand. And then he pinched her. Slowly, carefully, applying even pressure to one tightened bud. And then, he made it hard.

She cried out, pain radiating through her body, an answering echo between her thighs. And it was like an exultant hallelujah chorus. A burst of bright, sharp hope echoing through her body.

A wash of strength pouring itself over her like liquid gold, coating all that she was and reinforcing her.

She felt like a warrior in this moment.

Real. True.

She felt weightless. And she felt fearless. And then, he moved to the other side, but he did not build his pressure quite so slowly; this time he clamped down, his eyes making contact with hers as he did so.

Until she had to let her head fall back against the statue's abdomen and surrender. She closed her eyes and shivered, shook, as pleasure and pain mingled together until she could not sort one from the other. Indeed, she wondered if they were different.

For one showed her that she could withstand, and the other was the reward for that patience. For that endurance. Then he fastened his mouth to her neck, sucking hard, before returning to her lips and kissing her, kissing her until she couldn't breathe. Until she was senseless. But then, perhaps she had already been senseless. Then he bit her lip at the same time he pinched her again, and she felt something unravel inside her, and then bloom. And it radiated through her in a wave. On and on and she could barely breathe. Could barely think. And it reminded her of dying. Like when she would lose her breath and float towards that space where there was no sound, no light.

And then bursts of fireworks.

The vision of something bigger, greater than herself. And when it subsided, she shuddered. And slid down the statue. All the way to the ground.

And Briggs stood above her, his gaze something like triumphant, and something like terrifying.

He bent down, and gripped her chin. 'You did well.'

And she realised she was shaking. Shivering from the cold and from something else that she could not name. She found herself gathered up into his arms and held close to his chest. And then he lifted her up off the ground, and carried her into the house, carried her up the stairs. Her heart leapt like a wild thing. She didn't know where he was taking her. Or what would happen next. He took her to her room. And laid her gently on the bed, his manner suddenly soothing and entirely different to the way it had been moments before.

'Sleep,' he said.

'Briggs,' she whispered.

'Please,' he said. 'Do not speak.'

'But I need to… I need to know. Are you going back to the brothel?'

'No,' he said, his tone hard.

'Please don't.'

'I do not answer to you, darling wife.'

'I know. I do not wish you to go, though. And I would hope that that matters, whether or not you must obey me.'

'I will not return to the brothel tonight.'

And that she knew was the best she would get from him. But was that what he went to the brothel to do? To touch other women like that? To make them… She had no idea what he had done to her. She had never felt anything like it. It was like nothing she had ever experienced before, and she was desperate to experience it again. But also terrified. Because the way that it made her feel… Desperate and aching and restless inside… Well, she did not particularly care for that. That, she found, was almost entirely unbearable. She wanted him to hold her. She realised that with stunning clarity. But all of the confidence that she felt in that moment, all of the strength and brilliance and perfection seemed to fall away from her. She was simply… Undone. And she hated it. As much as she had loved all that had come before.

For a moment, she had felt strong. For a moment, she felt like a warrior. For a moment, she had felt like a woman. And now she was just back to being Beatrice. And it was enough to make her dissolve.

Chapter Eleven

Briggs was in hell. Because he had spectacularly ruined everything last night. And she had been... She had been a triumph. She was everything that he had suspected she was. And what a cruel joke that his best friend's younger sister should be made quite so perfectly in such a twisted, glorious fashion that she could fit up against every kink in him? It was a cruelty. But she had come apart in his arms from just a bit of pain and pleasure, and he had a feeling that were he to push her further, faster, they would find heights together that... It did not bear thinking about.

Today, he had to deal with his son.

Today, he would be taking him to see the sights around London. For they had endured the trip all for that. On one score he suspected Beatrice might be right. That if William had the distraction of those things which he was most interested in, he would weather everything else quite well.

And after that nightmare of the trip, there had to be some compensation. He was practised enough in the art of indulging himself in a bit of mastery and then going back to being the Duke of Brigham, and father to William, without allowing any of the night's previous indulgence to affect him in any way. Or to linger into the day. And yet he felt affected by this. By his indiscretion in the garden with Beatrice.

An indiscretion with your wife? A new low, and who knew you could still reach those?

He would laugh, but it wasn't funny. Nothing about the damned situation was funny.

He decided to find William and try to ply the boy with toast and drinking chocolate prior to presenting him with the day's itinerary. If he knew one thing about managing William, it was that an itinerary was very important, but he had to be sure to stick to it, because if he did not, then his son would be sure to let him know all the ways in which he had failed. And the point of this was not to fail.

But when he arrived at his son's room, Beatrice was already there, sitting on the floor beside him, engaged in what looked like a very intense conversation about shoes.

'Good morning,' he said.

She looked up at him, a deep blush staining her cheeks, and something inside him roared in satisfaction. She was remembering last night too.

She had been beautiful.

He could teach her.

Fire, excitement, licked along his veins. He could teach her. She would be a beautiful student. And she would...

No. *No.*

'William and I were discussing going for a walk,' she said.

'I have plans for the day,' Briggs said. 'No engagement scheduled whatsoever, because I am intent upon taking William to see London.'

William looked up at him, and there was visible excitement in his eyes. William was not a bubbly child. He did not show exuberance in the same way other children did, and while Briggs did not have experience with other children, he could see the differences between them and his own son. But he had learned to accept the excitement that William felt. To treasure those moments. For they were rare and precious when his son put his joy on full display. And sometimes he pitied other fathers, for he felt the outward joy of their children was so cheap they might never learn to value it. Briggs on the other hand treated every smile like a piece of gold.

'I have a complete list of what we might do today,' Briggs said.

'What time?' William asked.

'First it will be toast. And drinking chocolate. And then our day will begin.'

'What time?'

And Briggs knew that he had to choose his answer very carefully. He checked his timepiece. 'How about we leave the house at ten thirty?'

'Yes,' William agreed.

'But you must wear shoes,' Beatrice said, looking slightly triumphant.

'I will wear shoes,' William said, looking at Beatrice as if she had grown another head. And Briggs could only be amused by that.

'Can I join you?'

'For toast?' William asked.

'For the day?' She directed that question at Briggs.

He was about to issue a denial, when William turned to look him in the face, which was so rare that Briggs could not help but be completely taken back by it.

'She must come,' he said.

'I had thought,' Briggs said, 'that it would be just men.'

'But that would be boring,' William said. 'Because Beatrice is not boring.'

'*Beatrice*, is it?' Briggs asked, wondering what the boy should call her, but certain it should not be her first name.

'Yes,' she said. 'I asked him to call me Beatrice.'

'Because we are friends,' William said. 'She calls me William.'

He could not argue with this unassailable logic. It was quite annoying.

'Then of course Beatrice shall accompany us, but I will have hurt feelings that you think I'm boring.'

'I did not say you were boring,' William said. 'I said Beatrice was not boring.'

And he could not argue with that either. Instead, he found himself going down to breakfast with them, where toast for William, and coffee and eggs and meat awaited the three.

'I am pleased that we are going on an outing,' Beatrice said.

'I'm not an ogre,' he said. 'I would not bring William here and not take him to see the city.'

'But you would bring me and have me not see it?'

'You will see it in time. There will be balls...'

'That is not the same,' she said.

'Have you not been to London?'

'I have been to London once. I did not see the sites. I spent my days shut up in Hugh's town house. And I was sent home early. For he had concerns regarding my well-being, and the quality of the air.' She did not elaborate. But she looked like she might want to.

'And?'

'I had a fit with my breathing. It upset him greatly, it was the first time I had one in a very long time. And he sent me home.'

'You find your breathing well now?'

Anger burned through him.

She should tell him these things. She should tell him it was dangerous for her to be in London.

'I'm fine,' she said. 'I have not had the same sort of maladies that I had all those years ago. I was fourteen when that happened, and I have been quite well since. Please do not make this about my illness. I find that far too many things are.'

'I will not worry, but you will tell me if you feel ill.'

'I will.'

'Are you sick?' William asked, and he looked terribly concerned. 'My mother was very sick.'

Beatrice's face contorted with alarm.

'No, William. I am not sick like that. I was very sick when I was a young child. That's all.' Except she had no real idea what kind of sick Serena was. But then, neither did William.

'Good,' William said decisively. 'I do not wish for you to die.'

'I am glad to hear it,' Beatrice said.

He and Beatrice made eye contact, and her cheeks flushed again.

He looked at William, who was now absorbed in his toast, though he had a feeling that at exactly ten twenty-nine his son would emerge from wherever it was he went to let them know that they were in danger of running behind.

'You slept well?' he asked, where he was being provocative.

'No,' she responded. 'I did not.'

There were a great many things he could say in response to that, but he decided that none of them would be in particular aid of the situation.

'I'm sorry to hear it.'

'I was lonely.'

'I could not have stayed,' he said, hearing his voice go gruff.

She looked at him for a long while. A litany of questions was in her blue eyes and he did not wish to answer any of them. 'Why?'

'Do not ask questions you are not prepared to hear the answer to.'

'Do not assume what I am prepared for. You, like everyone else, underestimate me.'

'I do not underestimate you, but neither do I forget the reality of your health.'

'Is it truly me you worry for? Or are you simply obeying my brother's orders?'

He frowned. 'I worry for you. And of course I respect what Kendal has asked of me...'

'I know my brother made it clear you must watch out for me. But he is not here. And I am fine.'

'I do not trust you to always make the best decision when it comes to your own needs,' he said.

'That is a shame,' she said. 'Because I do. And I should like it if even one person gave me the benefit of being treated like a woman. You have done so once,' she said, her blue eyes meeting his, crackling with heat. 'Is it not hypocritical to treat me only as a woman when it suits you, and to otherwise relegate me to the position of ward?'

'Is it not hypocritical of you to ask for something and then attempt to use it against me?'

'I have asked for one thing,' she said. 'With consistency. To be treated as if I know my own mind, and to be given the freedom that I feel I deserve. I did not act counter to those wishes last night. I did what I wanted.'

She wanted.

He knew exactly what she wanted.

He could give it to her.

'It is time to go.' Just as Briggs had known he would, William returned to them as if an internal timepiece had told him that they were nearing the moment Briggs had said they would leave.

He was grateful. Because he did not wish to continue this conversation. He felt perilously close to the edges of dreams he'd had years ago. That perhaps he was not so bent, he only had to find the woman who would decide to bend around him.

He could pay women to do so, but part of him had always desired...

The hunger he saw in Beatrice's face.

And yet he could not. They could not.

With Alice and attendants, they got into the carriage.

It was not just the look of wonder on William's face that Briggs found himself captivated by. But Beatrice's.

He had forgotten what it was like to look around the world and see anything new, but everything was new to her.

The sights, the sounds, they were significant to her. Special. And it filled him with a deep sense of pride to be the person to have shown her.

And of course, it was unavoidable, he could not help but compare it to the pleasure that she had been shown last night. In his arms, she had fallen apart, and he had prevented her from splintering. He wanted to know if she had ever felt that manner of pleasure before. If she had found it with her own hand. He enjoyed that image very much.

Beatrice, laying on her bed, her hand between her thighs...

He wanted to know so many things, and he wanted to show her so much more, and yet, he knew that it was impossible.

Why? You said so yourself, there are many things that can be done without producing a child.

It was true. However, while he enjoyed games of self-control, there were limits. And while he believed himself to be a man of extreme control, and in fact enjoyed that as an aspect to his bed sport, eventually, he would need to be inside a woman. That was just how it worked. He was not a man who could forgo being inside a woman forever. And if he were to play with her physically, it was possible she would be hurt by his need to take his fulfilment with other women. And it was just best, easiest, if these things remained separate.

Is it not too late for that?

It was not too late. Not if he determined in himself that it wasn't.

They first stopped at Westminster, and walked around the outside, with William exclaiming about the architecture, and offering titbits about timelines in the construction.

They went to St James's afterwards, and took a distant look around the grounds. He had no wish to be accosted by the Duke of Cumberland and forced to take part in the conversation he did not wish to have.

William took equal delight in all aspects of the way the city was put together. From the intricate network of roads to the different buildings, whether or not they were famous. Briggs knew that his son's knowledge of architecture and infrastructure was astonishing, but he had truly had no idea of the breadth of it.

There were things that William knew about London that Briggs himself did not, and even if he had known it at some point, he would've forgotten it. William seemed to forget nothing. Particularly not if it involved numbers and dates.

'I have learned so much,' Beatrice said, beaming, tilting her head back and letting the sun wash over her face.

She was a rare beauty, was Beatrice.

If she had made a formal debut in society when she should have, she would have been a diamond of the first water. Would have been considered a triumph for any man. The sister of a duke, with a large dowry, incomparable innocence and extreme beauty. It was a farce that she should be limited as she was. An absolute injustice.

She seemed happy, though, and that pleased him. Right now, she was happy.

She could be happy with him. They did not have to be at odds. He thought of her as she'd been last night, furious with him, and then fire in his arms. No. There was no reason for them to play in extremes.

He could simply care for her. While he could no longer deny that he wanted her, there was a measure of satisfaction that stirred in him over the idea of simply...being with her.

Caring for her.

Showing her new sights, buying her new dresses.

'Rome is best,' William said matter-of-factly, with all the authority of a small boy who had only for the first time truly travelled away from home.

'I should like to see Rome some day,' Beatrice said, looking over at him.

'I have a feeling I will be outnumbered in votes for this venture,' Briggs said. 'However, I am a duke, so I don't know that I can truly be outnumbered.'

'I don't know,' Beatrice said. 'William is quite persuasive.'

'At times.'

Beatrice laughed. 'Isn't that true of all of us? It is said that you catch more flies with honey than vinegar, but sometimes it is so satisfying to speak with vinegar, that whatever the result might be is sincerely worth the diminished returns.'

'Is that so?'

'Yes. Anyway, being sweet eternally is terribly boring.'

'How would you know? You have never been endlessly sweet or biddable.'

She looked surprised by that. Did she not realise he always took note of her?

'Indeed not,' Beatrice said. 'Because I find the prospect so unappealing.'

'You are a wretched minx, do you know that?'

She wrinkled her nose. 'I quite like that. I shall take on the mantle of wretched minx for all of my days. For it is much more interesting than poor, sickly Beatrice.'

'I doubt anyone has ever referred to you as poor, sickly Beatrice.'

'Untrue,' she said. 'It is heavy in the tone of every servant in my brother's house, and in the way my own mother looks at me. She is filled with sorrow on my behalf. I find it tiring. All I hear is how sweet I am, but what that means is that I do not fight with those around me all day every day. I have no choice in my life, and that I do not kick constantly against it has earned me the label of sweet.'

'Beatrice,' he said. 'You're not a thing to be pitied. There is much in life set before us that we are shown is the right thing, but...' He looked down at William, who was focusing on the details carved into a parapet. And he allowed him. 'I achieved everything that I was meant to by the time I was twenty-three. I had my wife, my heir. It did not produce happiness. I do not speak of William. William has brought me...'

He felt *happiness* was an insipid word, and not truly the correct one. Being a father was not an endless parade of smiling. He was a duke who could have staff members see to William the entirety of the time if he so chose, but it would not make a difference, as William was ever present on his mind, as were his concerns for him. And so he found it was best to spend time with his son. Perhaps much more time than most men in his position would. But seeing him, understanding him in this way, rather than in relayed messages from staff, was truly the only thing that actually made him feel like William would be fine. For when he saw him like this, out in the world and filled with joy, when he was able to hear about the things that sparked his son's imagination, then they connected. And then, somehow, he had a glimmer of hope that all would be well.

Still, happiness was not...

'William added depth to me. That was not there before. Being his father is perhaps the greatest challenge of my life. But it has made me a better man. Still, there is happiness outside of these prescribed roles. And sometimes there is little happiness to be found in them. My first marriage did not produce happiness.'

He needed her to understand this. Perhaps just now. As

they were in public, as they were safe from it all becoming too intimate, even as he spoke of things he often left in the dark corners of his memory.

He was not being cruel for the sake of it.

It was clear to him Beatrice would welcome his touch. At least, as she understood it. But disquiet remained, in his soul.

For he had believed he had a connection with Serena, and he had been wrong.

For he had missed the signs that she was so deeply un-happy she no longer wanted to live. That she no longer loved him had been clear. But the rest...

He had not known.

And the feeling he had caused it, contributed to it, by tell-ing her of his desires to be dominant with her in their bed, stuck in him.

They continued to stroll along the walk, the sun filtering over the grass, the flowers and the gold of the palace.

'What of ours, Briggs? Is it to be more of what we had last night?' She did not look at him when she asked the question.

She might not look at him, but he did look at her. Her bravery, her honesty, lit brilliantly by the sun, amazed him.

Shamed him.

'An impossibility, I'm afraid.'

'You regret it so?'

'Beatrice...'

'Only I'm just beginning to understand. Desire. Desiring another person, and what that means. Is it that you do not desire me?'

He curled his hands into fists, for if he did not he did not think he could resist touching her. 'If I did not desire you, last night would not have occurred.'

'I am your wife. Why should it be a complication for you to desire me?'

'Because of the rules we must fulfil for each other. Be-cause of the way that I have been tasked with protecting you, and you can be angry about it all you like, but it does not change the way of things. I care for your brother a great deal, and promises were made to him.'

'It is not his life,' she said. 'It is mine.'

'And I'm your husband. So your life is mine now.'

'What a scintillating conclusion to have come to,' she said.

'You are mine, and that means I will care for you, as I said. I don't think you understand truly what that means.'

Of course she did. She didn't understand the deep... It was primal. The thing in him that demanded he care for that which was his. When he took a woman into his bed, her pleasure and her satisfaction, walking the line between pleasure and pain perfectly, was of the utmost importance to him. But even more, ensuring that Beatrice found happiness, that she was well-clothed and well fed, with her favourite foods...

Remember how you used to bring her sweets?

He stilled, locking his back teeth together.

And he refused to acknowledge that. The idea that all along he had been drawing her to him. Baiting her as if she were a small animal. Feeding her sweets.

None of what had happened between them was planned.

And when she threw herself at you in the library, and you slid your hand down to her arse, what exactly did you think you were doing?

He had known it was her.

Of course he had.

He was a man who paid great attention to detail.

A man who had been consumed with the details of her from the moment he'd met her.

And no, he had not thought of her beauty when she had been a girl. It had been her resilience, her sadness, her wildness.

But he had *known* her.

And he had known her when she'd gone into his arms.

'There is much you don't know of the world. We will find happiness together in it. But you must trust me.'

She looked up at him, her eyes filled with scepticism. And he could not stop himself. He reached out and took hold of her chin, gripping it tightly between his thumb and forefinger. 'You must trust me.'

She looked away. 'I don't think I can.'

'If you cannot trust me in this, you would not have been able to trust me with more.'

Her eyes flashed up to his. 'With...'

He released his hold on her. 'Let us walk this way, William. You wish to see St James's Park?'

'Yes,' William responded, never quicker with an answer than when everything was going his way.

That was not fair. It was not about getting his way, it was about being in this perfect space where there was no resistance being brought against him by the things that he found challenging in the world.

Briggs understood that. He remembered being a boy and finding peace only in books, and then in the hours spent seeing to the health of his orchids. He understood how engaging his own brain could be when it was occupied by things that were important to him.

And how difficult the world could feel when he did not connect with what was happening.

It was not a choice to be bad or misbehave, but a strange reordering of his brain, as if all of the pieces of his mind had been shoved into an overcrowded corner, leaving him in part overwhelmed and the other disconnected.

He had better control over these things now. But he still remembered when he was at the mercy of his emotions.

They turned and began to walk towards the park, Beatrice next to him, the wind now against her. And he did his best to ignore just how appealing she smelled to him. And it was nothing to do with the rose water she had likely placed just beneath her earlobes. And everything to do with the smell of her skin.

He had tasted her last night. She had been marvellous.

He would've thought that it would be the easiest thing in all the world to protect his best friend's younger sister in this position. For he had no interest in a wife, and he'd seen Beatrice as a child...

Did you?

He did not like this insidious voice searching inside himself for truth. He was not interested in his truth. He was interested, rather, in maintaining things as they were. And not allowing them to deteriorate.

St James's Park was filled with those intent on taking advantage of the sunshine, a veritable menu of societal elite, promenading so as to be seen by those who mattered. Briggs had never had the patience for such things. It was perhaps why he had married as quickly as he had done. For participating in the marriage mart, in these sorts of games, had not been his idea of intrigue at any point.

And now that he was back here, it was thankfully with a wife in tow, so as not to bring any marriage-minded mothers and their debutantes his way.

Beatrice herself looked delighted by the spectacle, and her delight only increased her beauty. He could feel the envious gazes of men around him.

Truly, these fashionable dresses with their boldly scooped necklines flattered Beatrice in an extreme fashion. Her tits were a glory. That he knew well, as he'd had them in his mouth.

Desire was like a raging beast in him, right here in the sunshine in the full view of so many people, with his son so near.

And that was something unfamiliar.

He separated these parts of his life. For him, sex and desire had nothing to do with what he did the rest of his days. It was disconnected. A service he bought. He had purposed that he would not expose himself again by sharing his desires with a woman who might not have the same needs.

Beatrice did.

She wanted the same things.

It was intoxicating.

It had been sufficient, keeping his intimate desires satisfied by whores. Beneficial for all involved.

But this was something he'd craved. Something he'd determined did not actually exist. The possibility of sharing his life with a woman who also wanted in the way he did.

It made him feel vulnerable.

It made him *feel*.

He didn't like it.

And yet he did not know if he could deny himself either.

William ran through the grass, though he did not join any of the groups of children that were about.

'Does he not like to be with other children?'

'He does not have much experience of them,' Briggs said. 'Though… I feel that if he wished to play with children, he would say.'

'He does not seem to long for inclusion.'

'No. I recall… I recall often feeling that way when I was in school.'

'When did you go to school?'

'When I was fourteen. I was taught at home by my governess until then.'

'Do you know why?'

He laughed. 'One does not question the Duke of Brigham, Your Grace. By which I mean my father. One does not speak to him also. I don't just mean now, because he is dead. He was ashamed of me, and he did not wish for me to be at school where I might reflect poorly on him.'

'Surely he did not…'

'He did. It was not until he died that my mother finally sent me.'

'What a terrible…horrible man,' she said.

'He was not a good man.'

'My father was the same.' She grimaced. 'Even if he was different with it. Though I do feel you must know a bit about the notorious Duke of Kendal, and all the ways in which Hugh has taken it upon himself to rehabilitate the name and title.'

'I do know,' Briggs said. 'It is one reason that I knew I must marry you. For there is nothing more important to Hugh than reputation. The doing right.'

'Right as society defines it.'

'It is the only way that matters.'

'Yes, so it would appear. But I wonder…'

'It does not benefit us to wonder, Beatrice.'

'But if it did.'

'But it does not.'

'But you said yourself…' She looked at William, overjoyed in his solitude at the moment, even when surrounded by others. 'That happiness is not always found there.'

'No. But you know, it is not a question of whether or not you are doing everything society dictates, but whether or not you appear to be. There are thriving parts of London that operate outside of this… This fear. Where people are… More themselves.'

'Really?' She looked very keen.

'Ladies do not go to them.'

'Do they really not?'

'Not if their husbands are responsible.'

Truth be told there were a number of ladies who went to the sort of clubs he frequented. Particularly widows. Either looking for a man in the market to satisfy them, or looking to buy a harlot themselves. Briggs found nothing particularly shocking in the gaming halls and brothels of London. But perhaps that was simply due to his own acceptance of his nature.

Of course, he had wondered, when he was young, if there was something terribly wrong with him.

That he felt equal desire to kiss a woman as he did to take a riding crop to her.

But it had not taken long for him to discover books and artwork that suggested he was not alone, and then brothels that confirmed he was not. His particular favourite memory was when he had been a young man of sixteen travelling on school holidays, and he had gone to a notorious brothel in Paris and been presented with a menu. There had been acts on it he had never even considered.

And he had tried most of them. He was a man with money and few hard limits, so there was little reason not to.

Brothels had provided the perfect venue for him to explore the darker facets of his desires, while providing him with rules.

Rules, he had learned, were essential for a man like him.

He knew the women enjoyed it too. It was why he had been so certain that Serena...

'The issue, Beatrice, is that these places truly are dens of immorality.'

'The kind of immorality I must be protected from because of my health?'

'And mine,' he said. 'If your brother had any idea that I took you...'

'To a brothel?'

Of course, it had been Hugh who'd accompanied him to the Parisian brothel all those years ago. He was becoming as annoyed with the hypocrisy of the world as Beatrice.

'Must you say that here?' he said, looking around. He knew William was not paying attention to them.

But others might be.

'He would kill you,' Beatrice said, sounding nearly cheerful. 'That is a fact.'

'I would like to avoid being killed by Hugh, and if I had wanted to be killed by him, I would have simply refused to marry you in the first place.'

'So there are all these rules of society, and half of the people in society simply do not observe them? Tell me, where is the logic in that?'

'I suppose this,' he said, looking around, 'is what separates us from the animals.'

'That and corsets, I imagine.'

'Definitely corsets.'

'I had hoped to find, when I grew up, when I married, that the world was perhaps not so mystifying and unfair. That things were not quite so inequitable between men and women. I had hoped, that there would be a magical moment when all knowledge, and all things, might be open to me. But it is not to be, is it? I will always be... I will always have to live my life half in fantasy. And not even a good fantasy, because I don't even know...' She looked up at him, her blue eyes suddenly filled with tears. 'I do not even know what I want. All these desires with you and me will be half formed. Except for that one moment. That one moment in the garden.'

She went away from him then, and knelt down beside William. Who began to speak to her in an animated fashion.

And he felt...

He felt perhaps like being a duke was pointless. Because with his status and power, he was unable to give Beatrice what she wanted without breaking his vows to Hugh, and William...

Well, none of it bore thinking about, really. He had never been the kind of man to rail at fate. The world did not care.

It simply unfolded, one step at a time, and you had to take it. Or die.

As his wife had chosen to do.

No. Serena was not his wife. Beatrice was his wife.

Beatrice was his wife, and that bore thinking about.

Chapter Twelve

On the second day in London, Beatrice had walked William endlessly around the little cluster of townhomes around Grosvenor Square. They had gone out to tea on the third day, though it was unfashionable to bring a child to such a venue.

He had not lasted long. He had become fractious and it had still been worth it, if only because they had left with cloth bags filled with scones.

Which she and William had elected to eat on the floor in his nursery.

Then she had gone to her bedchamber, to allow herself to be dressed to attend her very first ball as an actual lady.

Where she would dance.

But she would only be able to dance with Briggs, as he was her husband.

The partners did switch during many dances.

She had wanted this...

She had wanted it for a very long time.

All of her clothing fit perfectly, her measurements having gone to London ahead of her, the power of Briggs's fortune and status evident in each stitch of her clothing. The gown her lady's maid put her in was gold, with glittering beads stitched over a long, filmy skirt. The bodice was low-cut, with shimmering stars sewn around the neckline. Similar stars were fastened to her hair, which was arranged in beautiful, elaborate twists.

She felt beautiful. Truly beautiful. More so than she ever had in her life, with the exception of when Briggs had held her in his arms in the garden when her hair had been down in the simple braid, her body adorned in very little, and she had felt...

She had never thought about her own beauty. At first, she had always harboured anger against her body. For being weak. For failing her, and she had never much considered whether or not it was pleasing to look at. It just pleased her in its weakness, and that was what mattered. When she had found her secret strengths, the ways in which she endured pain...

She had begun to praise her body, for being stronger than all of the illnesses that had attempted to claim her.

A matter of perspective, she supposed. In the same way that being bled could have been nothing but an unendurable pain. She had allowed it to become something else. But this... This hurt, and not in a way that made her feel strong. Her throat ached as she stared at her reflection.

She was beautiful, and it did not matter. For she had a husband, and there would be no man that would look upon her and fall desperately in love. Least of all the man who had married her.

Briggs.

Her breath caught, sharp and hard, and she turned away from her reflection.

'Thank you,' she said to her lady's maid. 'I am ready.'

A beautiful, crimson-red pelisse was draped over her

shoulders, and she walked out through the door of her bed-chamber, at the same time Briggs walked out of his.

He was stunning. In black as ever, with breeches that moulded in a tantalising fashion to his body. She had so many more questions about that body than she had before. And such a great interest in what she might find beneath his clothes.

There was an intensity to his gaze when he looked at her, but just as quickly as she'd seen it, it vanished. Replaced by the cool detachment he preferred to treat her with.

'You are ready,' he said.

'Yes,' she said. 'A good observation, though I suppose I should be grateful that you did not ask if I was ready, which would imply that perhaps I did not appear to be so.'

'You appear more than ready to steal all of the attention at the ball.'

'How lovely for me. And what shall I do with the attention?'

'Allow yourself to bathe in the envy of others,' he said, his voice low, and rich. Rolling over her skin. 'For how often does one get to be the fixation of every man in a room, and the focal point of the fury of every woman?'

'I can say certainly that I have never.'

She felt as if he had just given her a compliment, but she also felt like she was trembling, so it was difficult to linger on the good feeling for too long.

'But isn't that just more fantasy? Imagining what it is others think?'

'Do you have something against fantasy?'

'Perhaps I am simply tired of it, because it is all I've ever had.' She wasn't hungry for more fantasy, she wanted real.

She wanted more of those moments she'd had with him before. Real and raw. Pleasure and pain. Physical. Not gauzy, sweet dreams.

But she did not know if he would ever touch her like that again.

It made her despair. She didn't want despair, not tonight.

She didn't want to dwell on what could be, or what might not be.

She wanted to live.

They made their way out of the house and down to the carriage. He, rather than his footman, opened the door for her. When they were ensconced inside, she felt as if all the air had been taken from her lungs. Being this close to him was... It was difficult. It created a tangle of desires inside her, and she felt beset by them.

'When I was a girl, all I could do was dream.'

'Tonight is not a dream,' he said. 'Tonight is very real.'

'You will dance with me?'

'I will share a dance with you.'

'No,' she said, firm. 'I have dreamt of this all of my life. I wanted to go to a ball and have a handsome man see me from across the room and know that his life would never be complete if he did not cross that space and take me into his arms. I will never have that. I have known that for a time now. I knew it even when I thought I was contriving to set myself up to marry James. I have had to let that go. But I ask you... I beg you... Please, give me this. If you can give me nothing else.'

She felt vaguely foolish, begging like this. But this was her life, *her life*. And everyone around her was making these decisions for her and she had tried to claim her freedom, and she had not been successful.

So if she had to beg to get what she wanted tonight, then she would.

'As many dances as you wish,' he said, his voice rough. And it sent a thrill through her body.

It was as if he cared.

And that made her hope.

* * *

When they arrived, they were swept into a glittering ball-room, replete with frescoes of cherubs, not half so lovely as the ones at Maynard Park. Nor as scandalous as the ones at Bybee House.

But they were nice all the same.

It was a thrill, to be in a new place, a new ballroom. To be at a party with different people.

And to actually be part of it, rather than standing on the fringes. It had not been long ago that she had been at her brother's house party and got herself ruined. And she did wonder how her reception might be.

It turned out, there was no need for worry. Briggs was ushered immediately into a group of men, and Beatrice was summarily captured by their wives.

'I did not think that he would ever marry,' said a woman who was introduced to Beatrice as Lady Smythe.

'No, assuredly not,' said Lady Hannibal. 'He had confirmed bachelor neatly stamped across him.'

'Well. Circumstances…'

'Oh, yes,' said the Viscountess Roxbury. 'We heard all about the circumstances.'

And Beatrice awaited the judgement.

'Clever girl,' the Viscountess said. 'It was the only way one could ever snag him. To catch him in such a fashion, particularly when he holds your brother in such esteem.'

And she had the feeling that she had been talked about, at length by this group of women, as she suddenly realised that the banter that went around the circle felt a bit rehearsed.

Still, she did not get the sense that they wished her ill, nor that they disliked her, only that they were fascinated by her.

'Well, I… I have known Briggs for a very long time.' She realised that she had referred to him by his rather familiar nickname, and that she ought not to have done so. Not in this group. 'The Duke of Brigham,' she said. 'His Grace. I have known him for quite some time. And he is a man I hold in great regard.'

'How can one not hold a man whose riding breeches fit him so in high regard?' said Lady Smythe with a curve to her lips.

Beatrice felt a rash of possessiveness. She did not appreciate the lady leering over her husband.

Particularly as Beatrice herself had not seen him out of his breeches.

The idea sent a slam of indignation and something else through her, and it made her feel warm all over.

Still, she found a way to keep her smile pasted on her face, and then, mercifully, the topic of conversation turned to other gossip, and Beatrice found she quite enjoyed it. She felt very much a part of this group in a way she had never much felt a part of anything.

It was a strange sort of revelation. She had not realised how much she wanted this. An evening of feeling enchanted. Of feeling… Normal.

They did not know that her and Briggs's marriage was not what it seemed.

They were treating her like a married woman. Like someone for whom the mysteries of the universe had been unveiled.

They were treating her like an equal, and not like a poor, sickly thing.

And then it was time for a waltz, and Briggs turned, his dark eyes connecting with hers as he closed the distance between them. 'If you'll excuse us,' he said to her new friends. 'I owe my wife a dance.' His eyes never left hers. 'More than one.'

A tremor went through her body, as he took her to the dance floor, and brought her into his arms. He had said he owed her a dance, but there was a promise beneath the words that felt heavy. That made her stomach go tight.

It was a lively dance, and she could not help but laugh, in part because she had forced him to partake.

And soon, he was laughing also. They spun and twirled across the floor, and she delighted in what a strong grip he had. And what a wonderful partner he was.

Oh, he was wonderful.

She studied the lines of his face, that square jaw, those dark eyes with long dark lashes.

And his mouth. She had tasted that mouth. Had shared intimacies with him only three days earlier that she had never even imagined, much less shared with anyone else.

And he'd felt hers.

But suddenly, she had the thought. That there were other women here who had tasted him. Who had perhaps experienced greater intimacies with him than she had done.

The very idea made her feel small. Ill. And terribly sad.

But she would not focus on that, not now. For that was fantasy. That was speculation. What was real was this moment. Where he held her in his arms. And the music wound itself around them.

A sweet, piercing melody that seemed made just for them.

It did not matter that there were other people here. None of that mattered. He had wanted her to focus on what it was like to be the envy of others, but she found she did not care. She did not care. She only cared what was. What was happening. And what was happening was that she was being held by Briggs. What was happening was that she was so close to him her air was made up almost entirely of that spicy masculine scent that was him, and only him.

She looked at the strong column of his throat, at his Adam's apple there. And she became unbearably conscious of wanting to lick him.

They danced together for longer than was fashionable. She was grateful for it. Because there was no other man she wanted.

And that, she realised, was the real sadness. Not that the fantasy of meeting someone else was dashed forever. Had she ever truly wanted to meet someone else? No. The saddest thing was that she had married Briggs. And it was something that part of her... A small corner of herself that she would never have allowed voice... Had secretly dreamed could be true. Because from the first moment he had ever brought her sweets, she had found him to be special. And she had wanted him most of all.

And there was not a fantasy left, because he was her husband, and yet she could still never truly have him.

But tonight he's dancing with you. Tonight you have this. You have lived in so many painful moments. Should you not fully live in this one?

And so she did. She allowed the music, and his arms, and the steps, to become the only thing there was.

Briggs was overwhelmed by her. She was beautiful, and when she had removed her pelisse upon entry, she had revealed the extent of the gown's secrets. He had wanted to kill the men he was speaking to, friends from school, for that matter, over the way they had allowed themselves to hungrily take their fill of her gloriously rounded bosom.

He couldn't blame them. He might've done the same had they possessed a wife of such great beauty. It was just that they did not. There was not a woman in the entire room that could hold a candle to Beatrice.

And the way that her face lit up as they danced... It ignited something inside him.

And he felt nothing but fury. At himself. At the world. But more than that, a fury at his own willingness to succumb to the helplessness of the situation. For he was not that man. It was certain he did not waste time railing at the world, but that did not mean giving in either.

He wanted her. He wanted her.

More than wanting to sink into her wet, willing body, though he did want that, he wanted her pleasure.

And he wanted her submission.

She had been made for him, as far as he could tell, nearly training herself in the art of pain all of her life.

She understood it. She understood it in the way that he did.

But there was an intense and rare gift to be found in the exchange of it.

And she was correct. It was her life. It was her life, and she had every right to decide what she wished it to be.

There would be nothing to stop her from taking her pleasure with other men, except that those men would not know how to satisfy her.

He did. They were perversely, innately made for each other.

And he wished to see just how far that went.

The only thing more unfashionable than dancing with one's wife for the entire evening was to be seen sneaking out of the ballroom with her.

But when that dance ended, he realised that it was the path he had decided on.

'Let us take a walk,' he said.

'A walk?'

He had this moment to turn back. But she was here, and she wanted to be his. He felt it. He knew it. She had said it with her mouth, had shown him with the way her body desired him and if he found her strong, and wild, and brilliant, ought he not also to believe her?

He knew there was a chance it was his weakness, his selfishness winning out. Remnants of the boy he'd once been, who had wanted nothing more than to meet a woman who might understand him.

That did not exist, that love he had once believed in. He was no longer naive enough to believe one person might accept all the ways in which he was different.

But Beatrice wanted this part of him. And so he would give it.

He was powerless to do anything else.

'Into the garden.'

'Is there a garden?'

'There always is,' he said.

'Oh,' she answered. 'Why is that?'

'Without a garden, there would be no garden path for rakes to lead innocent women down, would there?'

'Hugh has warned Eleanor about such things.'

'But never you?'

She laughed, hard. 'I think Hugh would never have thought he would have to.'

'He should have. Perhaps you would've stayed clear of me.'

'I did not know it was you.'

'Did you?' he whispered.

She shivered beneath his hold. He had not meant to issue that challenge, but he had done so. 'Walk with me.'

They walked out through the large double doors and into the dark of night. The moon was only a silver sliver, and the stars were all alike, but none of them were as compelling as the ones in Beatrice's hair.

They had entranced him all evening. Beckoning him to unpin her curls and fill his hands with them. With all of her stardust and glory.

'Briggs...'

'Didn't you want to live your fantasy tonight? Of going to a ball? Of having a man meet your eyes across the room and find you irresistible?'

'Yes,' she said, her voice a choked whisper.

'I find you irresistible.'

She looked at him, her eyes wide, glittering, even in the moonlight.

'You don't mean that.'

'I do, Beatrice, or we would not be out here.'

'I thought perhaps you just wanted to walk.'

'As much as I want to walk, I could take one in Grosvenor Square whenever I wished. I don't wish to *walk* with you.'

'What do you wish for me?' she asked, her voice hushed.

They walked deeper into the garden, and he knew that they had to be deeper there before he risked answering her question.

'What do I want from you?' he asked as soon as the hedgerows enshrouded them completely. 'Everything. Nothing less. I should have you kneel before me, Your Grace. I should have you do whatever I ask. Beg me to take you in hand and punish you for being such a temptress.'

Her breathing had quickened, he could hear it. Feel her pulse moving through the two of them. 'You are in bad need of a punishment for what you have done to us both, don't you agree?'

'I don't... I don't know.'

'You don't have to know. You must only answer, yes, Your Grace. That is the only answer that will do.'

The pause she took was only a breath. A twinkle of starlight and nothing more, but it felt like an eternity.

'Yes,' she whispered. 'Your Grace.'

Flames licked at his veins. Arousal pulsing through him so dark and heavy he thought he might be drowned by it.

They turned the corner, and he found a bench, perfectly situated there in the garden, such a private spot. And it was a bit early yet for others to be making their way out here for trysts. At least he hoped so.

And even if not.

She was his wife.

'But here we are in a garden,' he said. 'In all things I have in mind for you... Not here.'

'Why are you teasing me?' she asked, her voice breathless.

'I am very, very serious,' he said. 'I can assure you.'

He gripped her chin, tilted her face up, and kissed her. He

had kissed her before, but it had been nothing compared to this. This was… He was not being careful with her. For the way that she looked at him, the way that she acted as if he had done her harm by not finishing what they had started in his garden back at the town house…

Tonight would either inflame her desire for more or would cure her of her need for him altogether. Either way, it would be fun. The kiss was bruising. And she gasped as he licked deeper and deeper into her mouth, bit her lower lip, before sucking it hard.

She did not have any skill. But what she lacked there she made up for in enthusiasm. She was gasping, arching her body against his, trying to get closer. Trying to get everything.

'Be still,' he said.

And she responded. That note of authority in his voice made her entire body go limp against his.

'I will give you what you need. I promise.'

She whimpered, and he bit her lip again. 'Do not doubt me. Trust me.'

He moved his finger down to where the fabric of her dress met the plump flesh of her bosom. He pushed his finger beneath that gap, letting it drift around that curve, and he felt goose pimples break out over her skin.

He knew that her nipples would be tight beneath her undergarments. And he wanted deeply to pull the top of her dress down, reveal them and suck them again. But, not now. He would not risk exposing her so thoroughly here.

A light touch was not his preference, but he could tell that it tormented her, and that, he did enjoy.

'Please,' she begged. 'Please.'

'You will not get more until I say. You will not get release until I allow it. You are mine. My wife.' The words sent a lightning bolt of arousal through his body. 'Your satisfaction is my responsibility. It is also your reward. And it will not be claimed before I allow it.

'You know what I mean, don't you? Your release. What you experienced when you shattered in my arms in the garden.'

'Yes,' she whispered. 'I understand.'

'Have you ever felt that before? When you are alone in your room, did you ever put your hand between your legs and stroke yourself?'

'I…'

'You're a clever girl. You discovered that pain makes you feel powerful. That it thrills you. Did you discover how much touching yourself between your legs could thrill you?'

She shook her head. 'No.'

'I see. And what is it you do? When you're alone in your room? What is it you do when you cannot sleep?'

'Sometimes… Sometimes I dig my fingernails into my palms. I do that when I am afraid. I was doing it the night of the ball, when I was trying to get up the courage to…'

'I see. So you have given yourself pain, but never the pleasure to go with it.'

'I like it,' she said.

'Good. So do I.'

'Do you… Do you give yourself pain?'

He chuckled. 'No. I like to give it.'

And he could see, in that veiled expression, there in the garden, that his answer terrified and thrilled her all at once.

'But right now,' he said. 'There is something else. Something else I must do.'

He lowered his head and scraped his teeth along her collarbone, and he hoped, belatedly, that he had not left a mark. If so, she would have to retrieve her pelisse immediately.

He enjoyed residual marks on a woman's skin from lovemaking, but he admitted that marking one's own wife before having to go back into a ballroom was likely not the best thing.

He sat her down on the bench. And it was true, he preferred a woman on her knees before him, but, he had always known the power inherent in what he wished to do to her. So many men refused. Or were not skilled in the act.

And he had found that there was as much power to be had in branding a woman with pleasure, as guiding her in doing the same to him.

There was a tipping point, where pleasure could be used as torture, and this was one of the most effective ways he had found to do it.

They would not have infinite time here. But it would be enough.

He knelt before her and began to push her dress up over her knees. She locked them together.

'What is the matter?'

'I...'

'So sweet,' he said. 'You really are an innocent, aren't you?'

She nodded. 'You know that I am. The only ways in which I am not innocent are ways I was marked by your hands.'

'I delight in that,' he said. 'I should like to mark you all over.'

'Briggs,' she said, shivering.

'Spread your legs for me.'

'I...'

'Spread them.'

She did so, and he pushed her skirts up the rest of the way, revealing that delightful triangle of pale curls at the apex of her thighs.

And his mouth watered.

'You are beautiful,' he said.

He pressed his thumb against that source of her pleasure that he knew was there, smoothed it in a circle, and listened as she cried out in pleasure.

She was wet.

Their kiss had done its job. Their conversation had done its job.

He shifted, pressing two fingers against her swollen lips down there, trapping that little bud there between them, rubbing his fingers back and forth, careful to avoid what she really wanted.

She was moving her hips back and forth, desperately seeking more.

And he loved it. Gloried and revelled in it.

Then he put one leg of hers up over his shoulder, and another, bringing his face down so it was a scant inch from the glorious, wet heart of her.

'Briggs…'

But he did not allow her to speak. Did not allow her to say the next word. He fastened his mouth to her, moving his tongue in firm, rhythmic strokes across her flesh.

He knew what she wanted. And he would give it to her. Almost.

He feasted on her, deep, long. Until she was panting, her fingernails digging into his shoulders.

He found no particular pleasure in that, other than knowing that she was desperate for him. And for what only he could provide.

He took her close to the edge, then denied her. Pushing a finger inside her narrow, tight channel as he continued to feast on her. Took her to the edge, and then pulled back, pulled away.

She was mindless with need. Begging.

'Soon,' he said, working his finger in and out of her body. 'Soon you can come.'

'Please,' she said.

'Not yet.'

'Please, Your Grace.'

Her words shot all the way to his sex, causing it to pulse.

He wanted her. Wanted nothing more than to satisfy the

ache in his loins. Instead, he pushed another finger into her body, and bit down on her. She screamed, her orgasm sending a shock wave through her body, and then his.

And when it was done, he sat down on the bench, gathered her up in his arms and held her close while she sobbed out the rest of her pleasure. Held her until she quieted.

Then he rearranged her skirts, made sure that her hair was in place.

'I cannot possibly go back in,' she whispered.

'Why not?'

'I... Not after... You...'

'Yes,' he said. 'I have no such qualms.'

'How nice for you. But that was singular for me.'

'It was singular for me,' he said, tracing his thumb down the side of her face. 'You are extraordinary.'

'I don't understand.'

'You were right. You are mine. And...'

'I never said I was yours. You have said it. Frequently.'

'All right. You were right in that this is your life. And as I have some measure of control over it... Dammit. Beatrice, I like to see you happy. I did not like the idea that once we left here tonight the joy that I saw on your face here would end. And selfishly... The way you look in this dress...'

'You like the dress?'

'I am bewitched by it.' It was nothing less than the truth. Except, perhaps it was. Because perhaps it had less to do with the dress and more to do with her.

'Thank you,' she said, restless.

'Thank you,' he said, feeling amused. 'That's your response?'

'I am flattered,' she said.

'Beatrice...'

'What now?'

'Tonight? Tonight we will go back inside, and you will enjoy this ball all the way to the finish. We will go home.

You will sleep. Tomorrow morning, I will have your favourite breakfast made.'

'You would not ask what my favourite breakfast is?'

'What is it?'

'Eggs. Bacon. And I like pastries and jam.'

'All of them will be delivered to your room. Where you will take it as a queen. Then you and I will talk. And I will explain to you what will happen. What we will do. What I enjoy. And what our limits must be. And then... Tomorrow night after supper, when William is settled... I will show you.'

'Briggs...'

'Do you want this?' He could hear the intensity in his words, but this was the most important thing. That she was giving this freely. With no reservation.

For he would lay out his every desire. His very soul.

And he had to know she would accept.

'Yes,' she said.

'You don't even know what I offer you yet.'

'Because I trust you, Your Grace.'

The words sent a surge of desire through him.

'Wait until I tell you everything. And then you may agree to it. Or not.'

'I want more of this.'

'It will not all be this, little one.'

'Will it be more of what we had in the garden at the town house?'

'Yes. And more.'

'I enjoyed that.'

'Good.'

'What if I wanted...? Tonight. What if I wanted more tonight?' She leaned forward, placing her palm flat on his chest, and he nearly felt dizzy with desire. He felt nearly overcome by his need to have her, and that was... Unusual. Typically, he had much better control over himself than this. But she was doing something to him.

Something he could not afford to allow her.

'No,' he said, keeping his tone gentle.

'You wanted me to be honest with you. And I feel... Wonderful, but... Unsatisfied.'

He could relate.

'It is of no consequence what you feel. You will learn to wait. And you will learn to wait until I tell you that you may have more. You must prove that you are able. You will prove your strength by waiting.'

'I have always known I was strong,' she said. 'It is others who have assumed that I am weak.'

'Then prove it. Prove to me that you are strong enough. To wait. And take whatever I have in store for you.'

'Yes, Your Grace.'

When she woke the first thing she became conscious of was the smell of bacon.

She opened her eyes slowly and looked to see a tray beside the bed. A massive tray. Absolutely laden, not just with bacon, but with a near mountain of pastries that exceeded her every expectation, and certainly her every request.

The second thing she became conscious of was the fact that this meant he had kept his end of the bargain.

And that meant...

That meant the rest would be coming too. The rest. She still didn't know what all of it was. But he said that he would explain it to her.

A rush of giddy joy filled her as she sat up in bed and reached out for the bacon.

She felt both lighter and more carefree, and more mature than she ever had in her life. What had happened last night had been a fantasy brought to earth. The sort of garden she had found escape in as a girl.

She had now found true desire there as a woman. Had found the truth of dreams fashioned into reality.

A need created in her, and satisfied so thoroughly she would never be able to forget either.

He was giving her what she wanted. He was. This was a real life. This life with Briggs.

It was hardly like *Emma*.

Okay, perhaps not. Perhaps it was not like *Emma* at all. He was, of course, an older man who had known her for quite some time, but there was no... It was not love, this thing between them.

And she would not claim to have had great expectations of love, not in her life. Not when she had spent so much of it being so desperately aware that she was broken.

There were some similarities of course, between the novel and her life. In that Briggs was a long-time friend of her family, and several years her senior.

But... She could not help but think about all the qualities that she had always liked about Mr Knightley. He was assured in his authority. And that was what she liked about Briggs.

His certainty. His authority. It had been what had always drawn her to him. Like a magnet. It was not simply that he was the best-looking man that she had ever seen, though he was. It was more.

A strange sort of twist happened low in her stomach.

It was an odd thing, what he'd said to her last night. That he liked to give out pain.

But then, she supposed she liked to receive it, and if there was a person in the world who seemed made to receive pain, ought there not to be someone who enjoyed giving it?

It was as if they were two halves of a whole. Though that she and Briggs were each other's half seemed...

Overly romantic.

She did not know how to reconcile the soft romance of books she had read with what seemed to exist between herself and Briggs. Last night he had done things to her that she had not been aware existed. Exactly as he had done to her in the garden here only two days earlier.

He was teaching her, without ever saying so, that there was a dimension of life she was not conversant in, and she desperately wished to be. But he had promised that she would be so. After this.

After tonight.

The thought made her nearly wild with nerves.

It was also somewhat pleasing.

She did wish that Eleanor was here. She would like very much to speak to her. To warn her about the sorts of intimacies that men like to take. Eleanor would be shocked.

For the first time in quite some time, she thought of Penny. Her friend who had been engaged at one time to Hugh.

Had her Highlander done these things to her? That strange group who had carried her off?

Penny, by all accounts, was happy. At least, she had indicated as such in her letters, when she had arranged for them to find help for a young Scottish girl called Mairi. Hugh had generously provided a reference for her to get into a very good school. Even though he was not ever going to forgive Penny for what he viewed as a transgression, he would not pass on any sort of harm to an innocent girl.

And once he had heard of Mairi's plight, of the violation she had endured that had left her with child...

She sat there, stunned for a moment.

She had been left with child by a man who had... Taken something from her.

She had only vaguely understood these things, and her brother's fury. But now she understood slightly better. She had wanted everything that Briggs had done to her, and she wanted to get more. One thing that was evident when he held her was his strength. And how greatly it overpowered her own. How easily.

If a man wished to force his attentions on a woman, there

would be nothing she could do to stop it. How terrifying. How utterly horrible to have such intimacies taken when you were not desirous of the touch.

Oh, yes, she was discovering new pieces of the world.

She looked out at the pile of pastries, and the great brick of butter on the platter.

She smiled as she thought of Briggs.

He was... He was not gentle. It was what she enjoyed about his touch. It made her feel strong. He did not treat her as if she was breakable. When she was in his arms, she felt like a warrior. Like what she had always longed to feel like. But he was purposeful. Never once did she feel as if he might push her beyond that which she could stand. He seemed a man innately in touch with her limits. She trusted him implicitly.

When she had finished eating, her maid came into the room and told her that His Grace had requested she have a bath.

There were new scented oils to put in the water, and she luxuriated in them for a long moment, until she emerged soft and smelling like a rose garden. She was perfumed down beneath the first layer of her skin, and there was something about it that thrilled her. Because Briggs was preparing her for his touch. And she wondered... Would he strip her completely bare tonight? Press his body against hers. Would he be...?

She had yet to see him naked, and she wished greatly to do so. She had thought him beautiful all these many years, and to see the promise of all that beauty fulfilled...

It was a prospect that sent a thrill of need straight down between her thighs. She did not enjoy feeling cosseted, not usually. Because she associated it with being put away. Kept cloistered in her childhood bedroom.

This was different. She was being exceedingly pampered,

but it was in aid of being presented to him tonight. And so she allowed herself to revel in it in a way she never had.

She took her lunch on the terrace that overlooked the garden, the solitude beginning to press in on her. And she wondered when he would arrive to speak with her.

She did not fully realise when she began to understand. That this too was part of it. This anticipation that he built. The way that he positioned her, so that she spent these many hours wondering when he would appear, and exactly what would happen. The way that she obeyed him, even though nothing was stopping her from going wandering through the house and searching for him.

It was practice. For tonight. For the ways that she would need to obey. Because as he had said earlier, if she could not trust him in these sorts of things, then she would never trust him enough for the two of them to engage in greater intimacies.

She read, and lounged, and found indulgence in the act. Did not feel like a prisoner. Rather, she felt like royalty. She tried to see to her usual tasks. Spent some time with William and coaxed conversation from him about the sights he had liked best so far in London.

And all the while the anticipation built, excitement twisting her stomach, and also firing up that space between her legs.

Briggs.

His name was like her heartbeat. And, oh, how she wanted him.

Finally, at four o'clock, he came into her room.

He looked positively disreputable with his shirt collar open, and his strong chest visible there, a smattering of dark hair sprinkled over his muscles.

She was transfixed. By that white shirt, the tan skin beneath, the tight, black breeches, and his leather belt.

'You've been enjoying your day?'

'Yes,' she said.

'Good. You did exactly as I asked, which is also good.'

She felt replete with joy beneath his praise.

'Have I pleased you?'

'You have not begun to please me.'

He walked over to the bed. 'Explain to me all you know of the mechanics of what a man and woman do together.'

'Only what you have said. Only what we have done.'

'I see. So you do not understand that a man puts his cock inside of a woman and spills his seed in her and gets her with child?'

'I… I did not. No.'

'Where you were wet for me.'

She shifted. For she was wet. For him.

'I see.'

'That is the limit. We will not do that.'

'Oh,' she said, feeling hurt and disappointed, even knowing that she shouldn't.

'Last night, you were satisfied, were you not?'

'Yes,' she said.

'We will continue to endeavour to find your satisfaction, it is only that we will not fully consummate the union. Out of deference to your health.'

'I find that greatly disappointing.'

'We will recover. You may have my mouth there. Fingers. Mine and your own. I will pleasure you. And you will pleasure me.'

'And how might… How will I do that?'

'I will teach you to use your mouth on me.'

'You said… You said you might punish me.'

'Yes. Most especially for this situation we find ourselves in. I find that should be appropriate. You will tell me if it becomes too much.'

'Okay,' she said.

'I am not jesting. I will take you under my hand, and I will do so firmly, but if you do not tell me when you have been pushed to your limits, there can be no trust between us. And if there is no trust between us these games do not work. You and I must have the utmost respect for your limits or we cannot push you to them at all.'

'I promise,' she said, thrilling at being able to offer him this promise. At telling him the truth. He was very proud of her for all of the times that she had been truthful with him before. And she would continue to please him in this way.

'Then we will see one another again at dinner.'

She wanted him to stay. She wanted it to happen now. To push forward and get it over with.

She wanted the mystery unlocked. She wanted all to be revealed.

But he was going to keep her suspended in the rapture of anticipation, and she could not decide if it was brilliant, or a sort of torture. Perhaps both.

'Your brother cannot know,' he said.

'Do you honestly think that I'm going to speak to my brother of such things? He cannot even speak to me of the sorts of medical procedures that I have endured. For it all involves breaking open my skin and bleeding and things of that nature. And I dare say he does not wish to know so much about his own sister's body. He would not like to know what his friend wishes to do with it.'

To her surprise, Briggs chuckled. 'Yes. I suppose that's true. But I have no wish to be called out.'

'You've married me.'

'Your brother knows what I am. He knows how I am. He tolerates me, though he finds me to be debauched beyond what he personally would ever...'

'My brother is no saint, though he might conduct himself as one in public. I'm not a fool, Briggs. He could not maintain a friendship with you and remain a spotless lamb. It is only us ladies that are expected to be so.'

'By comparison to your father, Beatrice, believe me when I tell you that Hugh is exemplary.'

He defended her brother with great ferocity.

'Yes, I know.'

'I apologise. I should not have spoken out of turn about your father.'

'It is true, though. My father was a libertine. And perhaps… If I'm very honest, Briggs, I believe that there was more than enough information to be found around my house, and if one looked too deeply into the nude nymphs in the books at Bybee House, to educate me well enough.' She saw the real truth in that now. She had brushed against it earlier, but it hit her deeply now. Along with the reality of what her mother must have felt.

I want him and despise him in equal measure…

That made her ache, for she knew what it was to want now.

What her mother had lived with, always, was the reality of what she'd felt when Briggs had abandoned her for the brothel.

But Beatrice had been too sheltered then to know.

Her mother had known.

No wonder Beatrice had done her best to shield herself then.

She breathed out, a shaking sigh. 'But when it came to anything my father was involved in, I did not want to know. I sensed somehow that whatever capacity he… He disrespected my mother greatly. He disrespected the title. It is something that Hugh has worked a great deal to undo.'

'You are correct,' Briggs said. 'He has worked very hard to fix what your father has done, but it is not why I hold him in such esteem. I went to school late, as you know.'

'Yes.' She confirmed this with some hesitance, for he had mentioned it before but she could see now that she had missed something.

Something of what he had been trying to tell her.

'I did not know the other boys. I was the son of a duke, it was true. But I had not been raised around children, and I did not... I did not find it easy.'

She could not imagine that. Briggs was one of the most charming men she had ever known. At least, when he was intending to be. He could also be hard, and frightening, it was true. She liked him that way, if she were honest. But when he was engaged in discourse in public, he was nothing if not the consummate rake. Witty and delightful, and jolly good company.

'I did not find it easy,' he repeated. 'I did not understand how to speak to children my own age. I was left largely to my own devices, and my interests were... My own. Hugh practically trained me to make friends.'

'Hugh did? It seems to me that you are the one most likely to make friends of the two of you.'

'I am a fast learner,' Briggs said. 'A good study. A brilliant mimic.'

'Modest as well.'

'No. Never that. I will always be grateful to him. I will always owe him a debt. And this... Is surely a poor way to repay him.'

'Or,' Beatrice said, 'it has nothing to do with him. I should like it if what I want could be separated from him and what he wants. Utterly and absolutely.'

He looked at her, long and hard for a moment, his dark eyes glittering, darting back and forth as though he was doing some sort of mental calculus. 'I see you as a whole person, unto yourself,' he said. 'Please don't mistake me. But your brother will not. And... As I said before... He knows a bit too much about me for... For him to avoid making assumptions about our relationship should he discover we have one.'

'Of all the things, Briggs, who would've thought that the scandal you truly wish to avoid is someone thinking you have shared intimacies with your wife.'

His lips curved up at the corner. 'It only shocks you because you know so little about me.'

'You can tell me more.'

'We will speak after dinner.'

'I should hope that we will speak at dinner,' she said.

'Yes. But that is where people will see. And who we are away from others... That is where true honesty is, is it not?'

She shivered. He spoke the truth. She knew that he did.

It was as he'd said before, about polite society. All of these people who enforced proper behaviour... They did not necessarily engage in such behaviour themselves, and what was more, they knew fully that beneath the glittering veneer of the surface, many others did not. It was meant to corral the innocent and the powerless, more than anything else.

But who they were when they were alone... That was freedom.

And as long as she got a taste of it... She could endure it being between herself and Briggs only.

In fact, it felt lovely. Like a secret. No, not a secret, like a precious gem that you might conceal, so that it is not stolen or tarnished by anyone else. Like something too beautiful to give away.

And then he left her. And she knew that now, she had only to wait until after dinner.

Where he would make good on his promises, and she would find...

She did not know what exactly. Only that there was a certainty, bright and burning in the centre of her soul, that told her tonight she would find a piece of herself.

Chapter Thirteen

Dinner was a study in torture. But Beatrice had come to accept that torture was a part of all of this. At least, between herself and Briggs.

That feeling that she was guarding something precious and rare intensified. Yes, she was disappointed that he was going to withhold... Certain things from her. Not even thinking further down the road that he would be withholding a baby from her, but that there was an intimacy that was... That he was not willing to give.

But she had the sense that it was a common intimacy. Perhaps, the most common. And that what was about to take place between herself and Briggs was not common.

They ate dinner across the table from each other, and she did feel as if they were strangers, observing customs that simply didn't matter. That had nothing to do with the two of them. With Briggs and Beatrice and all that they could be. All that they would be.

For the first time she felt... Special. Not like she might be less, but that she might be more.

She was careful not to overfill herself, and when dinner was finished, she stood.

'I am ready to retire,' she said.

He looked up at her. 'Is that true?'

'Yes, Your Grace,' she said, using his title making her stomach tense. It should not. Only that there was a way he seemed to enjoy hearing it. And it was different, different to the way it was spoken in common conversation, where it was just an observation of his title, an expression of what was due to him. There was something else. Something deeper.

She went to her room, and her maid helped her dress for bed. She looked at herself in the mirror, and she wondered. If she was truly enough of a woman to entice him.

It had been one thing in the beautiful ball gown, with all those stars in her hair. She had been bewitched by her own reflection, so she imagined that she had a much better chance of bewitching Briggs in that state. But now... She just looked very much like herself.

The night that he had left the brothel, he had gone to engage in these activities, but had not done so. So no doubt that had played a part in his enticement towards her. That was why the nightgown had been sufficient then. But would it be enough now?

Would she be enough?

Or would she fall short?

No. You will not fall short. He trusts that you will not.

She looked at herself, and straightened her shoulders. He did not see her as an invalid. And she would not behave as if he should. This was what she had always wanted. For someone to see her as strong. As whole. Even recognising that he must... That he must behave differently with her... He was still not keeping himself from her entirely.

And that must be a testament to his desire. And to the way that he saw her.

And then the door opened. And he was here.

He was dressed fully for dinner, rather than in that state of partial undress that he'd been in when he had come into her room earlier today. For some reason, it gave him a look of unfettered authority, and that excited her all the more.

This man who seemed to be the embodiment of all she had ever wanted. It made her bold. If he was all she wanted, perhaps she could be all he wanted as well.

'Do you know,' she said, 'all of my life, men have stood in authority over me. I suppose that is the fate of all women. Whether it be my father, my brother, or the physicians who attended me when I was ill, men have always dictated my fate. And so I cannot fathom why it is your authority that I find so beautiful.'

He paused, a muscle in his square jaw jumping. 'There are two reasons. The first is that you know I will exert my authority in ways that will bring you pleasure. I take no joy in causing pain for the sake of it. Nor do I exert my will simply because I can. I was born with a title. I was born with authority. England is filled with spineless men who have been given power because of the structure of the world. And women must subject to this authority because of how they were born. You... You willingly submit. And that is what gives me the power. That is what makes it mean something. And I will not abuse that. The second thing is related. Choice. You choose this. You choose it because it is something you want. And I granted it because I know it is something you can handle. It is not the de facto power a man has over his wife. Nor the power society gives a man over a woman. Rather this is something we choose. Something we make the rules to. Yes, in this bed, you give the power to me. But when it comes to the rules of the game, the ultimate power lies with us. Not what anyone tells us we might have. And that is intoxicating indeed.'

She shivered, absolutely and completely held captive by his words. For he was right.

This was power, the likes of which she had never known. For the fire inside him was stoked high, taken to a place that he was not in utter command of. She had command of his desire. He was here because he wanted her, and she did not doubt it. She did not need stars in her hair or a dress that flattered her bosom. She simply needed to be her.

The right fit to who and what he was. And that was innate inside her. The same as the illness that had threatened to take all the joy from her life. It made her grateful for herself. For strength, for the innate pieces of who she was. All that she could be.

Beatrice was enough for this moment. And after being wrong, not enough, not strong enough, according to all of the people that surrounded her, for so many years of her life, it was more than a revelation.

'The first thing I think you are strong enough to handle, is learning to please me.'

He closed the distance between them, his gaze fierce. 'Turn around.'

She obeyed, turning her back to him, and she flinched slightly when he wrapped his fingers around her braid. But he did not tug her hair, as he had done before. Instead, he gently released it from its fastenings and let it fall loose around her shoulders. His touch was gentle, and it made her shiver. Because it wasn't gentle as if he was afraid she would break. It was gentle like a gift. The calm before a storm that she knew would rage and push them both to a breaking point.

Then he began to loosen the ties at the back of her nightgown, and it fell, slid down her body in a slither of silk, and pooled at her feet. Leaving her completely naked. His touch was gentle as his fingers skimmed down the line of her spine, down to her backside, where he squeezed her tightly, an echo of what had occurred in the library of her brother's house, though so much more intentional. And with no barrier between them.

Tears stung her eyes.

There was nothing between them. Nothing except for his own clothes.

And she thought that perhaps she should be embarrassed, but she wasn't.

Physicians had seen her nude from the time she was a child. It had been a necessity. Part of a life spent practically bedridden.

But he was not examining her body like a thing. Rather he touched her as if she mattered. As if she meant something. Rather he touched her as if she was both fragile and strong all at once. And beautiful.

She was not ashamed. Not embarrassed.

He dipped his fingers between her legs, stroking her in the most intimate of places.

She was wet, but she found that did not shame her either. He had made commentary about that. About her wetness. And he had made it only sound like a good thing. Something that pleased him. And she did so wish to please him.

He turned her to face him, and all the breath left her body in an exquisite rush as he examined her. His eyes filled with an intensity that she gloried in.

This was not the cold examination of a doctor. This was the desirous look of a man.

He took two steps away from her, never taking his eyes off her as he sat down in a chair positioned by the fireplace in her bedchamber. Without taking his eyes from hers his hands moved to the falls of his breeches, and he opened them. And her throat tightened, went dry, as he drew himself from his clothing. He was... Well, as suspected, the statuary in the garden had nothing to recommend it when compared to Briggs.

He was large and thick, and... He was beautiful.

How she longed to see all of his body, completely uncovered for her pleasure. But she had a feeling it was something she would have to earn. And she would do her very best. He said he was going to teach her to pleasure him, and suddenly she wanted that more than she wanted anything else. More than she had ever wanted anything before.

'Come to me,' he said.

'Yes,' she said.

'Your Grace,' he said.

She recognised that it was a correction. Firm and gentle. And it made her feel…everything.

'Yes, Your Grace.'

A smile curved his lips, and she took that short trip to stand right in front of him, feeling deliciously exposed beneath the intensity of his gaze.

'Get to your knees,' he said.

She obeyed, without thought, going down to her knees in front of him.

'Good,' he said. 'I'm going to teach you how to pleasure me. I want you to take me in your mouth.'

She was not shocked. After all, he had done the same to her in the garden and it had been exquisite. Why should he not enjoy the same intimacies? Their bodies were not the same, but surely there must be something in the taking of pleasure that they had in common.

And she wanted to… She wanted to give him some measure of what he had given to her. She did. She wanted him to feel the glory that she had felt. And if she could do for him what he had done for her, she would feel…

If she could make him shake, if she could make him cry out. If she could make his body unravel itself at that moment of release, then she would do so. It was all she wanted in that moment. The ultimate test of her strength.

And so she leaned forward, darting her tongue out over the head of his cock. He was lovely, and he tasted wonderful, something she would not have imagined. But she loved the feel of him beneath her tongue, beneath her hands. His skin soft and hot and hard all at once.

She had lived a life repressed. She had lived a life shut in. And this was her moment. The door was flung wide. And she was free. Running with no regard in the moonlight, her hair flying behind her as she swung as high as she wanted to on the swings. This was all of that, and it was more.

It was that thrill she had felt when she had first climbed a tree, when she had fallen. When she had sneaked away to be the person that she could only be when she was by herself. That girl who wanted to be daring. Who wanted to have everything that every other girl had.

She was that girl now. But she had Briggs. And she wasn't alone.

She took him deep into her mouth, and revelled in the groan of pleasure that escaped his lips. She had him. She had him, as he had her.

And the realisation emboldened her.

He put his hand on her back, centred at her shoulder blades, then wrapped his fingers tightly around her hair, before twisting it around his hand, and tugging.

She cried out.

'Don't stop,' he commanded. So she did not. She fought against his hold, and pinpricks of pain broke out across her scalp, delighting her, spurring her on.

And she found that his pleasure seemed to echo inside her. That his need was almost greater than her own, and the counterbalance of pain on an exquisite knife's edge that kept her present.

He began to arch his hips up to greet her, the tip of him touching the back of her throat.

She welcomed that too.

She was lost in it. In him. The tug of her hair, the thrust of his arousal, the escalating need between her thighs.

She moved to touch herself, to get some sort of relief from that building pressure there.

'No,' he said, tugging sharp and hard. 'You may not pleasure yourself. Not yet. I will take my pleasure first.'

She shivered, then went back to focusing all her energy
on him. And then suddenly, the bucking of his hips became
wild, and they both unravelled together. He growled his release, and she swallowed him down, as naturally as if she
had trained for it.

And then, she found herself being propelled back, as he
righted his breeches. Disguising himself from her.

'You did well,' he said. 'But it is not enough to redeem
you. You must receive your punishment.'

'Must I?'

'Yes. You must, because you were strong enough to withstand it.'

'Yes, Your Grace.'

And then she found herself being picked up, turned over
his lap. His large hand over the globe of her rear again. He
smoothed his hand over her skin, before removing it. And
when he brought it back down, it was with a resounding
crack.

She cried out. Pain spread over her body, wildfire. And
before she could catch her breath, he did it again, and again.
But something about the pain brought her focus between her
thighs, and the bright hot ache of pleasure there.

And she could not tell where the pain ended and the pleasure began. Where the heat turned from a violent fire to an
unending need. For it was all the same. Twisting and curling through her body. A torture she never wanted to end.
Except she couldn't endure it. She was wiggling, shifting
against him, trying to escape, and trying to get closer all at
once. Trying to grind the centre of her desire for him against
his muscular thighs.

'I need...'

'Not yet,' he said, bringing his hand down on her hard.

She trembled, shook.

And she found herself going to that place, that glorious place in her that she had built as a girl.

Where no one could touch her. No one and nothing. Because she was the queen of the palace inside her. Because she could handle anything. She could withstand.

Because she was strong.

Because she was a warrior.

She was not weak. She was not broken.

She could take this. She could take him.

It went on and on, and she began to find everything fuzzy around the edges, both more and less real. She felt wholly and completely connected to her body while also somewhere outside of it. But she was not alone. And that was the most revolutionary aspect of this. He was with her. They were in this together. It was not something being done to her, it was something they were both experiencing. Something holy and completely theirs. That brilliant diamond that she would protect from all else. From all others. It was Beatrice and Briggs, and only them.

And then, he moved his hand, pushing his fingers between her legs and thrusting them deep inside her. She cried out at the invasion, which was perfectly and wholly what she needed. She was slick and accepted him easily, and he thrust forward and withdrew in a steady rhythm, until the combination of being filled by him, and the lingering staying on her flesh tipped her over the edge into a total and complete release.

She found herself shaking violently, unable to stop, babbling incoherently. She grabbed for him, and he gathered her up in his arms. And oh, this was what had been missing. Always. Always.

There had been pain. There had been pleasure. And now he was cradling her as if she was the most precious, singular thing.

He picked her up and carried her over to the bed, where

he settled against the headboard, and cradled her naked body across his hard thighs, smoothing his hand up and down her bare back.

'You've done well,' he said.

And she went limp, burying her head in his chest as she wept. Piteously and gloriously.

Somehow it was both of those things all at once. As she became both weak and strong in his arms.

'Briggs,' she whispered.

'Sleep, Beatrice.'

'Will you stay with me?'

'Yes.'

And after that, she knew nothing more.

Chapter Fourteen

Briggs did not have a restful sleep. He stayed on top of the bedclothes, fully dressed, with Beatrice curled safely beneath the blankets, nude still.

She had been beautiful. Accepting everything he had given with more strength than he had imagined possible. It was not just that she had withstood it, but she had enjoyed it. Had wholly and completely been his in that moment.

She had surrendered to the pain, and had found that glorious place where pleasure intersected with it. And her release had been brilliant.

And he had felt...

He had given her pieces of himself he had worked for years to hide. The truth of his childhood.

The truths of his needs.

Had she rejected them...

It would have been a rejection of each and every piece of who he was.

He had never shared that part of himself so completely with a woman who knew him. He had only ever come close with Serena. And Serena had been... She had been horrified. She had rejected his touch, his...

Desires. She had found them and him far too animalistic. She had never been one to give herself over entirely to the marital act, but when he had attempted to introduce more she had...

She never would have taken him in her mouth the way that Beatrice had done. And Beatrice had done so with an enthusiasm unmatched by any whore.

Though the whores he had consorted with certainly evinced a certain measure of enthusiasm, when one paid for the pleasure, one could hardly be certain as to whether or not it was authentic.

It had never mattered to him. One thing he liked about the transaction was that there was no rejection involved. There were no grey areas.

He never felt exposed in his dealings with prostitutes because it was simple. He asked for what he wanted, and if they did not wish to provide, they were under no obligation to, but they did not get their money.

With a wife it was different.

He had been young, and he had been naive, and he had been certain that they could forge a marriage much different than his parents. One that included trust and fidelity.

And that she could see to all his needs. Instead, she had found his needs appalling. After that day she had never shared his bed again, and of course, he had never pressed himself upon her. He never would have.

An essential piece of his desire was the willing supplication of the woman he wanted. He would not, and had not, touched his wife in a manner she had found distasteful.

But Beatrice had not found his needs appalling.

Beatrice stirred, soft and sleepy, and he reached out and touched her.

And the moment his fingertips connected with her hair, so silken and lovely, he imagined gripping her hips from behind, then tugging her hair back as he thrust into her from that position.

No. That was...

It would endanger her. There was a risk, even with precautions, and he could not take those risks. He would not even allow himself to think of it.

It created in him too large of a feeling, and he did not wish it to exist in him.

They had found plenty of pleasure with each other. They had found plenty of pleasure last night.

She turned and looked at him, a slow smile spreading across her face.

'Good morning, Your Grace.'

He could not help himself. And it was not often that he could not help himself. So... He simply gave in. And he kissed her. On those soft, luscious lips. Her cheeks turned pink, and she smiled. 'It was not a dream.'

'No,' he said. His chest went tight. That she could find what had passed between them to be like a dream, rather than the waking nightmare his first wife had found it...

'I was afraid that I would wake up and I would be alone. And I would still be Beatrice.'

He frowned. 'What does that mean?'

'The same Beatrice. The Beatrice I always am. The Beatrice who is always alone, and certainly has never been touched so by a man.' She looked up at him. 'You make me feel... Incredible.'

And his stomach went tense, only because he understood.

It was why he was not Philip.

It was why he was Briggs.

So he did not have to feel the same.

Her lips curved into a smile and his thoughts stopped.

He could only stare at her, marvel at the fact that she fit with him in a way he could never have quite imagined. Had it been before him all this time?

'You astonish me,' he said. 'Innocence should not take to these acts with such fervour.'

'Do I offend you with my fervour?'

She looked upset, and he did not want her upset. He resisted giving her yet more honesty, but she had been accepting of him so far. And he would hate to cause her distress simply because he was unwilling to speak of the past.

'To the contrary. I find you exceptionally pleasing. It has just not been my experience.'

'Oh,' she said, looking away. 'Your wife.'

'I'm sorry. If it upsets you for me to speak of her...'

'I believe I said that to you last time she was mentioned. It does not upset me.'

'Are you jealous, Beatrice?' Beatrice's eyes suddenly filled with tears, and she looked away from him. He frowned. 'What is it?'

'She gave you things I cannot. She gave you a child and she...'

'*You* give me things that she would not,' he said. 'And that to me means more.'

She seemed pleased by that. And he was glad that he had found some way to ease her concerns. He did not want her to be concerned. He wished for her to feel utterly and completely safe and cared for. He wished for her to feel completely satisfied in the aftermath of all they had shared.

'We will go out today.'

'Did you have obligations?'

'Likely,' he said. 'But I am here in London with you and with William, and we should go again. To the park.'

'I would like that,' she said.

And he liked to see her smile.

* * *

They went their separate ways, dressing for the day, and he sought out William, and ensured that the boy ate his breakfast. He also decided to give the governess the afternoon off.

'We shall be together as a family today,' he said to William.

William looked pleased in that way that he often did. A small smile to himself. And Briggs felt as if he was... As if he was actually doing better than his father. It bothered him that the feeling mattered. It bothered him that it existed inside him, this desire to best his old man. And yet it did. He had not been aware it was quite so strong until now.

They got in their carriage and made their way to Grosvenor Square. They had packed a picnic for the afternoon, and he found himself slightly bemused by the fact that Beatrice had found a way to get both he and William to willingly participate in something both had said they would not. She might belong to him, but she had done a fair amount of changing the way that he lived.

She was very small for a revolutionary, and yet, he could not help but think of her as one.

'You are a warrior, Beatrice,' he said.

She looked at him, her eyes glowing. 'I am?'

'Yes.' He nodded. 'If I had to ride into battle, I would want you by my side.'

The flush of pleasure on her face pleased him immensely. And he was so focused on it, that he looked away from William for just a moment, and when he looked back, he was gone.

'William,' he said, looking around, trying to scan the group of children that were running about the edge of the water.

He spotted him finally, holding his deck of cards, and speaking seriously to three other boys. Something inside Briggs went tight. And he sat back, poised to act.

He would not intervene. Not if he wasn't needed. It was up to William to speak to other children if he wished to. And he ought to. It was a good thing. An expected thing.

But then one of the boys took hold of William's box, and flung it to the ground. And after the box, the cards.

'You're weird,' the other boy said. 'No one cares about Rome.'

'You're addled,' said another boy, and gave William a shove, and Briggs mobilised.

'You better find your governess,' he said, moving forward, and the boy looked up, his eyes going wide, and Briggs knew enough to know that the boy must have a father in the peerage, because he clearly identified Briggs as a man of great authority, his entire face going pale.

'I... I...'

'Is your governess about? Because she should seek to teach you manners, as you clearly have none.'

A woman came fluttering across the field. 'I am very sorry,' she said.

'You will do well to tell this boy's father when you give an account for his day, that he insulted the son of the Duke of Brigham. I will not allow for such a thing.'

'Sorry, Your Grace,' she said, 'so terribly sorry.'

He bent down and picked up the box, and all the cards, dumping them back in rather carelessly. And then he thrust them into William's hands. 'Take these.'

William was silent, his countenance dimmed.

They went back to the blanket where Beatrice was standing, looking outraged.

She knelt down. 'William,' she said. 'Are you all right?'

'He will be fine,' Briggs said. 'But you must...'

But then William shattered. He burst into tears, leaning against Beatrice as he wept.

'William,' she said, bringing him down to the blanket and holding him to her chest. 'It's all right. It's all right.'

'Don't cry,' Briggs said, his breath coming in shallow, angry bursts.

If the other children were to see William weeping, it would only make things more difficult for him later. He could not be remembered as that boy. And this was the exact thing he had feared. That he would find censure among other children, and it would be impossible for him to be known as anything else. And he might not be so lucky as to find a friend like Hugh who would come alongside him, who would be patient with him when he had outbursts. Who would...

'If you do not wish for other children to pour scorn on you, then you must learn to speak only of things that they care about. You must listen to them, not speak endlessly about things that they do not care about.'

'Briggs,' she said. 'He's a boy, and he loves those cards. The other boys, they were the ones at fault.'

Beatrice was angry at him. This she could not understand.

This part of him.

And what he knew.

Because of course she could not. No one could understand him quite so deeply.

'It doesn't matter,' Briggs said. 'It does not matter if they were at fault, and they were. They have the manners of jackals, and their fathers should beat them. But it does not change the fact that William's tears will only make the children think less of him. It does not change the fact that... The children will do what they do. And if you are different in any way, they will exploit that difference. They will make you miserable. They will make you wish you had not been born. And so you must learn to conceal it.

'We will finish our picnic,' Briggs said.

William was still weeping piteously against Beatrice. 'William,' he said sharply. 'We will finish our picnic.'

He had successfully startled his son into stopping his tears.

'You cannot let them see that they have made you hurt.'

'But it hurts,' William said.

'It does not matter. They do not deserve your tears. Remember that. Nor do they deserve to hear about your cards.'

They ate, but he took no pleasure in the taste of the food. Instead, he was consumed by his outrage, and the memories that it began to stir up inside him.

By the time the afternoon had worn on, everyone had left some of the incident behind. And he found some space to breathe around it.

But by the time they got back to the town house, he felt restless. And when William went to the nursery, he dragged Beatrice to her bedchamber, and unleashed more of the same on her from the night before. He took his pleasure, and she took hers, and when they were through, she laid her head on his lap, and spoke softly. 'Surely you cannot mean to have William never mention the things that he loves to the other children. You made it sound as if it was something he should be ashamed of.'

'It is not that he should be ashamed,' Briggs said. 'I am not ashamed of him. I'm not. But it does not matter if I am the proudest father in all the world, children will only see difference. And they will… Attack it like savages. It is who they are. It is what they do. They cannot help it, I suspect. It is innate. To make for the vulnerable, to make them wish they had not been born.'

He could remember being shoved to the ground by an older boy in the village when he'd been a lad. The boy's mother had been horrified because of who Briggs was, not because of the violence itself.

But the other boy had not cared who he was.

Imbecile.

He'd spat the word at Briggs.

All because he had asked Briggs about the weather and

Briggs had explained the ideal climate for orchids. On and on he'd talked until the other boy's fist had hit his face.

It had connected in his head, the weather and the flowers. He understood now why it had not to the other boy. But not then. Then he had not understood at all.

'Briggs...'

'No, Beatrice, you must trust me. I know of what I speak.'

'I'm sure that you do. You were right about the carriage ride, Briggs. You were. It was very hard for him. But look at how he has bloomed here in many ways. Exploring the city delights him, he adores the town house, his tantrums have slowed, the new environment is actually quite engaging for him, and it is clear he takes deep joy in it. So yes, you could've protected him from the carriage ride, but you would have also stopped him from experiencing all of this. And what a terrible tragedy it would've been. And think... If you would continue to protect me in all the ways my brother wished you to... We would've been protecting me from something that made me very happy.'

He shifted, his stomach going sour. 'I do not know that I do you any favours.'

'No,' she said. 'You do. I feel... Connected. To my body. To you. I do not know if I can explain. I spent my childhood very much as an observer. I felt as if I was not part of my family. I was always at home. While Hugh was away at school, I was at home. While he was away in London for the Season, I was at home. I was like a ghost in that house. My parents often acted as if I weren't there. Unless I was having some sort of episode.

'Sometimes my mother went away for the Season. My father would bring mistresses into the house, under the guise of...them being governesses for me. He did not speak to me. He did not... He acted as if I wouldn't tell. My mother wept outside my room often. Sometimes for me. Sometimes for herself. And I always felt as if I was pressing at a glass box, outside of all of it, controlled by everyone around me, and yet somehow completely distant from them. Closed off.

'Sometimes I would be left at home with only a governess, while they went to London for the Season, and the doctor said that my lungs would not be able to handle the city. And I learned to go places in my mind. I learned to dream. To read to find something happier than what I had in reality. But... Briggs, you must know that is such a miserable thing.

'And with you, I feel everything. When we are not separate. We are not distant. It is a revelation. It makes me feel like myself. In a good way. Not in the way I said the other morning. That I did not wish to be Beatrice. You make me feel as if Beatrice is a good thing to be. And I am always astonished by that. And I should take this feeling over protection always. Again and again.' She sighed heavily. 'You are a man who enjoys pain, and if you enjoy giving it you know someone else must enjoy receiving it. It is a balance. It is... life. How do you not see that sometimes to reach beautiful things, you must *endure* pain?'

'Because these are games, Beatrice. Games played in the bedroom, and they are not true to life.'

Her eyes were soft and filled with pity. 'They are not just games. Not to me. There's something so much more.'

'Beatrice,' he said. 'I have learned how to... Be the man that I must be. I have learned that I cannot simply... That I cannot simply follow every whim inside myself. There are places where I can be all that I feel.'

'Brothels,' she said.

'In the past that has been true. With women I have a transaction with, there is a certain expectation. I can meet them. And they meet mine. But I do not wonder about behaving this way to all and sundry.'

'Quite apart from anything else it would be very shocking,' she said.

'Yes. You cannot control the way others will treat you. But you do not need to needlessly expose yourself.'

'I do not wish to see William crushed.'

'I do not wish to see William crushed at all,' Briggs said. 'I would see him protected. From anything and everything. The best way to do that is to teach him how to... How to look like everybody else.'

He knew the pain of standing out. That boy...he had rallied other children to come after him whenever he ventured outside Maynard Park.

Eventually he had stopped leaving.

Eventually he had decided he preferred being alone.

It was Hugh who had taught him how to behave.

'Don't talk about flowers all the time, Briggs.'

'I don't. All the time.'

'No, but too often. And facts about soil and sun and things other boys don't care about.'

'I do not know what else to speak of.'

Hugh had looked confounded for a moment. *'Do you like the look of a woman's breasts?'*

Shock and shame had poured over him in equal measure, as he was still coming to grips with the shapes his fantasies were beginning to take. But that at least was an easy answer to give. *'Yes.'*

'That is something all those lot are interested in. If you can't think of something else to say, extol the virtues of a woman's figure.'

Be shocking. Be charming. He had learned how to do that. He had learned to be a rake.

And it had served him well.

'All I ever wanted was to be like all the rest. To be a girl like every other. To have the same expectations for my life. But it was not the path for me. If I were not born with my illness, then perhaps I would not... Perhaps the things that you and I do together would not be something I desired. But I cannot untangle those hardships with which I was born from who I am with you. From who I am all the time. So how can I say that I wish it were not so? How can I say that I wish I were not Beatrice? For if one thing in my life was changed, then I might not be the woman I am here and now. And while I might wish away my every hardship, while I might wish that you would allow me to fully be a wife to you… I cannot take away the risk, the concern, the terrible things that I have endured, and keep these precious things that we have found.'

He leaned his head back against the headboard, his thoughts a tangle. 'But perhaps if everything wrong in my past was undone, we would not need these things.'

'Perhaps. But they are not wrong,' she said. 'If we are both happy enough, they cannot be.'

'The only way to avoid my father's disdain was to be something completely different than what I was,' he said. 'My father despised me. And when I thought I had finally found the person who might care for me as I was, she also…found far more to despise than care for.'

He had not meant to carry on this path. Had not meant to continue on with this conversation. It was fruitless, after all. There was no point visiting any of these wounds in his past. He had bested his father by the simple virtue that he accepted William for who he was.

Something gouged his stomach.

Do you?

He did. What he had said to William was about keeping him safe. It had nothing to do with the way he thought the boy ought to behave. He loved the way that William thought. He was interested in the things that his son was, it was only that the rest of the world would never be. And it was not the same as what his father had done with him.

Serena had solidified these truths.

His father had been the one to teach them.

'I was not what he hoped for,' he said.

'Why?' She looked up at him, her gaze filled with genuine curiosity. 'You said before your father was ashamed of you. You seem everything a man could want his heir to be. You are handsome, and clever, and there is not a single person who does not enjoy rousing conversation with you. Why should your father not be proud of you?'

'I'm not the same as I was,' Briggs said. 'I learned. I learned to be the heir to the title. I learned to become the Duke of Brigham. Obsessions and specific curiosities, inflexibility, none of it allows you to connect with those around you. I had to learn. The other children in the village, they hurt me, Beatrice. They sought to punish me for my differences with words and fists. The boys at school did the same until Hugh taught me.'

'And so William must learn,' she said softly.

'It is not something you should concern yourself with.'

'Briggs... Tell me. Tell me about your father. Tell me about you.'

'There is nothing but the man before you,' he said, and when he said it, he almost believed it. Almost believed that he had successfully become something other than he had been.

'I am all that I must be. And that is all anyone ever need know.'

He got out of bed, and she reached for him.

'I cannot stay with you,' he said.

'Why?'

'You already know the answer.'

Perhaps she did know. Perhaps she didn't. It was not essential.

She could not become essential. And this could not become bigger than his responsibilities.

Bigger than what he'd made himself.

He had to remember. Even if Beatrice accepted him in her bed, it did not erase the way he had failed in the past.

He had become Briggs because Philip had been wrong.

And he stood there in the hall, by himself, imagining what it would be like for William when he was the Duke, and Briggs was gone. The idea, the image, made him feel hollow inside.

So he put it away, and he carried on. He knew what example he must set. He knew what he must be. In the meantime, he would take care of William and Beatrice.

Nothing else mattered.

Chapter Fifteen

For days Beatrice had been beset by what had happened at the park. By how badly Briggs had hurt William, even if unintentionally. She knew it had been unintentional. But William had been… Different since it happened. Quieter.

She wanted him to chatter again.

She had a feeling if it had only been those boys that had said those things to him, he would not have been cowed at all, but his own father had told him not to speak of those things, and that was what had silenced him.

She understood why Briggs had done it. She understood it was not out of any desire to hurt him or alter him in any way. 'William,' she said. 'Would you like to take a walk today?'

'No,' he said.

It made her chest hurt.

'What would you like to do?'

'Nothing,' he said.

'Come, let's go to the garden,' she said.

She found herself the focus of his irritation, but she did manage to cajole him outside to the garden, where he at the very least seemed contented by the presence of the statues.

She had not spent much time outside since coming to London, other than when they had gone touring. She hadn't been out in the garden in full daylight, she realised. And for the first time she noticed that there was a large glass building out in the corner.

'What is that?' she asked William.

'Oh,' William said, looking where she was gesturing. 'I don't know.'

It occurred to her then that the boy had never been here before. So asking him that question was silly at best.

'Sorry,' she said. 'I forgot that you have not been here before either.'

'It looks rather like the one at Maynard Park,' William said. 'It is a greenhouse. It is where the flowers are kept.'

'Flowers?'

'Yes. Orchids.'

She did not realise there was a greenhouse at Maynard Park. Briggs hadn't mentioned. Then she had not had a chance to explore the grounds thoroughly.

'Let's go look,' she said.

William was uninterested. But she considered it a mark of progress that she was able to extract him from the statues, and convince him to come with her. They went down the path and peered through the glass windows.

It was filled with flowers. Beautiful flowers.

She cracked open the door and walked inside, and looked around the room.

She did not know the name for all of these blooms. They were exotic and rare, brightly coloured.

'I'm not supposed to be in here,' William said.

'Why?'

'It is a rule.'

'How do you know you're not supposed to be in here if you've never been to the town house before?'

'It is the rule about the greenhouse in Maynard Park.'

'It seems a silly rule. I am with you, so you cannot get hurt.'

She grabbed his hand, just to be certain. And they began to stroll through the rows of exotic plants.

She saw movement outside the glass door, and then it opened, and in came Briggs, looking... Well, he looked furious.

'What is the meaning of this?'

'We were looking at the flowers,' she said.

'William is not allowed in the greenhouse.'

'So he said, but he's with me and...'

'Out,' Briggs said.

'Briggs...'

'Out,' Briggs said, his tone clipped.

She looked at him, at his handsome, angry face, and her heart squeezed.

She did not understand this man. This complicated man who made her feel like she was flying every night, and then who left her to try to find a place to land all on her own. Who both satisfied and left her aching with desire all at once.

Briggs...

And now he was angry with her, because she had done something wrong, but he had not laid out expectations for this. And she didn't know how he expected her to know exactly what he wanted her to do about everything if he did not tell her.

He could not be so picky if he wasn't going to be explicit in his instructions.

'The plants are very fragile,' he said.

And she stopped. Because she realised that this wasn't about William. It was about him. And it wasn't even about protecting the plants, there was something else.

'We will go,' she said. 'But you must take us on a walk, and you must entertain us,' she said.

'Must I?'

'You owe us, for behaving the part of an ogre,' she said. 'We did nothing to deserve your wrath. You did not leave clear instructions for me, and I was not given to understand there was any part of the garden that might be off limits. Now you have been an utter brute, and you must make up for it.'

'You are not an authority over me, Beatrice,' he said.

'Of course not, Your Grace,' she said, looking at him from beneath her lashes and knowing it would inflame his desire. Her confidence had grown in that at least.

She was rewarded with a flare of heat in his dark gaze.

She had been correct. He liked that. Liked her deference, even when it was hardened with an edge of defiance.

And that was how she finally got Briggs to take her and William out again, and how she got William slightly more out of his shell than he'd been over the past few days.

She would have to talk to Briggs about that. About the way he had been affected by what happened in the park. And about what she suspected was Briggs's part in it.

Afterward, they had dinner together, and then Briggs went, to his studies she presumed.

She had a letter from Hugh to read, and one from Eleanor as well. Both informing her that they were coming for the Season, and would be there in just a few days.

She knew that she should feel excited. To see her brother. See Eleanor. But… She felt selfishly upset that they were coming in and breaking up what was happening here.

She wondered how it would affect the way Briggs treated her. And what happened in her bedchamber at night.

She did not wish for that. She wanted to stay in her separate life, and she did not want Bybee House or her past to intrude.

She realised that was vile of her. But she could not help herself.

She waited for Briggs to come to her, but he did not. And finally, after becoming impatient, she went and looked in his study, but did not find him. And it was only intuition that led her down the stairs and out to the garden. Where she could see it. An amber light flickering back where she now knew the greenhouse was.

She had been right. She had been right, in her assessment of the fact that he had been trying to protect something when they had been in there earlier, but that it was not about the flowers.

This was him. There was a key here. A key to him. And she knew it. And so she stepped outside and followed the ambient glow of the light, and through the windows, she could see him. Inside, bent over one of the plants.

She pushed the door open. She did not knock, for fear that he would turn her away.

He might still turn her away, but she was already inside... He stiffened, then turned.

'Is this where you are? When I don't see you. I assumed you were in your study working away, but you're here, aren't you? William told me that there was a greenhouse in Maynard Park as well.'

'Not always,' he said.

'Briggs, why haven't you mentioned this?'

'I learned a long time ago that there are things people do not wish to hear about. It is not a mark against them, it is simply up to me to learn what people are interested in, and stick to those topics.'

'You like... You like flowers.'

'Horticulture and botany,' he said. 'The more complicated the better. The less suited to the English atmosphere, the better. I find it diverting.'

'For how long?'

He looked at her, his dark eyes intense. 'As long as I can remember.'

'These are your cards,' she said softly. She looked around. 'Briggs, do you not know that you're very like William?'

'He likes buildings. I like flowers. It is not the same.'

'It is the same. And that's why you reacted the way that you did when those boys were mean to him. People have been very unkind to you in the past, haven't they?'

'It is no matter.'

'But it is,' she said. 'Your father was unkind to you, wasn't he?'

He huffed out a laugh. 'Can you imagine how useless a man like my father would find this?'

'No,' she said. 'Because I did not know your father. You will have to tell me.'

'He hated this. He hated everything that I cared about. And I do not wish to speak further of it.'

'Why?'

'It will only bore you, and I reached my limit with how often I can possibly watch a person's eyes glaze over with boredom while I speak of things that matter to me. I reached the limit with how often I can disgust someone with who I am. I do not wish to do it any more.'

'I am not a child. I do not mock what I don't understand. I… I never had the chance to have friends, not when I was young. Maybe I would've been your friend.'

'No, Beatrice, if you had not lived a cloistered existence for you were forced to be different than others, you would not have been any different than the children that accosted William. For that is human nature. It is who we are.'

'I find that very grim.'

'Humanity is grim. There is no denying it.'

'I'm not a child now, though. I can certainly understand about this if you want me to.'

'I do not talk about myself. About…'

'I want to know, Briggs,' she said. 'I want to know you. It matters to me. You matter to me. And what matters to you will mean something. I can understand. Please, give me a chance to understand.'

'If I've learned one thing in this life it is that when you give too much of yourself away there will always be those standing by waiting to tear pieces from you. It is inevitable. My father...'

'I'm not your father.'

'Believe me, I did not confuse you with my father.'

'What got you interested in this?'

'Beatrice, this is not a wound that you can heal. I have learned to be different. I am content to see to my interests on my own time. It is not of any matter.'

'I want to understand you. And if you would deny us...'

'All right,' he said. 'You want to understand me?' He advanced towards her, and Beatrice shrank away. The intensity that radiated off him was confusing. For there was more happening inside him than she could fathom. There were things he was not saying. And it... It wounded her. Confronted her.

He grabbed hold of her arm and pulled her up against him. 'Do you pity me, Beatrice?'

'I don't understand,' she whispered.

'You pity my son, I think.'

'I don't,' she said. 'I don't pity William. I care for him. He is a wonderful... Unique child. He is not like everyone else, and that... I know what that's like. It doesn't matter whether it's because of buildings, or an illness, it amounts to the same thing. You end up on the outside looking in. And sometimes the loneliness is so bitter that you can do nothing to combat it. No, I don't pity him. And I don't pity you.'

'You might. If you knew the truth. About me.'

'Tell me, then?'

'My father wanted a son. He always wanted a son. When he had his son, his heir, his life was complete. And then he had his spare. The problem is, his heir died. His perfect, precious heir. And then he was left with... Well, they are spares for a reason.'

'Briggs... I had no idea. I didn't...'

'My brother died when he was ten. I was two. I don't remember him. But I already showed signs of lacking where he succeeded. In every way I was inferior to my brother. And my father took every opportunity to make sure that was known. My brother spoke in full sentences by his first birthday. I could not speak when I was four. I was lost in my own mind. Often turning over concepts and problems that I could not express. I became obsessed with small things. Knots for a while. Shoelaces. Small things. Eventually, I became entranced by gardens. Plants. I wished to know all about them, how they grew and where. So I learned. I became fixated on the orangery in my family home. And meanwhile, my father was trying to get me interested in other things. Trying to get me so that I could go to school and not be... Mocked brutally for the fact that I couldn't converse about anything more complex than an orchid.'

'But you...'

'Yes. I do well now. I learned. A bad combination of isolation and my natural self, I believe, made it harder for me for longer than it might have. If not for your brother, I would never have found my way at school. I'm certain of that.

'But it does not matter.'

'It does matter. It hurts you still.'

'My obsessiveness served me well in places in my life. In school, when it comes to managing the dukedom. With women.'

She flushed. She did not want to hear about him with women.

'I might always be the spare in the eyes of my father, the son that meant less to him. That he loved less. But... I have found other ways to gain appreciation. He used to punish me. When I could not speak on the topics he wished me to.'

'Oh,' she said. And of course she thought of the way that he had punished her. Of course she thought of that. How could she not?

'You feel out of control when you're a child.'

'You like to feel in control.'

'Yes. And I also like rare flowers. They are complicated. And one must know just how to care for them. You must take great care to observe, take into account every aspect of the environment. It is not so different than what I do with women. Finding the perfect balance of pleasure and pain. Watching your breathing. Your eyes.'

He took another step towards her, and she took a step away, her bottom hitting one of the platforms that held all the plants. That section was empty, the surface clear.

'You are like an orchid,' he said. 'You are in my care. And if I fail you, if you begin to lose your colour, the fault is with me.'

She could see. She could see it. He took total control, total responsibility, after a childhood spent feeling as if he had none. And she had felt... Insecure. Unsafe. She had wanted nothing more than to feel safe. As if she could trust all those in authority over her. But her father often acted in his own self-interest, her mother was distracted—even though it was her father's fault—the doctors... She simply had to trust that their training was as good as they said.

And all the while, things were simply done to her, and none of it... None of it with her permission.

While Briggs made her feel safe, taken care of. When he put his hand on her, she knew that it would be with the right kind of care.

She was his orchid. And he the master gardener.

'He said he wished I were dead,' Briggs said, his mouth now nearly pressed against hers. 'He said that he wished I were the one who had died.'

'Briggs...'

'And look at me, have I not done well? I've done better than him. It's only a shame that he's dead and he cannot see it.'

'Briggs.' She closed the distance between them and kissed

him. Kissed him fiercely. And he wrapped his arms tightly around her, kissing her as if she were the source of all life. As if... 'I want to know you,' she said, moving her hands to his cravat and undoing it, pulling his shirt open. She knew that this was outside the realm of their games. That she was not permitted to take his clothes off. She was not directed to do anything of the sort, and if she was not directed to do it, she did not do it. But she was lost in this. And his kiss. In her desperate need for him.

She opened his shirt, pushed it down his shoulders, and he tore at the front of her dress, exposing her breasts and pinching her ruthlessly. She cried out, arching against him. She reached desperately for the falls on his breeches, bringing his cock out and wrapping her fingers around it. She squeezed him, an answering desperation building between her thighs. By now, she knew what she wanted. He would respond by pushing his fingers into her, but he never gave her what she wanted. What she craved.

She was not an innocent. Not any more. She knew exactly what she wanted from Briggs. She knew exactly what he could make her feel. And she needed it. She did not know how to reconcile all that they were with what they both had to have. His desire to protect her. Her desire to be free. The honour that he felt when it came to his relationship with Hugh, and her desperate need to comfort him. To be all that he could possibly desire and more.

He pushed her skirts up her thighs, his fingers going between her legs as he stroked her.

'Please,' she whimpered. 'Please.' She arched forward, and he set her up on that platform, her thighs spread wide. He pressed the head of his arousal to her slick folds, stroked her, made her mad with her need for him. He was teasing her with what she wanted. Him. Inside her. That thick, masculine part of him. 'Please,' she whispered. 'Inside me. Please.'

He didn't. He was still.

And something stirred in her. A need.

His name.

She felt the head of him against her entrance, stretching her. He pushed in, a fraction of an inch and she gasped.

'Please,' she begged him. Because she was desperate. 'Philip. I need you.'

He growled and surged forward, and she cried out, his strong hands gripping her hips in a bruising fashion, the hard length of him pulsing inside her.

Whatever remained of her maidenhead was torn away by his invasion, and she revelled in the pain.

This new pain. This new closeness. Him. Inside her. So deep she could scarcely breathe.

And when he began to move, it was not gentle. His thrusts were hard and wild, the platform she was on hitting danger-ously against the glass walls, the sound mingling with their laboured breathing. With her gasps of pleasure. The surface of the table was rough, biting into the delicate skin of her thighs, and the sensation mingled with the feeling of him in her, and took her breath away. She was lost in this. In him. His every thrust electrifying that centralised source of her pleasure. He reached behind her, grabbed her hair and pulled as he thrust in hard, sending her over the edge, her release an endless wave that went on and on. Then he pulled away from her, stroking himself twice and finding his own release outside of her.

When it was through, he held her there, his breathing frac-tured. 'That should not have happened,' he growled.

She reached up and touched his cheek, a tender, swell-ing sensation overtaking her chest. 'But it was always going to happen,' she whispered. 'There was never anything else. Briggs, I was always going to need you like that.'

'It is not safe enough,' he said.

'You do not get to decide the level of risk I take with my life,' she said.

'No,' he said. 'You are mine.'

'I am not an orchid,' she said. 'You do not get to keep me in a glass case. I am not that fragile.'

'You were fine with the metaphor when it brought you pleasure,' he bit out.

'And it is a fine metaphor for pleasure,' she said. 'But not for my life. I ache for you. All night long. I want to be held by you, skin to skin. I wish to have you inside me. Are we not past these games? That I am an innocent and I must be protected from you. I am not an innocent. I cannot be a convenient release for your demons, and yet never receive any relief of mine.

'Do not treat me like a child,' she said. 'Please.'

'Do you not see? This is not treating you like a child, this is treating you as if you are mine, as if you matter. When I was a child I was not treated with such care. My father destroyed the flowers I spent years on. Everything. I was thirteen. He delighted in destroying my obsessions, but only after I had put enough work into them that the loss would be deeply felt. Nothing in that house was mine. Not really. I would hear my name. Echoing off the halls with rage every time he decided I had fallen short.'

His name.

His flowers.

His father had made every part of him into something he hated.

She put her hand on his face. 'I do not pity you because of the way your father treated you. I pity him. I pity that he did not know you. And what a great tragedy it would be if I did not know you either. Can you let someone know you? Just know you?'

'He knew more than anyone.'

'I should know more than anyone. I am your wife.'

'That is not what being a wife is, little one,' he said, touching her chin. Reflexively, she looked down. 'Serena did not wish to know every aspect of who I was. She wished only to be kept comfortable, to have her child...'

'You would deny me a child.'

'I am not the one who is denying you.'

'Can we not speak to physicians? Must we take the word of a man who has cared for me since I was a child, who made endless amounts of money from treating me? There must be someone else that we can speak to. At least try.' Her eyes met his, and suddenly her stomach went tight. 'Unless you do not wish to have a child with me.'

'Beatrice...'

'Is that it?' Her breath released on a jagged note. 'You do not wish to have a child with me.'

'I never intended to marry again. And my intent was to take you as my wife and never touch you. So perhaps you should just give me a moment to contend with the changes that have occurred since we initially took vows.'

She swallowed hard. 'Can we speak to a doctor?'

'Beatrice...'

'Will you take me to bed then? Take me to bed. Spill your seed outside of my body. But be with me.'

The look on his face was like torture. 'Please don't ever touch another woman.'

He picked her up from the table, then grabbed his coat that had been draped over another one. He wrapped it over her body, and carried her from the room. And then he took her into the house, up the stairs, and for the first time, into his bedchamber.

He laid her down in the centre of the bed and began to strip his clothes from his body. And she realised that she had never seen him fully naked. He never undressed entirely for their sessions.

She removed her own clothes, and lay back. Waiting. Then he joined her on the bed, the length of his naked body pressed to hers. And she thought she might weep. From how wonderful it felt. From how much it was… Everything. Everything that she needed. And then, for the first time, they slept together.

Chapter Sixteen

Beatrice felt something like a tentative happiness over the next few days. Briggs had made love to her the same as he had done in the greenhouse several times now. She found it thrilling each and every time. It was a revelation. Having him inside her. And while she wished that he did not have to withdraw when he found his own pleasure, she was determined to continue working on him regarding a second opinion.

But today, Hugh and Eleanor were arriving in London, and while Hugh was seeing about business with Briggs at the House of Lords, she and Eleanor would take tea.

She was very excited. To play lady of the house and dress for her friend.

She wasn't even playing. She really was the lady of the house. And properly now. She was truly Briggs's wife now.

Truly.

She wanted to call him Philip again, but he had let that one time pass without comment and she had a feeling that would not be true again, and she did not want to shake what they shared together.

She held that little spark of happiness close to her chest as she examined herself in the mirror. The mint-green gown that her maid had selected for the tea was wonderful. It made her feel fresh and beautiful. Or perhaps that was sleeping in Briggs's arms at night.

The door opened and the housekeeper arrived. 'Your Grace, Miss Eleanor Hastings is here to see you.'

She walked out of the bedchamber and went down to the morning room, where Eleanor was already seated.

'Eleanor,' Beatrice said, and her friend stood, crossing the room quickly and embracing her.

Eleanor was as delicate and beautiful as ever. The pale blue silk she was wearing suited her eyes and complexion perfectly.

'How are you?' Beatrice asked. 'Please tell me that Hugh isn't being an ogre.'

'No more so than usual,' Eleanor said, looking away.

Beatrice looked hard at her friend. 'What's wrong?'

'Nothing,' Eleanor said. 'I'm here for the Season. I will find a husband. That is a good thing.'

'Yes,' Beatrice said. 'If it is what you want.'

'I'm not like you, Beatrice. I do not have an assured place in this world whether I marry or not.' Eleanor sighed. 'I'm sorry. That was not a kind thing to say. I know that Hugh demanded you not marry.'

Beatrice shook her head. 'I'm not angry.'

The doors to the room opened and the maid came in with a tea service on a rolling tray. She laid it out before them, lovely sandwiches and cakes, and two pots of tea, along with two ornate teacups.

Beatrice smiled. 'I like being married.' She thought about Briggs, and the things that they did together, and her face went hot. 'I mean... I like... I'm pleased that I get to host you in my own home.'

'And what of Briggs?' Eleanor asked.

'He is... I care for him a great deal, Eleanor.'

'Of course you do,' Eleanor said. 'You always have.'

There was so much she wanted to say to Eleanor, but there was... She wasn't sure she could say it. Eleanor cared so deeply for Hugh that it might put her in a difficult position. But no, she would never speak of such things to him.

'I want to speak to a doctor again,' Beatrice said. 'About having a baby.'

Eleanor looked shocked. 'But they said you could not.'

'I know. But I...' She felt the colour mount in her face. She knew she wouldn't be able to hide it. 'I have been with him. Intimately.'

'Beatrice...'

'It could not... We could not... You don't understand, Eleanor. He is the other half of me. I...'

'You're in love with him,' Eleanor said softly.

The words struck a chord deep inside her that echoed like a bell in her head. Made her teeth ache, made her chest hurt.

Oh, no.

What a terrible thing to realise.

'I had hoped,' Beatrice said, slowly, 'that love would feel nicer.'

'Is he not nice?'

'He is... I cannot explain him. But please don't tell Hugh about us.'

'You are married,' Eleanor said. 'If he honestly thinks that he is going to control the way that you and Briggs are with one another now that you are... Now that you are married.'

'Just please do not tell him. He wanted Briggs to act as his stand-in, but it is not... That is not how we are with one another. I am not his ward. I'm his wife. I do not know if I love him. I... He makes me feel as if my heart is being cut out of my chest sometimes. And like I might die if I can't be near him.'

'As I understand it,' Eleanor said softly, 'that is love.'

'You are in love with my brother,' Beatrice said.

Eleanor looked at her. 'It is impossible.'

'It is only impossible because you think it is, and there is nothing that can be done once my brother decides something. That is the only reason, and it is not a very good one.'

'I should hope that you will tell him that. Maybe you can tell him while you proclaim your love for his best friend. And speak to him about your quest for a child.'

'You know that I can't. Once something is in his mind you cannot change it.'

'Yes,' Eleanor said. 'I do know that.'

'What is between Briggs and myself is very private. I think it is love,' she said, suddenly feeling upset. Because she had imagined that love would be more like the novel she'd read, and not this bright, sharp thing that stole her breath and made her feel like she was dying.

There was no sweet romance when they were in his bedchamber. Or hers. Or the greenhouse. It was fraught and desperate. And it contained everything. Exultant joy, deep sadness, pleasure and pain. They were a collection of their most shameful, messy parts when they were together. On full display and with nothing to conceal their sharp, jagged parts. They were... They were not a couple anyone would wish to write a novel about. For it would be unseemly. Too dark. Too hard.

And yet, so much of her life had been dark and hard and she had never thought that anyone could possibly find a way to make the sting of it make sense. To make all that she'd been through into something real. Into something that mattered. But he had done it. He made her feel.

'Maybe I will fall in love,' Eleanor said. 'With someone I can have. Maybe there will be a nice second son of an earl.'

'You do not want a nice second son of an earl.'

'No. Not because he is the second son of an earl,' Eleanor said. 'Simply because I don't know how to love someone other than… Other than His Grace.'

'Since when do you call him that?'

'I must. We are in London. And there is propriety to observe.'

'Has he scolded you? Has he put you in your place?'

'He is correct,' Eleanor said, her cheeks going pink. 'We are in society, and we must behave as if we are. I am not his sister.' Beatrice looked hard at Eleanor, and tried to see if she… Had something happened?

Beatrice knew that Hugh would find that sort of connection to his ward appalling. There were several reasons that Eleanor could never be suitable for him. But she wondered…

Because one thing Beatrice had learned was that unsuitable or not, it did not matter. Not when you desired someone. Not when they desired you. Not when you fit together in ways you had not even known were possible.

Love was inconvenient. And if there was one thing that she could learn from *Emma*, she supposed it was that. But it was often the person who infuriated you. The person who you least wanted to need.

'I'm glad you're here,' Beatrice said. 'I only have William and Briggs to speak to, and it's… I wanted someone to speak to. Really. I am sorry, I know that you… You are unmarried. But… Physical intimacy within marriage is wonderful,' she said.

Eleanor laughed. Actually laughed. 'I know about that,' Eleanor said.

'Eleanor!'

'I mean, I have not… I understand though.'

Beatrice thought that Eleanor probably did not understand all of the things that she and Briggs did together. But then, she doubted many people would. But they did. She would never share the details. They were far too personal. Far too intimate.

'I don't think he loves me,' Beatrice said. 'Or it's impossible to tell. He is...'

'What sort of father is he?' Eleanor asked.

'Lovely,' Beatrice said, a silly smile crossing her lips.

'Lovely?'

'He is. I don't know how else to say it.'

'It is hard for me to imagine him as a father. Given all I know about his reputation,' Eleanor said.

Beatrice thought about that for a moment. 'I've thought about Briggs's reputation. His reputation is both severely under-and over-exaggerated.'

It was true. Briggs was not a rake in the way that she had once imagined him to be. With her limited understanding of what that meant. He was a man of great intensity, and the desire that burned between them was anything but simple. It was the sort of thing that many people would find objectionable. Depraved even.

But it was theirs. It was theirs and it was not for anyone else to understand. Not for anyone else to approve of.

It was different, even, than the way that high society flaunted and enforced the rules they created at their own whims. For this was not about taking joy in debauchery, or in rebellion. It was about being what the other needed. It was about his honour of her strength. About her showing how safe he made her feel.

'I'm happy you're happy,' Eleanor said.

'I am not happy that you aren't,' Beatrice said.

'I will find a way,' Eleanor responded. 'You know, a woman such as myself... I have been very lucky to have been taken in by your family. It is... It is dishonourable of me to be so sad because I cannot have the impossible. I can no more take the stars down and hold them in my hands than I can aspire to be with your brother. My heart is foolish. I can go on loving him just fine married to another man.'

'You would be content with that?'

'I would be resigned to it,' she said.

'What of your husband?'

'I dare say very few men expect love from their marriages.'

Beatrice thought of that. 'I did not expect love from mine. But he is the very dearest thing in the world to me. He is so strong, so… Hard and remote. And yet I find I want to hold him in my arms and protect him from everything that has happened.'

'Does he grieve his wife?'

'No,' she said. 'He's…' She realised it as soon as she said, 'He is angry at his wife. Deeply and bitterly angry.'

'Oh,' Eleanor said.

'I know him better than I have ever known another person. I have let him do things that… And yet there is still so much I don't know.'

'I guess that is the fortunate thing about marriage being a lifetime.'

'Yes,' she said. 'I suppose that's true.'

'I can only hope I find that a remotely fortunate prospect when I'm faced with my own.'

'Let us hope a gallant and handsome man catches your eye tonight,' Beatrice said.

'Yes,' Eleanor said. 'Let us hope so.'

Briggs had not simply failed at what he had promised, he had jumped head first into an affair with his own wife.

He could not stay away from her.

Philip. Please.

It echoed in his head. When she had begged him. By name. To be taken.

He had not been able to resist. She was all tight heat and need, and every night when he sank into her he felt himself slipping further and further away from what he had promised he could be, and embracing the darkness of what he wanted.

He did not spill his seed inside her.

She was adamant that she would speak to a physician about the risk of her carrying a child.

Still, he knew that the precautions they took were no great assurance that there would be no baby.

He was primitively satisfied in the image that came into his head of Beatrice swollen with his child.

Serena had not wanted him to touch her when she'd been pregnant, and it was entirely possible that Beatrice might feel the same way. But she would not hide her body from him. That much he was certain of. He was deeply certain he would find the sight erotic.

Not thoughts he should be having in the carriage with his wife beside him on his way to a ball where her brother would be present.

She was leaning against him, her head on his shoulder. Those things were so easy for her. Casual touches.

She touched him all the time. She freely gave sweet affection to his son, and she gave it to him in equal measure. He had not realised how hungry he was for such a thing. Something as simple as touch. Not the sort of pleasurable touch they shared in the bedroom, but this simple close touch. That was simply pressure against his body, assurance that she was there.

In cutting these sorts of relationships from his life, he had lost that.

You've never had it.

'You look beautiful tonight,' he said, distracting himself by returning to her physical beauty.

The crimson gown she was wearing tonight felt wicked. It did not reveal any more of her body than anything else she wore, but there was something about the colour that felt an announcement of sin.

And he was so well acquainted with the kinds of sin that he could commit with Beatrice.

It was all he could think of. That and dragging her out

to the garden for re-enactment of previous interludes in the outdoors.

'When did you begin sneaking out of your house?'

It was something that he had puzzled over recently.

For when he had met her she had seemed a pale and drawn creature, and he did not know when those things had changed. Or if she was simply very good at putting up a smokescreen.

'When I was fourteen. I would climb out my bedroom window in the night. And sometimes I thought... Sometimes I thought it would be acceptable if it killed me. Because I was so very tired of those four walls.'

'I do not find it acceptable,' he said, looking at her. For he understood now, if reluctantly, what she thought about the baby really.

She was not concerned for her own safety. She was hungry. Hungry for experience. And perhaps he could find a way to be enough.

To be enough so that she did not feel the need to have a child.

'I understand,' she said. 'But you know, every day we take risk when rising from our beds.'

'For some it is a deeper risk,' he said.

'Perhaps,' she returned. 'But life is all the dearer to me for that reason. I fought for the chance to run in the moonlight. I had to engage in subterfuge to spend time swinging in my own garden. I had to beg for my husband's possession. I had to fight for a husband at all. Do you not see how much more dear these things are to me for that reason?'

'Beatrice,' he said, his voice rough. 'You are strong. I am in great admiration of it. But...'

'You wish to protect me.'

'Yes.'

'For Hugh's sake or for mine?'

The words caught in his throat for a moment. 'For mine.'

Her breath caught, she looked away from him, and said

nothing else. When they arrived at Lady Smythe's, they were announced upon entry to the ballroom, and he immediately spotted Hugh.

Beatrice was swept away by the gaggle of ladies that had taken a shine to her, and she took Eleanor along with her.

'And how are you finding London?' Briggs asked.

Hugh's expression was opaque. 'Eleanor's dance card is full. I suppose that is a victory.'

He rather sounded like he was being sent to the gallows, not like he was pleased with his ward's performance.

Something troubled him, and Briggs wished he could help. And also felt as if he did not deserve any additional insight into what Hugh was feeling, not when he had betrayed his trust as he'd done.

But you honoured Beatrice's desires.

He found that as much as he loved his friend, that mattered more.

'Full marks to you,' Briggs said.

Hugh cast an eye over him. 'And how are *you* finding London?'

'I am here. As ever. And Beatrice is getting her experience of the Season.'

'Good,' Hugh said, looking around.

'William is enjoying himself.' Normally he went out of his way to never speak of William. Not even to Hugh.

His friend lifted a brow, indicating his surprise.

'I'm glad to hear it.'

'Beatrice is a wonderful stepmother to him,' he said. 'He has… He has changed a great deal with her. I wonder what would've become of me if I'd had a mother who had cared for me so.'

He did not know why he was saying this to his friend, except that he knew what Briggs had been like when he had first gone to school. The lack of confidence he'd felt. The inability to speak to other children.

'I'm glad to hear it. That it has been something beneficial for you.'

'I would hope for all of us.'

'That is more than I expected to hear, I confess.'

'She is a strong woman, your sister,' Briggs said. It was difficult for him to keep the admiration from his voice, and then, why should he? Hugh should understand. He should understand what manner of woman Beatrice was. Woman. Because he got the feeling his friend still thought of her as a girl. And she was not. She was strong, and glorious. When the two of them made love they...

Hugh's head turned sharply, his focus suddenly diverted. Briggs followed his gaze. His ward had gone to the dance floor and was now in the arms of another man.

'I do not approve of that,' Hugh said.

'Abernathy? Why?'

'You know full well.'

'He frequents the sort of brothels that we do?' Briggs asked.

'He has a reputation for being quite perverse.'

'So do I, as you well know.'

The look that Hugh gave him went hard. 'Yes, and I have full confidence that you are not visiting such acts upon my sister or I would look at you much the same.'

Briggs ground his back teeth together. '*She* is not your sister,' he said, indicating Eleanor.

'No,' he said. 'Indeed she is not.'

Beatrice separated herself from her lady-friends, and fixed him with a bright smile. Then she looked at her brother. 'It is so good to see you.' He knew that were they not in the ballroom she would've flung herself at Hugh and given him a hug.

'And you. London suits you.'

'Yes,' Beatrice said defiantly. 'It does. I remember a time when you did not think that would be true.'

'I'm happy to be proven wrong,' Hugh said.

'Well, a strange thing indeed coming from you. I did not realise the Duke of Kendal ever thought he could be wrong.'

Her words were strong and clear. She was not saying this to him to goad him, rather she was not allowing him total control of the situation. He recognised a person playing at mastery when he saw it.

It was damnably impressive.

'In this instance,' he said, 'I am pleased to be.'

'My dear husband,' Beatrice said. 'Perhaps you should spare me a dance. We can keep an eye on Eleanor. Which I do think my brother would like. So that he can stop staring daggers in that direction.'

'I'm not staring daggers.'

'You are. Do not make this miserable for her,' Beatrice said, not allowing him to get away with it.

'Excuse me?'

'Do not make it miserable for her,' Beatrice repeated. 'Whether it be because of protection or because you do not want another man to have that which you will not take yourself, you must not make her miserable. Please let her be happy.'

'She will not be happy with him,' Kendal said, bristling, and Briggs felt utterly outclassed by his wife. Who had clearly identified something happening that he had not.

'You must let her determine that,' Beatrice said. 'You must let her decide what will make her happy.' Beatrice let out a harsh breath. 'You cannot protect people from everything. You cannot force everyone to live the life that you think is best.'

'Of course I can,' Kendal said. 'I'm a duke.'

'You are a stubborn ass is what you are,' Beatrice said. 'Come. Let us dance.'

Briggs shrugged, and allowed Beatrice to take him to the

dance floor, where he took her into his arms. 'Bold of you,' Briggs said.

'Eleanor is miserable with love for him. He cannot act a jealous lover when he has no intention of ever...'

'Beatrice,' Briggs said gently. 'Even if he did see her that way, which he has never indicated to me that he does, you know he never would. She is beneath his station in every way, and under his protection.'

'I know,' Beatrice said. 'And so does she. But it does not change the way that she feels. If he truly wishes to do a kind thing for her, he must let her be happy. He must let her be.'

'Human hearts are terribly inconvenient things,' Briggs said.

'Yes,' Beatrice agreed readily. 'They are.'

Her eyes took on a strange light, and he shifted uncomfortably.

Eleanor, for her part, looked like she was enjoying herself well enough, as she traded partners with frequency. She was extraordinarily beautiful, and even though her icy blonde beauty did not appeal to Briggs when he had Beatrice's lovely chestnut curls beneath his hands, he could see that she was just the sort of woman that many men would like. She did not have a title, or a dowry, but she was under the Duke of Kendal's protection, and he was offering quite the dowry. She should be able to find herself a good match.

Such a strange thing, to be at one of these events with a wife again. He had not fully appreciated it the first time.

He did not have to avoid women coyly trying to get his attention. Then indeed, even if there were women attempting to get his attention, he did not think he would notice.

He was brought back to the moment by Beatrice's hand on his cheek.

'You are missing from me.'

'I'm not,' he said. 'Never.'

Her cheeks flushed. 'I remember when I so looked forward

to experiencing a ball. And now I find myself impatient to leave so that you and I can be alone.'

'If your brother were not here, I might take you into the garden again.'

'That I would enjoy. But perhaps I would be the one to pleasure you.'

His desire had him in a chokehold. And he knew that he should not tease her like this, not so openly. But everyone around them was dancing, and they were far too interested in their own entanglements to worry at all about Briggs and his wife.

He moved his hand up between her shoulder blades, then up still to the back of her neck, his hold turning possessive. And he felt her shiver beneath his touch.

'A promise,' he said. 'For later.'

'I will hold you to that promise. I must warn you, I'm feeling particularly unruly tonight.'

'You shall require a firm hand.'

Her grin lit up the ballroom. And he felt it square at the centre of his chest.

'I do hope so.'

When he looked up it was because he felt, rather than saw, someone looking at him. And he was correct. The Duke of Kendal had fixed him with a thousand-yard stare that felt rather like a knife at the centre of his back.

He had been wrong then, about the interest of others. Hugh needed to find himself a woman to distract him, for Briggs had no interest in being the focus of his attention.

But then, Hugh would not find the sort of woman he liked here. While he did not share Briggs's specific affinities, what he knew was that his friend tended towards a level of roughness not ever visited upon gently bred ladies.

'Come on,' he said.

He led her out towards the back of the ballroom, to the terrace. And he sensed that Kendal was following them.

He was not in the mood to have a discussion with his friend about the details of his intimate life.

'What is it?'

'Oh, I imagine we will discover exactly what it is in just a few moments.'

'Why exactly was I watching as the two of you flirted outrageously on a dance floor?'

'We are married,' Beatrice pointed out. 'I cannot be ruined by my own husband.'

'Do not be incorrigible,' Hugh said. 'You and I both know the circumstances of your marriage.'

'Nobody knows the circumstances of our marriage but us,' Beatrice said.

And he did want to tell her to not play quite so grandly with his fate. He did like to be alive.

'Briggs, I asked one thing of you.'

'Yes. You asked me to take care of your sister. You asked me to treat her as a ward.'

'I have the sense things have changed.'

Briggs knew that he was about to cross a line. And he thought to himself for a long moment about whether or not he wished to turn back. He did not.

'Perhaps, it is simply that you are taking your feelings about what you would like to do with your ward and placing them on my shoulders.'

Hugh took a step forward. 'You bastard. You would question my honour.'

'I know what it looks like when a man burns with jealousy, Kendal. I'm not blind.'

'And I know what it looks like when a man is gazing at a woman in a way that suggests he has taken her to bed.'

'Are you accusing me of being bedded by my *husband*?' Beatrice asked. 'As if you have a say in that. As if it is yours to know? Because that is too far, Hugh. Even for you, it is too far. You may not control my life. You do not get a say in what I can endure.'

'Having a child could kill you.'

'Yes. But being married to Briggs and not having him would have killed me as well. Oh, I might've still drawn breath, but my broken heart would have hurt every time it beat.'

Hugh took a step back, a muscle jumping in his jaw. But he was only shocked enough to be set back for a moment. 'He is not a knight of the round table, Beatrice. He is a dragon. And you will end up burned.'

'Perhaps I like dragons. And fire in equal measure. You think me weak,' she said. 'And if you insist on inserting yourself into my life, then you will discover things that you may not wish to know. Not the least of which because you do not wish to know such things about your sister, but because you do not wish to find out you are wrong, and I think perhaps that is the thing that will burn the most. Do you think I fear the things that he wants? I run towards them. There are many things you don't know about me.'

'And you know exactly why his first wife died?'

Briggs took a step forward. 'That is too far.'

'If you laid a hand on my sister in the way you handle your whores then you have gone too far.'

'You would rather I stay married to a man who must seek out pleasure at a brothel, rather than giving myself to him? Even if it is what I want?'

'You cannot…'

'I cannot understand? I was bled. My skin was cut open, my… The process of saving my life was nothing but pain. Pain and isolation. What I wish to do with that life should be up to me. The cost that it took to get me here… You do not get to say how I will live. It is not your decision to make. And you will not speak so to my husband.'

'If you put my sister's life at risk, I can no longer call you a friend.'

'If you care so little for her happiness then perhaps I can no longer call you one either.'

And that was not even considering the fact that he had brought Serena into it. Her death. And his every feeling of guilt on the subject. 'Come, Beatrice. I think it is time we went home.'

'Yes,' she said.

But not before she put her hand on his face and kissed him boldly on the mouth. 'I should like to go home.'

She walked past Kendal without giving him a glance, and back into the ballroom.

Kendal stopped him with a hand on his chest. 'This is a betrayal.'

'It does not surprise me,' Briggs said, his chest feeling cut open. 'But in the end of all things, you find me as repellent as all others I have once called friends and family. But she does not.'

'For now.'

'For now,' Briggs said.

'And if she has a child, and she dies...'

The words stabbed straight through his chest. A knife to his heart. It was a deep fear, one that left him gasping for breath.

But he had seen her. What she wanted. What she was capable of.

What she craved.

He knew she would never be happy with half a life.

She wanted it all.

He would be damned if he was the one that kept her in chains.

'I will never forgive myself. But you have the luxury of turning her into an object. Of turning her into a child that you must guide and care for. I have a child. I have a son, and

I know the difference between being a father and being a husband. I am not her brother. I am not her father. She is my wife. And I am her life sentence.'

'Better than being her gallows.'

'She is not a child. I cannot look at her day in and day out and feel pleased with sentencing her to have a life where she is treated like she is weak and like she does not know her own desires.'

'That is a very noble way of saying you cannot control your cock.'

'Perhaps I cannot. Perhaps I want her. But you will find that she is not upset about that either. All she wanted was a Season, Kendal. For a man to look at her across the room and want her. I want her. She and I have been shaped and forged in a particular sort of fire, and I suppose the end result is that we suit each other better than we could've imagined. I am not ashamed of it. I refuse to be.'

'I wash my hands of you.'

'Then you wash your hands of her as well. For she is my wife. She is my family now. I protect mine.'

He walked away then, leaving behind the only real friend he had ever had.

And when he exited the ballroom, he saw her standing there, her arms wrapped tightly around herself. And he realised… He had her now. Whatever else.

In this moment. He had her.

They got into the carriage together, and she put her hand on his thigh. More of that casual sort of touch that lit him from within. 'I'm sorry,' Beatrice said. 'That was a terrible thing for him to say. It was a terrible thing for him to do. You are an honourable man, Briggs…'

'I'm not,' Briggs said. 'He is right. If I had honour, I wouldn't have touched you. But I did not have honour, what I had was a desire to see you happier than you were. And I wanted you. It was that simple.'

'I am not sorry about it.'

'I know,' he said.

'He should not have brought up your wife.'

No. But perhaps now was the time when he should speak to Beatrice about it.

But he did not. He did not. Instead when they got home they did not speak. He pulled her into his arms, and made a particularly punishing night of it.

The next day, she set out to find a physician to speak to.

And Briggs decided to have a picnic indoors with William.

'Where are your cards, William?' he asked, when they were midway through their meal and he realised that his son had not produced them.

'I do not play with them any more.'

'Why not?'

'I know all the answers on them. They're in my head. Where no one can see.'

Briggs felt a twist of regret inside him.

And there were so many things he wanted to say, but he did not know how to say them.

He thought of what his own father would've done, but he couldn't even get that far, because his father would not have been here sitting on the floor with him.

He did not know how to do this. He did not know how to… How to be the right thing for people. And he was trying. Trying for Beatrice, because she deserved it. But the cost was losing Hugh's friendship. He did not know how to protect his son, and make it feel like there was nothing wrong with him. He did not know what things to share of himself and what things to hold back. He did not understand how to make Briggs be a good father.

May I call you Philip?

No.

What sort of father would Philip have been? What if he turned around and started talking about orchids?

It was exhausting. This.

And he did not know the way around it.

Beatrice returned home; she was pale and large-eyed.

'How was your visit with the physician?' he asked.

'He said that there is always risk in having a child. And he cannot guarantee any woman that she will survive.'

Briggs laughed. But there was no humour in it. 'Quite a measured response.'

'He does not see why I should be any more vulnerable than any other woman. We talked extensively about my issues. The malady in my lungs, and how it has not been as bad in recent years. He said he does sometimes see this. The children who survive a childhood such as mine, with lungs that close off, sometimes fare much better as adults. He said it is difficult to get a firm grasp on how many, because very often they do not survive childhood.'

'I see.'

'He thinks that we can have a baby.'

He very suddenly, very fiercely did not wish to share her.

'Perhaps some day.'

'That is all right,' she said. 'I do not need one now. But I would like for there to be no restraint between us. At least tonight.'

Desire was a beast inside him. He knew what she was asking. And tonight... Tonight he felt willing, more than willing, to take the risk. 'Philip,' she said. 'I wish for you to take me to bed.'

It was still not yet dark, but he did not care. He picked her up, right there in the entry, and carried her up the stairs, in full view of all the servants, who undoubtedly knew exactly what he intended for his Duchess. He did not care. He simply did not care. For he was out of restraint. There was none left within him. And he wished to revel in that.

He had lost one of the most important people in his life for this. For her.

And he would make the decision again. Perhaps Kendal was right. And he simply had no control over his cock. But it felt like more. It felt deeper. 'Strip for me, little one.'

And she did, with no hesitation. Removing her layers with a coy look in her eye.

She gloried in his gaze. And it made him feel like a god. She was a lady. Gently bred, cosseted too. And she would be brazen for him.

'On your knees,' he said.

She approached him, dropping to her knees in front of him, her eyes intent on his. This was nothing like the studied submission of a whore. But a gift. A gift to him that he was not certain he deserved. No. He was certain he did not.

Because she did not know about Serena. Not the whole truth of it.

He freed himself from his breeches, gripped the back of her head and guided her to him, roughly thrusting inside her mouth.

As ever, she gave in to him. With absolute freedom.

Seeming to revel in all that he was.

He stopped her before he could come. Before he ended things.

Then he picked her up and moved her to the bed, depositing her on her knees and pressing his hand firmly between her shoulder blades, so that her breasts were against the mattress. And her ass was up in the air. She was lovely like this. And he did not think he would ever get enough.

'Is this what you want?'

'Yes,' she said.

'You want me,' he said. 'You want me, and all that I am?'

He brought his palm down hard on the plump global flesh, leaving a bright red mark behind.

She squirmed against him, the yelp that she made more one of pleasure than pain. 'Yes,' she said.

'For the rest of your life. You want me?'

'Yes,' she said in time with another strike of his hand.

'He was right. I am depraved. And you know that makes you depraved right along with me.'

'Yes,' she said. He timed it with another firm smack. Over and over until her every breath was in affirmation. Until she was marked by him.

Until she was shaking. And so was he.

'Philip,' she said. 'Please, Philip.'

And it was balm for his soul that she used his name. Because right in this moment he did not feel confused. Whether he was Philip or Briggs.

He was hers.

He pressed himself up against the wet entrance of her body and thrust hard. Claiming her over and over again, the only sound in the room flesh striking against flesh. And when her pleasure exploded around him, he could not keep himself back any longer. He released hold of his control. And he let himself spill inside her.

'Philip,' she whispered. 'Philip, I love you.'

Chapter Seventeen

Beatrice was rocked. Utterly shaken.

In the space of just a few hours she had found out that she could have a baby, had seduced her husband, and had told him that she loved him.

She was laying there in the aftermath of their desire, shattered and terrified. For she had not meant to say aloud that she loved him. Not yet.

But she could not keep it in. Not any more.

She was not… She was not sorry. She was not sad. It felt right. This. No matter what happened.

'I love you.'

'Love,' he said. 'I do not… I do not even understand what that means.'

'You do not understand what love means?'

'I do not understand what it has to do with this.'

'It has everything to do with this. You are my husband. My lover. My friend. I love you.'

'You love me,' he said, his tone sardonic. 'I do not think you do. Moreover, I do not wish to have this conversation. It is… It is foolish.'

'What is foolish about it?'

'No one has ever loved me. No one. No one has ever said those words to me.'

'Briggs,' she said. Her heart squeezed. 'Philip.'

'Do not call me that.'

'You have no issue with me calling you that when you're inside me.' She moved away from him, swinging her legs over the side of the bed frame and standing.

'It's different.' He sat up, getting out of bed and standing with the expanse of mattress between them.

'Philip, just because your father could not understand you…'

'You are not the least bit curious what your brother meant when he spoke of my wife?'

'I do not wish to pry. You have not shared about your wife and…'

'Serena did not die of some ailment. Serena took a bath and cut her wrists open with broken glass.'

Beatrice took a step backwards, her heart slamming against her breastbone. 'Philip…'

'Do you know why? Do you know why she needed to get away from me? I discussed it with her. She never loved me, Beatrice. But I thought that we could still be friends. I thought that we could… I was so young, and I believed, I truly believed in my heart that my wife would be fashioned for me in some way. That she would understand me. We were not friends. She despised me. She could not see a way to escape me.'

'Briggs, I know you. I know you, and I know you never did anything to harm your wife. I know you would never have forced yourself on her.'

'It doesn't matter. Knowing what kind of monster I was disgusted her so much that she could not look at me. She could scarcely share the same space as me.'

'I do not believe it. I do not believe that she left this world simply because of what you wished to do in bed.'

'It is not that. It is merely a facet. It is the whole of who I am that is wrong. My father was ashamed of me. So ashamed that he wouldn't send me to school. My own wife could not bear me. And now you want to tell me that you love me? You, who married me because you were caught with me when you did not intend to be.'

'Yes,' she said. 'Because perhaps I was meant to be your wife all along. You were right, Philip. There was a woman who would love you exactly as you are. For your orchids and your punishments. For the way you make her feel.' She looked down at her body, at the bruises left on her skin, fingerprints that lingered from his touch. And they marked her. As his. As strong.

'You were the only one who saw the warrior that I wanted to be. You are the only one who treats me like I am not broken. So do not now reject my love. Do not now tell me that I am not strong enough for you.'

'You do not understand.'

'I do understand. But you do not like to be Philip because you still think that he is a little boy who could not be loved. And so you became Briggs because you thought that he might be someone that people would accept. The Duke of Brigham. But I love every piece of you. I love you and your being a cordial rake, and I love you when you are in your greenhouse. And I love the way that you are with your son. With our son. I love him. Because he is a piece of you. Delightful and different and nothing at all to be ashamed of. In the exact same way that you are.'

'It is different...'

'It is not different. Would you ever look at William and tell him that he did not deserve to be loved? Would you ever tell him that he was so wrong...?'

'No. And you know I would not.'

'I know. So why do you do the same to yourself?'

'Because I…'

'Philip. Do you hate yourself so much, that you would punish yourself unto the end?'

He bowed his head for a moment, and then he turned away from her. 'Beatrice, I have wronged you. For I cannot be the man that you wish me to be. I cannot be what you desire. I can give you pleasure. But no more.'

'Can I give you my love?'

He shuddered. 'I cannot.'

'You cannot accept it. I… I am wounded by that. I will not tell you any lies. But I have spent my life locked away.' Even as she said it, she felt a deep pain stabbed her chest. 'I have spent my life being protected from all manner of pain. And you know that I now have come to seek it out. Oh, Briggs, I have felt so endlessly lost. So endlessly isolated. And I would rather stand here and live this moment than go back to Bybee House. I would rather love you and all this pain. I would rather love William. I would rather risk. And I will keep loving you.'

'Until you don't.'

His voice was flat. And he walked away. And Beatrice collapsed at the foot of the bed, weeping piteously. She felt… Utterly sad for him. For them. For all that they could be.

For all that he could have.

And even within the depths of her despair. She realised.

She was at war now. For his heart. For his very soul.

You always thought that you were strong enough to do this. You must not crumple now.

Briggs was drunk. And he was at a brothel.

He hated himself. Despised himself. And yet, he was doing everything he could think to do to push her away.

And you will devastate her if you touch another woman.

He knew that.

It was why he was simply in the dining area drinking. He had not gone up to one of the bedrooms yet, but he would. He would. He would do what he must in order to...

To what? Devastate her? So that you can prove your own point?

But it was the work. That was what he could not take. That was what he could not endure.

He did not know what magical combination of pieces of himself he had found to make Beatrice love him. He did not understand it. And he had no idea how to continue on with it.

And it would be like everyone. Everyone. Eventually, he would not be able to be the thing that she wanted, and then she would hate him. She would hate him.

As much as he hated himself.

He felt the same chilly presence that he had felt that night at the ball and looked up. Of course it was Kendal. He should've known better than to be seen at a brothel when his brother-in-law was in town.

'And what the hell are you doing here?'

'Leaving your sister alone. Is that not what you want?'

'Like hell. You bastard. I do not want you betraying my sister. That is certain.'

'A betrayal, is it? How so? If she is merely to be my ward.'

'And have you taken her innocence?'

He said nothing. Instead, he simply drank more whisky.

'You have. Wonderful.'

'What I have or haven't done is hardly your business. You must leave me to sort out the affairs of my marriage. After all, you will wash your hands of me.'

'It is only out of concern for Beatrice.'

'Do you want to know a cruel joke? Your sister thinks that she is in love with me.'

Hugh stopped. 'Does she?'

'Yes. She gave quite an impassioned speech to that effect earlier.'

'And now you're here. Drunk. Why is that?'

'Because you are right. There was no way she could possibly love me. How? How could she love me? I am debauched in every way. I am wrong. And I always have been. You helped me become the thing that people could tolerate. You helped turn me into a man who could at least walk into a room and have a conversation. One that was not about orchids. You took me to the brothel in Paris, and I found women there who enjoyed my particular vices. And with the exception of my late wife, with whom I made a terrible error in judgement, I have kept it there.

'Until Beatrice. And she thinks... She thinks that she loves me for it. For all that I am. For the orchids and everything else. How is that possible? And when will it end? Because it will end. It will have to end.'

A strange light entered his friend's eyes. 'I have little desire to think about the ways in which you connect with my sister. However, if she says that she loves you...'

'What? Now you believe it might be so?'

'You do not have a sister, so you are forgiven for not understanding why it was not something I wish to think about. The two of you together. I know too much about you. The hazard of being friends for as long as we have. We are now men who might deal in a bit more discretion. Whereas when we were boys, trying to figure out life's great mysteries, we were a bit more free.'

He could understand that. 'That is true. I'd...'

'It is not that I didn't think my sister could love you. It is that... You were right. I'm used to thinking of her as a child. I'm used to protecting her. Our father did nothing for us. She was merely a means for him to bring young women into the house under the guise of being her governess. He paid exorbitant fees to keep her alive. To physicians. That is all true. But he loved no one beyond himself.'

'And you have carried all of it.'

'I have carried all of it,' Kendal agreed. 'What I said about Serena was not fair.'

'It was something I had not told her.'

'Go home. You don't wish to be here.'

'I don't know where else to go.'

'You will not betray my sister.'

'No. Do you know... When we went to the brothel it was revolutionary for me. Because it was easy. I risked nothing to explore what I desired. It was a transaction. I have always found those things much easier than real life. But they do not last.'

'These things are not real. You cannot take them with you into your life. The women here... They don't know you.'

'Don't you see? I consider that a good thing.'

'Briggs, I never liked you for what you pretended to be. I of all people know exactly where you come from. Exactly who you are. Do you not know that?'

'It feels to me...'

'And if I did anything to harm the relationship between you and my sister, I am sorry. I handled it badly.'

'Does this have something to do with Eleanor?'

'I am everything my father was not. And that is my deepest source of pride in this life.'

'But that is not an answer.'

'It is the only answer I can give. Beatrice married you. She has taken you every way that you come. And she has said that she loved you first. If you cannot even be half as brave as my sister... Then perhaps you are not the man I thought you were.'

And after that, Hugh disappeared up the stairs, likely on his way to exorcise his own demons. And he left Briggs to do the same.

Philip.

He could only hear that name now on his wife's lips.

Philip. He had scorned himself back then. But now that

he heard the name spoken by her and not his father... It felt different.

He felt different.

He left and took his carriage back home. He could not see Beatrice like this.

And as he made his way up the stairs, he heard screaming. Crying.

William.

He went into the room and saw his son laying on the floor, his cards spread out all around him. He did not need to know the details of what happened to recognise that he was in a rage. A deep despair. And that Briggs was responsible for it.

And it broke him.

He sat down on the floor, his own misery beginning to overtake him. He was starting to lose hold of all that held him to the earth.

'William,' he said. 'What's wrong? William.'

He was met with nothing but tears.

'I am sorry.' On his hands and knees he began to pick the cards up and put them back in the box. Carefully. With all the reverence he showed his flowers.

All the reverence his father had never shown any of his things.

'I should not have made you feel badly about these. I was scared for you. Because those children were unkind. But they simply don't understand. And you will find someone. Someone who will. A friend.' He thought of Hugh. 'A wife. And in the meantime, you have me. And you have Beatrice. We understand you. And we... We are very proud of you. And all of the things that you know. All of the things that you are. I was afraid because... I was afraid because I'm like you. I know a great many things about my flowers that I grow in the greenhouse. And I am interested in all of the details. But so many people are not. And I decided to make myself different so that I would not be scorned. But it did not make me happy. My orchids make me happy. What makes me different makes me happy.'

His son had quieted now. And was looking at him. He did not know if the boy understood.

Then suddenly William's arms were around his neck. Holding him tight. 'I love you.'

And he felt as if he had been taken out at the knees. Two people loved him. And had told him so. In the space of just a few hours. And he could scarcely breathe.

And it seemed so clear now. What he must do. He had to be a warrior. Just like Beatrice.

'I love you too.'

Chapter Eighteen

Beatrice was determined. To demand nothing of Philip. To not push. Because she thought deeply about what he'd said. About the ways he had felt like he must change. And she did not wish to do that to him.

She wanted to accept him. Just as he was. She wanted to be a gift to him. Not a burden.

She was sitting in the morning room when he came in.

'Beatrice,' he said. He was wearing the clothes he had been wearing the night before, the neckline of his shirt open. His beard was overgrown. He looked tired.

'Will you come with me?'

'Of course I will.'

He held his hand out, and she took it. He led her outside into the garden, but she had the sense he was not leading her down the garden path.

Not the way that he had done the night of the ball. No. He was leading her to his greenhouse.

'I want to show you.'

And he did. Every plant. Every name. Latin and English.

All the ways that they were taken care of. Trivia about how they were discovered. All of it was in his brain.

'Which is your favourite?'

'I do not have a favourite. They are all of equal fascination to me.'

'You were brilliant.'

'There is nothing useful about orchids.'

'But you love them. That is why they are fascinating. It is the way that you see them that's extraordinary.'

'Beatrice…'

'Philip, thank you for showing me this.'

'I did not know how else to say… Except to say… I love you. I love you, and I am very sorry that I could not say it when you needed me to. Of the two of us, you are the stronger.'

Her chest burned. With joy. The satisfaction. With love.

'It is my joy to be a warrior for you.'

'I do not deserve you.'

'If there's one thing that I learned from being ill, it is that life is a gift. It is not about what you deserve or don't deserve. Bad things happen. The glorious things too. And what if we had not stumbled into each other's arms by the fire? That was a gift.'

'We both fought very hard to become something we were not in the end.'

'Did we?'

'Yes. You to become James's wife. Me to become Briggs. I think I will let the rest of the world continue to call me that. But as for you… I will be Philip. Only for you.'

'And I am Beatrice. And it makes me happy.'

'You are mine,' he said. 'And I care for what is mine.'

'I know you do.'

'I have some sweets for you.'

'Why do I feel as if I'm being tempted?'

'Because. You are. Now my darling wife… I feel that you should adequately show your love for me.'

'Of course, Your Grace.' She looked up at him, and their eyes met. 'Philip.'

Epilogue

There never was a man more frightened of his wife giving birth than the Duke of Brigham. Though perhaps her brother nearly matched him for anxiety. And when his daughter came into the world, with a healthy set of lungs, screaming, he could only give thanks that his wife's lungs seemed just as healthy.

The pregnancy had gone well. And the doctor said the labour was one of the easier he had ever seen.

It was true each time his Duchess gave birth. One thing he marvelled at was how different his children were, one from the other. And yet, he did not love any of them less.

William, for his part, proved to be a good big brother, though he did sometimes resent his siblings getting into his things, most particularly his cards.

The last of their children came when William was seventeen.

'I shall not like to be responsible for caring for this child when it cries,' William said.

He had just graduated first from Oxford. A brilliant mind.

He had never been the most popular at school, but the friends he did have were true indeed.

'Do not worry, William. You will benefit from the practice,' Beatrice said, patting him on the head. 'After all, you will be a father one day.'

'I shall need to travel more first,' William said. 'I have a plan to visit every country and territory.'

Beatrice smiled, if a bit sadly. 'I have no doubt you will. But I will very much look forward to your return.'

'You do not have to worry, Mother,' William said. 'I will always come back home.'

And such a home it was. Full. And never conventional. With orchids and cards filled with the places they dreamed of visiting. With toys all over the floor. And a riding crop in their bedchamber. His life might not be the life that his father thought the Duke of Brigham should have. And for that Briggs gave thanks every day.

Because he did not want to be the Duke of Brigham the way his father wished him to be. He only wished to be Philip. The man that Beatrice loved.

That was his greatest joy in all the world.

Beatrice had set out that day to be the architect of her own ruin. And instead, she had saved them both.

* * * * *

Historical Note

There are a great many elements in *Marriage Deal with the Devilish Duke* that were not understood widely in the era the book is set, and that is intentional on my part. Had Beatrice's childhood asthma been understood, and more easily treated, she would not have been weakened by the attempts to 'cure' her. If Briggs and his son's mild Autism Spectrum Disorder had been diagnosed, if their differences had been given a place in society, rather than the forced assimilation that was required, they would have had very different lives—especially Briggs, who I believe, with Beatrice's help, set about to make a better space in the world for William to be himself.

It is the same with Serena's mental health and James's sexuality, and Briggs's sexuality as well. As a society we ostracized and feared what we did not understand. In our modern times, there are labels for all and everything, but it is not labels (however helpful!) that truly advance society. It is empathy and human connection. Without labels, Beatrice was able to accept people as they were because of her position slightly outside society. She was willing to take someone just as they were, applying the kindest lens to them, which created space even in an era before labels. That is my deepest hope for the future. That we might meet on common ground, rather than focusing on differences. That we might greet people with love, and an open heart, for that is where real progress lies.

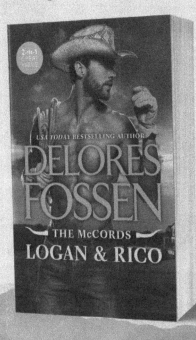

Subscribe and fall in love with a Mills & Boon series today!

You'll be among the first to read stories delivered to your door monthly and enjoy great savings.

WE SIMPLY LOVE ROMANCE